BY SUSAN RICHARDS SHREVE

Queen of Hearts

Dreaming of Heroes

Miracle Play

Children of Power

A Woman Like That

A Fortunate Madness

a novel by

Hearts

Susan Richards Shreve

Simon and Schuster
New York

Copyright © 1986 by Susan Richards Shreve

All rights reserved
including the right of reproduction
in whole or in part in any form
Published by Simon and Schuster
A Division of Simon & Schuster, Inc.
Simon & Schuster Building
Rockefeller Center
1230 Avenue of the Americas
New York, New York 10020
SIMON AND SCHUSTER and colophon are registered trademarks
of Simon & Schuster, Inc.

Designed by Levavi & Levavi

Manufactured in the United States of America

10   9   8   7   6   5   4   3   2   1

Library of Congress Cataloging in Publication Data
Shreve, Susan Richards.
   Queen of hearts.

   I. Title.
PS3569.H74Q4   1986   813'.54   86-15595
ISBN: 0-671-60102-4

To Po, Elizabeth, Caleb and Kate

"For the eyes are the scouts of the heart"

Book One

Prologue

*I*n late autumn, 1905, a woman arrived by train in Bethany,
Massachusetts, with one satchel held together by ship rope and
a belly large enough for a grown man to sit on. Her name,
Santa Francesca Allegra, which she had invented for its musical
sound, was a joke. Santa Francesca was no saint. She had left
Sicily pregnant by a Roman count, who did not accompany her on
the trip to America. She took a room on the second floor of
Rooster's Tavern beside the Leonora River, bore the child, whom she
named Sophia, and supported herself, she maintained, by telling
fortunes. According to stories told by the men who visited her, she
was strange and beautiful and generous with herself. There was no
doubt she lived by her favors to them.

Annually, the town of Bethany celebrated the arrival of spring
with a Festival of Fortunes, named to honor the role played by the
fortune-teller. There had not always been one. Bethany,
Massachusetts, had a reputation for bad luck. According to several
Colonial histories, the worst recorded massacre of Indians in the
Northeast during the settlement of America had taken place on the
hill where Bethany High School now stood. Beginning at the end of
the 17th century, coincident with the witch trials in Salem, ten
miles to the south, there had occurred in Bethany a series of
brutal and unsolved murders of young women. Hurricanes dashing
up the coast hit Bethany more frequently than other Eastern towns

before retreating out to sea. After a fire in 1912 burned out the riverfront and the commercial section, citizens decided to arm themselves against further disasters with a fortune-teller for good luck at the Spring Festival.

For years, Santa Francesca Allegra played the role of fortune-teller, sitting in a small dark booth dressed like a gypsy, skirt over skirt, imagining the patterns of lives in people's palms.

1.

The Festival of Fortunes: May 1, 1955

The Festival of Fortunes was held on the grounds of the high school in Bethany. Passions frozen during the long bleak winter surged out of control like the Leonora River, which in late spring swung a full skirt surrounding the town.

The Festival was actually a rite of spring. Winter in Bethany came before Thanksgiving and lasted until Spring, a damp, permanent cold from the sea. On the first of May, families broke out of their houses like flowers—full-bellied women impregnated in the lonely dark of November, children whose high spirits had been trapped too long in small rooms, young men anxious to feel the hard beating of life in their pulses. There were dancing and singing, games for the children, clowns and pony rides, a pocket lady with treasures in her apron, acrobats and jugglers. People drank merrily and made love into the next morning. And young women knew instinctively by the high prancing of the men that they could end their girlhood in some dark corner the night of the Festival.

Francesca Woodbine had lost her girlhood at the Festival in 1949, when she was fourteen years old. Her parents had gone home early after James, her twin brother, got into a fistfight with an older, larger boy. At dusk, when a thin rain began to fall, Francesca left her young friends to walk the back way home, a shortcut, down the hill and through a dense pine-woods to Hawthorne Street.

Three young men at the top of the hill just beyond the carousel watched Francesca take leave of her friends and walk alone down the steep incline towards the pinewoods. They had been watching her on and off since midday, when Johnny Trumbull, the principal's son, the youngest of the three, had seen her dancing.

"Look at Cesca Woodbine," he had said to his friend Tim Greenfield. "She's grown beautiful since the Festival last year." He blew her a kiss.

"She's grown breasts," Tim Greenfield said matter-of-factly. He jabbed his older cousin who had come north from Nashville for the occasion. "How would you like a young virgin like that one for tonight, George?"

"How old?" George Saunders asked.

"Fourteen," Tim Greenfield said. "But she's an *old* fourteen."

"Her grandmother was a whore. Did you know that?" Johnny asked.

"Everybody in town knows that," Tim said. "So what do you say, George?"

"A whore's granddaughter," George said contemplatively, looping his thumbs in his belt. He was twenty, with a reputation in Nashville for drinking and a disregard for women unusual in a Southern man. He had never had sex—although he lied about it to his friends and certainly to his younger Northern cousin Tim Greenfield.

"So how do I get the little girl for the evening?" he asked.

"Take her," Johnny said.

"Take her?" George asked.

"Any way you can." He took a twenty-dollar bill from his wallet. "Twenty dollars if you lay Francesca Woodbine by midnight."

Tim Greenfield took out his own twenty dollars and handed it to Johnny. "By bedtime you could be rich. Think of it."

Amongst friends sworn to secrecy, Tim Greenfield collected two hundred dollars for his cousin from Nashville. Only Billy Naylor, a plump, pale-skinned boy thought by his friends to be sexually ambivalent, refused to give out money. "Sometimes you guys make me sick," he said, but he promised not to tell anyone about the bet on Cesca Woodbine's virginity.

"You're talking about rape," George said to his cousin after the money had been put down.

"Any way you can get her," Tim said. "Maybe she'll think you're cute."

"I doubt that, very much," George said.

He hesitated. He had drunk too much. He didn't even know if he could take her.

"Nobody will ever know," Tim said. "Tomorrow you'll be back in Nashville, and if anyone heads into the woods after you, I can see them from here."

"What'll you do?"

"Shout that the British are coming."

"Big joke." He pulled out of his back pocket the three bandannas he had borrowed from Tim and watched Francesca disappear behind a thicket of trees.

"Don't let us down, George," Tim said.

"A piece of cake," George replied, and sauntered off down the hill, obscured at the bottom by the descending night.

The path through the pinewoods was always dark, even in daylight, and Francesca didn't see the figure of a man until he had hold of her. With one kerchief he tied her hands. He covered her eyes with another and stuffed the third bandanna into her mouth so that she couldn't scream. Although she kicked him with all her strength, he was much larger than she was. He pushed her down on the ground, straddled her body, pulling her panties to her knees. Then he hammered on top of her, pressing her small back against the hard pine-needle ground until she thought she was going to die. Years later, she could still hear his low voice speak in an unfamiliar accent, more Southern than Massachusetts: "Your grandmother was a whore."

After he untied her hands, he fled.

Francesca never saw him face to face. She pulled the kerchief out of her mouth, untied the bandanna from her eyes and ran home.

Her mother, Sophia, was at the door when Cesca arrived.

17

"Dinner is ready, darling," Sophia said in her melodious voice announcing safety. "Hurry."

"I got all muddy," Cesca said, dashing past her upstairs. "I'll be right down."

Francesca took her nightgown from the hook in the closet and locked the bathroom door. In the mirror, over the sink, her face, to her astonishment, looked exactly as it had looked that morning when she brushed her teeth. She turned on the shower extra hot as if to burn off the terrible germs. Then, standing under the stream of water, she touched herself where the man had been. And she was bleeding.

She put on her nightgown, combed her wet hair and went downstairs to dinner. She was shaken to the center of her being; but misunderstanding her own responsibility, her parents' fragility, she knew absolutely that she would never tell.

At the table, James sat across from her, bad-tempered, with a large purple bump under his eye.

"So, Cesca, I suppose you had a wonderful time at the Festival after I left," he said.

"Wonderful," she said,.

Her mother reached over and brushed her wet hair off her forehead.

"I'm glad, Cesca," Sophia said. "Did you have your fortune told?"

"I didn't. I never do at the Festival. I'm afraid I'll have a bad fortune, and then what can I do about it?" she said.

"You always have a choice of what to do with your fortune, even if it's bad," her father, Julian, said in his reasonable quiet way.

"What is the difference between a fortune and a choice?" Francesca asked, anxious to fill the room with conversation so no one would guess what had happened to her.

"Fortune is what happens to you," Julian said, "and choice is what you do about it."

Francesca's face darkened.

"I wish your relatives were a choice and not a fortune," she said. "And if I could choose, I'd find another grandmother than Francesca Allegra."

"Your grandmother was a lovely woman," Julian said softly.

18

"She was a whore," Francesca replied.

Julian and Sophia assumed their daughter had been ridiculed at the Festival by inconsiderate children. They explained about the life of Santa Francesca, and Sophia told stories about her mother to compensate for other stories her children would surely hear, so they could understand her condemned but remarkable life.

Like her grandmother, the Sicilian Francesca, Cesca grew up to be a warm and generous young woman, but aloof— damaged as the offspring of a woman with a reputation in a small and unforgiving town.

She would not understand for years the cost of history, the way in which one life is woven seamlessly into the pattern of a future generation until one day the threads, worn thin, unravel the secrets of the design.

On the morning of May 1, 1955, James and Francesca left early for the high school to set up the fortune-teller's booth. James, the elder by forty seconds, was as dark as his sister, with high cheekbones and startled hazel eyes. They were the same height, both very tall and slender, with the slight awkwardness of long and disobedient limbs.

"So, Cesca, what do you know about fortunes?" James asked, hauling the booth into the back of his pickup truck. "Can you tell mine?"

"I know you too well," Cesca said, pulling her long hair off her face in a ribbon. "Imagine if I could see my own life. I wouldn't want to live it, would I?"

James put the truck into reverse and backed out of the driveway, glancing at his sister reflected in the rearview mirror. She looked lovely, he thought, transformed in gypsy costume from the woman he knew almost as well as he knew himself into someone unfamiliar, strangely beautiful and provocative. He wondered why she had never had a love affair. At twenty, in her second year at Juilliard studying voice, Cesca was as intense as she had been when they were children, but

19

somehow more remote as she grew older. Perhaps, James guessed, her passions, like their mother's, were cautiously reserved for her music. She had an unusual voice for a young woman—already full and rich and warm.

"Do you have a date tonight?" he asked her.

"Not yet. No one has asked me," she said.

"Who are you hoping for?"

She didn't reply.

"You look very pretty, Ces," James said.

She was wearing a cranberry cotton skirt with petticoats in different colors, a sand-colored blouse and a white shawl which her mother had used when she was still playing the organ in church for funerals and weddings. She arranged her shawl in the side-view mirror of the truck. Usually, she didn't think about the way she looked; she was always surprised to see in a mirror in natural sunlight how golden-dark she was.

She watched her brother's profile, which was sharp and fine—Roman, according to Sophia, from his grandfather, the invented count, although it was of course the exact profile of her husband. Cesca thought James was handsome. She thought he was the most wonderful-looking man she knew except Colin Mallory, the son of the Mayor of Bethany.

She had not been with a man except for the terrible time when she was fourteen years old. She had never wanted to be, satisfied with the safety of daydreams in the arms of Colin Mallory.

Once, after she moved to New York, a young actor from Juilliard had taken her to his apartment. But when he undressed and his erection shot out at her, she had felt suddenly faint with fear and desire.

"I can't," she had said.

"Can't," he repeated, incredulous. "You can't."

She shook her head.

"Women always can."

He had turned her out of his apartment in her slip. Afterwards, she had conducted her social life in groups, cautious of the possible anger her own reserved passion could elicit in men.

At Elm Street, they waved as they passed Dr. Samuel Weaver's green Oldsmobile with the top down, going south towards the hospital. Sam was a large and commanding man, gone suddenly and prematurely white when his wife died, leaving him to raise three boys alone. He was a member of a family of old-fashioned physicians whose interest was in people more than in science. There were other doctors in Bethany, but Dr. Weaver was the only one who actually took care of lives, self-confident and gentle as a mother. He had come to the Woodbine house in February that year when Julian Woodbine found his wife unconscious in the study, where she practiced singing. According to Sam, she had taken sleeping pills he had prescribed for persistent insomnia. She had then gone into the study, where a book of Schubert lieder was opened to the fourth page. Perhaps she had even begun to practice. Afterwards, she remembered only drinking some whiskey to wash down the pills and waking up in the hospital with Sam Weaver's hand on her cheek.

"Did you know Sam Weaver loves Mother?" Cesca asked.

James slammed on his brakes at the stop sign on Elm.

"Still?"

"I think he has always loved her since they were young, only nothing came of it then."

Sophia Woodbine was a musician, perhaps one of genuine talent. According to Julian, who knew about music, she had an extraordinary soprano voice. But in Bethany, there was no place to play or sing except at church, sometimes for weddings and funerals—or at Rooster's Tavern on Saturdays. She sang like the sopranos on the Saturday radio broadcast of the opera—sang as nobody else who lived in Bethany could sing. When she sang in church on Sunday mornings, her full voice vibrating like a wire pulled tight, the children in the choir often laughed into their hymnbooks. She had a voice too rich for their limited experience.

"Please don't sing in church anymore," Cesca had said to her mother when she and James were small.

"But I love to sing in church," Sophia had said.

"The trouble is the children laugh at you." Cesca stood in the doorway of her mother's room watching Sophia dress for

21

church and pile her long hair into a soft brown nest at the back of her neck.

"Do they? Have you seen them?" Sophia asked. "I've never noticed—but then, I suppose, I am so pleased to be singing, I wouldn't notice anything else."

Sophia was the spirit of the Woodbine house, flying over her children's lives on angel's wings, promising a warm protection, a future in which they could be anything they wished to be. They blamed her illness on their father's coldness and restraint. On the distance he insisted on maintaining. On his clipping her wings and caging her in Bethany.

"You don't love her enough," Cesca had said to him when her mother was still in the hospital.

She understood that the love her mother needed was not to be found in a marriage. But she also knew her father retreated from Sophia when he felt himself inadequate to her needs.

"I love her the best I can," Julian had replied. Which was the truth.

Once when Francesca was in high school, she had come upon her parents dancing to her mother's singing in the morning. Sophia was in her nightgown, her robe open and flying behind her like wings. Her father, in a serious gray suit, was swinging her around the kitchen.

Cesca had stood watching, at the bottom step of the back stairs, but when her father saw her, he stopped dancing.

"I have to go to work," he said, self-conscious at being discovered.

"Don't leave now," Sophia said with real anguish. "We're having such a nice time."

"Why were you so upset to have him leave for work?" Cesca asked her mother at breakfast.

"Some mornings I'm afraid to be alone," Sophia said.

"I'll stay," Cesca said quickly. "There's nothing important in school today."

Her mother brushed the curls, still damp from dancing, off her face.

"That's sweet of you to offer, darling," she said. "But you can't stay forever."

At the stop sign at Beech Street, Will Weaver, Dr. Weaver's strange son, rounded the corner carrying two large mesh cages of brown snakes. He raised them, along with small turtles and a variety of lizards, in the second-floor bathroom of the family's house on Hickory Hill.

Ever since he could remember, Will Weaver had liked to watch the cold-blooded snakes of the Leonora River moving like lightning through the bushes along the muddy banks.

When he was small, he and his mother used to spend hours together in her sewing room, going through a huge jungle-green book titled simply *Reptiles*. The pictures reminded her of her own childhood in the Georgia swamps.

"There were more snakes in those swamps than you could shake a stick at. More than by the Leonora River," she'd tell him, full of affection for the memory and for him as well. "On Shyla Island, where I used to go for summer vacation, there was every variety of snake on the North American continent. And lizards and alligators were as common as weeds in Massachusetts."

After his mother died, Will started to keep snakes, mainly the ones he found in abundance along the Leonora River. But he also had a boa constrictor, which ate mice that Will raised in a large cage on the radiator. He particularly liked to watch the way the boa swallowed a mouse, working the round fur ball down its long gullet. For a while, he had a small alligator, sent to him by post from his oldest brother on vacation in Florida; week after week, the alligator lay stupidly in the bathtub, its eyes fixed, growing perceptibly until finally Dr. Weaver said the alligator would have to go.

In the afternoons after school, Will would come home to an empty house, make a double chocolate malt and take it upstairs. In his bedroom, with the door closed, he'd open the cages and his snakes would escape, slithering swiftly across the floor, then stopping suddenly. Still as statues, they'd lift their heads in a high arch and flash a black and bright pink tongue from their tiny mouths. Sometimes, to his father's consternation, he filled his bedroom with low branches broken off the oak and elm trees, a few from the willows and rhododendron, occasionally some bright azaleas from his mother's enduring garden, making a jungle of his room for his snakes.

"Want a ride to the high school, Will?" James called out pleasantly.

"I like to walk," Will said.

James smiled at Cesca. "What do you think? Crazy as a loon?"

"On and off, he is," Cesca said.

In fact, Will Weaver was crazy. He was seized with craziness like an epileptic. But there were no visible signs of his state of mind; nobody knew. He daydreamed of killing. He had strangled kittens in his father's barn, burying them in the dirt floor. Once, playing at the Woodbines' house, he had locked himself in the bathroom and broken the head off one of Francesca's dolls, pretending it was a young girl. Then he had dropped the doll down the laundry chute, where days later Sophia had found it amongst the children's clothes. He slept with a lock of his dead mother's black hair which he had asked his Uncle Rhoddy to cut for him when it was Uncle Rhoddy's turn to sit by the casket before the wake.

If anyone had known the terrible dramas played out in Will Weaver's damaged brain, the boy would have been put away. As it was, his real nature was camouflaged by the town's invention of him. After Grace Weaver died, families in Bethany claimed him as their own. He was beautiful, with wide blue eyes, high color in his cheeks and a surprising capacity for sweetness.

He had a hold on people, especially women. It would take years before people finally understood that what had drawn them to Will Weaver was not his free spirit, as they had supposed, but the dark recesses of his troubled mind.

James turned into Bridge Street, where Maud Hanrahan lived in an apartment above Hanrahan's Market. It was with Maud that James had first lain naked, spring vacation of his freshman year at Harvard, making love in the woods behind the market, spilling his semen on her belly, where it solidified like confectioner's sugar in the chilly air.

"Maud Hanrahan was the only girl in my class in high school who thought about ideas instead of boys," Cesca said.

"She thinks about boys now," James said.

"She may sleep with them, if that's what you're suggesting; but while she does, she's thinking about the theory of relativity or whether man is born innocent or whether there's such a thing as salvation. That kind of thing."

James laughed. "While she's making love?"

"She's *very* smart."

Colin Mallory was standing on the first step of the high school in blue jeans and a white dress shirt unbuttoned half-way. He was the only son in a family of daughters of the Mayor of Bethany. Like his father, he was a black Irishman of high temper and sex. He had thick hair, which he wore long over his collar, and eyes the color of the sea.

James sensed the alteration in Francesca as they drove by the high school and she waved shyly to Colin Mallory.

"Do you like Colin Mallory?" He stopped the truck at the end of the road and turned off the engine.

"Not exactly," Cesca replied.

"I'm glad for that. I can't imagine you wanting the same man every other woman in Bethany wants."

She turned away, looking out the open window, over the river. She wasn't going to tell James anything about Colin.

Cesca had been in love with Colin for years. Before she knew desire, she memorized the patterns of his daily life so they could meet as if by accident on Elm Street; or by the baseball field, where she just happened to be riding her bike; at Sunny's Ice Cream Parlor on Saturday mornings; in the line outside the Leonora Movie Theatre at the matinee. Since the beginning of her last year at Bethany High, however,

Cesca had been obsessed with Colin Mallory—short of breath when she saw him, her chest muscles constricting, denying air to her lungs. Light-headed, she would cross Main Street against the traffic. Once, preoccupied, she walked directly into a telephone pole. There was hardly a moment during which Colin Mallory wasn't life-size in her brain.

Senior year her grades fell and rose depending on the level of his attentions: an occasional smile or wave as they passed in the high school corridors if he wasn't talking to someone else. "Hiya, Cesca" when they arrived at Sunny's at the same time. Just the sound of Colin saying her name used to make her stomach turn over, and she'd dump the maple-nut ice cream cone she'd bought in the trash can, unable to eat it.

Once, he had stopped her outside the theater while she was looking at the posters for *Rebel Without a Cause* and asked her had she seen the movie and did she like James Dean. She had seen it two Saturdays in a row, but she said no, she hadn't, in case he asked her, which he did not. She said James Dean was all right but a little pudgy in the stomach, and his eyes were intentionally sexy. She wanted Colin to know she had high standards and would not fall in love without serious consideration.

Francesca got out of the truck onto the thick grass which was still wet with spring dew; the air was sweet with the smell of early lilacs lining the high cliffs over the Leonora River, and the willows, just leaved, made crinolines around their broad and craggy trunks.

James lifted the fortune-teller's booth out of the truck. It was a simple structure made of two-by-fours, painted dark brown with artificial shutters on painted windows. A velvet curtain, heavy with the odor of mothballs, served as a door; inside, on a small platform floor, was a stool on which Francesca would sit in semidarkness with the curtain drawn, her skirts filling the tiny room.

She tried out the stool, setting it up in the back of the room with just enough space for one full-grown man to sit opposite her on another stool. Between the stools was an orange crate

26

with a lace-shawl tablecloth and a small bayberry candle. James drew the curtains.

"Too dark?" he called in.

"Pretty dark." She lit the candle; the sweet smell filled the small room.

He ducked under the curtain and sat down on the stool, putting out both his hands palm up.

"So?" he asked.

Francesca had never thought of telling fortunes. That February, the committee in charge of the Festival had in fact asked her mother first, and Sophia had refused.

"I don't have my mother's instinct for fortunes," she had told the committee. "But I believe my daughter Francesca does."

Francesca had read a book on tarot cards and palms. She knew something to say about the confusion of lines on the hand, the life line interrupted halfway down the palm. She read about astrology. But none of it held any interest for her. She had no faith in those mysteries or in her reading of them. She was not by nature a receiver of information but rather an inventor. She simply believed in her capacity to see into the lives of people she knew.

She had always known secrets. At night, she used to tell bedtime stories to her mother and brothers. Sitting against the headboard of her four-poster, her knees tight to her chest, she'd tell stories about the people in Bethany.

"Mrs. O'Malley has a man who comes to see her in a milk truck pretending to deliver milk," she'd say.

Or "Frank Adler beats Mrs. Adler with the dog's leash on Thursday when he comes back from Rooster's Tavern drunk."

Or "Anna Wheeler is in love with her cleaning woman. I saw them kissing."

Or "Mama," she'd say, "Sam Weaver loves you."

And Sophia's lovely face would rise in color.

"Honestly, Cesca, I don't know where you find these stories."

"She peers into people's houses." James was a born disbeliever. "I see her do it when we walk to school."

"Cesca lies," said Prince Hal, her younger brother, nicknamed from Shakespeare by his father.

"I don't lie," she said. "These are stories I just know."

Cesca took her brother's hands.

"Oh, James. Such bad news I see," she said. "Impotent at twenty-one, give or take a month. I'm sorry."

"Is that all you see?"

"Let me look closer."

"What about love? Look close enough to find some love on my hand."

Cesca leaned right down to his palm, heating it with her breath. "Shh," she whispered, and bit it lightly right in the center. "So much for love."

James got up and pulled back the velvet curtain.

"Fraud," he said, and kicked over the stool in mock anger; but he didn't climb into the pickup truck immediately. Instead, he ducked back under the curtain of the fortune-teller's booth and caught her practicing mysterious expressions on her face.

"If Colin asks you to the dance tonight, be careful."

"How come?"

"I don't trust him," James said.

"Never mind about that. He won't ask," she said.

James didn't know about his sister's relationships with men, and he worried about her, sensing she was somehow sexually fragile in a way he did not understand. Once he had watched from his bedroom window as Tim Greenfield gave her a long, awkward kiss under the porch light. When she came upstairs and passed his bedroom door, she had made a face.

"I wouldn't want to kiss Tim Greenfield either," James had said.

The last fistfight of many he had had in high school was sparked by Johnny Trumbull calling Francesca "a cold fish— probably frigid."

"What do you know about frigid?" James said, hitting Johnny Trumbull straight in the mouth. "A rabbit would be frigid with you."

"Maybe I am," Cesca said when James told her the reason for the fight.

"You're afraid is what you are," James said. "With Tim Greenfield and Johnny Trumbull around, it's a good thing you are afraid."

Francesca shrugged. "What I'd honestly like to do is spend the rest of my life with you," she said. James understood exactly. The only safe relationship he himself had was with his sister.

He drove his pickup truck down the hill towards the parking lot thinking of her. If she had never been with a man before, as he suspected, Colin Mallory was certainly not the sort of man with whom to begin.

Will Weaver walked up the hill to the high school past Colin Mallory standing alone on the high school steps, admiring himself as if he were a mindless alley cat, past the men setting up the merry-go-round outside the science wing of the high school, past the women closing in on middle age who had been baking sweets for days, past James Woodbine driving his pickup truck down the hill. He stopped at the largest willow tree on the high school grounds and set down his cages, twenty-five yards away from the fortune-teller's booth, where Francesca Woodbine, whom he loved with a passion that filled his nights and days, was leaning against the corner of her tiny building.

She was taller than he was, with soft black hair pulled carelessly away from a broad face with wide-set eyes. It was a striking face but not uncommonly beautiful. She looked like his mother the last time he had seen her—a blackbird lying on the white, white pillow of her final bed at Mercy Funeral Home, Atlanta. Every woman that Will loved looked like his memory of his mother.

He liked to look at Cesca's breasts. They were soft and full, not like the solid unripe cantaloupes of other girls Will knew.

Her many crinolines spread her narrow body so that she looked wide-hipped. He liked the rich cranberry-colored skirt she wore with a teal blue sash. He loved colors. On his night to make supper at the Weaver house, Will spent hours arranging the meal not to eat but to look at, as if it were done in oils. He liked avocados for the rich green and brown lying in wedges against a slender tomato and black pitted olive. He liked red lettuce studded with pearls of water; he liked white mushrooms and raspberries and firm peaches pitted and sliced.

He thought of undressing Francesca Woodbine—of sitting on the high-canopied bed in his father's room and unbuttoning her sand-colored blouse—of taking it off one arm at a time so her breasts, unencumbered, fell from the soft folds of the blouse—of taking off the teal blue sash while she sat shyly, letting her long hair down from the ribbons so it fell over her bare breasts. He would take off the cranberry skirt, and crinoline after crinoline would fall on the floor while he knelt at her ankles pulling the skirts into a heap, until she was naked except for a triangle of silk panty. Then, as he had seen men do in some of the magazines his brother bought in Boston and Will kept hidden in his bottom drawer beneath his old chemistry papers, he would slip her panties down to her thighs and kiss the soft black wire nest of hair.

He felt his sex rise in the worn blue jeans he was wearing, reached down to hold himself and slid beneath the leaf curtain of the willow tree where he could still see Francesca, a filigree of color through the leaves.

For a moment before he came, he wanted to kill her, squeeze the breath out of her as he had done with the soft kittens in his father's barn. But the moment passed. He zipped his pants and picked up the two cages of snakes. There were Penelope and Odysseus, Samson and Delilah, Daniel, Susannah, Joachim, Persephone, Demetrius, Lysistrata, Hedda Gabler and Hamlet—snakes named according to his reading in English.

"How in God's name can you tell them apart?" his father had asked. "They're all brown and ugly."

"If you'd get to know them, you'd know the difference," Will said.

It was the kind of remark that people in Bethany would think funny, but Sam Weaver was not amused.

"Get rid of those miserable snakes immediately," he said.

"I will. I'll sell them at the Festival," Will said agreeably.

He walked by Francesca's booth on the way down the hill to set up his own booth for Snake Charming and Selling. CHARMED SNAKES FOR SALE, his sign read.

"Want to tell my fortune?" he asked Cesca. He wondered whether his hands would shake if he put them in hers, whether his pulse would be pounding too hard for him to hear her.

He put down the snake cages and went inside the booth with Cesca.

He put out his hands, which were small and white, striped with a pale blue. She took them in her own larger hands, rubbed her thumb across his palms and examined them with great seriousness.

She had a lovely smile, he thought.

"Do you read palms?" he asked.

"Do you really want to know?" She traced her forefinger down the curved line on his right hand. "That's the life line, interrupted there." She pointed to a straight intersecting line. "There's some kind of abrupt disaster, but you see—the line continues after the disaster almost to your wrist, so you'll survive and live a very long life."

"Unhappy?"

Cesca shrugged. "No. I don't read palms, since you asked. I read a book about it and the whole idea didn't make sense."

"So how are you going to tell fortunes today?" Will asked.

"I'll make them up."

She was curious about Will Weaver; even, she sometimes thought, attracted to him. When her mother had been ill, he had written her a strange and moving letter in red pen on Corrasable Bond typing paper which read: *I am sorry that your mother is ill. I know exactly how it feels. When my mother died, I died with her. Love, Will Weaver.*

"Tell me what you know about me," Will asked her.

"I *don't* know about you." She had known Will Weaver since he was small and had come to play with Prince Hal, although he was a lot older than her brother. For hours, the two of them used to play invented games with heroic possibilities.

"I know things about your family but not about you. There's no predictability to your life. You are capable of doing anything."

"What do you mean, 'anything'?"

Francesca stood and drew the curtain back. The Festival was beginning. Cars were winding up the long drive to the high school and the grounds were filling with people. The sun, closer than it had been since autumn, was warm and bright.

"Nothing you might ever do would surprise me."

She walked outside and stretched, took the ribbons out of her hair, took off her shawl.

"I didn't like my fortune," Will said, picking up his cages of snakes.

"I didn't give you one, Will Weaver, because I can't figure you out. I'm not magic, you know."

Colin Mallory was dancing. There were fiddlers by the flagpole in front of the high school playing Irish music, and Colin was dancing to the high-stepping tunes, sometimes alone, sometimes with one of the young and pretty girls hunched together like mushrooms around the fiddlers. He would reach into the crowd of girls, take one in his arms, and she would suddenly flower. He was wonderfully handsome with a kind of careless magnetism, dangerous in a small town whose thin surface of civilization is easily stirred.

"Colin Mallory is the kind of man who causes catfights," James said to Cesca the first time he was aware of his sister's attraction.

"You're simply jealous," Cesca said.

"You're wrong, Ces. It doesn't appeal to me to have a bunch of kittens howling and dying over me."

When James walked up the hill from the parking lot, Maud Hanrahan was standing alone in the crowd around the dancers. She was a small, soft, black-haired Irish girl with an open face, ordinary as marigolds, sunny and comforting with a temperament which offered the unexpected pleasure of simplicity. She was not simple, but James, whose instincts were inclined to the predictability of plants and sciences, did not know that.

He walked up behind her, brushing his body against her back. "H'lo," he said. "I see you're falling in love with Colin Mallory."

Colin, without a partner, was dancing an Irish jig with complicated footwork. He caught sight of James out of the corner of his eye and reached out for Maud Hanrahan.

"The prince beckons," James whispered in her ear.

Colin took her in his arms, and they danced together. James watched Colin's hand slip below Maud Hanrahan's hipbone and move forward almost imperceptibly until his broad thumb touched her belly.

When Colin swung her back to him as if he and James were in collusion, sharing her bounty, James stood at a distance and didn't respond.

"Colin is like that with everyone—men and women alike," Maud said. "It's not that I feel anything for him, James. I just can't help myself."

"That's very encouraging news, Maud. Fills a man with confidence."

"I wouldn't do anything with him, you know." Maud reached into James's trouser pocket to take his hand.

"We've no bargain of fidelity."

James folded his arms across his chest and watched Colin Mallory dance with Louisa Natale, who was wearing a hat, as she always did, a fine white broad-brim with royal blue ribbons to the waist. Louisa was the only woman James knew with whom he sometimes imagined himself when he was making love to Maud.

There are people who in manner and temperament express their time exactly. Louisa Natale was one of these. She was conventionally pretty, high-spirited, with a sense of style and daring. Her friends found her appealing and copied the way she dressed and walked and wore her hair or spoke with a slight almost Southern lilt. She was sure of herself and gave the impression of a ranging life without conventional limits. She was sexy and like a dancer, surprisingly at ease with her body. And so she grew up self-centered, avid to have what she wanted immediately, not anticipating cost.

Maud had taken James's hand again, running her finger light as silk across his palm. In spite of himself, he could feel the rushes in his pulse, the brief shock of electricity between them announcing the plans for the evening.

"I want your sister to tell my fortune," Maud said, and pulled him away from the group of dancers, up the hill to the fortune-teller's booth where Francesca was sitting with Sam Weaver.

"Palms up," Cesca said, taking Dr. Weaver's hands in hers. "I have to see the lines."

"There are too many lines, full of bad news I don't want to hear." His hands were small and deeply creased. "You probably can't even find my life line in that confusion," he said in his soft Southern voice, borrowed from his wife during the years of his marriage.

"Cup your hands," Cesca said. "You see, there's your life line." She leaned back against the wall.

Sam tugged at her long hair gently. Ever since she was a child, Cesca Woodbine had moved him. He had delivered her and James—a birth he remembered not just because they were twins but because, to his great surprise, Cesca was born with a membrane covering her face. According to a story Grace Weaver had told him, in the South, especially in Georgia and among the colored, a baby born with a membrane covering its face is believed to have second sight. Sam used to tell Francesca the story of her birth: how he had swiftly pulled off the fine mucous membrane, clearing the nasal passages so she could breathe; how he had carried her wrapped in a terry-cloth towel to Sophia with news of her unusual birth. "Just like your mother," he had said to Sophia. "A girl with magical sight."

"You don't need to see the lines in people's hands to read palms," Sam said to her. "Now tell me about your mother."

In February, after Sophia tried to kill herself, she had begun to hallucinate that mockingbirds with beautiful yellow breasts were filling her hospital room with song. A psychiatrist from Boston, called in by Sam Weaver for consultation, told the Woodbine family Sophia needed to find a satisfactory outlet for her music besides weddings or funerals. If she didn't, she'd go mad.

"It's a little late to tell us that," James said crossly to his father. "She's mad already." But Julian insisted he would find a way for Sophia to sing. He turned the attic on the third floor into a large room lit by skylights and long windows, with her piano and chaise overlooking the back garden. There was also a bed to rest in, where, in fact, she decided to sleep when she got out of the hospital. She never came downstairs at all, even to meals.

"She's singing again," Cesca told Sam. "The piano is on the third floor and she practices there. She's even composed a love song."

"Sing it to me."

And Francesca did. In a clear lyrical alto voice, she sang a song that was as sweet and simple as an ancient ballad. She stood up to sing, as if for performance, her head touching the rafters of the fortune-teller's booth, her hands folded in front of her: an overgrown child.

Sam Weaver reached out to touch her waist.

"You have a beautiful voice," he said.

She pulled the curtain open for him to leave, coquettish, knowing with some confusion that she had stirred this man her mother had loved.

At fifty, Sam Weaver was still handsome, with the dark countenance of a Welsh coal miner, worn by winters underground, yet warm and intense. "As if his heart is always unlocked," Sophia had once said of him to Cesca, and she knew her mother had a longing for a man who was not remote.

After Sam Weaver had left, Cesca sat down on the stool in

the fortune-teller's booth. She had never been as conscious of Samuel Weaver's Southern voice before, but in the tiny dark closet of the fortune-teller's booth, his accent intensified and called up an old, disturbing memory.

Once, when Francesca was seventeen, she remembered waking suddenly in the midst of a nightmare about the Festival of 1949. In the dream, her eyes were uncovered and she knew the man who had raped her, although she couldn't name him. When she woke up, he was still there, hovering in the corner of her room. And she screamed.

Julian came. He turned on the light. In the place where the man had been lurking was her familiar blue chintz chair with piles of clothes on the back.

"It's okay," Cesca said. "You can turn off the light now."

Her father did. Cesca kept her eyes fixed on the chair and with the lights off, the man came back again.

"Do you mind turning on the light once more?" she asked.

"What does your chair look like in the dark?" Julian asked. "A man?"

"How did you know?"

"When you were small, you used to think that same chair was a man," he said. "It's common in darkness to imagine shapes."

"Perhaps you could leave the light on for a while," Cesca said softly.

She turned on her side so she could look at the chair. Each time she turned off the light, the man came back. Finally, in desperation, unable to sleep, she got up, put on her robe and slippers and sat in the blue chintz chair until morning.

She got up and pulled back the curtain for Maud Hanrahan.

Francesca had not had close friends while she was growing up, although she longed for the chance to share secrets. She had James. And she had Sophia. She was an adult before she realized that her mother, not unkindly but in desperation, had kept her children hostages to her own needs. James and Cesca were everything to her—her husband and best friend, confidant, mother and father and children: they provided an endlessly changing variation on all of the possible relationships a grown woman can know, safely contained in her own flesh. She did not mean to do it. She would have been deeply sad to know the cost to them of her terrible loneliness, and they protected her from any responsibility.

If, however, Cesca had been free to form a deep attachment, Maud Hanrahan would have been the girl she chose. Maud had a rare and genuine maternal warmth and curiosity. People, even strangers, told her personal stories.

In many ways, her life was dreary. She had worked at the market since finishing high school, ordering produce and meat, sorting and cleaning, paying the bills when her mother went to bed with the change of life, driving the truck to Salem for produce when her father had a hangover. Her bedroom, where she lived out a rich interior life, was directly over the butcher shop, and even in summer, it smelled of blood.

Maud slid into the seat across from Cesca, put out her hands, checking them first in candlelight to see if they were clean enough to show.

"I'll tell you the fortune I want," she said quickly.

"To marry my brother and live on Hickory Hill in the Weaver house and have scads of children. I'll give it to you."

"I want to go to France."

"France?" Cesca felt a sudden sadness for James, longing after this girl who wanted only to leave him and go to France.

"I want to go to France as soon as possible. Not even to Paris but to a small village in the South. Maybe on a river, but not like this awful river full of snakes."

"Going to France is not a fortune but a choice," Cesca said, moving the candle so the light caught Maud's face just below the chin, illuminating her head.

"I want to compose, like your mother," Maud said. "Did she choose to stay in Bethany, or was that her fortune?"

"My mother is not exactly well." She turned Maud's hands over, palms down. "I don't know about making choices when you're ill."

"I don't want to marry," Maud said, leaning forward on her stool.

"Not even James?"

"I don't want to marry James," Maud said. "What about France? Do you see France in my hands?"

Cesca laughed. "Your hands are full of France. You'll go to France soon and stay for years in a village on a wonderful river without snakes and then you'll come back to Bethany."

She touched Maud's cheek.

"If you want to go to France, you'll go."

Sam Weaver sat down next to the Snake Charmer's booth thinking of Sophia. Often he asked himself, what would have happened to her if they had married—could he have rescued her, as he had always believed? At seventeen, when he had fallen in love with Sophia, he hadn't had the courage to defy his Anglo-Saxon parents and court the daughter of an Italian prostitute.

As a young woman, Sophia had sung on Saturday nights at Rooster's Tavern, often for sailors who had docked in a nearby town and come to Bethany for a night's carousing. Rooster's was legendary on the North Shore of Massachusetts. The women available for sailors from out of town, as well as for the men in Bethany, were said to be softer and less used than the women in the other coastal towns. The entertainment at Rooster's was always good, and everybody in town went there, even the older high school students.

Sophia was a virgin until she married at twenty-six; she knew the prostitutes who worked at Rooster's Tavern, and they protected her girlhood. She sang ballads in a high, clear soprano voice without accompaniment, sitting on the piano in a full-length challis dress which covered her arms to the wrist, her hands folded in her lap like a late-Victorian painting of a child, inviolate. Often Sam and his brothers, still in their teens, would come just to listen to Sophia Allegra sing. And then they'd go home full of sex, each one in love with her, and fight in the front yard until their father shouted out of the second-story window to break up the fight and go to bed.

When his older brothers had left for college, Sam went one

night to Rooster's alone and sat at a table right in front of the piano, thinking as he watched her that Sophia was too beautiful to spoil by touching. He had drunk too much, and before Sophia stopped singing the bartender asked him to leave.

He did leave, but he didn't go home, He walked up and down the dock in back of the tavern, the cold clearing his head. Once or twice he thought he heard a scream or a shout, but his senses were dulled by ale. Just as he was ready to go home, Sophia opened the fire door on the second floor back of the tavern, scrambled down the black wrought-iron steps and ran along the dock in a long ivory slip and blouse but no coat. Sam Weaver caught her. In the dock lights, he saw that her face was bleeding below the eye and her cheek was bruised.

"What happened?" he asked.

"I want you to come back upstairs with me," she said. "Someone broke into my room."

"A sailor?" he asked, feeling at once full of importance.

"Of course," she said.

"Did he take advantage of you?" he asked.

"No," she said. "I would have killed him."

"I doubt that," Sam had said, pleased with the opportunity to save her. He took her arm and led her back up the fire escape.

He followed her through the door, down the corridor to the room next to her mother's where Sophia had lived since she was born. The room was an ordinary girl's room for the early 1930s, with *Water Babies* prints on the wall done in pen and ink washed with pastels, lace curtains over the windows and an organdy bedspread in a heap on the floor. She sat down on the bed, pale in the yellow lamplight from her dresser.

"I want you to stay with me," she said.

Immediately, Sam Weaver, still too drunk to be clearheaded, had imagined obligations. At seventeen, he had never been with a woman. He was thrilled and afraid.

Sophia fixed the bed, putting the bedspread on. Then, still in her slip and blouse, she climbed under the covers, moving over towards the wall to make room for Sam, who was not sure what to do but believed what was called for was to take off his clothes. He began to unbuckle his belt.

"I want you to sleep with me in your clothes," Sophia said.

Sam climbed in under the covers with her, put his head on the pillow next to hers and folded his arms over his chest, as she instructed him to do.

"I don't want to be touched," she said.

"What are we doing, then?" Sam asked.

"I'm afraid to be in here alone," Sophia said.

When he woke in the morning, she was already up and dressed.

"I suppose you'll be in trouble with your father," she said to him.

"I probably will be."

"You won't tell him you were with me, will you?"

Sam looked at her and laughed. "I wasn't with you, was I?"

Sam thought about Sophia's daughter. He had certainly wanted a young girl before, but never had the wanting been so powerful as it was in the fortune-teller's dark booth. He wondered how much this turbulence two weeks before his fifty-first birthday had to do with Francesca's mother and how much to do with the mystery of the young woman herself.

When the snake show for the children was over, Will put all but one of his snakes back into the cages.

"Persephone," he said solemnly to his father. Persephone was wrapped once around his waist, resting her cylindrical head on Will's hand.

"How do you know it's a girl?" Sam asked, seldom able to conceal his annoyance with Will's snakes.

"She lays eggs, of course," Will said. "So far today, I've sold two snakes and made twenty dollars. Not too good. Did you have your fortune told?"

"Not really."

"I saw you up there." Will sat down next to his father, leaning against him, which he often did, like a much younger boy.

"Put her away, please, Will," Sam said, moving away from the snake that Will was holding.

"She's my absolute favorite," Will said, opening the cage door, kissing the top of Persephone's head.

"Isn't she beautiful?" Will asked.

"Persephone?"

"Francesca."

"Yes, she is."

Sam was surprised that Will had noticed. He had never thought of his son as having any sexual interests and was disturbed to hear that Francesca had attracted him.

"She looks like Mother, don't you think?" Will asked.

"If everyone with black hair looks alike, then they are similar," Sam said.

"She looks exactly like my memory of Mother," Will said.

When Sam found himself irrationally angry at Will, it had to do with his son's associations with his mother.

At noon, James bought lunch at one of the booths and sat with Cesca and Maud on the hill beside the fortune-teller's booth overlooking the town.

Located on a peninsula on the coast of Massachusetts, separated from the other towns by marshes, Bethany was settled originally by the English and later drew outcasts from Eastern Europe, Italy, Wales and Ireland, who crossed the Atlantic at the bottom of ships—third-class citizens even for America. They settled on the peninsula because no one was there who would reject them and re-created Europe in pockets of Poles and Welshmen and Italians, with lines of demarcation. Their children played out familial wars with wooden guns in alleys and backyards. They married each other, and even if they left the town, they remained like flying buttresses on a cathedral, attached top and bottom to home.

Hanging precariously over the river, Bethany was a town full of hidden surprises. There were back streets, narrow lanes and tiny bungalows with one-story saloons, cottages in the Catholic section surrounded by flower gardens with birdbaths and winter-worn Madonnas. From the sea, the town looked beautiful with rocky slopes peppered by craggy bushes and slender, angular evergreens. The snake-filled river was dark not from pollution but from spillage of the black earth from the riverbanks. There were small tributaries, warm and gentle

41

enough in summer for swimming, frozen in winter for skating.

To a stranger, Bethany was an unexceptional American town whose major trade was fishing. Lives were bound by values of economy and moderation. Families were brooding and earnest, even self-righteous, but in the manner of people afraid of their own capacity to imagine, whose dark secrets fester away like internal wounds. The most profound emotion was shame. Amongst other things, it had to do with our treatment of the Indians, according to the minister of First Presbyterian, Main Street, who used that subject as the basis for his sermons during Lent.

The successful families lived at the top of the town on hills in large clapboard houses, painted white with pine green shutters, built in the 19th century on wide streets with towering trees.

The Woodbines lived there, and the Weavers, on a large property which had been a farm. As the hill descended towards Main Street and the center of town, the houses were closer together, often stucco, painted in deep yellows, vermilion, sometimes pink. And along the river, there were frame bungalows with wide front porches, usually unscreened.

In the attic of the Woodbines' house, James and Francesca had found a history of Colonial America handwritten in the late 19th century by a man named Morton who had at one time lived in the house. There were several pages at the beginning of the history recording the rape of Indian women by colonists during the settlement of eastern Massachusetts. On afternoons late in the summer when James and Cesca were fourteen, they sat in the garden behind the house reading Morton's history of America out loud to each other.

"What do you know about rape?" Cesca had asked James that summer.

"Everything," James said.

They were lying on the grass carpet beneath a large crepe myrtle, languid, almost sleepy in the smooth summer air.

"So do I," Cesca said. She rested her face in her arms, wishing to ask James a lot of questions but carefully, so that the conversation between them would seem to be casual. "Why do you think men rape women? They don't have to." She

42

rolled over on her back and looked at the sky through the lace curtain of tree branches and leaves.

"Of course they don't have to," James said.

"Then why?" She watched her brother stretched out on his stomach with his eyes closed.

"Why rape? Jeez, Francesca, I can't know everything," James said.

"I suppose it's to make a woman or an Indian feel like nothing," she said.

"Maybe." He jumped up. "I wouldn't know. I'm not going to have to be an Indian or a woman." He raced across the back lawn and leaped up, catching the lowest branch of a large elm, swinging into the tree. Then he scrambled to the top and sat on the highest safe branch.

"Cesca!" he called.

She didn't answer.

"I can see everything from here," he said.

"I don't have to be in a tree to see everything," she replied. But James couldn't hear her.

The people in Bethany had learned to be conventional; they lived careful lives and guarded their secrets.

"If we ever have trouble in our family, don't tell," Sophia warned her children. "When someone asks 'How are you?' Always say Fine, thank you. Fine, fine, fine. And smile."

So Mrs. O'Malley, who lived at the mouth of the Leonora River in the Irish section, went to Mass on Sundays and Wednesdays without fail, raised her children to be good and obedient. Nobody but a child like Cesca Woodbine, who peered into windows at people's lives, would have guessed in a million years that a man who came to see Mrs. O'Malley in a milk truck was not delivering milk.

And Mrs. Adler wouldn't have dreamed of telling a soul in Bethany that Mr. Adler beat her regularly with a dog's leash when he was drunk. Mr. and Mrs. Adler went to the Methodist church at Main and Hawthorne and were active on committees.

Anna Wheeler was head nurse at Mercy Hospital, one of

the few married women in the town to have a paying job. There were people in Bethany who asked particularly for Anna when they were ill. Certainly no one would have been pleased to hear that Anna took Thursday mornings off from work and that after Mr. Wheeler left for the First National Bank of Massachusetts, where he was a teller, the cleaning woman arrived full of an affection for Anna Wheeler which her neighbors would not have understood.

People in Bethany did, however, guess about Sophia and Sam Weaver. They would not blame Sam Weaver for any indiscretions, because he was a beloved physician and a widower besides. If anything had gone on between them, it would have been Sophia Woodbine's fault.

In a town of smoldering allegiances, the descendants of Santa Francesca Allegra were high, fixed points—certain in an electrical storm to attract lightning.

There was a popular story in town about Cesca. Both she and James, when they were young, had trouble with authority, James because he got into fights. Cesca's difficulty was with teachers, old maids in early middle age whose affection for children diminished year after year in their bitterness at knowing they would not likely have children of their own.

Cesca did not usually talk back to teachers. Neither, however, did she do what she was told. The children in the class were fascinated by her silent rebellions. Often she was sent out of the room to sit on a stool in the corridor or asked to write *I will do exactly what I am told to do* a hundred times in perfect script. Once she was suspended for insolence. When she was twelve years old and in frequent trouble with her music teacher, Miss Jones, she was sent out of class for the month of March.

"I didn't ridicule Miss Jones," she told James, who was standing with a group of friends on the playground outside the elementary school. "I wouldn't bother ridiculing such a silly woman. I hope she drops dead."

Which is exactly what she did.

The next morning James and his friends, remembering Cesca's remark on the playground, were very surprised to learn that Miss Jones, aged thirty-one and seemingly in perfect health, had dropped dead of a brain hemorrhage eating supper at her grandmother's house the night before.

"Cesca Woodbine's a witch," James's friends had said, and even James had told his father at supper that Cesca had willed Miss Jones dead.

"So," James said, sitting down next to Cesca with a boxed lunch. "How is the witch of Bethany, Massachusetts?"

"She gave me a good fortune," Maud said.

"That was a choice," Cesca said.

At high noon, the sun was bright and warm, filtering through the clear air. The green hills were full of color, and women and children wore bright summer clothes in advance of the season. A group of string musicians strolled among the picnickers sitting on blankets. Mr. and Mrs. Clarence Peartree, dressed in costume, were carrying trays of jams and preserves; and Mrs. Adler sold sweet cakes baked that morning and vegetables she put up every fall.

Dressed in black and white as harlequins, Tommy Doyle and his sister rode unicycles through the crowd, dodging the children, falling occasionally. The high school band in maroon uniforms with gold tassels played patriotic music. Contests were going on on the football field—sack races, three-legged races, tugs-of-war, eggs in spoons. A crowd of little children raced after Louisa Natale, dancing behind her, reaching for the blue streamers on her broad-brimmed hat. Colin Mallory, strolling in front of a group of boys who followed him, stopped Louisa, took off her broad-brim and kissed the top of her head.

"They ought to marry," James said of Louisa.

"They're too much alike," Cesca said. "He'll marry someone very different."

"Why do you worry about marrying?" Maud asked. "We're too young."

"What else do people in Bethany worry about?" Cesca asked. "We go to college if we're lucky and then we marry."

"Will you come back here after Juilliard?" Maud asked Cesca.

"I plan to go to France," Cesca said, and the two girls laughed, leaning against each other like sisters.

Because of the holiday, Julian Woodbine got up late. Since Sophia had become ill, he didn't like holidays, preferring the carefully planned structure of his working day. He filled the noon spaces on his calendar with lunch, the evenings after supper with meetings. People liked Julian Woodbine. Young men thought of him as a father; his contemporaries looked on him as a brother, wanting to claim a personal relationship. His well-controlled intensity excited their interest. He was a successful man in worldly terms. But on the few occasions when he permitted the indulgence of self-examination, he concluded that the Woodbine men were a common breed in America whose success in the world was matched dollar for dollar by failures of the heart.

He was darkly funny, with an acerbic wit, self-contained and enigmatic, inviting, by his mannered distance, people's curiosity. No one knew him well, although he could be charming. Often he forgot names, particularly of women whom he had known for years, as if he enjoyed these people as objects for observation but had no interest in them personally. Except for Sophia. Sophia Allegra had set his heart on fire. He had been forty-four and a widower when he met her at Rooster's Tavern, where he'd gone in a fit of loneliness. Rooster's was not a place to find a man like Julian—a lawyer, a judge in the county seat, whose English family had been in America since the 17th century. In Bethany, an unlikely town for Woodbines, his family had maintained a distance, keeping company primarily with one another. Their passions dissipated after twenty and thinned to sentimentality.

Julian married Sophia in a month in spite of objections. After seeing her, he could hardly remember his first wife, a pale apparition, imperceptible as a spring breeze, floating through the large Victorian house.

Their love affair did not last beyond the birth of the children—not because Julian did not love Sophia, but because his expression of love for her was never satisfactory. Although she loved him, there was never enough intensity

46

between them to compensate for the long loneliness of her isolated childhood.

"You always make me feel as if I'm a greedy monster," she told him once, "wanting more, more, more while you fall back on the pillow exhausted saying, enough, enough, enough. That's all there is left of me."

Julian had more to give, but his own emotions were blocked by a childhood of strictness and restraint. He had inherited a long history of hurt feelings.

Nevertheless, there was more than enough love between them to sustain their children with the belief in a family, at least within the confines of their own home.

Prince Hal was feeding his trained cats tuna fish in the kitchen.

"How many times do I have to tell you we can't afford solid white-meat tuna fish for cats, Hal?" Julian said, taking down the coffee.

"Now watch this," Hal said, paying no attention to his father. He held up a large chunk of tuna, and the cats, purring and rubbing against one another's fur, stood up on their hind legs.

"Meow," Hal said.

"Meow," the cats replied.

Hal put the tuna behind his back.

"Lie down," he commanded the cats, and they lay down, rolling on their backs, purring uniformly.

"Meow," the cats replied, and Hal dropped a bit of tuna for each of them.

"Aren't they amazing?"

"Absolutely amazing," Julian said drily.

At seven years old, Hal was a gentle, funny boy, full of high-minded adventures which he played out, sometimes with friends, more often alone, in the Woodbines' long garden. Because the life he lived in his mind was more exciting than life with friends, he tended not to form attachments beyond his family and the cats.

Hal had raised the cats himself from two mothers who had

two litters each. He spent hours with them, filching tuna from the larder as a prize for tricks. They followed him around from room to room, outside in the garden, even occasionally to school. All eight of them slept on his bed at night, on his pillow, under the blankets, against his back and stomach, a sleeping bag of cats.

When Julian went downstairs to leave for the Festival, he found Prince Hal standing on the couch examining his collection of World War II guns. In periods of his life, Julian had become a collector—once of stamps and early postcards, another time of old foreign coins, and after he returned from World War II, he had collected the guns, which lined the wall opposite his desk in the study.

"I thought you had one loaded gun," Hal said when Julian came in. "Cesca told me you kept one because there was a robbery when they were small."

"It's in my desk drawer."

"She said you taught her and James how to shoot when they were my age."

"Would you like to learn?"

"I'd hate it," Hal said. "I just wanted to see the loaded gun."

In the car on the way to the Festival, Hal brought up the subject of the gun again.

"Does Mother know the gun is there?" he asked offhandedly.

"Of course," Julian said, understanding what his son was asking. "She wouldn't use it. Like you, she hates guns."

Colin Mallory was leading a group of young men around the fairgrounds, a Revolutionary War general. He raised his hand in the air, pointed his forefinger towards the clowns or marionettes, the bake sale or hot dog stand, and off they'd all go, swaggering behind him, imitating his high-hipped gait, the way he put his left thumb in the slender pocket beneath the waist of his blue jeans, the way he swung his head so that his hair fell just over his eye like a swag curtain.

The parade of the Revolutionary Army was not without design. The soldiers' march around the fairgrounds was less to see than to be seen. Afterwards, they gathered in the parking lot behind the high school to discuss their plans for the evening. They sat on the hoods of cars, smoked cigarettes, spit out smoke.

"So Colin, do you have a date tonight?" Billy Naylor was pygmy-size and fat, but very tough. "Not at all nice," according to James, who had fought with him when they were in high school.

"Not yet, Billy. I hate to rush into things," Colin said. He was lying on the hood of his father's station wagon blowing smoke rings. "Why? Are you free?"

There was a long, unsteady laughter in the group. Sexual jokes were favored among the young men in Bethany in 1955, particularly homosexual ones, and Billy was often the target.

"I was thinking of Francesca Woodbine for you, Colin," Billy Naylor said.

Colin closed his mouth. He watched the smoke curl out of his nostrils.

"Yeah, Colin, what do you think?" Tim Greenfield asked.

Colin sat up. "Now, I favor virgins, I'll have to tell you."

"At least you can get your fortune told," Billy said.

"Anybody here had his fortune told?" Colin called out.

There was a chorus of "No."

"Chicken?"

No one replied.

"What about you, Tim? Chicken?"

Tim Greenfield shrugged. He was a tall, angular boy and smart, but he kept his sharp intelligence well hidden so as not to be left out.

"She honest-to-God scares me. Ever since she killed the music teacher in sixth grade," Tim said.

"Cesca didn't kill the music teacher. The woman died on her own," Colin said. "So, who's going to get his fortune told? Come on. Billy?"

"I'm scared shitless of her, if you want to know the truth,"

49

Billy said. "I think she can see straight through your head with her eyes closed. She knows stories in this town you wouldn't believe. Ask her brother."

"What you got to hide, Billy?" Tim Greenfield asked.

"What he's got to hide is that he wants to go to bed with me, Timmy, but don't you tell anyone. It's our secret."

Billy Naylor lit a long black cigarette. "Turkish," he said cockily. "If I want a boy lover, Colin, he'll have to have a longer dick than you. And not so purple."

"Oh, Billy boy," Colin said. "God made my dick the exact right size for women, and purple is a color they're mad for."

"So you gonna get your fortune told or not?" Tim asked.

"Come on, Colin. Chicken?" Billy asked.

"Not a bit chicken," Colin said, standing, brushing off his blue jeans, putting out his cigarette on the driveway.

"You're looking good," Billy said. "Hope she doesn't guess you want to screw her."

"It could be, Billy darling, that she wants the same thing," Colin said, and walked up the hill behind the high school towards the fortune-teller's booth.

Colin Mallory had been graced from childhood with good fortune and attention. He was arrogant, certainly, and unaltered by grief.

After he first took hold of himself under the soft cotton sheets with a bright full moon staring at him over the Leonora—"Forgive me, Father, for I have sinned"—he ran his fingers through the warm pool of semen and fell asleep smelling the clean odor in his prayer-cupped hands.

He was fourteen when he made love with a woman—and she was a woman: Maia Perrault, who used to baby-sit the Mallory children when the Mayor and his wife went to Boston. One night at supper, Maia put her hand on Colin's thigh and saw his erection. He was awake when she came in to him that night in her long soft flannel nightgown. She knelt by his bed and kissed him gently on the lips, holding him as he rose. Then she took him in her mouth with such sweetness that he was overwhelmed, as if all the secret and forbidden pleasures of silk and roses and velvet had come to him in a waking dream.

Will Weaver was just finishing a snake show when Colin passed. He stood very straight, bound by snakes, one wrapped around his calves, one around his thighs, one binding his arms flat against his torso.

"'Lo, Will," Colin called out. "Comfortable?"

Will bent slightly at the waist, and the snake tying his arms unraveled in a leisurely fashion.

"Want to try it?" Will asked.

"No, thanks, though it's very kind of you to offer."

"Scared?" The snake around his waist caught itself on the branch of the tree and wrapped around it.

"You bet. I'm getting my fortune told now, and if it looks good enough to risk snakebites, I may take you up on the snakes."

"Cesca wouldn't tell my fortune," Will said, putting his snakes back into the cages.

In spite of the affection the town of Bethany felt for Will Weaver, Colin did not like him.

"He's crazy," Colin had told his oldest sister, Miranda, who was particularly fond of Will.

"Honestly, Colin, he's sweet and funny," Miranda had said. "You never know what he'll do next."

Colin opened the curtain of the fortune-teller's booth. He sat down on the stool across from Cesca and put his hands on the table between them.

"I've come on a dare."

She took his large and capable hands in her own, turned them over and looked at the palms, which were deeply lined.

"What's the dare?"

"That I let you tell my fortune." He made his hands shake in hers. "So here I am, not a bit worried, as you can see."

Francesca was beautiful in candlelight, he thought; her face had the deep, rich colors of the woman in the painting of the

Virgin Mary at Our Mother of Mercies Roman Catholic Church. She was restless and seductive, and he wanted her there on the floor of the fortune-teller's booth; he wanted to scramble under the layers and layers of muslin and satin skirts until he got at her.

"You know some people—especially the boys who graduated high school in your class—are afraid of you," Colin said, moving his stool closer.

"Because of my grandmother and the fortunes."

"Not because of your grandmother but the fortunes. Friends of mine believe you actually can predict the future."

"But you don't."

"Of course not."

Impulsively, he blew on her hand holding his, and she laughed.

"Well, I can't predict the future." She examined his hands, the color rising in her face, her heart like a bass drum in her chest.

"I have a short life line, right?"

The curve across his palm called the life line stopped halfway and Cesca traced it with her forefinger.

"Miranda has told me it's very short. She thinks that's amusing, of course."

"It's short," Cesca said. "But look at everything else on your palm. You have more lines than anyone our age I've seen. See?" She picked out a horizontal line. "You'll go to law school, probably Harvard."

"My grades are bad."

"Well, you'll go somewhere, and you'll do very well for a year or so, until . . . Look." She pointed to a broad vertical line intersecting the horizontal one. "You'll meet a lovely and dangerous woman."

"Terrific. Soon, I hope." He pointed to a short line on his palm. "Is that the woman? She looks fat to me."

"She's tall and slender and dark, and you'll fall in love with her."

"And get married and live happily ever after here in Bethany?"

"No, no, no," Cesca said, pointing to another line. "She

isn't going to be the kind of girl you marry at all. She's going to be a traveler. She'll take you to Spain and Africa—all over the world. And even though you know she's dangerous, you'll be so wild for her you simply can't leave her."

"Do I ever graduate from law school?"

"In time."

"And become a lawyer?"

"After you leave the girl in Morocco. The two of you have run out of money and you're living in a tiny room in a small hotel and she's become a belly dancer to make ends meet. She dances all night in casinos and in the morning she comes to you."

"And I don't do anything all day?"

"Except in the morning," Cesca said.

"I certainly hope the sex is good."

"Wonderful. That's why you can't leave her."

"My father is going to be very pleased with this fortune."

"You'll get back to America eventually. One morning, she won't arrive home from the casino and you'll search all over town for her and then you'll leave by boat to Spain and fly to America."

"And you'll be waiting for me here in Bethany, won't you?"

"Oh, no," Cesca said. "I'm the girl in Morocco."

"Tell me more."

"That's all I see." She put his hands down on the table, her own hands placed gently on top of them.

"You mean it's *kaput* for me after the girl in Morocco."

Cesca smiled.

"You are something," he said.

She felt blown up, a helium balloon, ten feet off the ground and rising. She was beautiful, her face hot and rosy, her breasts growing, filling the soft sand-colored blouse.

"You're coming to the dance tonight?" he asked.

"Perhaps."

"With me?"

She looked away.

"Will you come with me?"

"Maybe," she replied.

"I'll come back to get you at six o'clock exactly," he said.

53

He leaned across the table. She thought he was going to kiss her. Instead, he kissed his own finger and touched the tip of her breast with the imagined kiss.

Will Weaver was in a temper. He had watched Colin Mallory slide behind the curtain and sit down across from Francesca. Then he had watched the curtain close and pictured them behind it. She must be holding his hands in hers now, he thought, touching the palms with her soft fingers. Their heads were close together. He could kiss her if she would let him. And why wouldn't she let him. Every woman in Bethany would be happy to have Colin Mallory make love to her.

In a sudden fury, he reached into the cage and grabbed Odysseus—a large brown snake broad in the middle. With Odysseus wrapped lazily around his waist, he walked up the back of the hill beside the Leonora towards the fortune-teller's booth. His plan was to interrupt the love affair. He'd thrust Odysseus into a crack in the fortune-teller's booth behind the stool where Cesca was sitting. No one would see him.

When he reached the back of the booth, he could hear their voices whispering to each other, and through the spaces in the two-by-fours, he could see Francesca's cranberry skirt.

He held Odysseus around the neck and lay down on his stomach. He picked up a twig, which he slid between the open slats to lift Francesca's skirt. Odysseus, when he put him through the boards, would slither under the long cranberry tent.

The talking inside the booth had stopped; there was a commotion as Colin stood up, knocking over the stool. And Will slipped Odysseus through the crack just beside the stool where Cesca was sitting.

The fine brown warrior wriggled forward under the layers of skirt. Will crouched low to the ground, moving like an Indian, and scrambled back down to the Snake Booth. By the time Odysseus had reached the obstacle of Francesca's long and slender right leg, Will was back with his snakes preparing to put on another performance.

Odysseus examined Cesca's leg, his head arched, alert with

interest. Then he whipped quickly up her calf, winding his rope body around it, stopping at her bent knee. All this before she had a chance to scream.

"I thought she had cracked up," Colin reported later.

Her eyes were set as if she had lost consciousness, and then she screamed.

Without moving, she lifted her petticoats and stretched out her leg, around which Odysseus had wound himself so that his arched head extended like a branch from her knee.

Cesca was still screaming when Will burst through the curtain. A crowd had begun to gather.

"Oh, God, Cesca, I'm so sorry," Will said, taking Odysseus. "I didn't even notice he'd gotten out."

"For chrissake, Will, you ought to be sent to a zoo someplace," Colin said.

"He wouldn't have hurt you, Ces," Will said. "You know that I'd never hurt you."

Cesca couldn't speak.

"I'm really sorry. You'll have to forgive me," Will said.

"Are you all right?" Colin asked after Will had left.

She leaned against the outside of the booth, still white.

"Will Weaver's a lunatic," Colin said.

"It wasn't his fault," Cesca said; but she was glad when Colin put his hand gently on the side of her head and left it there long enough to stop the pounding in her temple.

By late afternoon, the Festival was at its height. Children ran or rolled down the hills surrounding the high school, colliding at the bottom, full of merriment. There was a maypole dance around the flagpole, with green and yellow and rose streamers pulled into the shape of an inverted ice cream cone by the children dancing. There were pony rides and acrobats, young girls wandering through the crowds in aprons selling daffodils. The line outside Francesca's booth had shortened. Maud passed by to ask Cesca to join her and James for a picnic supper at dusk. "I may be busy," Cesca said. She wondered if Colin Mallory would come back for her.

Will packed up his snakes and closed his booth. He had finally sold all his snakes but Persephone, his take for the Snake Show larger than he had anticipated. And, he thought, quite pleased with himself, he'd broken up the romance that might have been starting between Francesca and Colin Mallory.

"I saw you danced all evening with Colin Mallory," James said when he picked Francesca up at ten and loaded the booth onto the back of the pickup truck.

"Not all evening."

"He was the only one you danced with. I was watching," James said.

James was right. She had danced with Colin all evening. Slow dancing to the music played by wandering musicians on the blacktop where the younger boys shot baskets after school. She and Colin had fit together perfectly. He was taller, but her head came above his shoulder, so their faces touched. When he talked to her, his breath brushed her long hair, and he held his hand strongly against the small of her back; she could feel him just above her pubic bone. Warm with longing, she pressed against his chest.

They drove down the high school hill in silence.

"Are you going out again?" James asked.

Colin had asked her to meet him after midnight. He'd said he had the job of cleaning up the high school lawn after the Festival was over, but he'd come for her in his father's car, park at the bottom of the Woodbines' driveway and honk once. She'd have to listen carefully for the honk.

"I'm not going out again tonight," she said to James. "Are you?"

"Yes," James said. "Colin asked you, didn't he?" James was angry. He turned the radio to classical, the knob at top volume, and gripped the steering wheel with both hands.

"He asked me," Cesca said. "I don't do everything I'm asked, you know."

He opened the window on his side completely so the sound of the wind whipping behind their necks was as loud as the music.

Julian and Hal were already back, and Hal's light was off. Francesca sat in the cab of the truck and waited for James to turn off the radio and talk to her.

"What I do is none of your business," she said when he could hear her.

Julian had been drinking. He was standing in the living room, looking at his own reflection in the windowpane.

"Darling," he called when Cesca came in. "I'm glad you're back."

The sight of Cesca occasionally filled Julian with unspecific longings; he embraced her, stirred by emotions he couldn't name. And she pulled away from him.

He followed her upstairs. He had not thought he had drunk so much, but he seemed to sail up the steps, his feet not touching the ground. The door to Francesca's room was shut, and James had just come out of his room in a change of clothes.

"I'm going out," he said.

"At eleven?" Julian asked.

"It's Festival night. I'll be back at two. May I take the pickup?"

Francesca was sitting on her bed when Julian knocked and opened the door.

"Are you in for the night, Ces?"

She hesitated.

"I'm going to bed now," she said. "I'll turn off the lights except one for James."

"How was telling fortunes?"

"Okay," she said abstractedly. She didn't want him to know she was going out. "Good night."

She listened as he walked down the hallway to his bedroom. She heard him bang around his dresser and lose his balance as he slipped out of his trousers. She went to the door of her bedroom so she could see when his light went out. He usually

57

read, but he'd drunk too much for reading. She hated it when he had too much to drink.

Upstairs, she heard her mother on the piano tentatively composing. Once or twice she thought she heard Sophia's high soprano voice trying out a song. Cesca slipped a light wool challis robe over her clothes and went up the back stairs beside Hal's room to her mother's studio.

The lights there were arranged for performance—one gentle lamp by the bed diffusing softly through the room and one bright floor lamp shining on the piano like a spotlight. When Cesca knocked, her mother was standing at the piano, playing a melody lightly with her right hand. She was dressed in a long peach gown which she had bought in 1933, when she was first married, to go to a dance in Boston. She looked lovely and young in the suffused light.

"Hello, darling," she said, smiling at Cesca. "I could hear the Festival from here. Was it nice?"

"Mmm," Cesca said, nodding. "All right. Telling fortunes was a little odd. Sam Weaver came."

"Did he?"

Sophia didn't color with the mention of Sam Weaver's name as she'd used to do before her breakdown.

"He told me about the membrane on my face when I was born."

"Again." Sophia laughed. Her laugh was easy—perfectly normal, Cesca thought.

Everyone, even James, tiptoed around Sophia as if she were a fragile china figurine, the delicate French kind with fluted lace skirts which can break at the slightest touch. But since the studio had been built, Sophia had seemed fine to Cesca.

"It doesn't seem fine to me that she spends every day in the attic, seeing her children only when we go upstairs to see her," James said.

"It's not the attic," Cesca said. "It's a studio, and she's happy there."

James thought his mother was crazy. And what bothered him in particular, perhaps because he was a man, was the fact that she slept in a small single bed with a white fluff comforter—and never in bed with Julian.

"Sam always asks about you," Cesca said,

"I know he does. I haven't wanted to talk with him since I was ill," Sophia said. "I'm not sure why."

Sam Weaver had been her imaginary refuge for years—her lover, although they had never had sex. Once he had kissed her with intention after a party at which they had both had too much to drink. But since she had moved to the studio, people had fallen away like veils—Julian and Sam; even, she had to confess, her children—and she was left to herself. Which had become entirely satisfactory.

She pulled Cesca by the lapels of her flowered robe.

"I see you're still dressed underneath your robe," she said. "Are you going out again?"

Cesca blushed.

"I have been asked."

Sophia kissed her on the forehead.

"I know you're twenty and have been to New York, but that's still young, Cesca. I was twenty-six before I'd been with a man, and then only when I married your father. Be careful with yourself. It is something for a woman to make love to a man. Entirely different than for a man."

"I'm not going to make love," Cesca said quickly.

Sophia ignored her.

"A woman can be touched in a place of too much tenderness."

"Don't worry. Nothing will happen," Cesca insisted. "I probably won't even go out."

She kissed her mother good night.

Going down the narrow steps from the studio to the second floor, she did wonder, however, what her mother was saying to her and whether the tenderness Sophia mentioned had to do with the body or the heart. She wanted to know why her mother, still young and lovely as she was, had decided to sleep alone. She wondered if desire left the body in small rushes with age or simply fell into a long snow-white sleep.

It was midnight. She put her old stuffed animals from childhood and two pillows under the quilt so if James peered into the moonlit room, he would think she was sleeping on her stomach. She turned out her bedside lamp, took off her shoes, put on the old cape which had belonged to Francesca Allegra and crept down the hall. Prince Hal was sleeping in a heap amidst his cats, and her father kept up his warrior's steady snore. Cesca slipped down the back steps, opened the kitchen door, took a flashlight from the toolshed, put on her shoes and went down the driveway to where Colin Mallory was parked in his father's car with the lights out.

"I came."

He laughed. "So I see."

He turned on the engine and drove without lights until he came to a stop sign.

At the stop sign, he reached over and touched her right breast, pressing the nipple gently between his fingers.

She was afraid and thrilled and wondered if he was feeling as she felt, at once very wise and innocent as a child curling catlike into sex.

They drove down Elm and across Tulip, behind the high school and into Maple Avenue, where the Mayor lived. Colin took a side road to a small frame cottage on a bank of the Leonora. He had been there already. Candles were lit, the couch had been opened into a bed and a bottle of dark red wine was on the table.

He kissed her, and his lips had the softness of a girl's. She felt him pressing insistently against her belly. He undressed her while she stood, taking off her cape, which he tossed on the bed as a blanket, then her blouse, which buttoned in the back, until she faced him in a full cranberry-colored skirt naked above the waist.

"You are beautiful," he said to her. He made her shy.

She untied the ribbon in her hair and lay with him. He kissed her breasts, hiding his eyes in her long hair. He took off her skirt and petticoat and panties with such gentleness that she was neither frightened nor sick with the confusions of longing, and when he kissed her, running his warm tongue along the folded petals of her vagina, she was burning and wanted him to fill her.

They awoke at dawn in each other's arms, with the smell

of candle wax heavy in the small damp room.

"It's almost light," she whispered. And they dressed quickly, ran to the car and drove off. She was racing up the driveway of her house just as the grandfather's clock in the hallway sounded five.

When James opened her bedroom door at eight to wake her for breakfast, Cesca was sleeping, her arms around the deceptive lump of pillows she had left of herself, wrapped in the cape Francesca Allegra had used as a protection against the cold, cold air crossing the Atlantic.

2.

The Wedding of
Francesca Woodbine

The summer of 1956 swooped into Bethany with an un-forgivable heat. Even in June and on the Leonora River, the air hung over the town heavy as brocade curtains. In the morning, Cesca would wake at dawn stirred to consciousness by a tingling in her body, softened by desire thin and fine as silk. She was in step with the season.

She had called James at Harvard in May of his junior year to tell him she was getting married.

"At twenty-one," he said crossly. "What about your singing?"

"Married people sing," Cesca replied.

"I think it's a catastrophe," James said.

"Colin Mallory is not a nice man," James told his father.

"He's arrogant, perhaps, but perfectly agreeable," Julian said. "Cesca is strong and full of temper. No one is going to hurt her."

"Right now, Cesca could be hurt by a flea," James said.

He was right.

In the year Cesca had loved Colin Mallory, she had shed her skins. She was high-spirited with unfettered happiness and certain of herself. The world, as she saw it, had been perfectly designed, and she fell seamlessly into place in the pattern.

That spring, after she had dropped out of Juilliard, she danced from room to room of the large frame house. Whirling into a bedroom, she'd embrace the heavy cherry four-poster or kiss her own lips in the Sheraton mirror over her mother's dresser or fly down the banister into the arms of an imagined Colin Mallory waiting at the bottom of the steps.

"Cesca is driving me crazy," Hal said at dinner when James had come home from college.

"Don't let her near you. She's mentally ill," James said.

"Her state of mind won't last," Julian said. "Women are like this when they're in love. She'll be herself again."

"Disappointed. Probably unhappy," James said crossly.

"Disappointed maybe. There's nothing quite like falling in love. If it lasted, we'd be incompetent to live our normal lives. But not unhappy, I hope."

James could not be consoled. He no longer felt towards Cesca as he had when their lives were woven into one material. He was bad-tempered at her silliness and shortsighted affections. Sometimes before he fell asleep at night, he wanted to shake Francesca until her head fell off.

When Cesca came home in May, she had been three months pregnant. Julian had shielded his own anguish with conversations about money. Would there be enough if she and Colin married right away? What would be the cost of an abortion? Or the cost of sending Cesca to one of those homes away from Bethany where she could have the baby and put it up for adoption?—as though the cost in emotions could somehow be held in escrow.

"Colin wants to marry me," Francesca said. "We wanted this baby."

The truth was Colin didn't want to marry anybody. Francesca had called him in May from New York to say she was pregnant and would he come down to the city, which he did on the next bus out of Kingston, Rhode Island, where he was in his last year at the University of Rhode Island. He was

63

pleased with himself. He was behaving responsibly, facing the consequences of his actions. He was certain that he'd be rewarded by an easy solution. From a friend in Providence, he'd found the name of a doctor who would perform an illegal abortion under safe conditions for three hundred and fifty dollars, which he borrowed and took with him in cash on his trip to New York.

He never had a chance to bring up the subject of an abortion. Cesca met him at the Port Authority bus terminal, flushed the color of holly berries, full of such love for him and his gift to her that he forgot his resolve. He fell into marriage, a drunk, conscious of events and how they were overtaking him but too weak-limbed and thickheaded to resist.

By June, however, with the wedding lowering on him like the unbearable heat, Colin was restless.

One sultry night, two weeks before the ceremony, he went with Cesca to Rooster's Tavern. At the next table he saw Louisa Natale with a group of young men including James Woodbine. She had matured since he had last seen her, grown more beautiful; he smiled at her directly across the tables.

He was not a man to be satisfied with the mind's imaginings. The next day he called Louisa Natale and asked her would she come over to the cottage on Monday afternoon for lunch.

On Monday he was supposed to begin a summer job on a fishing boat, but he called in sick. His parents and sisters were away for a few days in New Hampshire. Francesca was driving to Boston with James to pick up her wedding dress, which had been altered to fit her growing waist.

Certainly Louisa knew what Colin Mallory had in mind, but she didn't feel responsible for Cesca Woodbine's heart. In fact, she had no great sympathy for other people; like a Himalayan cat, that rare breed of unusual beauty, she was an object for admiring.

On Monday, she dressed for work, where she was a guide at the House of the Seven Gables, in a white lawn dress just skirting her ankles, with a broad lavender tie around the waist. From the top of her closet, where she kept her collection of hats—broad-brims, pillboxes, net-and-lace ones, tiny cloches, cylindrical boxes from the thirties, calico bonnets, a home-made one of pigeon feathers and one made of mauve ribbons; always since she was thirteen or fourteen, she had worn hats, even to school—she took down her particular favorite, a broad-brimmed white straw decorated with a swan's head, rising in a lovely arch, made out of stuffed silk.

As soon as the liquor store opened Monday morning, Colin Mallory went to buy champagne. At noon, he called Francesca's house to make sure she had gone to Boston as she had planned to do. When no one answered, he assumed that she had left with James, who was picking up some things at Harvard. Colin showered and dressed in blue jeans and a white shirt unbuttoned to his chest. He looked quite wonderful, he thought, examining himself in the mirror on the bathroom door—a fine figure, too young and full of life to suffocate in a closed box of a house with a wife and baby. He was not inclined to self-examination or reflection, but if he had been, he would have known that despite his resentment, Cesca Woodbine had a hold on him, not through entrapment but by his own desire for her.

Francesca left the house on Monday just before noon to cool herself in a walk along the river. She had risen late, and when she came down to breakfast, James was already in the kitchen and Hal had left for school. James told her that the pickup was at the Sunoco station in town for repairs and wouldn't be ready until late. They'd go to Boston in the after-noon. She went down the long drive to Hawthorne and straight down Hawthorne to the bank of the Leonora. There was always a current, even in summer, and children were dis-couraged from swimming there. Cesca walked along the bank in her bare feet with the water up to her ankles.

As she walked, she thought about James and picked long-stemmed periwinkle wildflowers, which she wound together in a wreath. Since her pregnancy, her brother's feelings for

65

her had been different, as if she were an object for ridicule, not love.

She walked over the small bridge below the town, behind the Mayor's house, passing through a thick path of cattails and yellow reeds as tall as she was. She saw the cottage where in two weeks she would be living as Colin Mallory's wife. Colin's truck was parked outside. Behind it was another car she didn't recognize. She was surprised and pleased. The other car must belong to a fellow fisherman—she had never seen it before. She put the periwinkle wreath in her hair and hurried down the path.

At the small table in the center of the room, Louisa Natale sat naked except for her swan hat, drinking champagne.

"To your great beauty," Colin said, pouring his glass of cool champagne between her long and tawny legs.

"To your great freedom." Louisa smiled.

What Francesca saw when she crested the hill beside the cottage and passed alongside the window was Louisa Natale in her swan hat. Her bare arms swung above her head in a slow dance.

Cesca stood for a moment, temporarily stunned, and then she ran down the hill to the river, her belly tight and throbbing. When it was too hot to run any longer, she simply fell in a heap of soft cotton dress and yellow reeds. The sun was a pale curtain, a thick gauze-like haze which spread over the river, smothering Cesca so she couldn't breathe. She lay against the bank as if unconscious.

Then a hot stream of adrenaline began its swift voyage through her body and she was convulsed with rage.

Every thought was swept out of her mind, tornado-struck by Colin Mallory's betrayal.

She was going to kill him.

Colin was resting, half-sleeping, on the couch when Francesca knocked. He was light-headed with champagne and thinking mainly of Cesca. Wanting her. The afternoon with Louisa, the swan woman, had left him bereft.

"Cesca? Is that you?" he called. "Door's open."

She had taken her father's .22 revolver from the desk drawer. She knew very well how to shoot it. This particular revolver she had used for target practice when she and James were taught to shoot. Since the gun was kept in the desk drawer for protection, it was always loaded except for the first chamber. She had run down the drive from the house and along the river holding the revolver in her deep pocket. Only when she reached the door to the cottage—Louisa Natale's car was no longer there—did she take the revolver from her pocket and pull the trigger once, past the empty chamber. The revolver in her hand was as familiar to her as the feel of shoes or gloves in winter. She pushed the door open with her shoulder.

Nothing else was in her mind but killing Colin Mallory. She was alert and in control. In the last hour, the old comfortable world, a set design made of quickly dispensable materials, had fallen away.

"Cesca!" Colin said in horror when he saw her. She had wanted him to see her shoot him.

"Cesca, don't!" He jumped up from the couch, perhaps in the sudden realization of what she must have seen with Louisa.

She fired the revolver, holding her right hand absolutely steady with her left. And then she ran out the front door, down the hill, through the cattails and the yellow reeds by the river. She put the revolver, still hot from firing, in her pocket and held her hand on it to keep it from hopping—even after she had slowed to a walk. She continued along the bank to Hawthorne, turned on Elm and up the hill towards her own drive.

She walked by the house, down the long path through a small apple orchard which opened at the back of the property to a meadow, a fishpond without fish, a cement bench, an old rope swing and the tiny graveyard where Hal had buried a litter of kittens that had died of fleas the previous spring.

There she knelt quickly and dug a hole with a stick. When it was too deep for the stick, she dug some more with her hand, burying the revolver. She heard James pull up the driveway in the pickup. When he stopped the truck, she was just emerging from the trees.

"Want to leave for Boston now?" he called out.

"Sure," she said. "Let's go to Boston, now, now, now as soon as I get my shoes."

She walked on air into the house and upstairs to her room. She looked in the mirror at a woman whom she had never seen before, whose black hair she brushed with a silver brush. Then she washed her hands and went downstairs, where James was writing a note to Hal saying they were on their way to Boston and would be home after supper.

"What time is it?" Cesca asked.

"About two thirty," James said.

"Exactly?"

"Two thirty-three and two seconds. Let's go."

"To Boston, to Boston, to buy a fine pig. Home again, home again, jiggity, jig," she said flatly as they coasted down the driveway.

James looked at his sister. She sat with her head straight ahead, her hands on her lap and an expression on her face, even in profile, that suggested she had had a large portion of her brain removed or else she was dead.

All the way to Boston, they didn't talk.

At Charles Street, James let Cesca out of the car just in front of Sweet Nellie's Dress Shop.

"I'll be back in an hour," he said. "You okay?"

"One hundred percent," she said. "Fine, fine, fine."

She told Miss Nellie she didn't want to try on the dress. In fact, she felt a little sick from the drive in. She was sure it fit.

But Miss Nellie insisted, helping Cesca take off the thin cotton shift she was wearing. The wedding gown was simple white linen with a deep round neck, tiny sleeves capping her shoulders, a scalloped hem like inverted tulips.

"There," Miss Nellie said, buttoning up the back, pulling the material over the swell of baby at the waist. "It's beautiful."

She called her seamstress. "You are a picture. So pretty. See, Tonia. Lovely as an Easter lily." She handed Francesca an artificial bridal bouquet to try. "Here. Just look at yourself. It takes my breath away."

Cesca stared without recognition at the strange woman repeated in the three-way mirror. What she saw reflected was a young bride in a white, white dress. She was disconnected from her own fragile brain.

Colin Mallory died slowly. When Cesca shot him, he started after her before pitching forward. And then he pulled himself through his own blood to the front door, calling for help.

Cesca took the wedding dress out of its box and hung it on her closet door. She was ill, she told James when they got back from Boston. "The flu," she told her father when she climbed into bed, wishing for total darkness without delay.

"Something is the matter with Cesca," James said. "You should call Dr. Weaver."

"The flu is going around," Julian said.

"Billy Knowlton threw up on his desk," Prince Hal said, pleased to inform his family.

Later James checked on Cesca, but she was too deeply asleep for him to wake her.

When James went downstairs to talk to his father, Julian was sitting at the dining-room table with a glass of wine.

"Did Colin call today?" James asked.

Julian shook his head.

"Today was his first day on the fishing boat. He's probably exhausted."

"I can't wake Cesca. Something is the matter with her," James said. His father followed him upstairs.

"Cesca," James said, shaking her shoulders gently. "See?"

"She's breathing normally," Julian said.

"Of course she's breathing. I didn't say she was dead."

James turned on the light on her desk. "Did you see her dress?"

"I didn't." Julian touched the linen dress hanging on the closet door. "It's lovely. She'll look lovely, don't you think?"

The heat broke with small staccato storms during the night. The storms continued all of Tuesday, turning the town of Bethany as gray as a room with the shades permanently drawn.

Colin was discovered just before midnight by his father when he returned with the family from New Hampshire. The Mayor called Sam Weaver, who confirmed what was perfectly clear: that Colin Mallory had been dead for several hours.

Dr. Weaver brought the news of Colin's death to Francesca. The Sheriff, who had come with him, stayed downstairs and talked to Julian and James.

According to the Sheriff, Colin had probably died between five and nine Monday evening, but the Coroner's report would be more specific. He had been shot in the abdomen at close range with a common .22-caliber revolver.

The Sheriff of Bethany, with the assistance of the county police and the only county detective, searched the cottage Tuesday morning. The only things they discovered were an empty bottle of brut champagne in the kitchen wastebasket and evidence that champagne had been spilled on a wooden dining-room chair. There were no fingerprints on the front door, but they took specimens from the cottage. The Mayor told the police that Colin was supposed to have begun work on the *Maid of Gloucester* that morning, and they knew from the captain of *Maid of Gloucester* that he'd called in sick.

Tuesday afternoon the Sheriff and one police officer stopped into Bethany Liquors, Ltd., to ask about the champagne. Anna Wheeler was there buying a bottle of Scotch for a patient in the hospital, and Sam Weaver came in to buy wine. Mr. Havens, who owned the store, told the Sheriff he hadn't been in on Monday, because of the heat and his bad heart. He said that Colin's murder was the worst thing that had happened in the community since he was twelve years old and the drugstore caught fire and burned to the ground. Mr. Havens' assistant came out from the back room where he was unpacking stock to say that yes, he'd sold champagne to Colin Mallory Monday morning early—Colin said he was buying it to try it out for the wedding. Which was odd, the assistant said, since Mr. Woodbine had already ordered thirty cases of Spanish champagne for a hefty sum.

"He couldn't have been too sick," the county detective said to the Sheriff once they were back in the patrol car.

"Not if he was the one drinking the champagne," the Sheriff said. "We can find out easy enough if he was drinking."

"I can't imagine a good-looking boy like that drinking champagne alone," the detective said.

The Sheriff called the Coroner and asked him to check Colin's alcohol consumption on the day of the murder and include that in his report.

"Now we find out who was at the cottage yesterday," the Sheriff said, "and I suppose that means we see Francesca Woodbine first."

Francesca had gone upstairs at about noon on Tuesday after Sam Weaver had come with the news of Colin's death. So tired she could barely make the steps to her mother's studio, she climbed under the soft comforter on her mother's bed and watched the day advance through the studio window. From time to time, Sophia left the piano, sat down on the bed next to her daughter and stroked Francesca's face or kissed her forehead. Once she put her hand on Cesca's belly between the pelvic bones so the uterus pulled taut and the embryo crested above the flat line of the stomach.

She didn't talk to Cesca except to murmur sweet words as if to an infant—"Oh, darling," she'd whisper. Francesca didn't cry. In fact, she felt absolutely nothing but the diffused terror of being found out. Nothing for Colin Mallory whatsoever. Her mind's slate had been erased even of the memory of emotion. Outside the studio, a fine wind was blowing the willows and the blue jays were making a terrible racket on the side lawn.

The small details beyond the window stood out in the gray

day, pale green leaves and black branches finely drawn, a squirrel perched foolishly on the electric wires, testing his luck.

"I feel nothing," she said to her mother once.

"Better to feel nothing, my darling," Sophia said.

"But I'm not dead," Cesca said. "Everything I see is clear, like the willow, as if I'm seeing it for the first time. Do you suppose I could be crazy?" she asked Sophia.

"You are in shock," Sophia said.

When the Sheriff came at three Tuesday afternoon, Cesca was having tea with her mother at the small wicker table next to the window. James came up to get Cesca, took her hand and helped her down the stairs. She was too weak to walk alone.

"Creeps," James said. "You'd think they could have left you alone for a couple of days."

"What do they want?" Cesca asked.

"They want to question you," James said. "They have to question everyone."

Cesca had decided about questions. How she was going to lie.

The Sheriff and the Chief of Police were in Julian's study with the county detective, whom Cesca had never seen. He was a small man with a crew cut who lit one cigarette off the next, putting out the stubs in the large ashtray on the coffee table.

Cesca was struck by the deep lines in his boyish face; she found her mind locked on his face, forgetting the others in the room.

"She's terribly distraught," Julian said quietly to the Sheriff.

"I'm sorry, Miss Woodbine, I know this is a terrible time for you."

"Terrible. Terrible. Terrible," Cesca repeated in her head. The word had a nice sound to it—not like terrible at all. Horrible was a better word for her time. Horror.

"Horrible," Cesca said without realizing she was going to speak.

72

"I'm sorry," the detective said. His name was Bill, he told her. The Sheriff's name was Bill as well.

> Oh where have you been Billy boy Billy boy
> Oh where have you been charming Billy
> I have been to seek a wife
> She's the joy of my life
> She's a young thing and cannot leave her mother

Francesca repeated her story to the Sheriff and the Chief of Police and the detective. On Monday, she had gotten up late and had breakfast, cleaned the house, taken her mother tea and biscuits, read in the garden, walked to the river and gone with James to Boston to pick up her wedding dress.

The Sheriff listened and made notes. When Cesca had finished speaking, he said in as gentle a voice as he possibly could: "Colin Mallory called in sick in the morning; he went to Bethany Liquors and bought a bottle of champagne, which we found in the kitchen wastebasket."

"I didn't talk to him Monday morning. I thought he was at work."

"You didn't see him at all on Monday?"

"No."

"He didn't call you?"

"He thought I was in Boston all day. James's truck had to be fixed, so we left later than we had planned to leave."

"Do you know of anyone who might have been with him? An old pal from high school or college?"

"No."

"Was anyone angry at him for any reason?"

"I don't think so."

"Were there any other girls who might have been jealous of you?"

"Colin and I have been together constantly for a year. All we wanted to do was get married," Cesca said in a flat voice.

Julian said that was enough. Cesca couldn't be questioned any longer. He told her to go back to the studio, which she did like an obedient child, nodding goodbye to the Chief of

Police as she passed through the study door.

"I'm sorry," the Sheriff said to Julian.

They shook hands.

"I haven't been to this house since you were robbed several years ago and I told you that you ought to keep a gun."

"I remember that," Julian said. He did not say he had taken the Sheriff's advice. He walked the men to the back door and watched them pull out of the drive in the Sheriff's patrol car. Then he went back to his study.

Instinctively, he went to his desk and opened the left-hand drawer where he had kept the loaded revolver. Inside were a legal pad with information on a case he had been trying in the fall, four ball-point pens, loose paper clips, a hymnal which Sophia had used at church before her illness, a picture of him in front of the county courthouse with his father after he became a judge and a valentine made by Francesca from red construction paper and white doilies. The revolver wasn't there.

He pulled the drawer all the way out. He looked in the second drawer, which was full of photographs which he spilled on the floor in his haste, and he looked in the longer middle drawer, where there were pencil shavings and business cards, letters from James when he went to camp. He checked the collection of guns on the wall, which was intact.

His mind leaped past the dangerous possibility of Francesca to Anthony, who did yard work and carpentry for the Woodbines and was always asking could he borrow a gun for shooting beaver out behind his place. Perhaps Anthony had taken the gun without asking, had meant to tell Julian later but forgotten. He'd speak to him on Friday when he came to trim the hemlocks.

Certainly it wasn't James. James had no interest in guns. Cesca, when they'd learned to shoot, had been much better at it than her brother. Julian closed the door of the study and went upstairs past Cesca's and Hal's bedrooms up the back stairs to the studio.

When Julian entered the room, Cesca was sitting on her mother's bed staring out the window at late spring. Sophia was standing at the long desk filling in notes in a musical composition book. The mood in the room was conspiratorial. He sat down on the rocker across from Cesca, feeling like an intruder.

"I won't talk to anybody else," Cesca said to her father.

"I don't want you to have to," her father said.

"I just won't." She was full of intention. All day, her mind had kept in view a specific picture of the last time she'd seen Colin Mallory before she killed him. She could remember the expression on his face as he got up from the couch. It was not horror exactly. Perhaps surprise. She ought to have told him what she saw with Louisa.

"I was walking by the cottage and saw Louisa in the window and she was naked," she should have said. But then he would have had time to wrest the gun away from her and she wouldn't have been able to kill him. "You have already killed me," she should have said to him. And as these thoughts were marching in double time through her brain, Julian was watching her and wondering if it was at all possible that Francesca had taken the gun from his desk drawer. She looked like a small child stricken by a disease of the brain; the expression in her hazel-colored eyes was unrecognizable.

"The Mallorys called. They are coming to see you tonight," Julian said.

"Okay." She would see the Mallorys, she thought. She'd do the things she had to do.

Downstairs, Julian went into his study and stood there for a long time examining the collection of guns on the wall across from his desk. There were two German Lugers, several Walther P-38s and three .22-caliber revolvers similar to the one missing from his desk drawer. He took one and loaded it, except for the first chamber, with cartridges he kept in a highboy under the collection, then placed the gun on the yellow legal pad in the top left-hand drawer of his desk. It was almost six o'clock when he left for his office to pick up some papers he needed to work on that night.

When Cesca went downstairs, the house was empty. James had left a note saying he and Hal were at the Mallorys' and would be back at six. Upstairs Sophia was resting.

She wandered into her father's study and stood sightless beside his desk waiting for something to disturb her—the telephone, perhaps; her mother's call. It had occurred to her that she should replace the revolver she had taken. For a long time she looked at the gun collection over the highboy. If she took one off the wall now, certainly her father would notice because it would leave a mark. And he might not notice the gun in his desk was gone for months. She was too weary to consider alternatives.

She went upstairs and took off her dress and slip, threw them in the bottom of her closet and ran a hot, hot bath. She lay in the water up to her chin until it cooled. Then she dressed for the Mallorys in a pale lavender summer cotton with a huge sash like the one she used to wear to church when she was a child.

Combing her hair in the mirror on her mother's dresser, she was astonished at her detachment. She had turned into a woman she didn't recognize. Perhaps she was even capable of murder with her wits about her. Anything seemed possible; she would not have believed her state of mind two days ago, so sure had she been of the sweet and quiet contents of her heart.

When she came home from work in Salem on Tuesday, Louisa Natale took down all her hats. Now she stood at the full-length mirror on her bedroom door. She put her hair in a rubber band and tried on the pigeon-feather hat at an angle.

"What are you doing?" her mother asked when she came upstairs.

"What does it look like?" Louisa said.

"Well, supper's ready," her mother said.

"I'm not hungry," Louisa said.

"You are hungry, Louisa. You have to eat. Everybody has to eat."

Louisa rolled her eyes.

She had found out about Colin's death at lunchtime. The

girl who sold sandwiches at the Salem Deli told her.

"The Mayor of Bethany's son was murdered last night," the girl said, with the pleasure some people have as the bearers of bad news. "Aren't you from Bethany?"

Louisa had nodded.

"Did you know the Mayor's son?"

"I went to school with him," Louisa said coolly.

All afternoon she maintained a strange calm. When the other guides in Salem began to talk about Colin's death, she said nothing, going about her business. She didn't want to know what had happened, certain that she was implicated in a terrible event and would be found out.

"What's the matter, Louisa?" her mother asked. "Just tell me why you don't want to eat and if the reason's good, you don't have to."

Louisa took off the hat with pigeon feathers and put it on the head of her baby doll. She picked up the one with streamers she had worn to the Festival two years before.

"I don't want to tell you."

"So you have to eat."

The Chief of Police called just as Mr. and Mrs. Natale sat down at the kitchen table for supper. He wanted to talk to Louisa.

Louisa took the phone upstairs.

"So what do you think he wants?" Mrs. Natale said to her husband. "Is she in some kind of trouble?"

"I can't believe Louisa's in trouble," Mr. Natale said from behind the evening news which separated him from his wife.

"I could hear trouble in the Chief's voice," Mrs. Natale said.

"He's a policeman, Lucilia."

Louisa came back into the kitchen after she had talked with the police. She dished herself out a bowl of stew from the small red pot on top of the stove, avoiding the potatoes.

"Are you going to say what happened?" Mrs. Natale asked.

Louisa sat down between her parents.

"You know Colin Mallory was killed," she said.

"An awful thing," Mrs. Natale said.

"I was probably one of the last people to see him alive," Louisa said evenly. "The Chief of Police is coming over now to question me."

"What do they think you did?" Mrs. Natale asked.

"I suppose they must think there's a chance that I killed him," Louisa said evenly.

She sat down at the table, eating in very small bites.

"It's policy to question everyone." Mr. Natale folded the sports page and put it under his chair. "What the police are doing is policy. Why were you the last person to see Colin Mallory? What were you doing at his cottage?"

"I went for lunch," Louisa said.

She had been frightened when the Chief of Police called. Perhaps someone had seen them through the window of the cottage. Perhaps, after she left, Colin had bragged to one of his friends about fucking Louisa Natale. The possibilities were endless. She did not have any idea who might have killed him.

If the police asked her, she would lie about the sex.

"Why go alone for lunch to the cottage of a man about to marry, Louisa? That was foolish in a town as small as Bethany," Mr. Natale said.

When he appeared, the Chief of Police, like every man, was very pleased to look at Louisa sitting across from him in her parents' living room. He told her that a neighbor of the Mayor's had seen a white Buick go into the driveway of the Mayor's house at noon on Monday and they had traced white Buicks and were questioning the owners.

"I went to lunch at Colin's," Louisa said.

"Was it lunch or champagne?"

Louisa hesitated. There had been lunch. "Both," she said.

"What were you celebrating?"

"He was trying out champagnes to take on his honeymoon with Francesca Woodbine."

As she was speaking, Louisa thought how easy it was to lie.

"Can you tell me the time you got there and left?"

"I had an hour and a half for lunch. I probably arrived about twelve thirty. I had to be back at work by one forty-five. The House of the Seven Gables can verify those times. I had a tour at two."

The other questions seemed odd to Louisa. What was Colin wearing, and what had they had for lunch, and was his shirt open because of the heat, or did he have a shirt on?

When the Police Chief left, he was satisfied that Louisa had been telling the truth.

At the office, the Police Chief checked Louisa's story. Her supervisor said she was back at work at one forty-five and had worked until five o'clock.

When he was a young officer the Police Chief had been told to look carefully for an inside job when you are investigating a murder. Seventy-three percent of murders are crimes of passion.

The Police Chief called the Woodbines' house at seven thirty Tuesday evening. Julian said the Mallorys were there and could the Police Chief wait until after eight to come.

The detective from the county and the Chief of Police returned to the county office together, but the Chief went to the Woodbine house alone, arriving just as the Mallorys were leaving.

Cesca was walking back to the house with James. In her pale lavender shift, she looked very young, almost frail, and the Chief waited until she was back inside the house to knock.

Julian answered. "I hate to do this, Judge," the Police Chief said, asking to see the loaded gun in Julian Woodbine's study. "Since people know you keep a loaded gun, I have to be sure it is still where you put it."

"You don't have to explain," Julian said. He opened the top left-hand drawer of his desk.

"Here it is," he said calmly, handing the gun to the Chief of Police.

"Good," the officer said. "Now I need to find out exactly what Francesca was doing from one o'clock to three when she left for Boston. Someone saw Colin at one o'clock."

Julian hesitated.

"I'll be very brief."

79

Cesca sat on the blue chintz couch in the study with her hands folded in her lap. She said that at one o'clock she was probably cutting flowers from her mother's garden. Lilacs, which she had put in a vase in the living room. "There are some in my mother's room, too." She spoke as if the subject were lilacs. And then she said she had walked down to the river to cool off. She had stood there for a long time feeling the water rush over her ankles, thinking about the wedding. She had made a periwinkle wreath like the ones she used to make when she was a child. Even as she spoke, she wondered what had happened to the wreath. She had been wearing it when she walked up to the cottage and that was the last she remembered it.

"Did anybody see you at the river?" the Sheriff asked.

"No, it must have been too hot. Everybody was inside."

"Did you do anything else?"

"I went to the fishpond in our yard; and when I came back to the house, James had arrived with the truck and was ready to leave."

James followed Francesca upstairs and sat down on her bed. She did look different, he thought, especially her eyes. When he'd found his mother after she had tried to kill herself, her eyes were as fixed as Cesca's appeared now—glass eyes in a china doll's head.

She took her wedding dress down from the door and hung it in her closet. She examined the perfume bottles on her dresser, opening them, sniffing them one by one, trying the contents of the last one behind her ears. Then she looked at herself in the mirror on her closet door, this time pulling a piece of her hair over her eyes, in a half-mask.

"Lots of people have sent flowers," she said absently.

"I know," James said. "Louisa Natale just called while you were with the Police Chief. Hal told me."

"Don't talk about it," she said. "I'm going upstairs with Mother."

James lay back on his sister's bed and closed his eyes.

Sophia was sitting in her rocker looking like a portrait of a woman in repose, shimmering in the soft light.

For a moment, Cesca wanted to tell her mother what had happened in Colin Mallory's cottage on Monday afternoon; but just as she was about to give away the terrible news, Sophia spoke first, saying she hoped everyone would let Cesca alone until after the funeral.

Francesca buried her face in her mother's dress, and Sophia braided and unbraided her long hair.

The temptation to talk had passed.

Downstairs, James joined his father for a drink.

"Do you want a beer?" James asked.

"I'm drinking Scotch," Julian said. He had had several already. "Sometimes even too much is not enough to drink."

At nine on Tuesday night, Will Weaver sat down with his father for a dinner he had cooked himself. At eighteen, he had suddenly taken on aspects of manhood. He was thinner than he had been, his boyish face had shape and he moved without the leggy awkwardness of boyhood. Otherwise, he had not grown up. He still kept snakes and played with them for hours on end in his room. He had flunked high school physics and French and was not allowed to graduate with his class.

"Certainly he's smart enough," the counselor had told Sam Weaver. "He simply doesn't want to graduate and leave home." Sam resolved to make Will repeat his final year.

"So Colin Mallory's dead," Will said dispassionately when his father sat down at the dinner table.

Sam Weaver didn't respond.

"I thought he was immortal." Will served pork chops and fried apples. "Have you seen Francesca?"

"I saw her this morning."

"Is she okay?"

"She was stunned today, of course."

81

"Are you going to the funeral?" Will tossed the salad and served his father. "I am, even though I didn't feel awful when I heard that he was dead."

Will had learned of Colin's death at noon on Tuesday when he stopped by Sunny's to get an ice cream cone. He asked Gloria at the counter all about the murder, seeking pleasure in the details. He wanted to know how Colin had died and whether he had suffered and what he looked like when he was discovered. But Gloria had only heard about Colin Mallory from the last customer and could not supply details.

Will and his father ate in silence, Will reading science fiction and Sam thinking of patients or women or just Sophia. Now he found his mind wandering to revolvers. He wondered whether Will had access to a gun; whether his older brothers had taught Will to shoot summers when they came home. Both of them had learned to use guns early, hunting turkeys in the woods, birds in the low marshes near Bethany. He wondered if Will had the capacity to kill. Certainly most people who knew him would say absolutely not. Will Weaver didn't have it in him to harm a flea. What he did have, and of this Sam was sure, was a peculiar combination of gentleness and violence. Sam had never seen the violence, but he felt it in Will's presence, an undercurrent invisible on the surface. Anything with Will seemed possible.

"Where were you yesterday?" Sam asked, cross for no apparent reason.

"In the morning, I was at school cleaning out my locker."

"And in the afternoon?"

"I had lunch at Sunny's and then went to the two-o'clock movie."

"I thought you were going to look for a job."

"I am, but yesterday I wanted to see a movie," Will said evenly.

At ten o'clock Tuesday night, Chief of Police Bill Becker went home. He had learned very little about the circumstances surrounding Colin Mallory's death. The neighbor who had seen Louisa Natale's car had left the house at one; she had heard no shots and was the only neighbor close enough to have heard anything. Nevertheless, driving home to his wife's baked-ham dinner, Bill Becker couldn't get Francesca off his mind.

On Wednesday morning after Colin's death, Sophia woke up restored. She arose at daylight, went downstairs and for the first time since her breakdown cooked breakfast for the children.

Julian was moved to see Sophia, much her old self, floating with ease and familiarity through the kitchen. He kissed her neck. There was no longer any sex between them, but a gentle affection remained.

"You did this for Cesca?" he asked of her new self-possession.

"I did it to repair our lives," she said, and brushed his face with her lips.

Hal was practicing tricks with his twin cats when his father called him for breakfast. He was using a red terry-cloth towel like a bullfighter; the two bored cats sat on matching kitchen stools licking their chests.

"Watch!" he called to James as he passed the bedroom.

"Beg," he said to the cats, who leaped in unison off the stools, ran to the flapping terry-cloth towel and stood on their hind legs.

"They are brilliant cats, Hal. You ought to take them on tour."

Hal tossed two chunks of tuna to his pets, who returned to their stools.

"I'm going to be a lion tamer for Ringling Brothers," Hal said, throwing the towel on his bed and following his brother down the back stairs. "Mother thinks it's a terrific idea."

"I doubt Daddy will be so enthusiastic," James said.

At breakfast, Sophia talked. She told stories about James and Cesca when they were small, about her mother, about Hal's plans to be a lion tamer, about her music. On and on she went in a soft lyrical voice, lifting the spirits of her household.

"I think we should have a toast," Hal said, raising his orange-juice glass.

"A toast to what?" Julian, always a literalist, asked.

"To us," Hal said, and drank his orange juice with a flourish. "Here together at breakfast."

Colin Mallory's funeral was on Wednesday. After the Mass, a lunch was held at the Mayor's house under the blue-and-white-striped tent that Mrs. Mallory had ordered for the rehearsal dinner which had been scheduled at their house the night before the wedding.

During the lunch, Cesca took a walk behind the cottage, through the reeds and yellow cattails along the river. A hundred yards, maybe more, from the cottage, she found a wet, flat, broken periwinkle wreath, which she ripped into small sections and threw into the center of a bayberry bush. Again and again in the last few days, she had been astonished at her self-possession.

She had decided that morning about the gun. To let well enough alone. To leave it buried near the fishpond, and should her father by chance happen to find his revolver missing, perhaps one of the workmen always around the house for the garden or to fix the roof or to redo the kitchen floor had taken it.

All of June and July, the investigation of the murder continued, day after day with diminishing results.

During the long summer, the swelling beneath her wide skirts grew larger, and Cesca was glad for the baby's life, as if the blood from the unborn child ran in reverse, flowing from his heart to her veins.

All summer she kept the house filled with scarlet and pale yellow flowers, perennials from her mother's garden which maintained their strength in the dark wet earth of winter and returned year after year as young green shoots unblighted at their roots.

Prologue

*S*anta Francesca gave Sophia the long cape she had worn crossing the Atlantic for her twenty-first birthday. It was a black wool cape with a stiff mandarin collar lined in scarlet silk, and handmade.

"Given to me by the Count," Francesca told her daughter. "A lucky choice of presents, because a girl from Sicily would not have had the proper clothing to keep warm on the North Atlantic. And there was a terrible storm. I stood in my cape at the cabin entrance holding tight to a brass railing while people on the deck were washed overboard."

"A good-luck cape," said Sophia, whose interest in her mother's story had to do with the Count.

"Why didn't he come to America with you?" she would ask when she was small. "Was he afraid of storms or seasickness? Didn't he want a baby?" she'd ask. "Tell me what he was like and can I see him."

One afternoon, Santa Francesca spread out her fingers palms up. "You want to see your father?" she said. "Choose any of my ten fingers."

"Each of these fingers is my father?" Sophia asked.

"One of them is your father," Francesca said. "One has black curly hair and one of them is musical and one of them has eyes dark as a crow's and one is generous with gifts."

"And which one is the Count?" Sophia had asked, bewildered, examining the fingers.

Francesca pulled her daughter onto her plump lap and kissed her small lips.

"They are all of them counts, Sophia," she said.

1.

Storm Warnings: August, 1961

Francesca lay on her back with Tobias straddling her belly, waiting for the promised storm. The air was still and hushed as death in a room of a funeral parlor. Nothing moved against the horizon. The leaves on the oak and willow trees, the high grasses were ocher and emerald green, bright with the unreality of oil paint. The air grew rancid.

The town of Bethany had never completely recovered from Colin Mallory's death. In five years, his killer had not been discovered. People began to believe he was at large and one of them. How else, they asked one another, would he have known to find Colin in the cottage instead of the large house? And why would he have bothered to kill Colin?—there was no evidence whatsoever of robbery. In small ways, they began to distrust one another—first in groups: the Poles distrusting the Italians, the Welsh uneasy with the Portuguese. And then a quiet and pervasive paranoia spread through the town, seeping like stagnant floodwaters underneath the cracks of houses. The Mayor resigned three months after his son's death and moved his family to Salem. When Tobias was born, the Mayor's family was cordial to Francesca but did not seem interested in developing a relationship with Colin's son.

At four and a half, Tobias looked like the childhood photographs of his father, with black curly hair and blue eyes, wide-set and dreamy. He was the only passion in his young mother's life.

"If it weren't for Toby, you'd be dead," James told his sister when he came home from medical school the summer of 1961 to assist Dr. Weaver in his practice.

Cesca had stopped singing. She lived at home in the room where she had grown up, and Tobias slept there too, first in a crib and then in the other twin bed. She cooked the meals, except for dinner, did the gardening and marketing for her mother and played with Toby, sitting on the floor with him, capable of living only within the emotional dimensions of a child's world.

There wasn't a waking moment in which the memory of Colin Mallory, angling towards her, clutching the wound in his stomach, was not in her peripheral vision. There wasn't a time in which she was free of the fear of being found out. Occasionally the Sheriff stopped by to see her father, and she would lurk upstairs expecting him at any moment to take her into custody. She was sure that people knew and looked at her suspiciously when she went to Hanrahan's or Sunny's Ice Cream or the movie theater for an afternoon show.

"Your behavior is unnatural," her father said to her in a rare outburst during the summer of 1961.

She shrugged, saying blandly she was sorry and would try to do better.

She knew her behavior was unnatural. When she took Tobias to the park, she sat on the edge of the sandbox, sometimes in the sandbox making castles with him, always apart from the other mothers. She did not join their domestic conversations. Other women her age in Bethany had babies. They gave dinner parties and went to football games and occasional dances. Sometimes Cesca was invited to join them, but she had accepted only one invitation, to a picnic by the river on the Fourth of July. Most of her high school class who had married and stayed on in Bethany were at that picnic with their children. Cesca arrived late, just as people were beginning to eat. She sat down on a picnic bench and lifted Toby up next to Tommy Tyler's little boy, who announced himself immediately as "Tommy Boom Boom" and added, "I can beat you up, if you want to know."

Tobias contemplated that information and decided not to reply.

"So," Tommy Boom Boom said. "Is that your mommy?"

Tobias nodded.

"Where's your daddy?"

"Dead," Tobias said.

Tommy Boom Boom eyed him suspiciously.

"My daddy is huge," he said combatively. He pointed to Tommy Tyler, who was in fact small and round, with an ample belly and a reputation for a bad temper. "Why is your daddy dead?"

"He got killed," Tobias said, taking a chicken leg when the plate was passed. "I think I want to go home," he said to Francesca.

Tommy Boom Boom turned to his mother, who was sitting next to him. "His father got killed," he said in a loud voice which caught the attention of everyone at the picnic table.

"Yes, he did." Lyn Tyler smiled at Francesca. "I knew his daddy. He was very handsome," she said.

"He was enormous," Tobias said. He turned to Cesca and added in a loud voice, "I am going to throw up." He put the drumstick in his pocket and took his mother's hand. In a broad and intentional gesture, Cesca knocked over a large cup of beer, soaking Tommy Boom Boom's supper with beer, which poured through the cracks in the table onto his corduroys.

"She spilled!" Tommy cried. "She spilled all over me." But Cesca walked up the hill from the river with Tobias and did not even turn around.

When Julian walked the familiar streets of Bethany in the years after Colin's murder, he was sensitive to perceptible changes in the town; people, even his friends, had retreated into a state of undeclared civil war.

"If the Sheriff could only find Colin's murderer, we'd all

feel better about one another," Sophia had said to Julian.

"Perhaps," Julian replied. He had never spoken to anyone about his suspicions—certainly not Sophia. He didn't allow himself to think about the murder or consider Francesca's implication. But he would be glad if something could happen in Bethany to displace the insistent memories of Colin's death.

Only Prince Hal, playing imaginary games with his multitude of cats, was free of a growing dark spirit.

"What we've been needing in Bethany is some kind of natural disaster," Sam Weaver said to James one afternoon as they were doing rounds in the hospital. "In a state of emergency, people are remarkable."

The gods of wind and rain must have been listening. Hurricane Elsie hit the North Shore of Massachusetts on the thirtieth of August in the worst New England disaster in one hundred and twelve years. The eye of the storm, tumbling up the coastline in a mad dance towards the ocean, struck Bethany by surprise at four forty-five in the afternoon. Radio and television had reported a Storm Watch and by four o'clock Storm Warning; but Bethany expected to be only brushed by Elsie's long train. So people were unprepared for the terrible force with which the storm plunged into their center just as businesses and shops were beginning to close for the evening.

At four forty-five Sophia was in her studio, working at the piano on a musical composition, when the room went suddenly crow-black. She stood, knocking over the chair in which she had been sitting.

"Cesca!" she called, frightened at the darkness. A sudden gust through the open windows blew her papers into the air; she could hear them flapping.

"Cesca!" She started towards the stairs, feeling her way across the room.

Initially the rain was soft and uneven, falling in fat drops. But the wind galloped through the trees, tearing off the leaves and smaller branches, bending the willows double, ripping out the small azaleas and rhododendrons. Then the rains came with a cruel force, slapping the windows of the Woodbines' frame house, breaking the panes in the studio.

The electricity was gone.

Cesca and Toby stood with Sophia at the bottom of the studio stairs and listened to the storm tear through the floor above them.

"The piano," Sophia said, and started back up the steps.

Cesca took her mother's hand. "We should go in the bathroom," she said. "It's the safest place."

"The radio said it wasn't going to hit at all," Sophia said to Cesca. "That it was going out to sea."

Cesca closed the window in the bathroom. Already the rain had soaked the floor and she stood in a small pool. Blindly, she reached into the linen closet and put towels down to mop the water.

"It's night forever," Tobias said solemnly, and he sat on the toilet seat.

"Not forever," Cesca said. "Until the storm is over."

"Maybe forever," Tobias said darkly.

"We should have candles in the downstairs buffet," Sophia said. "I'll get them."

"Never mind. We ought to stay here until the wind lets up. This kind of storm can't last long."

Sophia leaned against the bathroom door. Upstairs, she could hear the sounds of devastation.

"I believe all the windows in the studio have been broken." She put up her hands to cover her ears so she didn't have to hear.

And then she remembered Hal.

"Where's Hal?" She sank to the floor and put her head in her arms.

Cesca didn't answer. They both knew exactly where Prince Hal was. He had left the house at two in his usual high spirits, ready for whatever adventure might come his way. Now he was on the Leonora River with Will Weaver catching snakes. He had promised to come back before the storm began, but the warning had not come in time.

"Hal is careful, Mama. He'll do the smart thing."

But Sophia shook her head. "No, he isn't careful," she said. "You know that."

Hal Woodbine was thirteen and small. He had not begun to mature; his body, thinned from baby fat at ten, was not broadening like the bodies of other boys in his class. Occasionally Sophia worried about hormones and considered asking Sam Weaver whether something was the matter with Hal. Certainly James had matured by fourteen. According to Cesca, who might have made it up, James had had sex before his fifteenth birthday. But Hal showed none of the usual signs of puberty.

When Hurricane Elsie arrived, Hal was sitting on the bank of the Leonora thinking about Will Weaver.

Will was nine years older than Hal, but they seemed the same age—in fact, they seemed no age at all, just boys who would not grow up. As he watched Will wade into the water, dragging his arms along the bottom in search of snakes, Hal wondered if Will would ever do ordinary grown-up things— like finish college or have a real job or marry—or whether both he and Will would always be children. Each fall for the past two, Will Weaver had gone off to a new college and by winter had been asked to leave—once for grades and the last time for a sexual incident when he was a second-semester freshman at Boston University.

On a snowy Wednesday afternoon, during winter exam time, he had been standing on a street corner outside his dorm watching a small sports car with two girls trying to move off a thin sheet of ice. As he watched them, particularly the yellow-haired girl in the passenger seat, he felt the coming of an erection. And then without thought, or so he later said, he knocked on the sports-car window. The girl in the passenger seat, thinking he had knocked to offer assistance, opened the window, to find Will Weaver's penis pointing directly at her from the folds of his overcoat.

94

She screamed and rolled the window back up. The girl in the seat next to her screamed. Will stuffed his resistant penis back into his pants and ran. But the girls had seen him clearly, and he was discovered two days later after the girl in the passenger seat identified his picture in the freshman handbook.

No one in Bethany knew about the incident in Boston. Everyone was simply glad to have Will Weaver back in town.

"Did you ever have girlfriends?" Hal asked Will when he walked out of the river carrying a small brown snake wrapped once around his waist.

"Your sister and Maud Hanrahan." Will put the snake in the cage and went back into the river.

"I didn't know you liked Cesca," Hal said.

"I sort of love Cesca," Will said.

Hal didn't have a girlfriend himself. There were girls he liked in an ordinary way, but nobody he was hot for, the way boys in his class described feeling for certain girls. Sometimes he worried about himself, but not a lot.

When the sky darkened, Will Weaver was standing in the water to his waist. At first the rain danced softly on the water. Then they could hear the wind roar down the river. Will had just stepped out of the water when the full force of the hurricane hit the center of town above them.

"Lie flat!" Will shouted to Hal as the rains began.

Hal was already lying flat, but not by choice. The wind had thrown him to the ground and he lay stunned, his face rubbed against the bark of a large elm tree.

"Hal!" Will called. "You okay?"

Above them, branches were spinning and flying down the river. There was a loud and terrible crack in the tree against which Hal was lying, and the sound of lightning striking, although there was no light. Will could see the place where the lightning had split the elm tree and called, "For chrissake, watch it!" just as the large elm fell slowly towards the river.

Anna Wheeler was lying with Maria in the aftermath of lovemaking when the sky darkened and the electricity went out. Her first thought was the hospital; Ray Hanrahan was on a respirator after heart surgery that morning. When she picked up the telephone to check if the hospital needed her, the lines were dead. Still naked, her soft middle-aged flesh moving as she walked, she made her way downstairs to the chest in the living room where candles and matches were kept.

Anna Wheeler's house was on Tennyson Street, above the town, not as high as the Weavers' and the Woodbines' and therefore protected from some of the force of the hurricane by its location in the middle. It was the house where Anna had been born and where she had lived on and off for fifty-two years, except for three years in nursing school in Providence and the year that Mr. Wheeler had taken a bank job in Concord, New Hampshire. Their first baby, born sickly, had died at three months. There had been two other babies: one carried full term and born dead; the other, the last, dead in the womb. When Anna was in the hospital in Salem for the third baby, she met Maria, visiting a cousin in the maternity ward. Maria happened to be there when the obstetrician told Anna there would be no more babies. Something in her glands, no doubt her thyroid, kept the fetuses from developing properly. Maria stayed with Anna that afternoon, rubbing her arms, running her fingers through the older woman's hair. Every day for the week that Anna was in the hospital, Maria would come to her room and rub her back and arms and head. One day in an automatic gesture, Anna took Maria's hand and put it on her breast.

What developed between them was sweet and surprising and had lasted twenty-one years. Maria married and had children of her own. Anna and Mr. Wheeler lived an ordinary life of moderation and friendship; but once a week, with Maria, Anna Wheeler came to life.

She got the matches and candles out of the drawer and was making her way back up the stairs with a lit candle when the doorbell rang.

Julian Woodbine had left work early with the flu. He was driving through the center of town when the sky turned. The streetlights flickered on automatically and then went off. By

96

the time he turned left towards home, the rain and wind were coming with such force, he could hardly see to drive. Just beyond Anna Wheeler's house a tree was down, blocking the street. He pulled into the Wheeler driveway, jumped out of the car and rang the doorbell.

"It's awful out there," Julian said.

"I wish I could get to the hospital. Ray Hanrahan is on a respirator after surgery." She got Julian a dry shirt and jacket of Bob Wheeler's.

"He'll be all right. There's auxiliary electricity."

"But with this storm?" Anna's voice trailed.

"It can't last," Julian said. "A storm with these winds has a twenty-minute life, no more. I read it in *National Geographic.*" But Julian was wrong. Hurricane Elsie was immortal.

When the electricity went out, Sam Weaver was in intensive care with Ray Hanrahan.

"You'll be okay," he said to Ray, who, semiconscious, had panicked when the respirator stopped.

The problem was not the respirator, Sam explained to Maud Hanrahan, who was sitting in the intensive-care waiting room. The auxiliary electrical system had taken over there. The problem was her father's terror of the storm and the fact that fright was dangerous for a heart patient.

"I wish my mother would get back," Maud said to James when he came out of intensive care. Mrs. Hanrahan had left at three to close the store.

"Well, she won't get back now." James followed Maud into the room with her father. What she really wished in the dark recesses of her mind was that her father would die.

Ray Hanrahan was not a man fond of women; he had an Irish Catholic's affection for male companionship coupled with a complicated mixture of fear, distrust and earthly pleasure in women, which often made him mean, especially to his wife but even to his daughters. And to his great disappointment, Maud, a menopausal baby, had been an arbitrary trick. He had expected a son. Why else would God have sent him an-

97

other child when his wife was forty-five if not to finally give him a boy?

Maud sat down in the chair and took her father's hand. It was cold and pasty white; the feel of it gave her a terrible chill. She could not look at his face, which was gray and hollow. Instead, she watched the way in which the respirator made his chest rise and fall foolishly, an empty chest.

The Leonora River was rising above its banks. Prince Hal lay on his stomach several feet above the riverbank with his legs pinned underneath the fallen elm. Twice Will had tried to move the tree without success. He pulled Hal's legs, but they were firmly lodged beneath the center of the split tree. Then he dug in the shallow riverbed underneath his legs to free them from below.

"I think my right leg is broken," Hal said. He was thinking about the river, what it would be like to drown. He hoped it wouldn't hurt and that Sophia would be all right without him. Cesca would take care of the cats.

"I'll go for help," Will said, scrambling up the bank; but there was no moving forward against the wind. At the top of the small hill, exhausted by his struggle, Will lay flat on his stomach and watched the river rise towards Hal Woodbine.

Frank Adler was drunk. It was early in the day for him to drink, but he'd been fired from the newspaper on Friday for continued incompetence, and he planned to take a week off before he looked for another job. Some days, he was angry. He had been angry for as long as he could remember at a lot of things—the cost of groceries, and the stink in the basement from perpetual dampness and rodents, the way his mother had favored the girls, the stupid strawberry chintz Dottie Adler had bought for the matching set in the living room.

"You're not an angry man," Dottie told him patiently. "You're an angry drunk."

"I'm not a drunk. Occasionally, I have too much to drink," he had replied.

In fact, as Dottie Adler told her sister with her tendency for Hallmark Card lines, Frank Adler was by nature a sweet man gone sour from being kept out too long in the bright sun.

"I like a man I can count on," her sister had said.

"In an emergency, you can count on Frank," Dottie Adler said confidently.

When Hurricane Elsie struck Bethany, Frank was watching television. He had not even noticed the sky go dark or Dottie Adler come in from work at four o'clock, but when the electricity went and the television sizzled and died, he lost his temper.

The Adlers' house was at the bottom of Hawthorne Street, just above the river, which was why the basement was always damp. It was a modest frame cottage, the closest to the river, with a view straight down the Leonora. Always during hurricane season, if the storms were moving as far north as New England, the Adlers worried for the safety of their house.

"They said on television that Elsie was going out to sea," Frank said when Dottie Adler came down with candles. "They said we'd get some rain and wind. This is a disaster."

They stood in the center of the living room listening to the upstairs windows shattering in the wind. The round table with a glass top and framed pictures of relatives turned over next to the couch. The standing lamp beside the window slid across the room.

"Oh, brother," Frank said quietly. He had to have his wits about him, he thought. He took a candle from his wife and made his way to the kitchen with the intention of splashing cold water on his face, but when he turned on the spigot, the water was off. The coffee was still hot, and he poured himself a mug, drinking it quickly. He was in the kitchen when he heard the elm tree crack and fall into the river, pinning Hal Woodbine's legs.

"Was that lightning?" Dottie Adler asked. Frank went to the window. He couldn't see in the darkness, but after the thunderclap he could hear the tree crack and knew that sound well enough.

"The storm is taking down trees," he said.

Above them came the sound of a mountain-size vacuum

cleaner, and the Adlers guessed correctly that their roof had blown off and was on its way downriver.

"If we don't get into the basement, we're going to fly out of the top of this house," Mr. Adler said, and he took his wife's hand. They carried the candles and made their way carefully down the basement steps. The basement floor was dirt; river rats, traveling to higher ground in the rainy season, lived there.

"I don't want to go all the way down," Dottie said. "Listen to them running. I'd die if one of them ran across my feet in the dark."

They sat side by side in the middle of the staircase; their candles illuminated a small circle of light.

The Adlers were in their late thirties and childless, but they seemed old and weary with a life that had held no surprises. Mrs. Adler had grown up in Salem and gone to Salem High, where she was beauty queen in her senior year and then Miss Salem and then runner-up for Miss Massachusetts. She lost, she said, because she had no talents and the winner had been an acceptable pianist. She was probably right about the talents, but she certainly was pretty, even at thirty-eight, bleached with the years of diminished promise. Mr. Adler had been a football player who dropped out of Bethany High when he broke his leg in October of his senior year. He was not particularly handsome, but he was a touching man complicated by failed childhood dreams of heroism. He had no idea how to make even the small world he inhabited work for him, and so, in time, he fled it.

"It's too bad we've had to live in a place like this," he said to Mrs. Adler as he pressed close to her on the basement steps. "We could have been very happy."

"Always 'could have been,'" Dottie Adler said. "What about now?"

"Now, we haven't got a roof over our head and that's the honest-to-God truth," Frank said, but not bitterly. Something about the roof of the house flying down the river pleased him and gave him a sense of purpose.

The wind had abated, but the rain still fell in sheets. The sky was lighter, dull gray now, and Will Weaver, lying face down on the riverbank, could barely see Prince Hal, but he could hear him moaning.

"Hal!" he called. He got up on his hands and knees. "You still okay?" He could see Hal halfway up the bank, perpendicular; the river was up to his waist.

"I'm going to get help!" Will shouted. "Hold on!"

He saw the Adlers' cottage when he stood. Half of the roof was gone. He pulled himself up the hill towards the cottage hanging on to trees and low branches that had been blown down, crawled on the ground beneath the force of the wind until he reached the cottage. Flat on his stomach, wriggling like his beloved snakes through the mud, he moved the last ten yards along open ground and knocked on the basement window.

"Help!" he shouted. His voice was paper-thin. *"Help!"*

The Adlers heard.

"Dottie?"

"I hear it," she said.

"I'm going." Frank groped up the basement steps.

"Not alone." She went behind him.

Where had the voice come from? They listened. In the distance, they could hear a low wail, the sound of a cat perhaps. Frank opened the back door. What had been Dottie Adler's vegetable garden was now a dump; the trash and garbage cans from the houses up the street had blown into the Adlers' backyard, stopped by the tree line that separated the Adler property from the river.

"Listen," Frank said.

But Mrs. Adler covered her eyes. She was thinking of the hours of work to clear the garden, of the maimed eggplants and zucchinis and tomatoes.

"Look," she said to Frank. "Just look."

But Frank was listening, and he could hear that the sound came from the side of the house near the river. He stepped out onto the back porch.

"Don't go," she said. "You could be killed."

But he went down the steps.

"Please, Frank."

"Someone's in trouble," he said.

She stopped halfway down the back steps.

"Oh, God, the stink." She was weeping. She didn't know whether she cried for the garden, for the terrible smell imposing itself upon her backyard or for Frank's safety. She couldn't any longer remember whether she loved him or not, but she was tied to him as if he were her limbs, lame without his life, and that was fact.

"Be careful," she called wearily.

Frank made his way through the garbage, waded in the awful stuff, grown soft and vile in the steady rain. The rats would be out soon, having a picnic. Dottie wouldn't touch an eggplant or broccoli or lettuce if the rats ran over her garden.

Will stood up when Frank Adler came around the side of the house and saw him.

The bank was soft mud, and slippery; it was difficult to keep their balance, but Will and Frank Adler climbed down to the fallen tree. Prince Hal had to hold himself up by his arms to keep his face out of the muddy water. Frank slid his own body underneath Hal's head and torso, making a shelf for him to lie on. Once again, Will tried to move the tree. The water was too deep for him to dig under Hal's legs without submerging his head.

"We're going to stay here with you, Hal," Frank said.

"You okay?" Will asked.

Hal nodded, resting his head on Frank's lap.

"What time is it?" Hal asked.

"Getting on towards six," Frank said.

"I promised I'd be home by six," Hal said.

With the rain coming as it was, filling the river, Hal Woodbine would be underwater by seven o'clock unless, by some miracle, they could move the tree. Frank Adler made up his mind to stay with Hal as long as he could.

"I'm staying too," Will said to Frank.

When the wind stopped, Sophia wanted to go to the studio.

"I'll check," Cesca said to her mother. "And then I'll go to the river and find Hal."

"Me too," Tobias said.

"No, you stay here with your grandmother."

Sophia sat on the floor of the bathroom, her knees up, her head in her arms, as she had been sitting since the beginning of the storm, when the possibility of Hal's death had occurred to her.

"Right, Mama?" Cesca asked.

Sophia nodded. Toby, in the bathtub, zoomed his Matchbox cars up and down the sides of the bathtub. "Right, Grand-mama?"

Sophia worried about losing Hal. She had never worried about the twins, who seemed to her not so much stronger than Hal as more present in the world. Hal had no compre-hension of danger or ill will. In the world of his imagination, people were generous to one another and lived forever. By nature, he didn't anticipate misfortune or bad luck or danger. He was a child who could die easily. Right now, in spite of Francesca's vision of Hal's safety, Sophia saw her son floating face down in the tide towards the mouth of the Leonora.

Sophia's studio had become a large rectangular bowl filled with water to above the floor moldings. The bookcases and pictures were down; compositions, carefully notated scores in blue-black ink on which she had been working since her ill-ness, floated in the artificial pool. The ink ran across the pages in abstract designs. All the windows were gone, broken in pieces and shards. The room smelled of wet roses and the damp cherry wood of the piano.

Francesca went downstairs. The smaller furniture, lamps and tables, pictures, bric-a-brac, were blown about; some win-dows were gone, and a slender chorus line of rain danced wickedly through the living room and down the hall. It was cold, and Cesca wrapped her grandmother's black cape around her shoulders. The kitchen was lower than the rest of the house. The windows over the sink were out, and the rain had filled the kitchen so the water was above her ankles. Barefoot, she crossed the floor, careful of glass from the windows; she took a flashlight out of the cabinet. It crossed her mind that Hal's new litter of kittens was in the pantry, settled in an empty Michelob case, but she hurried out the door without allowing her mind to rest on the lives of kittens.

It was dark, not black as it had been. The rain was heavy. Even on the hill of Hawthorne, the water was high. The empty streets were littered with branches and debris; pieces of roofs and furniture blown out of windows, children's toys, uprooted plants floated on the surface of the running water, and garbage rushed down the hill towards the center of town. There was no sign of life, no light, only the sound of rain, a low wind and the slosh of water against her galoshes. She kept her flashlight pointed straight ahead. She didn't want to see a familiar corpse, some friend or neighbor stricken by the storm, floating downstream towards the river.

In fact, she felt wonderfully alone and exhilarated, cut loose by the storm. She had left her child and mother and house, the memory of Colin Mallory ghosting the rooms of her life so there wasn't enough room to breathe.

The damage was worse and worse as she made her way down Hawthorne. Roofs were completely off the houses closer to the river; the side of the Bradys' cottage was gone, half of the Adlers' roof; the yews in front of the Thompsons' were down, and the McIntires had lost their front porch. The town stank of garbage.

Beyond the Adlers' house, she stopped. Will hunted snakes at the bottom of Hawthorne, usually near the Adlers'; she leaned against a tree to get her bearings. The river sounded like the ocean, slapping the shoreline furiously. She thought she heard voices, but she couldn't be sure.

"Hal!" she called. Her voice was strangely soft against the storm. "Hal!" she called again, and she heard a reply—either "Here" or "Help." She pointed the beam of the flashlight towards the river and moved the light along the line of the bank until she saw the fallen tree, the shadows of people. With the flashlight, she followed the waterline up the bank to the figure of Will Weaver on his haunches, leaning beside another figure she didn't recognize. She slid down the thick mudbank, unable to keep her balance on the slippery surface. On the way down the hill she dropped her flashlight, and it lay like a small yellow moon in the darkness.

"Cesca," Will said. "Is that you?"

"Yes," she answered.

Then she saw Frank Adler with Prince Hal's head in his lap. The Leonora River splashed around his slender neck, and he had to lift his face to keep from swallowing too much water.

"His leg is pinned underneath the tree," Will said. "We think it's broken."

Cesca leaned down and kissed Hal's cool lips. "You're going to be okay," she said.

"Did you check the kittens?" he asked.

"They're okay too," she lied. She didn't allow herself to think, as her mother was at that moment thinking, that Prince Hal was going to die.

Louisa Natale should not have left Salem, where she was curator of the Witches' Museum. Everybody told her to wait. Weather reports were unpredictable. The storm could hit Bethany or Salem or one of the towns on the coastal road where she would be driving. But Louisa left anyway. If there was going to be trouble, she wanted to be at home in her own room. Since Colin Mallory's murder, she had been plagued by a quiet sense of doom. All she needed any longer was safety. She had stopped wearing hats. She didn't wish to call attention to herself. She had slept with other men since Colin's murder, but there had been no real pleasure, only a sense of accommodation and the wish that the sex would be fast, without demands for tenderness afterwards.

Often she thought about Colin Mallory and what one careless afternoon with him had cost her in peace of mind. She didn't want to contend with the aftermath of desire. At Smith

College, where she had gone on scholarship to study art history, she had lived for the most part like a nun.

There was a strange, unfamiliar purple over the ocean. At almost five o'clock, she turned onto the coastal road and heard the weather report interrupt the all-music station on the radio. The weatherman reported storm warnings on the North Shore and in the Boston area until 11 P.M., although Hurricane Elsie should be out to sea by 5. Heavy winds and rains were predicted for the Massachusetts coastal towns. There had been property damage earlier in the day in New York State and Connecticut. Four deaths related to the hurricane were reported.

For no clear reason except perhaps the purple sky over the ocean, Louisa turned off the coastal road onto a back road through an area of woods and marshlands which wound circuitously towards Bethany.

On several occasions, Mrs. Natale had offered an explanation to Louisa of the town of Bethany's strong reaction to Colin's murder. He had seemed invincible, she told her daughter, the epitome of a kind of masculine virility. His murder made everyone in town vulnerable to violent death. Mrs. Natale had her own theory. She thought James Woodbine had done it out of jealousy.

"Jealousy of whom?" Louisa had asked.

"I always thought he had unnatural feelings towards his sister," Mrs. Natale had said.

"James Woodbine hasn't an unnatural feeling in this world," Louisa said, but Mrs. Natale shook her head.

"All of us have unnatural feelings, Louisa," she said.

Sometimes Louisa thought Francesca had killed Colin, but she never told anyone, certainly not her mother. She would find herself, sitting at Sunny's or with a group of friends at Rooster's or shopping at Hanrahan's, staring at Cesca and wondering was it possible for a woman of such gentleness to commit murder. Her mind wandered to what might have happened the afternoon of Colin's murder. Colin and Francesca were in the cottage after she had left and they were arguing about Colin's betrayal. The scene, as Louisa imagined it, always involved betrayal, although she knew her imagi-

106

nation must be responding to guilt. There was no reason for Francesca to be carrying a gun—unless, of course, she had seen Louisa and Colin together, perhaps through a window.

It was beginning to rain unevenly. The wind had picked up, lifting the tree limbs like chorus dancers. Every time Louisa turned a curve, the storm gathered momentum and she found herself driving faster. As she rounded a bend, her tires screeched. The tail of her car careened into the opposite lane. She should slow down, she told herself, but she was afraid.

The road to Bethany called Marsh Road was named for a long section of marshland, a bird retreat, just before the last bridge over the Leonora River into town. The marsh, even in August, was three or four feet deep, thick with reeds and muddy. A path along the highway led to an interior path where bird-watchers walked in the fall. Just as Louisa drove around the last curve into a stretch of straight road through the center of the marshes, the sky turned pitch-black and the wind rushed by her at a terrifying speed.

Halfway between the beginning and the end of the flat section of Marsh Road, Louisa's car sailed sideways. She turned the steering wheel hard left, but the gesture was useless. The car, under its own direction, was headed towards the marshes. It landed intact on four wheels, ten feet from the road, sinking gently into the muddy bed. The reeds rose up around the windows, and the birds were making a terrible racket, which Louisa heard indistinctly from what felt like a deep, narrow hole into which she had fallen. Through the worst of the storm, she slipped into and out of consciousness, too dazed to panic.

Bethany Hospital was dark. The storm raged around the building, attacking with unprecedented force, but inside the corridors and rooms half-full of patients, pantries and large supply closets, kitchens and operating rooms, everyone was quiet. Sam Weaver and James were the only doctors in attendance. Dinner trays had just been put on the long six-foot-high dollies when the storm broke. The orderlies, even with flashlights, couldn't see well enough to push the dollies down the corridors. An orderly in the elevator with two dollies full of food trays was stuck between the second and third floors. In the course of hours, the orderly, a man of extraordinary calm, ate two of the dinners, one salt-free, and fell asleep.

There were one hundred and forty-five patients in the three-hundred-bed hospital. Thirty nurses and nurse's aides were on duty. A resident physician from Boston was supposed to be in the emergency room, but he had not arrived by the time the storm hit Bethany. There were twenty-two other staff, including orderlies, kitchen help and technicians. James and Dr. Weaver sat together at the main desk in the central corridor and read the patients' charts with flashlights to determine priorities.

Anna Abel had a baby girl born August 28 called Hannah.

Mr. Morton Asher was in his third day recovering from surgery for a hernia.

Terry Barnes had had an emergency appendectomy on August 29.

Tom Barnes was in traction with a broken leg.

Alice Bates was slipping slowly out of the world with terminal cancer.

Mrs. Mary Carson had taken an overdose of very old sleeping pills, but was recovering.

Tommy Castman had been hit by a car at Elm and Main two days before and had a concussion. Dr. Weaver pulled his chart. There were going to be real emergencies as soon as the storm abated.

They had just left the main desk to go to the emergency room when Maud Hanrahan burst through a door shining her flashlight in her own face so they could recognize her.

"Something's the matter," she said. "The nurse in intensive care came out to tell me."

They followed her up the two flights of stairs to the cardiac wing of the hospital, down the long corridor to intensive care, a large room broken only by curtains, with ten beds, four occupied. Three nurses were standing around Ray Hanrahan's bed. He lay flat with his head tilted slightly backward; his mouth, bone-dry after hours on a respirator, was open to accommodate the absent oxygen tube. His heart had stopped.

James told Maud that her father was dead.

"Do you want to see him?" James asked.

She shook her head. "I'll just sit here until the storm is over and I can get home to tell my mother," she said.

The water had risen above Hal's head. He had to hold his breath between the waves, and gradually the time between breaths was lengthening. Francesca held her own breath while Hal was underwater, testing her brother's future. She couldn't hold it for as long as Hal did; not long enough to stay alive if she were in her brother's place.

Hal was imagining the circus. He had been frightened when the tree fell and pinned him in the rising water, but he wasn't afraid any longer. He didn't think about dying. He was lost in a color daydream of circuses—of himself with the lions who were doing fine tricks, nuzzling him in the chest and belly while the audience screamed in fear and delight.

Francesca had been gone half an hour when Sophia stood up and opened the bathroom door. It was possible for her to see down the corridor—not well, but enough to move around in the silver-gray light which had followed the eye of the storm. She took Tobias' hand.

"Where's Mommy?" he asked.

"Gone to find Hal," Sophia said.

Tobias' eyes, dilated in darkness, looked like the eyes of a nocturnal animal, and in a sudden wave of maternal compassion, Sophia lifted him up.

"Do you hear noises?" he asked.

"I hear the wind."

"Downstairs," he said.

"I hear the wind upstairs and downstairs," she said. But she did hear something unlike the storm, and then she heard Julian's voice shouting distinctly, "For chrissake—Sophia?"

She made her way downstairs carrying Toby, holding on to the banister.

Julian stood in the center of the hall in a gray suit, soaked to the skin.

"The town is ruined," Julian said. "Where're the children?"

"Ruined?" Sophia asked.

"I was driving home when the storm hit. I got as far as Anna Wheeler's, where a tree was down."

"What's ruined?" Sophia insisted.

She fell against him.

"It has been an awful storm. I had to walk from the Wheelers'. You can't drive."

"Mommy's gone," Tobias said. "Will she be back soon?" he asked bravely. Tobias knew that Colin Mallory had been shot with a gun in the stomach. Although he had no emotional attachment to this man he had never known—Francesca did not talk about Colin at all except to show Tobias pictures of him—the absence of a father made life seem more fragile to Toby than to other children his age.

"Of course she'll be back," Julian said.

"Cesca went to look for Hal," Sophia said. "She left after the worst of the storm. James is at the hospital with Sam."

"Where is Hal?" Julian asked.

"At the river," she said weakly.

Julian could imagine without any difficulty the height of the Leonora River after such a storm. He took Sophia's hand and they went upstairs.

"Hal is sensible," he said quickly.

"No one fearless is sensible," Sophia said. She sat down on her bed and picked Tobias up.

"Do you want me to read you a story?" She took a copy of *Le Petit Prince* from the bookcase over the bed. It must have been Cesca's from French class in high school. Sophia didn't know languages except from listening to operas in Italian and German.

"Read," Tobias said. He gave her the flashlight he held.

She read the unfamiliar French, guessing at pronunciations, in a soft, musical voice.

"What are you saying to me?" Tobias asked after a few moments.

"I am reading a story to you," Sophia said simply.

Julian checked the second floor. The windows on the north side of the house had been blown out. Hal's and Cesca's rooms were in complete disarray, but otherwise the second floor had not been as damaged as the first. Anticipating, he thought, the worst, he went up the stairs to Sophia's studio. The door was shut, but a small stream of water poured down the steps. When he opened the door, a rush of water splashed over him. His inexpressible love for Sophia was in this studio he had built for her. He shut the door and went back downstairs followed by the running stream of water.

Frank Adler was contemplating his own life. He could sense that Hal was giving up. His grip on Frank's hand had relaxed, and he no longer struggled for air when his head bobbed above the river.

The sky was considerably lighter, and Frank noticed that the tree was larger than it had seemed in darkness. No wonder it couldn't be moved.

"Let's give it another try," he said.

First he had to slip free of Hal's body. It wasn't heavy in itself, but with the weight of the water and of the tree, Frank was trapped. He grabbed hold of a large exposed root of a pine tree and pulled with the old strength of a former all-state tackle. Slowly he dislodged his body; his legs felt paralyzed with cold, but he was free.

Hal felt Frank Adler go. Briefly, he panicked as he sank beneath the surface of the river. Then he stopped fighting.

"I'll pull; you two push the tree," Frank said.

On his haunches, his right foot lodged in the deep web of a pine root, Frank Adler leaned forward just far enough to be out of balance. He grabbed under Hal's wet and muddy arms. Initially, Hal was immovable, pulling Frank into the water with him. Unless the pine root held Frank's foot, he was going to pitch forward and lose his balance altogether.

"Push!" Frank shouted. In the river, Will and Francesca pressed their shoulders against the fallen tree and pushed. "Again!" Frank called. "Again!"

And something happened.

There was a heavy and reluctant groan and the elm tree shifted in the water, moving just enough downstream to release its hold on Hal Woodbine's leg.

"I pulled at the right moment," Frank said later. "The storm had softened the riverbed."

"You saved Hal's life," Francesca said.

"The tree moved," Frank said. "How could I have predicted a gully?"

But Francesca insisted Frank had pulled Hal from under the tree. "It wasn't chance," she said.

It was seven o'clock by the grandfather's clock in the hall when Cesca walked into the Woodbine house. The front door had blown off and was lying over the porch banister. The porch was full of broken glass, and two pillars had split in half.

"Mama?" she called. "Toby?"

"Mommy's home," Tobias said. He scrambled off the bed, ran down the steps and jumped into Francesca's arms.

"Hal's okay, Mama!" Cesca shouted.

Sophia ran to the top of the steps.

"Fine?" she asked.

"Okay," Cesca said. "A tree fell on his leg and broke it, but he's okay. James drove the ambulance to take him to the hospital."

"He's fine?" Sophia asked.

"He's fine."

Sophia sat down on the top step and put her head against her knees.

Julian was standing in the kitchen with water halfway up his calves.

"Don't come in, Cesca," he said sternly.

But Francesca, carrying Tobias, was already at the door to the kitchen.

"Why?" she asked. And she saw what her father had not wanted her to see.

112

Floating sideways in a foot of water just in front of Julian was a small yellow-striped kitten.

"Did you hear me say Hal's okay?" Cesca said.

"I heard," Julian said.

"That's all I wanted to tell you." And Cesca pressed Tobias' head against her shoulder so he wouldn't have to see Prince Hal's kitten.

2.

Recovery:
August, 1961

The morning that followed the arrival of Hurricane Elsie slipped over the horizon bright and clear; people were stunned by its beauty.

Francesca awoke with the first rectangle of light through the windows of her parents' room, where she had slept because her own room was full of shattered glass. She had been dreaming. In her dream, she had died. She passed through a long cylindrical tunnel on the other side of which was a town exactly like Bethany, only empty. She had been sent with instructions to populate the town with parents and children, ministers and shopkeepers, schoolteachers, gasoline attendants, policemen, physicians, electricians. And an angel. "Every town needs an angel," the instructor had told her before she set off on her journey. "I am the angel," she had replied indignantly, and left.

She got up and stretched, not wishing to prolong the dream into nightmare, as her dreams, especially those at dawn, had become since Colin's death. Tobias still slept face down next to her, and Sophia sat quietly in a chair beside the window.

"I suppose Daddy stayed the night at the hospital," she said.

"He must have," Sophia said.

"I'm sure he's fine. Everyone is." Cesca sensed her mother's concern.

"Of course," Sophia said. "The day is lovely. Don't you think it's a lovely day?"

Cesca could tell that her mother had gone off again since the hurricane; her mind, unmoored, had splintered in the storm. And she wanted to shake her.

"I'm going to the hospital," Cesca said. "I'm sure they need help. Do you mind staying with Toby?"

"I'd like to, darling," Sophia said. "We were reading quite a good book when you came last night. You know your book about the little prince? Only it was in French."

"I didn't know you read French." Cesca brushed her hair and tied it back with a ribbon.

"I don't," Sophia said.

Francesca hesitated. Her mother's mind had snapped entirely before, and she was worried. "You're sure you're all right to stay with Toby?"

"I'm fine," Sophia said. "Completely fine."

"Call me if you need me." She kissed her goodbye, forgetting until much later that the telephone lines were dead.

Outside, in the bright sunlight, the town was in ruins. The river rushed merrily downstream, full of debris—parts of houses, automobiles, large limbs from the giant oaks along the banks, the headboard of a four-poster bed, an upholstered chair. Sophia's rose garden had been ripped out by the roots; all over the front lawn the pale pink and yellow petals of tea roses in full bloom were confetti in Cesca's path. Above her, in an elm tree stripped almost naked of branches, an ordinary family of brown swallows voiced their disapproval back and forth.

The neighbors on Hawthorne Street were on the sidewalk with brooms and shovels and rakes, cleaning up and in high spirits.

"Good morning, Francesca," Mrs. Appleton, next door, said as she passed. "Do you have any news?"

"James is at the hospital helping Dr. Weaver, and my father went over last night. My little brother broke his leg. That's all the news I have."

"Well, the water's off and the electricity, and you can't go

115

through the center of town except in a boat." Mrs. Appleton sat down on her blue velvet couch, which had blown out the front window, her broom across her lap. "I was folding laundry when it hit and I stayed in the basement for the duration," she said. "I wonder if anyone was killed."

"I'm off to the hospital now," Cesca said. "I'll let you know the news."

The day, hanging like a splendid tapestry over the wreckage of Bethany, was too beautiful for imagining the deaths of friends.

As Cesca passed the Wheelers' house, Maria, the cleaning lady she had seen kissing Anna Wheeler when she was a girl, came out and waved. She was soft, not plump exactly but ample, and sweet-looking. Cesca wondered if they had been making love when the storm came. And her mind wandered to lovemaking between women, suddenly aroused by the thought of a woman lying against her thigh.

She had been celibate. In the months after she killed Colin, the thought of sex had filled her with an anguished longing for some impossible promise she had destroyed. Then thoughts of making love fell away. Except for nursing Tobias, taking pleasure in the closeness of his small body, erotic pleasure in the contractions which accompanied his languorous pull on her nipples, she stopped thinking about sex at all. Now, on this brilliant summer morning full of hidden surprises, she began to awaken from a long, long sleep to the silent explosions of desire.

Overhead there was an unfamiliar whirring, and Francesca looked up to see a helicopter, just above the tree line, coming from the direction of Salem.

The marshes where Louisa Natale's car rested had flooded during the night. She slept secured against the high back of the front seat. The windows were up on both sides, with a few inches of air space on the driver's side. Occasionally, during the night, she was conscious of water rising, but mostly she was lost in a deep and unnatural sleep.

The helicopter dispatched from Boston to check the access roads to Bethany discovered Louisa's white Mustang—just the top of it, like a beach blanket in the marsh grasses, but visible from above because of its whiteness.

The aircraft hovered just above the marshes, flushing the mallards and savage crows which had returned in daylight. Hendrik Andrews opened the helicopter door, dropped down the several feet and landed on the top of Louisa Natale's car. Kneeling, he leaned over and looked in the window.

"It's a girl!" he called up to the pilot, who could not hear him above the engine. "A woman."

He was a young man accustomed to emergencies and assessed the situation quickly. The marsh water was too deep for him to open the car door. There was just enough space for him to reach his arm through the window, unwind it, which he did, and with great gentleness lift the woman, whom he thought dead, through the window. The pilot dropped a rope pulley and lifted Hendrik and the woman up to the helicopter. In a matter of minutes, Louisa, stirred to consciousness, was strapped on the stretcher on the floor of the helicopter, and the pilot had ascended and headed in the direction of Bethany Hospital, approximately six miles away.

Hendrik knelt beside the woman, brushed the damp black hair off her forehead and took her pulse, which was abnormally slow. He pulled back her eyelids to check her pupils and rested his head against her chest to listen to her breathing. "A concussion," he said quietly to the pilot, strapping himself into the passenger seat. "Perhaps there's hemorrhaging."

"You a doctor?" the pilot asked. They had not met before that morning, although they were both assigned to the medical-emergency division of the National Guard, Hendrik in his last month of a seven-year reserve commitment. He had been asleep with an unfamiliar woman beside him, as usual, when the telephone message came from his commanding officer that the President had called in the National Guard to Bethany, Massachusetts, and he was to report for duty.

"Yes, I am a doctor," he replied, lying with surprising ease.

Later, in the safekeeping of recollected terror, he couldn't imagine why he had been so stupid as to tell that dangerous lie.

He would, in fact, have made a remarkable physician. All his professors in the three years he had spent at medical school had told him that. His mother had told him he had special gifts for healing. But his father, whose own particular gift for laziness maintained the Andrews family at bare subsistence level in the boom years after the Second World War, insisted that doctors were devils and quacks and he wasn't going to lay out money for a son of his to be one. He had wanted to be a physician since Elena's accident when he was seven. Occasionally he fabricated a life of heroic rescues in his mind, but he had never lied about it until that morning on the way to Bethany.

"Lucky thing you're trained," the pilot was saying. "They're going to need doctors in Bethany. Look at the place."

Hendrik looked out the window as the helicopter followed the river into town. The small village was a disaster of buildings lopsided or split in two, doors and couches, tables and toys in the middle of streets, on front lawns or floating down the center of town with the rescue boats.

"I used to want to be a doctor," the pilot said as he slowed and lowered the helicopter over the long expanse of lawn in front of the hospital. "But I was bad in science."

"My trouble with medicine was never science but people dying," Hendrik said.

"Yeah," the pilot agreed. "But what can you do? People die. If I'd been good in science, I wouldn't have minded the dying."

He turned off the engine and opened the helicopter door.

Francesca had just arrived at the hospital when the helicopter landed, and she stood on the lawn with James, who had been sent out by Dr. Weaver to meet the plane.

"We have a woman," the pilot called out the open door.

"Hurt badly?" James asked.

"Yup," the pilot said, taking hold of one end of the stretcher. "We have a doctor, too."

Hendrik caught his breath. This was just what he had been afraid would happen. He should say now that he had lied. Listen, guys, he should say, I'm not a doctor—can't you tell? I'm A.W.O.L. from medicine. I split at the end of my third year. He lifted the stretcher.

The pilot nodded in the direction of Hendrik. "The doctor's coming."

"No kidding." James helped them lift Louisa out of the helicopter. "We're desperate for a doctor. There're only two of us here, and I'm in medical school."

Francesca recognized Louisa Natale even before the stretcher was out of the helicopter, and her heart beat as if her fury at Louisa had finally killed her.

"Dead?"

"Unconscious," Hendrik said. He introduced himself.

Since Colin's death, Cesca had had nothing to do with Louisa. They hadn't been friends after grade school, so there was no friendship to cut off. Nevertheless, she held Louisa somehow responsible not for Colin's betrayal exactly but for her own guilt. She had never been sorry about Colin's death. She couldn't even remember how it had felt to love him and was glad that he was off the earth. She simply wished that he had been struck dead by natural forces, and Louisa's presence in Bethany was a physical reminder of Francesca's capacity for violence, although the act of killing Colin had always seemed less a decision of will than inevitable, a kind of natural disaster.

James led the group into the emergency room.

"You'll stay, won't you?" he said to Hendrik Andrews.

"Of course," Hendrik said.

Francesca watched Louisa's lovely white face; her eyes were closed and she lay very still, breathing slowly, a shallow rise and fall of her stomach under the sheet.

"Did you check her?" James asked Hendrik.

"You have a look," Hendrik said. "Concussion, I think."

Emergency was a large room with fifteen beds around a center island which was the nurses' station. The beds were separated by curtains, which were open so the patients were visible. There were four high stretchers and three low stretchers from ambulances with victims from the hurricane. A long space of floor beyond the nurses' station had been readied with rows of mattresses from beds not in use in the rest of the hospital. The staff were expecting hundreds of injuries.

Francesca went with James and Hendrik to check on patients. In the first bed, plump Billy Naylor lay curled in a fetal position sucking his fist to combat the pain. He had been hit in the chest and stomach by flying boards at the filling station on Main Street where he worked. He was bleeding internally, James said.

In the second bed, a young boy, perhaps twelve, from the Polish section of town, had broken his arm, and Dr. Weaver was setting it.

"I want to get out of here," the boy told Cesca. "I don't like trouble. I didn't even have breakfast."

"Hold Cesca's hand while I set your arm," Sam instructed the boy.

"Will it hurt?"

"It will hurt," Dr. Weaver said.

"Then give me a shot so it won't."

"We're saving those shots for people who can't stand the pain. We're short on supplies. This will hurt for a minute or two, but you're a strong boy."

The boy bit Cesca's hand.

"Would you pull the curtains so I don't have to see any blood?" he asked Cesca while a nurse wrapped his arm in plaster.

Cesca closed the curtains and moved on.

The man in the next bed was dead. She could see the bottoms of his bare feet protruding from the sheet, and they were blue.

Louisa lay on the stretcher next to the entrance, belted at the chest and legs so she wouldn't roll off. Cesca wanted to touch her, to brush her wet hair off her forehead, to pinch her pale cheeks. She ran her fingers across Louisa's lips just as James and Hendrik Andrews came up.

"Louisa?" James said. He opened her eyes with his fingers. The irises were rolled back, half-visible. With a tiny high-beam flashlight, he examined the dilation of the pupils. He took her pulse and wrote the information on the chart on her stomach, as if she were a table. Then he slapped her cheek. "Louisa."

Her eyelids opened. Only the whites were there, small eggs in the middle of her head.

"No, Colin," she said distinctly.

James frowned. "Didn't she say Colin?"

Francesca's heart was pounding.

"Maybe her boyfriend," Hendrik said.

"Francesca's." James checked Louisa with a stethoscope. "Cesca's husband."

"He's dead," Cesca said. "And he was never really my husband."

"I'm sorry," Hendrik said quickly, confused by the personal conversation.

"Don't worry," Cesca said, touching him lightly on the arm with new feelings lost since girlhood, akin to pleasure or curiosity, excitement even. "He's been dead forever."

She watched Hendrik examine an unfamiliar woman. There was something at once strong and sweetly hesitant about him, as if he had decided to be a physician only that morning and were inventing the profession while he went along. She liked the way he looked, very dark like James with hair so black, it seemed wet. He covered the woman with a sheet, touched her cheek lightly in consolation and followed James to another patient.

The chart said *"Robert Olsson, broken ribs,"* but Mr. Olsson's pulse was too faint, his blood pressure too low for him to be suffering simply broken ribs. "Another internal bleeding, don't you think?" James said to Hendrik Andrews. "I wish the next helicopter would bring blood."

"What do you do for a concussion?" Francesca asked, and sat with James at the nurses' station while he checked charts.

"Rest."

"Will she die?"

"Not likely."

"Who is dead?" She nodded in the direction of the first man she had seen under the sheet.

"Mr. Wheeler. You know, Mr. Wheeler at the bank." James put down the charts. "He drowned. He must have been knocked in the head as he tried to leave the bank last night."

"Hal was very lucky, wasn't he?" Cesca said.

"It was a miracle."

Louisa was moaning. Francesca walked over and stood at the foot of her stretcher, fascinated by the materialization of this woman, always, in the shadows of her mind, naked and in a swan hat. She wondered if Colin had loved her—or if, when they made love, he had been thinking instead of Louisa.

Cesca touched her foot under the sheet and Louisa stirred. Her eyes flew open. She focused enough to recognize Francesca, and then she screamed. It was a long, low scream, not piercing, more like a groan.

In Louisa's nightmare, Francesca Woodbine was trying to kill her.

"What happened?" James asked.

"I touched her foot." Cesca was frightened by the response. "You heard what happened."

He took Louisa's face in his hands. She had stopped screaming, and although her eyes were open, they didn't register.

"She must have had an automatic response." James brushed Francesca's face with his hand, sensing her dismay. "She was probably having a bad dream," James said.

"The scream seemed personal." Cesca followed James and Hendrik upstairs to the wing where Hal was staying.

Outside the picture window of Hal Woodbine's room, a solitary cloud in the form of a lion in repose floated across his vision. He was reminded of his childhood, when clouds always took on the forms he wished them to have, mainly those of circus animals.

"Look at the elephant," or the lion or the chimpanzee, he'd say to Francesca when he was small.

"Honestly, Hal, I don't see anything but a cloud," Francesca would reply.

"Of course you see a cloud, but it's also an elephant," Hal had said. "Can't you believe in anything?"

His leg throbbed and he was hot with fever. Dr. Weaver had said last night that he worried about infection, and surgery might be necessary because the fracture was compound.

"You could have died," Sam Weaver said.

Hal knew very well he could have died.

People, especially his family, thought he was a child with a capacity to imagine unlimited happiness, but the fact was that his imagination had grown in self-defense against a world which he suspected held out promises of sorrow.

Once when he was seven years old, he had gone unannounced into his mother's room and she was sitting on the bed cutting out the people in a magazine. He climbed up on the bed with her and she continued to cut.

"What are you doing?" he asked.

"Cutting paper dolls," she replied.

"To play?" he asked.

"I suppose to play." She lined them up on the bedspread. There was a yellow-haired woman in an evening dress smoking a very long cigarette and one in underwear with her hand jauntily on a hip, a man in a business suit with a thin tie, his arms folded across his chest. There was a child on a bicycle and another dressed for Easter in a straw hat carrying a basket of eggs and chocolate rabbits.

"What do you pretend when you play with them?" Hal asked her.

"I pretend I am in charge," his mother had replied.

He was going to join the circus, he resolved. He tried to turn towards the window without moving his elevated leg. As long as he remained in his family's house, he would be kept a child. "My darling boy" his mother called him still, suggesting his boyhood was a permanent affliction. Now that he had almost died and knew inexactly his own fragility, he wanted to take a turn at being grown up. Perhaps if he left home, his body would respond to such a change. The tiny testicles hidden inside, disguised like a girl's sex, might drop and hair grow on his chest and face and underarms. He might even want to be with a girl.

Francesca came into his room looking beautiful and hugged him.

"Don't tell me I'm lucky," he said to her.

She lifted the sheet and looked at his leg, secured in position with pillows and sandbags.

"Don't mention miracles," he said.

She laughed. "Is everyone driving you crazy?" She sat down in the chair beside the bed and kissed his hand. "It *was* a miracle, you know."

"I know everything. More than you can imagine. Did you check the cats before you left home this morning?" he said.

"Yes, I have," she told him. One by one, she listed the grown cats, all of whom had survived the storm, and then she told him about the kittens, but not in detail.

"Did you see them?" he asked evenly.

"I saw one."

"Don't tell me," he said. "I understand that drowning is not a terrible death." He looked out the window at the lion cloud which lingered there. "You just go to sleep."

"I guess that's true."

"I wonder why Daddy didn't tell me about the kittens last night."

"Because he can't bear bad news. You know that."

"He lied to me," Hal said.

"Not exactly. He just didn't tell you the truth."

Hal closed his eyes. "I'm thinking of leaving home," he said.

Francesca got up, pulled the sheet up to Hal's chin. She blew him a kiss. She wasn't going to listen to bad news either—certainly not from Prince Hal, who she had believed was immune to sadness.

"I'm going to go to work," she said, and left to join James and Hendrik Andrews in Emergency.

Hendrik Andrews had taken charge of Emergency. Someone had to. Dr. Weaver was in surgery, and he had, besides, been up forty-eight hours without sleep; James was only a medical student and not prepared to take over. Doctors had been requested from Boston, but by midday none had arrived.

"I need help," Hendrik said to Cesca when she came in.

Emergency was a battlefield. All the mattresses on the floor were occupied, as well as the beds. People moaned and cried out in long, thin voices. Many of the patients had superficial injuries, but there was a lot of blood. The last helicopter had estimated many more injuries, and there was no way to determine the number of drownings. Only one supply of blood had come from Boston. Hendrik and Cesca went from bed to bed. Hendrik checked the vital signs, the heart and lungs and pupils; he examined people for broken limbs. Cesca washed them off and checked the extent of wounds and bandaged them. She talked on and on to each one for comfort.

"Sing to me, Francesca," Billy Naylor said when they came to his cubicle. "Remember how you used to sing."

"Later," Cesca whispered. "I haven't sung anything since Colin."

"But you will sing to me today," Billy said.

"You're a singer?" Hendrik asked after they had left Billy Naylor.

"I was on my way to being a singer," she said. "And stopped."

He might have told her that he had been on his way to being a doctor and stopped if a patient suffering cardiac arrest hadn't arrived at that moment. He had had first aid as a medic with the National Guard and knew how to treat a heart patient, but this one, an elderly woman with a history of heart trouble, according to James, was past saving.

"As soon as the doctors come from Boston, I'll have to leave," Hendrik said to James after they gave up on the woman heart patient, covered her with a sheet and moved her into the corridor outside Emergency.

"She's the only one who's died since we came," Cesca said when they took a break in midafternoon. "We've been lucky."

"You're a good nurse," he said. "That's why."

She smiled at him.

"Sometimes this morning I've thought you were something other than a doctor. I don't know, like a piano player."

Hendrik started. "You mean I don't seem competent."

"Oh, no, you seem very competent."

"Well," he said breathing deeply, "I'm not a piano player."

"You are secretive, though."

"And you are very pretty," he said.

Francesca stood up. "I should cut my hair."

On his way downtown, Will Weaver met the new girl who worked at the bookstore. He was light-headed from lack of sleep, drunk with rushing adrenaline. And there was this lovely woman from the Cheshire Cat Bookstore walking up the hill towards the hospital. They met climbing over the tree down just above the Wheelers' house. She looked as if she had been in a fight. Her white cotton full skirt was ripped at the waistband; her pale yellow peasant blouse was covered with dried black mud and the white hairs of an animal. Her long hair was matted in large wet clumps, and she was barefoot.

He saw his mother in her eyes.

"Hello," Will said. "I've seen you before." He introduced himself. She nodded and said her name was Celia Hamilton and she had just moved to the Irish section down by the river, although she wasn't Irish. The hair on her blouse and the mud, she said, were from her dog, which had been frightened by the storm. She told Will her family had moved from Norton, Massachusetts, to be on the water because her parents thought the town of Bethany was sweet.

"Sweet," she said bitterly. "The town is cursed."

She was on her way to the hospital, she said. Will, in fact, was on his way downtown to help the cleanup crews who had been working just above the main flooding. Two people besides Mr. Wheeler had been brought by helicopter dead from drowning.

"The hospital is full of emergencies," Will said. "Downtown must be a wreck."

The girl glared at him.

"Destroyed," she said. "Shipwrecked. I hate this town."

He walked up the hill with her.

"Is that the helicopter?" she asked. "Do you hear it?"

"I think I hear it," Will said. He looked up. The helicopter moved across the clear sky sideways and began its descent on the hospital grounds.

"I hope that's the helicopter with my brother," she said. "It better be; if it's not, he certainly will be dead. He may be already." She went on and on.

Will wanted to hold her; he wanted to take her hand—poor, frail blackbird. He followed her across the street just as the helicopter touched down on the hospital lawn. Hendrik Andrews and James were there to meet it.

"It's him," Celia said. "He's only ten. Yesterday was his birthday," she said. "And the house fell on him." She leaned against Will, hiding her eyes in his shirt so she didn't have to watch her brother lifted from the helicopter. "The whole house. We were in the kitchen getting ready for dinner. Philip was in his bedroom, and *slam*. There he was in the bedroom playing with toy soldiers, and he was crushed."

Will put his arms around her, powerful unclear emotions swimming drunkenly inside him.

When the boy was on the stretcher, Celia went over to Hendrik Andrews.

"That's my brother, Philip Hamilton," she said. "He's been unconscious since last night when the roof of our house caved in on him, trapping him on the floor of the bedroom."

Hendrik pushed Philip's stretcher across the lawn and through the doors of Emergency.

"My mother was too upset to come," Celia said absently. "My father didn't even get home last night."

"Go with Will," James said to Celia. "Emergency is too busy. You can help upstairs while we check your brother."

"Philip was a change-of-life baby," she said to Will. "I'm twelve years older—almost thirteen." She stopped by the ladies' room.

"There's no water," Will said.

"That's okay. I just want to see how awful I look."

"You look beautiful," he said. "You are beautiful."

She smiled a little.

"I've heard about you." Celia pushed open the door to the ladies'. "You keep snakes."

"I used to."

"People in town talk about you like you're a pet," she said.

"I was young—the youngest in my family—when my mother died, and my father was always busy. The town adopted me," he said. "You look like my mother."

The ladies' closed behind her.

Dizzily, Will went into the men's, which was dark and windowless; he went into one of the cubicles, urgent with the pressure of desire, and brought himself quickly to climax.

Celia was waiting for him when he came out.

"Show me where I can help," she said, and followed Will upstairs to the nurses' station, where Anna Wheeler put her to work filling paper cups with bottled water.

Will left.

"I have to go to town to help out," he told Celia.

He was too stirred up by the sight of the young woman to concentrate, but he wandered back to the entrance and down the hill toward town. He would buy her a dozen long-stemmed roses as soon as the town was cleaned up and the florist opened. His mind filled with visions of soft closed-petaled roses as he walked.

Billy Naylor was dying.

"From internal bleeding," James said to Hendrik Andrews. "His liver must have been severely injured by the blow."

"Can't you do something?" Cesca asked.

"Not without more blood," James said. "Even with more blood." Three years of medical school had not prepared him for the events of this day, and he was beginning to retreat to a kind of silent fatalism.

"I'll sit with him, then. Will that help?" Francesca asked.

"That's probably the most useful thing you can do today, Ces. Stay in Emergency and talk to people. Hendrik will be here. I'm going to surgery to help Dr. Weaver."

"How long might he live?" Cesca asked James, not wishing to witness a dramatic death.

"Maybe for hours, but he'll just slip away. It won't be awful," he said, sensing her fear.

Francesca slid between the curtains now drawn around Billy Naylor's bed and took his hand.

"It's Francesca," she said.

"I had hoped you'd come back." His eyes were closed.

She talked to him. After Colin's death, she had wanted for someone, particularly her mother, to talk to her endlessly, talk her to sleep at night. She told him about the storm, how the windows were blown out of her mother's studio, how some of the houses had tumbled into the river, how the emergency room was full of injured people but a lot of doctors were supposed to arrive from Boston. In the middle of her conversation, his eyes opened.

"You know Colin Mallory was a shit," he said.

She was shocked to hear Colin's name brought up for the second time and didn't reply.

"What time is it?" Billy asked.

"About eleven."

"In the morning?"

"Yes."

"The next morning?"

"The storm was last night," she said. "This is the next morning."

"I'll tell you about Colin if you want to know," he said quietly.

"I suppose I do."

James met Julian in the corridor on his way upstairs to help Sam Weaver.

"I hear Cesca's here," Julian said.

"She's been here for a couple of hours, helping in Emergency mainly."

"Then Sophia must be home alone," Julian said severely.

"She's with Tobias."

Julian was not a man inclined to imagine catastrophes, but moments ago while he rested in Hal's room after a night without sleep, he had had a premonition about Sophia.

"Did Cesca say how your mother was this morning?" Julian asked.

Francesca had. As they waited for Louisa Natale to arrive by helicopter, she had told James that Sophia had come unglued again, as if their mother had never been properly assembled in the first place. But with the demands of the day, James had forgotten Sophia altogether.

"Cesca said your mother was unwell, didn't she?"

"She left Tobias with Mama. She must have thought Mama was well enough for that."

"I'm going home," Julian said.

Sophia put Toby in tennis shoes and swim trunks, dressed herself in tennis shoes of Cesca's and a skirt whose length was tucked into the waistband.

"We're going to fix the studio, which got broken last night," she said to Toby. "And I need you to help me."

He was pleased to help. He carried two buckets and metal cups up the back steps, following Sophia.

She was not prepared for the damage.

"A lot of water," Toby said earnestly as the water splashed over the steps onto his legs.

She stepped down into the room. The water was above her ankles.

"We'll fix it," Toby said.

Her desk had been cleared by the wind. Everything was strewn through the room like paper sailboats. She picked up two of the boxed tapes of her compositions. The writing on the boxes was smeared, the boxes water-soaked. Surely the tapes were ruined.

Toby filled the buckets with his tin cup.

"Not too full," Sophia said. "We have to be able to carry them."

She picked up a sheet of music whose notes were indecipherable and dropped it into the water again.

"See," Toby said, happily pointing to the sun pouring through the window. "The sun will dry your music. Everything will be fine and good," he said, finishing with one bucket and beginning on the other.

Sophia sat down on her desk chair, exhausted.

130

"Fine and good. Is that so?" she asked.

"It's so." Toby picked up another sheet of music and put it carefully in the sun to dry.

"Do you think I'm dying?" Billy Naylor asked.

Francesca hesitated.

"I don't mind dying," he said. "Since I was about twelve, I haven't been so happy living. Except for my mother."

He had always been fat. Short and fat since the fourth grade. Children at school laughed at him until he learned to fight, and then they stopped laughing because he could beat their brains in and they knew it. When he was twelve or thirteen, he used to hang around the Sunoco station in the summers. That was where he'd had his first experience with another boy, about seventeen, who worked there. And it was nice, although he felt terrible, of course, knowing it was wrong. But that didn't stop him. He and the other boy went at it all summer until the boy left for college and got a girlfriend and pretended he'd never seen Billy before in his life when he came home vacations.

"I wanted to like girls," he said to Cesca. He was perspiring from the pain. "Could you get me another shot and rub my hair?" he asked.

His hair was thick and curly. Cesca ran her fingers through it, rubbing his scalp. Hendrik brought the injection, took Billy's pulse, listened to his heart.

"No tricks," Billy said.

"Tricks?"

"Don't tell me things are looking good," Billy said.

He curled up and turned to face Francesca. "It's all genes, you know. And what can you do about genes? If my father had knocked up my mother another night besides the one they got me, I might have liked girls. I could have been good at sports like he was before he got fat."

Sometimes Billy slept, but even sleeping, he held Francesca's hand. Just as he would begin to sink into a different level of sleep, a permanent unconsciousness, he'd bring himself back to the world.

"Francesca," he'd say.

"I won't leave," she said.

"Promise."

"Never," she said.

The last story he told her before he went to sleep for good was about Colin Mallory.

"I'm glad he got killed," Billy said.

"I thought you were friends."

"The morning after he was murdered, I woke up afraid that I'd been the one who'd done it," Billy said. "That's how much I hated him. I began to believe my nightmares were real."

Billy Naylor had not gone to college. For a while he was a waiter at a restaurant in Salem, and then he took jobs in Provincetown, at restaurants or shops, in filling stations, wherever he could find work.

Memorial Day, three summers before Colin died, Billy was home for the weekend. He had gone drinking with old friends at Rooster's Tavern, had drunk too much and had gone home early. He was sleeping when Colin Mallory with two of his friends, Tim Greenfield and Jimmy Turnbull, arrived by the side window of his bedroom at the back of the one-story shingle cottage where his mother lived.

"Let's go," they whispered.

He stumbled out of bed. He couldn't even remember what they said they were going to do, but he followed them out the window into a cold rain, which sobered him quickly. Colin was driving and they all got into his car. Colin said there was a party in Milltown, a small Portuguese coastal town, below Bethany. Billy would love it, Colin said.

They never got to the town. They took Marsh Road, and several miles outside Bethany, Colin stopped the car, pretending car trouble, and everybody got out. Billy was not sufficiently sober to sense trouble until Colin said, *"Strip."*

"Not on your life," Billy said.

"I think you might change your mind, Billy boy," Colin said, picking up a slender metal pipe from the floor of his father's car. "Just start with your shirt."

Billy took off his Moose Lodge T-shirt. He was barefoot, and the air was cold.

132

"What's up?" Billy asked, trying to be lighthearted. "You boys a little bored tonight? Can't get anyone to go down on you?"

"Nobody but you, Billy," Colin said. "Now the pants."

Billy took off his blue jeans; they were wet and stuck to his fleshy body, so he pulled down his undershorts when he finally got them off. Then Colin was behind him, pulling his arms back. Tim Greenfield tied his wrists with rope and Jimmy Turnbull, strong as an ox, tied his legs so he couldn't move.

Colin turned his flashlight on him.

"There," he said softly, and he passed his flashlight over the soft rolls of flesh, the small, retreating penis. "No balls, Billy?" He pressed the flashlight between Billy's plump legs. "Aha, there they are—pink and prickly and very small."

"The word's around that you make it with boys, Billy," Jimmy said.

Billy didn't reply.

"So do it to Tim."

Billy shook his head.

They were all but Billy drunk beyond reserves.

Tim dropped his trousers.

They put Billy out of the car at the bridge into Bethany. He was naked and still tied when the Chief of Police found him at five fifteen. They had told him never to say a word about what had happened or else they would tell everyone in Bethany about him.

A prank, he told the Chief of Police. A bunch of college students. He didn't know any of them.

The Chief of Police, guessing the reason for Billy Naylor's humiliation, took him home and did not press for more information.

When, three years later, Colin Mallory was murdered, Tim Greenfield and Jimmy Turnbull suspected Billy. They even told him so, but they never dreamed of saying a word to anybody else, not wishing to implicate themselves.

"If I'd been going to kill Colin, I'd have done it straight off when I was hot. You understand?" Billy said.

"Yes," Francesca said. "I understand exactly."

The tiny cubicle was too warm; she was aware that the emergency room smelled of blood like a butcher's shop, sweet and sickening in the heat. Dizzily she got up and called for Hendrik.

"I feel ill," she said. "Please stay with him a minute."

She walked through the lines of mattresses on the floor and out the door. In the corridor, a nurse stood with Philip Hamilton, who had regained consciousness. She turned the corner and leaned against the double doors which read in big white letters: DANGER: X-RAY IN USE.

"So," she thought, breathless with emotion, "Billy Naylor could have killed Colin. And he didn't."

"In a war zone, every danger is equal," her father had said one night at dinner, describing his own brief service in the United States Army at the beginning of World War II. "There is no guarantee that a man, even one with a reputation for courage, will behave well in an emergency," he added.

"How did *you* behave in emergencies?" Francesca had asked, young enough at the time to risk personal conversations with her father.

"I was only on the periphery of the war zone," Julian had replied. "But at night, I'd go to sleep rehearsing courageous behavior in the hope that should the occasion arise, I could depend on rehearsals."

"Did you ever kill anyone?" she had asked.

"Different rules apply in war, of course," he had said. "But no, I never killed anyone."

She didn't quite believe him.

Hendrik Andrews pulled the curtain closed behind him. Billy lay on his side, curled up, his knees drawn, his hands fisted and close to his chest. His pale green eyes were open and opaque, clouded by approaching death. Hendrik was struck by how swiftly the blinds drop across the pupils and distort, perhaps obliterate the objects of the visible world so the only sight which lingers to the end is internal.

When Hendrik was young, he had played surgeon after

school in the cold attic of the Andrews' row house in South Boston so his father, who sat in a plump upholstered chair next to the kitchen stove and listened to the soaps on a console radio, would not know his son's preoccupation. He collected dolls and stuffed animals discarded in the trash cans in the alley behind his house and repaired them in the attic. He had an operating table and scissors, needles and wire thread, red finger paint which he had stolen from the kindergarten room at South Side Elementary for blood. He became proficient at repairing dolls. He could repaint their faces, rehinge their arms and legs, glue on hair and patch up flaked skin or broken fingers, missing ears.

In the world of physicians where he lived weekday afternoons, Hendrik Andrews was a magician. He made new kidneys and artificial hearts before such inventions were a part of medical research. He operated on ruptured spleens and broken legs and brains. He built a laboratory on top of the trunk where his mother stored her wedding dress and their baby clothes and christening dress and developed cures for polio, rheumatic fever and acne, which was his cousin's particular affliction. His patients never died.

Outside on the streets and alleys of South Boston, Massachusetts, his friends from grade school played army or Robin Hood or cowboys while Hendrik played out his own heroic role as a starched-white-coated knight saving children from the jaws of certain death.

At five, he'd come downstairs for supper, take out the trash, do the dishes, walk the dog around the block, listen to *Spider-Man* at his friend Mickey's house and go to bed in the room behind his parents' with his arms wrapped around a portable radio, daydreaming of the children in the attic above him whose lives he had rescued that very afternoon.

He never thought of Elena, although certainly he knew the life he had invented had to do with her.

"I want you to tell me what's going to happen. The truth about it," Billy Naylor asked.

Hendrik sat down and pulled his chair next to Billy's bed.

"The I.V. you're getting has some medication to stop the bleeding."

"Is it working?" Billy asked.

"We can't really tell. It's supposed to work."

Billy closed his eyes.

"It's not working," he said. "I'm on fire inside. Tell me, will I just go to sleep or will it hurt? Are you a doctor or not?"

Hendrik had bolted in 1954 in his third year of medical school at Tufts. It was winter, late afternoon on a Friday in January, and Hendrik's class had just finished the first lecture of the new term in Obstetrics and Gynecology when the medical alert sounded and all the doctors and students were called to the emergency room.

A school bus full of children and traveling too fast for the icy road conditions had gone out of control on a bridge over the Charles River and plunged into the shallow end of the river. Hendrik arrived in Emergency just as the first ambulances pulled up and the children were rushed in on stretchers. The attendants in wet suits or parkas, bundled against the winter, brought them in, wrapped in blankets. In a matter of minutes, the beds were full. In the distance, Hendrik could hear the long wail of more ambulances bearing down on the small supply of doctors available in Emergency that afternoon. They worked through the night in Emergency, in Surgery, on the floor.

Just as a gray light softened the darkness and broke through the glass doors of Emergency and the last ambulance load of children arrived, Hendrik Andrews simply cracked.

On and off all night he had been attending a small child who called him Uncle Ben whenever she slipped into consciousness. "Uncle Ben," she'd say softly. "Uncle Ben. Uncle Ben."

Even as a student physician, he certainly knew that she was going to die. When her parents arrived, he was with the doctor who told them. At one point he asked the child's mother shouldn't she call Uncle Ben, since the little girl kept asking for him.

A brief smile flew across the mother's face. "There's no

Uncle Ben," she said. "Laurie made him up."

Hendrik had just finished setting up a transfusion for a young boy in shock when Laurie's mother appeared at the foot of the bed.

"I think she's gone," the mother said.

She was gone. As he took her pulse, Hendrik's hand shook. His legs began to shake and he lost feeling in his feet and hands. His chest and throat tightened and he started to perspire. He thought he was going to be sick.

"I'll get a doctor," he said to the mother.

"I thought you were one," the mother replied. She followed him as he got one of the residents.

"Laurie must have thought that you were Uncle Ben," the mother said.

He told her he was sorry, and excused himself. He ran through the doors of Emergency into the long corridor which led past Oncology, up the steps, out the back door, across the parking lot to his room. In minutes, he had packed a few possessions, called a taxicab and left for home. He went back to Tufts only once, months later, to withdraw formally and in person after he had joined the medical branch of the National Guard for six months' service in Texas and seven years' reserve.

Hendrik took a wet cloth and wiped the perspiration from Billy Naylor's face. He soaked the cloth in water and wet his blistered lips. His hands began to shake as they had years before at Tufts. His feet were numb.

"I'm not a doctor," he said quickly.

Billy's eyes fluttered open.

He put his hand on Billy's soft, fleshy wrist. "I can give you something for pain. You'll go to sleep and it won't hurt as much as it does now."

"Please," Billy said. "And get Cesca. I'd like her to sing."

Hendrik found Francesca at the telephone.

"The lines are dead," she said. "I just tried to call."

"Didn't you know that? Everything's gone."

"I guess I forgot. I wanted to check on my child."

137

"Don't worry," he said gently. "Nothing more can happen today. You've had a hurricane." He ran his hand over her long hair. "I think you should leave your hair long," he said.

The sun was directly overhead—high noon—when Julian walked in the front door and called Sophia. Toby, with his yellow blanket, sat on the first-floor landing.

"Tobias."

Toby stood, the blanket clutched in his fist. "The studio is broken," he said earnestly.

"I know it is," Julian said. "Where is your grandmother?" He imagined the worst. His legs were heavy as pipes and his breath was short as he walked up the steps.

"Sleeping," Toby said quietly.

"In bed?"

Toby shook his head.

"In the studio?"

"Yes," Toby said.

He followed his grandfather down the corridor to the steps up to the studio.

"Coming?" Julian asked, himself afraid to go alone.

"No," Toby said, standing firmly at the bottom of the steps.

"Sophia?" Julian called as he walked up the steps, but his voice hardly carried.

She sat in the white rocker, facing the windows now entirely open to the weather. Her arms were on the rocker arms. He assumed that she was dead.

"Sophia."

She was wearing a pale blue summer sundress with the skirt hiked into the elastic legs of her underpants, showing the length of her long and lovely legs. Her eyes were open. Her hair, damp with perspiration, was in a floppy bun on top of her head, and she was still.

"Sophia." Julian leaned over. "Say something."

Her eyes rolled up so she was looking at him, but she didn't speak. He wanted to slap her.

"This is cruel of you to do. I was so worried." He took her hand and lifted her up from the chair. "Pull yourself together.

We're going to the hospital to see Hal and help out."

Julian had seldom spoken harshly to Sophia; but the madness he was witnessing in his wife was no absolute condition, and he was angry at her self-indulgence.

Sophia dressed. She picked out a pale gray linen skirt and blouse she had not worn for years, since before her illness. She brushed her long, thick black hair laced with silver into a French roll and tied a bright scarf around her neck. She put on Francesca's plum lipstick and colored her cheeks.

"Ready," she said quietly, and followed Julian and Tobias downstairs. She ran her hand over the cherry library table in the hall and brushed off slivers of broken glass.

"There's a lot to do to clean up," she said.

"Most of the people in Bethany have suffered irretrievable losses," Julian said crossly.

They walked down the path littered with tea rose petals to the sidewalk.

"I'm sorry Julian," she said. She watched him walk stiffly just ahead of her; he looked aged. "You are too old to stay up all night."

"Don't ever do that to me again," he said.

When she had looked at the destruction of her studio this morning and considered the time it would take to restore her neatly ordered life, she simply hadn't been willing to accommodate a turn of fortune; so she pretended to be mad.

"I won't do that again." She reached out and took his hand.

James wheeled the stretcher with Louisa Natale into a semi-private room on the same floor as Emergency. In the other bed, Sylvia Olmstead was recovering from a hysterectomy. He pulled the curtain between their beds. From the cupboard of the bedside table he took a white hospital gown, a metal bowl which held a thin terry-cloth towel and washcloth, a wrapped rectangle of soap. There was water in the thermos pitcher, which he poured into the bowl. Then he undressed Louisa. He took off the tight sundress she had been wearing, wiped the dried mud off her arms and shoulders. She was slender, thinner than he had imagined, with sharp pelvic triangles rising above her belly and small breasts which fell flat, soft cookies with tiny lavender centers. He lifted her on the bed. Just before he covered her with a hospital gown, he touched one lavender nipple. She stirred, the trace of a smile on her lips, lost in some reverie of lovemaking.

James, shaken by the look of her and by his own unprofessional gesture, was in an actual sweat. He raised the sides of the hospital bed so Louisa wouldn't tumble out, and left.

Shortly after noon, the helicopters arrived with blood, water and supplies as well as volunteer physicians. Hendrik Andrews was grateful. He was ready to leave.

Behind the curtains of Billy Naylor's cubicle, Francesca Woodbine sang in a clear lyrical voice which filled the emergency room with song. Just before he fell into a final sleep, Billy Naylor asked her to write a song about him.

"I will. I'll write a ballad and sing it at Rooster's on Saturday nights," she said.

Hendrik left without telling her goodbye. The helicopter in which he had arrived that morning was amongst those which had come from Boston with supplies and doctors.

"We're ordered to help out in the center of town," the pilot said to Hendrik, locking the door from inside and preparing to lift off. "So how was it?"

"A mess. Terrible."

"A lot dead?"

"Some."

"Too bad. Lucky you were there."

Hendrik shrugged. He wished he had said goodbye to Francesca. If he happened to see her again, he planned to tell her that he had fallen in love with her beautiful voice.

At one, Sam Weaver found Francesca with Billy Naylor. She rested her head in her arms against the side of the bed and sang to Billy. But he was dead.

"When?" Cesca asked. "I've been here the whole time. There wasn't any noise."

Dr. Weaver turned Billy on his back, straightened his legs, crossed his arms on his chest and gently closed his eyelids.

"Probably minutes ago," Sam said. "There wouldn't have been any noise."

And to his astonishment, Francesca cried out. Later she would describe to her mother what overcame her as an attack like a gunshot wound or a heart seizure or transition during labor when the baby's head is in the birth canal. The sound she made was no ordinary cry. Doctors and nurses in Emergency stopped what they were doing. The patients held their breaths. The depth of her anguish portended further disasters.

"Leave me alone," Cesca said when Sam tried to take hold of her. He led her down the corridor into his office across from X-Ray and closed the door.

"I'll be right back," he said. He found James on the second floor setting up an I.V. for Louisa Natale.

"Francesca is in my office," he said. "Something's the matter with her."

A couple of nurses lingered outside the door to Sam's office.

"Is she okay?" they asked when James ran down the hall.

"I don't know." He had never heard such an awful sound before.

"Don't touch me," Cesca said when he went into the room and sat down in the chair across from her.

"What happened?" he asked when her crying had subsided.

"I don't know," she said. "You know Billy Naylor died," she said.

"I didn't know. Is that what happened to you?"

Francesca stood and rubbed her tingling hands together.

"I don't know what happened to me," she said, and looked at her brother directly. "If you fall for Louisa Natale, I'll die," she said.

"Jesus, Francesca." The memory of touching Louisa's nipple flew by, and he shuddered. "For chrissake." Sometimes he thought she was a witch with eyes that shot straight through his brain.

"I have to go home to get Tobias," Francesca said.

"He's here." James was glad to change the subject. "Mama brought him a few minutes ago."

Later that day on the way home from the hospital, Sophia told Francesca a story about her mother when Sophia was small, perhaps only five or six. Sophia had been sitting at the bar at Rooster's eating her usual dinner of beef stew from the big pot always on the burner. Two or three of the women who worked upstairs at Rooster's were with her—one in particular called Sweet Sally Lou who lived in the room next to Sophia's. Francesca Allegra was under the weather, as she told her daughter, which meant she had her monthly period, but Sophia always imagined "under the weather" defined by invisible storm clouds which hovered over her mother's bed where she lay.

"My mother's under the weather," she said to the company at the bar in explanation of Francesca's absence. Those days of the month were Sophia's absolute favorites. They meant Francesca didn't work and she had her mother to herself. She ate her dinner quickly so she could go back upstairs. Sweet Sally Lou was telling a funny story about a man from Boston when a terrible sound came from one of the rooms.

"Someone's in trouble up there," Sweet Sally Lou said, "or else having a baby."

The sound came from Francesca's room.

Sophia slid off the bench, but Sweet Sally Lou held her back while Redblade, the bartender, raced up the back steps. By the time Redblade came back downstairs, the cries had stopped.

Sophia pushed away her plate of stew. "Was Mama, wasn't it?"

Redblade nodded. "Some awful sadness came over her, she said."

"She's crying about the Count," Sophia said matter-of-factly, and everyone at the bar agreed that Sophia was probably right.

"Well," Francesca said when her mother had finished telling the story. "There is no count for me cry about."

Just before six the night after the hurricane, Sam Weaver sat down at the large desk in Emergency to assess the damage to Bethany, Massachusetts.

The National Guard were in the center of town to help in the cleanup. All the businesses along Main Street had been

142

leveled except the few brick buildings. The water was thick as soup with produce—bananas and oranges, broccoli, cucumbers and lettuce—and furniture, clothing, ice cream tables from Sunny's. There was the heavy smell of rotting food. Occasionally, an animal, a dog perhaps, caught unaware, floated by. People who had not spoken for years stood side by side joking or sharing tragedies from the night before.

Supplies had arrived, and Anna Wheeler's house, with two others on Elm Street, was designated as a way station for dispensing food and water. The access roads to Bethany had been cleared by sundown, so Anna's friend Maria had gone home to Salem, as well as other people stranded by the storm. The auxiliary electrical system at the hospital was still in operation, although electricity, water and telephones were still out of order in the rest of the town. It would be days before the wreckage was cleaned up and three years before the center of town was restored to its original form.

Sixteen deaths were reported in Bethany on the seven-o'clock national news the night after the storm.

Robert Wheeler, age 54, died of drowning.

Sandra Mason, age 18, died of drowning.

Anne Terp, age 81, died of congestive heart failure.

Billy Naylor, age 26, died of internal injuries.

Tom Jackson, age 35, died of drowning.

Timmy Wright, age 56, died of head injuries.

Saki Olson, age 2, died of head injuries.

Marie Mason, age 20, died of drowning.

Theresa DeAngelo, age 19, cause of death unknown.

Ray Hanrahan, age 71, died of heart failure.

Martha Jackson, age 92, died of a cerebral hemorrhage.

Julie Karsh, age 42, died of complications from a fall.

Caroline Biscuit, age 12, died of drowning.

Seth James, age 47, died of a heart attack.

Terry Wriger, age 58, died of suffocation.

Dr. Joshua Marin, age 41, died of head injuries.

The last fatality, Dr. Joshua Marin, had died on his way to work. A large limb broken by the storm had fallen as the doctor walked along the shore road.

There were three hundred and forty-seven hospitalized injuries, seventeen critical. Intensive Care was full. Emergency was full. Twenty-five relief doctors had been sent from Boston and Providence.

The estimate of damages to the town was in the millions.

Anna Wheeler checked off a list she had compiled with Dr. Weaver of people to notify. Billy Naylor's mother, who was in Marblehead visiting her sister. Mrs. Hamilton, whose son, Phillip, had been admitted to Boston Children's in critical condition. Will Weaver handled most of the notification of next of kin, accompanied by Bill Becker, Chief of Police. Will seemed to like the job, Bill Becker told his wife the night after the storm.

Just after midnight, the town dark, Sam Weaver lay down on his bed in the hospital and was asleep before he had a chance to remove his gown.

Anna Wheeler went to the small room behind the nurses' station reserved for occasions when she stayed the night, took off her uniform and pulled the pins from her hair. Then she turned off the overhead light, lay down on top of the sheets in her slip and wept. She wished Maria were there to comfort her. Bob Wheeler had been like her brother. She would miss him terribly.

In his dark room, Prince Hal couldn't sleep. His leg throbbed. He wished James would stop by once more before he went to bed just to talk so Hal could forget the dead kittens.

James was too tired to sleep. Sam's gentle snoring in the next bed took on the strength of thunder. He'd make tea, he thought, getting up.

Hal lay on his back, his eyes open, when James came in with a small flashlight.

"I thought you'd come," he said.

"I can't sleep. I've been awake too long, I suppose."

"Me neither."

James sat down on his brother's bed. "I have always thought you could sleep through a ground attack, Hal."

"Aren't you going to take my pulse?"

James laughed.

144

"Your pulse is fine."

He patted his brother's cast.

"See you in the morning." He leaned down and kissed Hal on the head. He couldn't remember ever kissing him before.

Louisa was also awake when James went in.

"Okay?" he asked.

"Am I?"

"You will be in a couple of days. You have a concussion." He picked up her wrist. Her pulse was almost normal. "I was just doing a final bed check before I went to bed," he said.

"What day is it?"

The storm was yesterday afternoon."

"Have my parents been told?"

"They've been here. They were here this afternoon, but you were out of it."

"I can't remember anything since I left Salem. Not even driving through the storm."

He told her what had happened.

"When you've finished seeing everyone else, will you sit with me?"

He hesitated, remembering Francesca's warning.

"You're the last patient I have to see." He pulled a chair next to her bed.

"Just hold my hand," she said.

He must have fallen asleep immediately, with such tiredness he didn't feel himself slip off the chair. One of the nurses found him at dawn curled up on the floor beside Louisa's bed.

"I thought you were another fatality," she said, helping him to his feet.

At midnight, Will Weaver finally went home for the first time since the storm. The Weavers' house was in disarray but not badly damaged. There were broken windows, and tiles from the roof had blown off and decorated the lawn. Two trees were down—one large mulberry which Sam had particularly disliked because of the soft fat berries carpeting the sidewalk every summer.

Today, Will decided, had been the most wonderful day of

his life. He lay down on the couch and thinking of Celia Hamilton, fell immediately asleep.

Francesca lay on Tobias' bed rubbing his back so he could sleep. Every time he was almost asleep, a nightmare flashed across his brain and he raised his head.

"Shh," she'd say, pressing his head gently on the pillow.

"Why don't you tell me about my father?" he asked.

"Because I didn't know him very well."

Tobias turned on his back so he could see his mother's face in the moonlight.

"Do you know me very well?"

"Of course I know you. You are my darling boy."

"How come you didn't know him, then?" he asked.

"Knowing people isn't so easy, Toby. Sometimes I don't even know myself."

In her own bed, she lay on her back and thought of Colin Mallory. He was standing on the high school steps in blue jeans and a white oxford-cloth shirt which was unbuttoned halfway down. He had not been shot.

She could not get the living memory of him out of her mind. He had captured the imagination of young women in Bethany. She could feel his energy now in an unlit room holding a feather pillow in her arms. Surely, she had loved him—a wrongheaded love, because he was not a kind man and she had been too tender. But as she lay in an absolute darkness, the streetlights on Main out of commission, she could not believe she had killed him.

If she had gone instead into the cottage and caught Louisa Natale in her swan hat with champagne wet on her naked thighs—and said, *"Get out"* or said nothing whatever but stood there implacable, he would have been sorry. If she had had the courage and foresight for that gesture, *she* at least would be free of this endless brooding on an irreversible life.

Or if, after she had seen them in the cottage, she had waited in the marsh grasses for the madness to pass—it would have

146

passed, certainly—she might not have had the fury to go home and get her father's revolver from the desk drawer.

She sat up in bed. She had not thought about the revolver for a very long time, but now it occurred to her that the storm might have washed the gun out of hiding. Trees and bushes in the garden had flown down Hawthorne Street. The gun had not been buried deeper than the roots of bushes. Hadn't she buried it beside a rhododendron? She got out of bed and sat in the bathroom in the dark until dawn. In the morning, she would go to her parents' garden.

The large oak tree that had held the rope swing was down across the fishpond, which was full of water, flattening the rhododendrons and azaleas. Cesca sat on the cement bench and tried to get her bearings. She had come up the path through the line of boxwood to the fishpond and buried the revolver just there, she thought, next to a large rhododendron, still intact. The ground was spongy, full of debris, but unturned. She did not see the skeletons of the kittens that had died of fleas the spring before Colin and had been buried by Hal next to the place she had chosen to bury the revolver. Certainly, then, the gun was still underground.

She went to the house, in the back way, taking off her galoshes in the pantry. Her father was at breakfast reading a stack of papers for work.

"I was checking the damage to the garden," she said.

"Mama's not good," he said as if he had not heard her properly.

"I know."

She wandered down the hall; a light wind was blowing through the broken windows into her father's study.

So the gun was safe in the ground where she had left it. If that storm had left the gun in place, then certainly it would remain where she had put it for her lifetime. She flopped down on the leather couch and put her feet on the arm. The curtains were down in the study, the windows on the west side were out, but otherwise the room was as it had been before the storm. Her eyes wandered beyond the west window, past where the Woodbine-family hunting prints hung cockeyed, to the gun collection over the highboy. When she had first learned to shoot, she used to spend hours examining the gun collection pretending she was a pioneer woman or an anthropologist in an uncivilized country or a woman at war. She remembered once in particular when she had taken the German Luger; her father discovered her standing on his armchair with the gun pointed at the south window against an imaginary enemy. He had sent her to bed without dinner or conversation except the warning not ever to touch a gun of his again except the one in his drawer in the event of an emergency.

Julian walked in and put the papers on which he had been working in his middle drawer.

"Check on Mama today, if you will, Ces," he said to her.

"Of course."

"The phones are working again," he said. "You can reach me at the courthouse if you need me."

He caught her looking at the gun collection.

"What are you looking for?" he asked.

"Have you rearranged things from the days I used to play in here?"

"I do from time to time," he said. "That's my domestic contribution to this household."

"I used to shoot that one, didn't I?" She pointed to one of the revolvers.

"You were an accomplished marksman," he said sharply, uncertain of the reason for his quick anger.

"I don't like guns any longer," she said.

"Just as well," he replied. On the way to the office he decided to get rid of the gun collection altogether.

Much later, she had the energy to turn her attention away from the wall with the guns to get up from the couch and call James to ask him about Prince Hal.

As she sat at her father's desk waiting for the hospital to answer, it occurred to her to open the left-hand desk drawer where her father had kept his revolver. Had he ever looked in that drawer since Colin died and wondered what had become of his revolver, or had he forgotten the gun kept there for so many years? And if he had found it missing, what would he have done? Kept it a secret, or as a judge and known

148

for personal integrity as well, would he have gone to the Chief of Police?

Hal was fine, the nurse on his floor said.

"I'll be over soon," Cesca said, and hung up the telephone. She opened the other drawers, which were full of papers and paper clips and pencils and photographs and bank statements. But her hand only touched the handle of the top left-hand drawer. She did not pull it, knowing instinctively that it held news she was not prepared to see.

Before she left, she checked on Sophia, who sat up in bed, pale-faced as a patient. She promised to be back soon and went downstairs with Toby and out the back door.

As she walked down Hawthorne in the bright sunlight, Colin Mallory was back again, shaking her internally. She could not continue to feel this anxious and survive, she decided, unless a portion of her brain were excised and she could forget. She sat down on the steps of the Maykins' house and waited for the shaking to cease. A natural lobotomy was what she wished for immediately.

Then she went on. Some time before she reached the hospital, a different state of mind slipped in like weather, and the memory of Colin Mallory was denied admission.

After Billy Naylor was buried and Mrs. Naylor had moved to Salem to get away from memories, word got around that Billy Naylor had been the one who killed Colin. Cesca heard bits and pieces of the story Billy had told her before he died and assumed that Tim Greenfield and Jimmy Turnbull had spread the tale. They no doubt believed that Billy had been the one to do it and now that he was dead, there was no chance that they would be implicated. But no one in Bethany seemed interested in Colin Mallory's murder any longer. Hurricane Elsie had overtaken their imaginations, drawn them together like family. And with the storm, the memory of Colin Mallory blew down the Leonora River at last and out to sea.

The next bright morning after the storm, Francesca woke early and took Tobias on a walk to see the wreckage of the

149

town. They went the back route into Main Street by way of Rooster's Tavern, which was located at the far north end of Bethany. To Francesca's astonishment, the tavern was untouched except for flooding up to the front door, as if the storm had simply leaped over Rooster's Tavern and landed on the other side.

"That's where my grandmother lived and where your grandmother was born," she told Toby, walking along the high road above the river. They came to the beginning of downtown Main Street in a shambles. "And here is where I was born and you were born. Bethany, Massachusetts."

At the bottom of the hill next to Hanrahan's Market, a group of National Guardsmen were hauling the debris out of the devastated market. Amongst them, Francesca recognized Hendrik Andrews. He saw her immediately and smiled as she passed by the store.

"Hello," he called to her. "You sing like an angel." He was very glad he had a chance to tell her.

"I am an angel," she replied, full of pleasure.

Book Three

Prologue

*O*ne *afternoon early in the summer of 1933 when Santa*
Francesca's life was winding down, Sophia found the
occasion to ask her mother about her profession.

They were having coffee, as they often did, in Francesca's living
room on the second floor of Rooster's Tavern — a rectangular room
with long windows decorated in rich Florentine yellows and deep
green velvets and patterned rugs. There were fresh wildflowers in
smoky vases and pictures, mainly dark miniatures in gilt frames, of
the family Francesca had left behind in Sicily.

"Why?" Sophia had asked. "You could have been a shopkeeper."

"I was a shopkeeper in Sicily, before you were born. It was
always the same, hour after hour. There was nothing by which to
remember the days," she said.

She sat in a wooden rocker next to a window which overlooked
the Leonora River, dressed, as she often was, in costume, with
bright-colored full skirts to her ankles and full-sleeved blouses. She
had never cut her hair, and even as an old woman, she sometimes
wore it in a long braid woven with ribbons as if she were a girl.

"What was it like?" Sophia asked.

"I didn't think of myself as a prostitute," Francesca replied.

Sophia had thought of her that way. In grammar school when
she felt the sharp critical eyes of other children, she used to wish
herself away.

"You could have been anything, Mama," she said. "Even married."

Santa Francesca laughed. "I suppose I could have married. But sometime when I was still young, I lost the desire to make certain accommodations," she said. "Work is only how you think of it. And so, I thought of my work as a gift. Besides," she added, "I always had fortunes to tell."

1.

Mating Calls:
July 4, 1964

The summer of 1964 was glorious in all of New England, and especially along the coast. The bright, clear days were warm enough to soften even the dark tempers of the Welsh in Bethany. Nights were cool and windless. Seabirds, swallows and warblers, mockingbirds and blue jays draped the branches of elms and sang into the night as if their hearts would burst with joy.

It was a perfect summer to celebrate the restoration of Bethany. The week before the Fourth of July, workmen removed the last of the scaffolding from the shops along Main Street. Painters put up green shutters on the clapboard storefronts and finished painting the black wrought iron on the block of Italian stucco buildings closest to the river. Shopkeepers planted their small square gardens with begonias and impatiens, bright red geraniums and periwinkle. In the long days of early summer, the streets of Bethany, Massachusetts, sparkled like highgloss picture postcards sold in drugstores of small New England villages.

Citizens wandered smugly along Main Street mentally supervising the final details of the town's reconstruction as if its design were their own invention. Relatives were invited from out of town. Friends from Salem or Northside or Ewes came for dinner, and for recreation they were taken on a walk from

Rooster's Tavern, at the mouth of the Leonora, along Main Street, which was dominated at the northern end by the First Congregational Church, white and steepled, built to a benevolent God and located directly across the street from Our Mother of Mercies R.C.

Father John Meagher had been, with interruptions, priest of Our Mother of Mercies since the First World War. He was a striking man with a splendid mass of wild and curly hair, a long angular face flushed by a childhood in a village on the Irish Sea. "He's a man full of mysteries," Frank Adler said once to Francesca, who was captured with curiosity about Father John. The priest must know firsthand the confessions of generations in Bethany, Francesca decided, perhaps even those of her grandmother. Sometimes she wandered up and down Main Street, like a lover, lying in wait for Father John to come out of the chapel door so she could persuade him to tell her secrets.

He had left Bethany twice in his long priesthood at Our Mother of Mercies, missing the years of Francesca's growing up. In the thirties, he had returned to the small village in Northern Ireland to witness his parents' long dying. And then for fifteen years before the summer of the hurricane, he had worked as a missionary in Africa, not out of a sense of mission—he was a priest stirred only by the individual soul, not the general human condition—but because the life fell out of Bethany, Massachusetts, when Santa Francesca died.

At seventy-five, his mind still leaped with the spirit of an ancient child, and people were drawn by his wonderful energy.

Since spring, Father John had been in a bad temper. First it was his arthritis. Sometimes he couldn't get up in the morning for the pain in his knees. Other times he couldn't go to bed at night, so he'd pace back and forth in his apartment or up and down Main Street at three in the morning. There were days he celebrated 6 A.M. Mass without a bit of sleep. Then there was the trouble he'd been having with the new minister of First Congregational who took an interest in arguments about birth control and the sexual revolution, although he certainly didn't look like the sort of man who'd have an opportunity to participate in either. It wasn't that he disliked Protestantism, Father John decided. To each his own. The Protestants had their reasons, and who can escape history, after all? as he told Frank Adler. But he'd come to the conclusion that with a few exceptions like Frank Adler, he disliked Protestants. However, in the summer of 1964, the real reason for Father John's bad temper was the restoration of Bethany.

Sunny afternoons, he and Frank would sit on the wood-slat bench in front of the First Congregational Church and talk about failed promises.

Failed promises was Father John's favorite subject for private discussions. The expression had been given to him by Santa Francesca Allegra when she first told his fortune years ago. After the fortune was given and the sex, he had asked her what she thought of heaven, curious about the nature of a woman, a prostitute, who had true faith in God as certainly she did and faith in her own surprising powers of sight as well.

"You're a good Catholic woman, Santa Francesca," he had said to her. "Surely you believe in heaven."

"Promises," Santa Francesca had said, taking the young priest's hand over her breast like a cup. "Failed promises. Just like America, the beautiful."

"I don't like the way the town is being remade on the same old foundations mortared in Indian bones," Father John said to Frank.

"But Main Street looks nice, don't you think?" Frank Adler said, always remarkable for his patience.

"False fronts. All of these buildings now," Father John said. "Even your own."

Frank Adler had taken over Hanrahan's Market, next door to the church, although only the foundation of the building remained, so the shop was new and smelled more of fresh pine and paint than butchered meat, as it had when Ray Hanrahan was alive. There was a delicatessen in the back, with tables for lunch and early supper, but people stopped in all day for coffee or hot chocolate and conversation with Frank or Dottie or each other. Prince Hal stopped by many after-noons to talk about the circus and his plan to leave home.

"Finish high school," Frank said, knowing Hal had only one more year. "I didn't, and that was a mistake. I had dreams at your age and no way to get at them."

"You have your own shop now," Hal said. "That's some-thing. And a baby."

Frank had stopped drinking after the hurricane. When his hangover from the night of the storm faded, he never had another drink. And Dottie, girlish, almost young again with the pleasure of his continued sobriety, agreed to have a baby.

"The hurricane changed my life," Frank said.

"Mine too," Hal agreed. "Only I haven't done anything about it yet." Which was not entirely true. For almost three years, he had been in correspondence with Amal, the blond, bearded, slack-skinned and aging lion tamer for Ringling Brothers Circus. *"I want to be your apprentice,"* he had written to Amal. "HURRY. COME SOON," Amal's letters would say in bold capital letters. "I NEED AN APPRENTICE BEFORE MY HEART GIVES OUT."

Julian had discovered one of the letters on Hal's desk and at supper that night, colored by anger, he said, "You can think whether or not you're going to join the circus when your body fills out like a man's."

Sometimes Julian couldn't help himself.

"I'll probably join the circus after high school," Hal said to Frank, but he doubted he could wait.

Next door to Hanrahan's, Mrs. O'Malley had a dress shop for middle-aged women like herself with simple lives. She sold linen suits for church and cotton dresses with sleeves, belted at the waist, A-line skirts in primary colors and print blouses. She kept only a few styles in stock, since the women in Be-thany were not inclined to be imaginative about clothes. And women liked to go for their lunch hour simply to try on clothes, not with the intention of buying but for the company.

Sunnys' Ice Cream Parlor, still owned by Sunny, a dark Welsh woman as sunny as winter in a northern sea town, had been restored without changes to the original shop. Reluctantly, Sunny carried more flavors of ice cream than she had before the storm—bubble-gum, praline, maple-walnut, peppermint, rum-raisin. A chain ice cream store had moved in next to Rooster's and she had to compete.

Will Weaver owned a book and record shop called Leonora's next to Sunny's. When the shops were put up for sale after the storm, Sam Weaver, with tempered optimism, bought the shop to ensure his son's employment. Celia, the girl Will had met during the hurricane, worked in the children's section called The Snake Bed, painted by Will to resemble the bottom of the Leonora River. There were snakes wound around the roots of trees, coiled amongst the vegetation, slithering along the mud bottom. At the entrance to The Snake Bed there was a large cage with several living but languid and uninterested snakes. Children poked their fingers through the cage or pressed their noses against the mesh, often more delighted to come to Leonora's for the snakes than for books.

On the second floor of Leonora's Books and Records, Francesca Woodbine had an apartment which she shared with Tobias and Maud Hanrahan.

The evening of July 3, as Father John, crabby about the approaching Fourth of July celebrations, sat on the bench in front of First Congregational with Frank, Francesca Woodbine came around the corner of Main with Tobias in hand. She had on her grandmother's bright purple skirt and a loose silk sash in Roman stripes, her feet were bare and under the arm that was not holding Toby's hand she carried a full-size shiny cardboard replica of herself in the exact outfit she was now wearing, only with black ballet slippers on the cardboard feet.

"She's lovely," Frank said, and he did think Francesca was lovely, but he spoke for Father John, sensing the priest's response to her as soon as she rounded the corner.

"Yes," Father John said. "I knew her grandmother."

"They looked alike?"

"Santa Francesca was small," he reconsidered. The early-summer air was still, the evening comfortably warm, there was no traffic on the street at dusk to diffuse the priest's unspoken confession. "Even small, she was the most beautiful woman I have known."

"I suppose Cesca's going to be famous," Frank Adler said, embarrassed by the intimacy of the moment.

"She is already." Father John adjusted the collar at his neck. "I hear her songs on the radio as I turn the dial to Classical."

"You should stop and listen," Frank said.

"I do. I listen."

Francesca stopped by the bench and held up the paper doll by the top of its head. "Myself," she said gaily.

"So I see," Father John said.

"It's to advertise her album which will be out soon. Right, Cesca?" Frank said.

Father John was pensive. "I know about your album. Aren't you singing it tomorrow night at Rooster's for the Fourth of July?"

Cesca nodded.

"Why Rooster's?" Father John asked. "It's such an ordinary place for a girl who is already on the radio even in places like Kansas and Minnesota to sing."

Francesca sat down beside him and put her hand on his skirted knee.

"Because of my grandmother. She lived at Rooster's," Cesca said. "She had to live there."

"Your grandmother was a good woman, Cesca; she doesn't need atonement," the priest said, understanding exactly the nature of retribution. "Santa Francesca didn't have to live there at all. She liked Rooster's."

She put an arm around Tobias. "Did you know her?"

"Somewhat."

"Did she come to you for confession?" she asked.

"And if she did, would I tell you?"

Cesca laughed. "I'd know," she said wickedly. "You wouldn't have to tell me. I inherited her sight."

Father John lifted the soft cotton skirt. "Hers?"

"Everything I have on was hers." She stood and turned, modeling the gypsy outfit.

"She liked color," Father John said.

"You knew her well, then," Cesca said.

"She was a parishioner," he said.

Frank Adler and the priest watched Francesca walk down Main Street with a small skip, swinging Toby's hand, and turn into Leonora's.

"Do you believe in seeing the future, Father?" Frank asked.

"If the news is good," the priest replied. "Otherwise I only believe in God."

When Francesca arrived at Leonora's, Will Weaver was unpacking the boxes of *Mating Calls* which had just come from Columbia Records that day. She leaned in the front door.

"H'lo, Will," she called to him.

He carried a stack of records and put them in the bay window already decorated with the cardboard advertisement of Francesca.

"Did you listen to *Mating Calls*?" she asked.

"I listened," Will said, slicing open the second box of albums. "You're very good."

"Well?" She walked into the shop. "Is that all?"

"Did you write 'Billy's Love Song'?"

"I did."

"And you're going to sing it tomorrow night at Rooster's?" She nodded.

"You're going to cause a riot, Francesca," Will said matter-of-factly.

"You'll be at the concert?"

"Of course I'll be there."

"I'm not worried." And she went up the outside steps to her second-story apartment. Already Maud was at the piano practicing for their last rehearsal before the Fourth of July.

Early on the morning of July 4, Tim Greenfield walked down Main Street with his cousin George from Nashville, whose yearly visit north coincided this year with restoration celebrations in Bethany. Tim had become a lawyer in Boston, married now to a girl he had met at Radcliffe, and they had

161

a child. He lived a simple, ordinary life, with court work and dinner parties and Saturday afternoons in the park with his daughter. When his wife found a cache of erotic magazines in his underwear drawer beneath a neat stack of Jockey shorts, he agreed to put aside boyish indulgences and tossed the magazines into the trash. Only occasionally were his thoughts about women disturbing. Weekends, he came to Bethany for Sunday dinner at his parents' house, and always when his mother's family from Tennessee visited, he stayed the night— frequently, as was true this time, without his wife, who was not fond of Bethany.

Tim and George had gone to Hanrahan's for milk and bread and stayed awhile to talk with Frank Adler; they were walking towards the river when Tim stopped at Leonora's Books and Records. He had already seen the full-size cardboard replica of Francesca Woodbine on display in Leonora's window, but he wanted to show George.

"You know who that is," Tim said to his cousin.

"I've never heard of her," George said. "She isn't well known in Nashville."

"You may not have heard of her," Tim said, giving his cousin a significant look. "But I imagine that you remember her."

With a terrible sinking, George Saunders recalled the Festival of 1949. He had been very drunk. In fact, he had little recollection of Francesca. Even now, the memory was a nightmare held over from childhood, no more real than the attack of demons as the brain begins to surface from uneventful sleep.

"She's the girl," George said.

"Right," Tim replied. "She lives up there." He pointed to the white sash windows of the apartment above Leonora's.

"I don't want to see her." He started down Main Street. "I was drunk. I hardly remember what I did."

"We were young," Tim said. "We did a lot of stupid things when we were young." They turned right towards Tim's house. "So you aren't familiar with her music."

"I don't think so."

"You've heard the song 'Betrayal,' I'm sure." He hummed the melody.

"Yes, I have." George had heard "Betrayal" on the radio.

"Of course. I simply didn't remember her name, if I ever knew it."

"The song is in the top ten or twenty. I can't be sure. I don't keep up. But she's done very well."

"Good," George said absently. He was considering the possibility of returning to Nashville that afternoon.

"You'll get to see her," Tim said. "There's going to be a dance at Rooster's Tavern tonight."

"I think I'll pass," George said.

"Everyone will be there," Tim said. "You may change your mind."

On the morning of July 4, Francesca woke up late. The light beams from a full sun shimmered along the crisp white sheets like dancers. She heard Tobias in the kitchen getting cereal, and in the next room Maud was with someone. She could hear them talking in stage whispers. Unlike Cesca, Maud was often with someone, usually a man quite a lot older than she was and married, who was gone by morning. By the clock radio beside her bed, it was nine o'clock. She switched the knob to ON; already the dial was at WQRM, Boston's all-music station, and the end of "Betrayal" was playing. She pulled the sheet over her face and closed her eyes.

Sometimes she could not believe her good fortune.

She had returned to Juilliard after Hurricane Elsie in 1961. She wanted to develop as a contralto and intended to finish her degree in Fine Arts; but many afternoons at Juilliard instead of practicing voice she slipped away to her bedroom and wrote songs. She had a lovely voice—"excellent," according to her professors; "strong and vibrant," they said—but in fact she knew herself that even when her voice matured she could be very good but she would never be great. And she had little interest in a life begging jobs, grateful for minor operatic roles, accepting the conditions of backstage as a matter of course. Besides, what she really loved was to write about the secret lives of ordinary people. And such composition

163

was not considered a serious occupation for music students at Juilliard.

The summer of 1962 between semesters, Cesca worked with Sophia on melodies. The studio, obliterated by Hurricane Elsie, was under construction again, and the piano was in Julian's study. On the heavy days of August, Sophia and Cesca sat together on the piano bench trying out ideas for compositions. Sometimes they lay head to foot on the couch under Julian's gun collection and listened to Mozart while Toby played in the garden with his friends. Slowly through those months Sophia wove her life into Francesca's, recovering from the internal losses the hurricane had wrought, and at the end of the summer, color was back in Sophia's cheeks and for the first time in years, she wanted to make love.

"Your songs have made a difference to my life," Sophia said.

"Your songs too, Mama," Cesca said. With her mother's help, Francesca had completed her first scores of original music.

By luck, folk songs were popular when she graduated from Juilliard in 1963. She began to sing in coffeehouses in coastal Massachusetts, sometimes in Boston and Providence. A scout from Columbia Records who had heard Cesca sing in concert at Juilliard made a special trip the summer of 1963 to hear her at a coffeehouse in Boston, with Maud Hanrahan accompanying on the piano. She had a warm and sensual voice. "Stirring" was how the young scout, paper-thin and nervous, himself a musician of a cerebral disposition, described Francesca to producers at Columbia records. The producers decided to do an album of traditional and original songs, preceded, a few months before, by the release of a single original.

So that fall Francesca wrote "Betrayal."

"Is 'Betrayal' true?" Maud had asked Cesca when they first began to practice the score together.

"Every woman knows about betrayal," Francesca said, "but the story isn't personal."

They didn't speak about Cesca's life with Colin Mallory. She had killed him in her mind as well. His memory had

164

dropped into a dark hole lost in the recesses of consciousness. She could not face the internal consequences of her act, and certainly she could not confess. From time to time, Maud sensed in Cesca a complication more subtle than simply the loss of Colin, but she was a woman of remarkable sensibility, trained to caution growing up in a house full of trouble. She wanted to please people and would go to lengths to maintain a certain peace.

"And 'Billy's Love Song'?" Maud had asked. "You write strange stories for a girl who grew up in Bethany."

Cesca had written "Billy's Love Song" at Juilliard right after Hurricane Elsie. She changed the names of Tim Greenfield and Johnny Trumbull and Colin; she called the town Baytown and the boy Little Billy Brown. But otherwise it was the story Billy Naylor had told her before he died.

"I made the lyrics up," Cesca said. She had considered telling Maud the truth. "Not from scratch, of course."

Maud had been sitting at the piano, her legs apart as they were when she played, like a man's, a jazz pianist, her hands poised, her back unnaturally straight, about to begin. She didn't change her position or look at Francesca but continued to study the lead sheet for "Billy's Love Song" in front of her.

"Tell me about seeing, Ces."

"What do you mean?" Francesca asked, knowing exactly.

"Billy Naylor liked boys, so everybody says." She played the melody slowly.

"Some of the stories I make up are true, I'm sure," Francesca said.

"Lucky I have a boring life." Maud played the opening bars of "Billy's Love Song" for Cesca to sing.

In April Cesca and Tobias had moved with Maud to the three-bedroom flat located above Leonora's Books and Records because there was a living room large enough for Maud's grand piano. Francesca liked the location above Leonora's. She could imagine people stopping along Main Street to look at the card-board Francesca. "That's her," they'd say to one another. "She lives upstairs." And they'd look up at the line of second-floor

165

windows hoping to get a glimpse of Cesca as she practiced with Maud. Besides, she and Will Weaver had become close friends, insofar as a friendship with Will was possible. Many afternoons he came upstairs for lunch and listened to her practice a new song. Once, when Maud was out, he had kissed her.

Trouble at home had forced her to move. In the early spring Julian began to fight with Prince Hal in earnest. He complained about the state of Hal's room and the cat smell in the house. One of Hal's old cats urinated on the couch in Julian's study, and the odor was so bad that the couch had to be stripped to the wood frame and restuffed. "I don't even like cats," he said. He didn't approve of the way Hal dressed in embroidered Indian shirts—"like a girl," he said. Or the length of his hair, which was black and curled over his ears and at the nape of his neck.

"Please, Julian," Sophia would say at supper when he returned from a day at court and attacked Hal like a picador, "let Hal alone."

"I simply can't," he told her with terrible honesty.

So Francesca knew she would have to move.

"It's time for me to go," she said. "I'll be thirty-one."

"Of course," Julian agreed.

"It will be better for Tobias too," Sophia said.

But her family understood she did not want to watch them splinter at the supper table or hear her father late at night drawn irresistibly to battle in Hal's room.

"It will be hard for you to be alone in the house with Daddy like he's been," she said to her mother one evening as they cooked together.

"It's a large house," Sophia said. "And Hal's here."

"He won't be here for long if Daddy keeps up," Francesca said "He may not even finish high school."

Sophia sat down in a kitchen chair and rested her head in her hand. "Your father thinks I'm responsible for keeping him a boy, but it's hormones, you know," she said. "An actual disease that keeps him from developing. I asked James to find out about it."

Julian grew worse. At night, he'd sit in the dark in a large

166

leather chair beside the fireplace and drink until his nerves were calmed and he could sleep.

"I'm turning into a kind of animal," he said one night to Sophia, genuinely concerned about himself.

Sophia was half-sleeping, propped up in bed. "I remember from Mr. Biggs's biology in high school that some animals kill their weaker babies out of a sense of protection," she said. "Do you remember?"

He stood up and took off his robe. "I'm not killing Hal, for chrissake."

Sometimes, quietly drunk, he would stand in the archway to Hal's room and watch him sleep in the silver light from the moon.

Tobias came into his mother's bedroom with a bowl of cornflakes and sat down on Cesca's bed.

"Don't spill," she said lazily. "Night before last I slept with soggy Cheerios."

"The person who slept with Maud was very old." Tobias balanced his bowl on crossed legs. "He had curly hair in his ears."

Cesca laughed.

"He had a mustache," Tobias said. "I wouldn't like to kiss someone with a mustache."

"Me neither." Francesca got out of bed and brushed her hair into a long braid bound with ribbons such as her grandmother used to wear.

"Who do *you* kiss?" Tobias asked. The question was serious. He had watched his mother since they'd moved away from the protection of his grandmother's house. Maud had boyfriends almost every night, different ones who came after dinner and stayed in her room. As far as he knew, his mother had no one except Will Weaver for lunch. He didn't especially want her to have a boyfriend—certainly not Will Weaver—but he didn't want her to be left out either.

"I don't kiss anyone but you," Francesca said.

Maud knocked and came in. She was barefoot, in a long

167

gown; she wore her hair short so it fitted like a choir cap around her sweet face.

"Brother." She rolled her eyes. "He was boring."

"Old," Tobias said. "He had hair in his ears. I looked."

"So did I." Maud fell across the bed and buried her face in the quilt. In the sunlight, her red hair glittered with gold sprinkles and her white Irish skin was transparent. She looked like a child. Francesca leaned over and kissed her.

They were close with an intimacy that comes between women who live out similar interior lives, a wordless friendship. To be in each other's company was entirely satisfactory.

Sometimes Tobias wanted them to marry each other and seal his future.

"I've been thinking." Maud turned on her back. "Everybody's going to be drinking tonight. Probably drunk. Why don't you do another song than 'Billy's Love Song'?"

"I've decided to sing 'Billy's Love Song' last," Cesca said.

"People in Bethany are afraid of homosexuals," Maud said.

"You've been talking to Will Weaver. He already told me last night."

"I don't need to talk to Will for decisions," Maud said.

"The fact is people in Bethany are afraid of sex," Cesca replied.

Francesca opened the windows over Main Street. Already the sidewalk was full of people and the air smelled sweetly of pastries from the bakeshop.

"I promised Billy Naylor that I'd write a song about him and sing it at Rooster's." She sat down in one of Santa Francesca's old and uncomfortable chairs, put her feet up on the coffee table. "So that's that."

She had imagined this evening at Rooster's nights before she went to sleep. Tim Greenfield would be there with his young intellectual wife. James would be in the far corner in a booth, shaded by the crowd in front of him. Johnny Trumbull, grown fat with beer and mean-minded at twenty-eight, would sit directly in front of her. The Adlers were there with her parents—perhaps not Julian—and Prince Hal.

The room would be full and dark and smoky. The bar girls had to raise their trays in the air, inch their way through the enormous crowd. People would be drinking too much, lulled to sweetness by Francesca's voice, to a feeling of camaraderie and warmth for the occasion.

And then she would sing "Billy's Love Song."

She didn't know what she expected to happen. She simply knew that something would.

She wanted to take the stage at Rooster's in Santa Francesca's gypsy skirts and disturb the peace. Ground warfare was what she was after, armed with true stories against the ordinary enemies of the human heart.

Francesca's love affair with her grandmother had come upon her with the wonderful surprise of an actual romance the spring before Julian and Hal began to fight.

One morning during a break from Juilliard, she and Sophia searched a steamer trunk of treasures for old toys, particularly James's train set, with which Tobias might like to play. At the bottom of the trunk, Francesca discovered a shoe box with the pictures of Italian relatives which Santa Francesca had kept on a round table in her living room at Rooster's.

"Do you remember these people?" Cesca asked. "Are they cousins?"

Sophia sat down on one of the horsehair chairs and went through the pictures. "This one is my grandmother whose name I have. And my grandfather, who died when my mother was very small. And an aunt called Anna, who was well known in Sicily for seeing the future and taught my mother tricks before she came to America. And that's an uncle, her brother, who always wrote her sentimental letters on saints' days when I was young. And that"—she handed Cesca a small photograph in a silver frame of a man; it must have been a man, although the photograph was too dark to convey actual features except for a long straight nose and a high white round collar—"is the Count," she said.

Francesca took the picture from her mother and examined it under the bright white light in the basement. "I can't tell what he looked like," she said.

"The picture has always been faded," Sophia said. "I'm not

even sure it's of a man. My mother was peculiar. She could have found this photograph on the street or in the trash and just decided to pretend." She gestured—a leftover Italian turn of the hands. "Who knows?"

"It's the Count." Francesca slipped the picture into the pocket of her trousers and put the shoe box back in the steamer trunk.

"Whatever," Sophia said with a rare edge to her voice. "My father, whoever he may have been, was responsible for my mother's choice of work."

"Choice?" Francesca asked, intrigued by this new information. "What kind of choice was that?"

"The choice of a woman who has little faith in counts," Sophia said, and the subject was lost between them when Tobias came into the kitchen to play with James's old train set.

But a picture came to Cesca which she might have imagined or might have seen once amongst the boxes of photograph albums her mother had kept. In the picture, Santa Francesca stood in profile by a window in her room at Rooster's Tavern and she was pregnant, although in the wide skirt she wore she simply looked overweight. The picture was washed in light, perhaps overexposed, and showed a woman almost serene, sufficient unto herself. Her hair was down in a long braid, the end of which she held in her hand, brushing her cheek with the bristles as if she were her own lover. The other hand lay on her belly, supported by it.

That afternoon Cesca tried on her grandmother's gypsy clothes which her mother had saved for dress-up or to wear for the Festival.

"You don't look like her except perhaps the eyes," Sophia said. "She was much shorter, and plump, with little round hands like a cherub's."

"That's all right," Cesca said combatively. "Her clothes fit exactly."

After that day, Francesca wore her grandmother's clothes. They had been packed away in a round-topped steamer trunk and they smelled thickly of gardenias even after washings. The waists were too large and hung wide on Cesca's fleshless hips; the skirts, full-length on Santa Francesca, wavered mid-calf on Cesca and dipped unevenly. The colors of the cottons, even faded by years, were splendid and surprising—dyes, according to Sophia, that her mother mixed from ordinary dye and berries to dip the lengths of muslin in before she stitched them into a gathered skirt or full blouse or a robe which she wore for serious occasions. There were skirts in magenta and lavender, vermilion, fuchsia, cornflower blue and violet. Colors mixed from the imagination of a woman who had sustained a memory of extraordinary light in spite of years on a northern sea in a sullen climate. Francesca, never interested in clothes at all, spent hours dressing—braiding her long hair with ribbons, ironing the heavy cottons, restitching the dried and broken seams.

In daydreams, she saw herself on the backs of albums and the front Arts sections of newspapers; interviewed on television or by the music critics of local papers; in an article in a women's magazine on the unwed gypsy singer and her child.

"Why do you dress in these peculiar clothes too large for you and smelling of the past?" the reporters asked in her reverie.

"They are my grandmother's," she replied combatively. "She was a whore."

"I can't even look at Cesca now that she's taken on the aspects of a tramp," Julian said.

"Singers need a memorable style," Sophia replied. "And Cesca has found one."

"Your mother was fat. Her clothes don't suit Cesca." It was all that Julian could think of to say.

Sometimes Francesca stood in front of the long mirror on the back of her closet door, an unencumbered stranger, cut loose, as if the string which bound her to responsibility for present time had been cut and she floated weightless backwards into the past.

171

When "Betrayal" came on WQRM, Hendrik Andrews turned the radio up. He stretched across the double bed, moving the legs of the woman who still slept on the other side, and closed his eyes.

In late June, he had passed a record shop on Boston Common and in the window was a cardboard Francesca, shorter than he remembered and plumper. But she had the same angular face, flushed rose, the same wide investigative eyes, a certain child-like awkwardness about her presence, even in cardboard. Or else his memory of Francesca Woodbine was that strong. He had gone into the shop and bought two albums, a new needle for his stereo, a copy of *Music Times*. And casually he had asked could he have the display Francesca Woodbine when the advertising campaign for her album was over.

"We have an extra," the boy behind the counter said. "I'll ask my father if you can have it."

A long-haired and bemused young man, notable for the thickness of his eyebrows and not old enough certainly to be the boy's father, came to the front of the store.

"He wants that girl, Bert," the boy said.

The shopkeeper shook his head in amusement.

"I'm sure he does," the man said. "Pretty soon a lot of men are going to feel the same way."

"I *know* her." Hendrik was embarrassed.

"That's nice for you." The man called Bert crouched down behind the counter and came up with Francesca Woodbine in three pieces with a stand to fit under her skirt so she could be upright.

"I won't charge you." The man dropped Francesca into a shopping bag.

"That's very kind."

"Not kind at all. She came free to me, so she may as well go free to you."

Hendrik asked when *Mating Calls* would be in the shop.

"In July," the man said. "Have you heard it yet, her being your buddy?"

"Only 'Betrayal,'" Hendrik said. "I don't think she's done anything else."

172

"There's one song on this album about a queer named Billy that will knock your socks off."

"She has a lovely voice," Hendrik said, not anxious to pursue a personal relationship.

"Nobody writes about queers." Bert walked to the door with Hendrik. "Put the girl next to your bed," he said. "Like a guardian angel."

He put her up in the living room next to the camellia tree. The woman, Emily, who lived with him did not approve.

"It just looks stupid to have a cardboard folksinger in the living room," she said.

Hendrik didn't take issue. The apartment was his. Emily was a short-term visitor. Nor did he tell her that he knew Francesca Woodbine.

Sometimes he danced with Francesca, waltzing comically through the living room, avoiding the chairs and couch with a dramatic turn, or he kissed her paper lips or took her on his lap so she loomed stiff and placid above him. It drove Emily crazy to see him cavorting like that.

"Someday you'll come home and she'll be gone or burned up or eaten by my pet raccoon which I'm going to keep in the bathroom," she said furiously.

"That wouldn't be a very good idea," Hendrik replied.

"If it were just a joke, I wouldn't mind," she said. "But it's not just a joke."

"That's right, it's not," Hendrik said.

"Sometimes I think you're mental," Emily said.

Whenever Hendrik made love to a woman—anyone— even the first splendid time full of lust with a new woman— Francesca's face flitted in and out of the shadows of his mind.

"You're a dreamer, Hendrik, always waiting for the right girl. The perfect girl," his mother said. "She won't come. There's no such thing on earth. Men get ruined by stupid dreams, so you better go back to medical school and have a useful profession."

"Your mother's right," his father said in a rare acknowledgment of his wife's wisdom. "Besides, you should get married before you lose your looks. At thirty, all the Andrews men go to fat," he added, full of the usual bad news.

Emily woke up and kicked Hendrik gently, "Turn down the radio," she said from under the covers. "It's too loud."

"When the song is over," Hendrik replied.

She groaned and covered her eyes with her long straw hair. "You always stop the world when Betrayal Shmayal is on as if it's a personal story. Please, Hendrik, I have a headache."

She leaned over and kissed him, through the last verse of "Betrayal," and when it was over, he wriggled under her to turn the radio down.

She sat up with the sheets drawn over her breasts and watched him dress. They had been together for four months and she thought she loved him, although she knew he didn't love her except when they slept together.

"Sometimes I think you're only half here," she said to him.

"Maybe the half you see is all there is," Hendrik replied.

He was not a man to press for commitments. He could ask her to leave.

"You're a cold man," she said to him another time. He didn't disagree, but she was wrong. He was reserved by nature, but he could be deeply stirred. He had been only with women who couldn't touch him, and that by choice.

She got up and followed him to the living room.

"When will you be back?" she asked. "It's a holiday."

"I'm going to be working."

She sat down on the couch naked with her knees up under her chin. He wished she'd dress, he thought.

"Are we going out tonight?" she asked.

He took an apple from the basket on the kitchen table.

"I'm going to drop by to see Elena after I finish," he said.

She stiffened. "Why?" She couldn't help herself. "It's Saturday night."

"I'll be back around eight," he said.

"I thought you were going to sell the toy store and finish medical school." She followed him to the apartment door. "Aren't you going to kiss me goodbye?"

He started to lean towards her and changed his mind. "Please get dressed, Emily," he said, and left.

Uncle Ben's was on Arch Street, at the end of the block—half on Arch, half on Second. Hendrik let himself in the front door. Uncle Ben's was his own. It had been an old warehouse for ties when he bought the building in 1959 shortly after he left medical school. He had in mind opening a toy shop.

"A toy store," his father said as if Hendrik had announced the death of a favorite relative.

"You were against my being a doctor. Remember?" Hendrik said.

"I was against the expense. But a man selling toys?" his father said.

Uncle Ben's was not an ordinary toy shop. It was a huge and wonderful playhouse. The main room downstairs had been made into a town called Middlemarch with shops and a hospital and school and houses with mothers and fathers and children and traffic lights and firehouses and police cars and regular cars and puppet theaters and grocery stores and a butcher shop and a bakery and a drugstore. A child could come to Uncle Ben's with his mother, who planned to shop for Christmas upstairs. He'd leap into a fire truck, rush off to put out a fire at the local school, jump into his small metal car with bicycle-pedal drive, pick up toothpaste at the drugstore and then *vroom vroom*, drive home and kiss his pint-sized wife with yellow ringlets and the plastic baby in her arms. In the pure mad rush of childhood, a boy could play at being grown up without cost.

"How can you make any money if you're running a playground?" his father asked him.

But in fact, he did quite well. Mothers sometimes brought their children two or three times a week to play in Middlemarch, and always, not wishing to take advantage, they'd purchase toys as well.

Hendrik turned on the main lights and went upstairs. He made coffee and sat down on a cardboard carton in the stockroom to read *The Boston Globe*. In the second section, there was a notice about Fourth of July celebrations including a picture of Bethany, Massachusetts, restored. In the small print under the picture, there was a list of events. Francesca Woodbine, in performance, 8 P.M., Rooster's Tavern, River Street.

He picked up the telephone and dialed. Emily answered at the first ring.

"I'd like to go to Bethany tonight to hear Francesca Woodbine sing," he said, anticipating Emily's reply.

"Well," she said, "I wouldn't." And she hung up the phone.

He made one other telephone call, to the Boston Home for Disturbed Children, and asked for Elena. She could not come to the telephone, the supervisor said. He told the supervisor that he'd be there on Sunday to spend the afternoon with her.

Then he left the phone off the hook in case Emily reconsidered later and decided to go to Bethany too.

In Newton Saturday morning, James Woodbine woke up suddenly to the clock radio turned too loud and reached for Louisa. She wasn't there. The sheets on her side of the bed had been pulled tight, her pillow fluffed and in place. He could hear the shower splashing against her bare back. He rolled on his side and held a pillow against him.

He wanted her. He always wanted her in the morning, by daylight so he could watch her lovely body as they made love. But by daylight, she didn't even want to kiss him. Her lips would tighten into a thin pencil line like a girl's; she'd close her eyes against the evidence of his desire.

Sometimes he was furious at her inhibitions—at least, he supposed they were inhibitions and not a problem—although just the other day he had looked up frigidity in his medical text, and she had symptoms.

He knocked on the bathroom door and went in without waiting for an answer.

"I'll be out in a second," Louisa said over the sound of water splashing.

James pulled the shower curtain and stepped in. Her head was full of soap, pouring in a long white river over her

176

breasts. He leaned over and kissed a soapy nipple with his tongue.

"Blah!" He wiped the soap out of his mouth.

"Serves you right," she said, bending her head back to rinse her hair.

He reached down gently between her legs.

"Please, James." She moved his hand. "I can't."

When she came out of the shower wrapped at the waist in a large towel, he was sitting at the end of their bed.

"I know I make you angry." She sat down next to him.

He slipped on his shoes, tied the drawstring of his green medical pants and brushed his hair without a mirror. "I'll adjust. I understand it's downhill after thirty."

She sighed. "So what time will you be home?"

"Four thirty," he said. "We'll have to leave by five or so."

"What time is Cesca singing?"

"In the evening."

Louisa lay back on the made bed and watched James collect his change from the bureau, strap on his watch, put his wallet into the small back pocket of the medical trousers.

"James," she started, wanting to detain him but not for long.

He checked the time.

"I don't want you to say anything to our parents about us if we go to Bethany tonight."

James covered his face with his hands. "I was under the impression that we were getting married in September, and sometime before the actual day, we ought to let them know."

"The fourth of September," she said quietly. "I don't know. I'm not sure."

They had been together secretly on and off since the hurricane. First Louisa had moved to Boston and got a job at the Children's Museum and her own apartment in Cambridge.

"I can't make a commitment," she said to James. But she was always glad to see him. The next year James was an intern at Mass General. They saw each other only one night a week, but regularly, although Louisa never agreed to stay the night.

Suddenly in December, she wanted to get married. It was entirely her idea. She pored over *Bride's Magazine* and window-shopped along the main streets of Boston mentally furnishing an apartment. She made lists of babies' names even before she knew she was pregnant. Clarissa and Clara, Eleanora, Mariamne. Benjamin, Theodore, Nicholas. She tried them out with Woodbine for sound. Louisa Woodbine. Perhaps she should use her middle name. Louisa Anne Woodbine. Or just Anne Woodbine. She thought of herself at thirty in an elegant dress with a picture-book daughter and son and a physician husband—an excellent physician well known in Boston for saving lives.

She knew in January she was pregnant, but she put it out of mind. In February she told James, although she had already made arrangements for an abortion.

"Don't," he said. "It's too awful. If we weren't going to get married, an abortion would be another thing."

"I don't want to *have* to get married," she said.

"But we *are* getting married," he said. She could drive him crazy.

"We're *planning* to get married. By choice," she said. "I'd hate to have happen to me what happened to your sister."

"I haven't in mind getting murdered," James said. "I take every precaution."

At Louisa's strange but absolute insistence, they had managed to keep their relationship secret from their families for two years.

"When do you plan to tell our families? Twenty minutes before the wedding?"

He insisted on going to the doctor with her, and she pretended to relent. She told him the appointment was at four, knowing she would be home recovering by then. She didn't want him there. She didn't want a baby either, she had decided. She wasn't even sure she wanted to be married, although such feelings had nothing specific to do with James. She loved the idea of relationships—the still-life pictures in her mind, as if, in time, her memory would be an album of imagined events which had never occurred.

There were complications at the abortion clinic, although the physician had come well recommended. James got a call at Mass General to say that Louisa was in Ob-Gyn at the hospital in fair condition.

"Why did you lie to me?" he asked her days later. "Why didn't you want me there?"

"I just didn't," she said.

Louisa followed James to the apartment door in bare feet, her hair in a wet cap around her face. He didn't kiss her.

"The plan has been to tell everyone this evening," he said to her quietly. "If you've changed your mind, let me know by the time I get back from the hospital so I can make other arrangements."

"Other arrangements?"

"I'm getting married on the fourth of September. It doesn't matter to whom." He slammed the door.

Louisa opened the window and stretched out across the bed. She could go swimming at the Y, she thought, or cut out recipes from *Ladies' Home Journal*, or hem the new skirt she'd got at Bonwit's June sale. Except for the brief excitement in December and January, a metabolic condition, she had felt nothing since Colin's murder except small rushes of pleasure in details: the work at the museum, a new dress, a French meal she made from scratch with real butter and cream— those things.

She would get married, of course. Pull herself together and stare Francesca down while James told her their wedding plans after the concert at Rooster's tonight. Although Francesca, the witch, had probably sniffed out their romance already.

She was hemming the red-striped cotton skirt when "Betrayal" came up on WQRM. She didn't even hear the announcer or she would have turned it off immediately, as she always did when they played "Betrayal" unless James was in the room, and then she went into the bathroom and turned on the water and counted slowly to two hundred. Now the song caught her unaware. Full of unexpected fury, she dashed across the room and turned off the radio. And then, because the absence of Francesca's voice was not sufficient, she yanked the plug out of the wall and threw the radio across the room. It hit the wall over the bed, just missing Picasso's happy

179

flowers, and shattered. Still angry, she picked up the pieces and put them in the wastebasket. What a stupid idea to marry James, she thought.

But by the time James came home that evening, she had readjusted.

"Unless you're determined to make other arrangements, we'll tell our families tonight," he said.

She looked very pretty, like a girl, in her red-striped skirt and white piqué blouse. He kissed her in the sunlight, and she kissed him back.

Rooster's Tavern was a large 19th-century barn of a building with a horseshoe bar added in the thirties and a small stage with space enough for a piano which had been there since Santa Francesca arrived from Italy. The room was dark-paneled, with old-fashioned mustard-colored lights, high-polished round tables, gloomy booths with leather seats and a tendency to dankness because of the tavern's proximity to the river. There was a dance floor, although seldom at Rooster's did anyone dance except the sailors and occasionally a formal long-married and middle-aged couple from Bethany who had grown up with the grace of the waltz.

At dusk on the Fourth of July, Francesca and Maud sat on the fire escape on the second floor of Rooster's out of sight and watched the crowd arrive. They sat like girls, close together, their shoulders pressed tight, their knees drawn up under their chins. They didn't speak at first, but if they had, what they would have said was "Look at us. Look at us. Look at us."

Small heroines in their own hometown, flying above the treetops.

"Nathan Elks," Maud whispered to Cesca as Nathan Elks came down River Street.

"Sarah Wheeler and Joe Murphy," Cesca whispered back.

"Jimmy Walker."

"And Alice."

"Johnny Trumbull."

Back and forth, just the names of people, like prayers, were whispered as they arrived.

Tim Greenfield had always liked his cousin George because George would take a dare. No matter how risky, he'd do it. Perhaps for friendship or admiration or simply the pleasure of danger. Even age and a certain sense of appropriateness had not altered George's essential character, and by noon on the Fourth of July, he had agreed to go to Rooster's to hear Francesca sing.

"Maybe we'll have a drink afterwards," Tim said wickedly.

"One thing at a time," George insisted, but he was not beyond persuading.

"There's Tim Greenfield," Maud said to Cesca. "Who's the other man?"

"His cousin, I think." So, Tim Greenfield had come, just as Francesca thought. She knew him as a young man with remarkable self-possession. His reaction to "Billy's Love Song" would be restrained.

"I remember Tim's cousin. He comes up every year and slinks around Roster's looking for girls," Maud said.

Johnny Trumbull in his police uniform came with his girlfriend from Salem whom, it was rumored, he had saved when she fell through the ice on Salem Pond.

The Woodbines came with Hal and Frank and Dottie Adler. They were not social friends, but since the hurricane there was a bond of unspoken friendship between the families.

"I never did like Rooster's," Julian said as they walked in the front door of the tavern. He was overdressed for the occasion and uncomfortable.

"We met at Rooster's, darling," Sophia said as if that recollection would suffice.

The room was crowded with young people in blue jeans and long hair, flaccid and lethargic. They were dressed like Prince Hal in Indian shirts, and the men sat with their legs crossed at the knee like women. Julian was apprehensive. The scene was foreign and made him wish he were at home in his study with a Scotch.

James and Louisa had announced their engagement to the Natales at dinner. Mr. Natale was pleased.

"A hometown boy," he said. "What more could a father want?"

"He means a hometown boy whose father is a judge," Louisa said later. "Not any hometown boy would do."

Mrs. Natale was reserved. At dinner, James could feel her eyes rest on him even when the conversation had turned to someone else.

"I can't get used to the idea," she said, implying that she didn't plan to accept the news.

At dessert, she brought up Francesca.

"I suppose she has known all along," Mrs. Natale said. "Just kept it a secret from your parents."

"No," James said. "In fact, we haven't told her yet."

"No?" Mrs. Natale considered. "She might be jealous, right? Off goes her beloved brother to another woman. You didn't want trouble to gct in the way." The conclusion seemed to satisfy her misgivings. She even kissed James on the cheek when he left.

"Brother," James said, taking Louisa's hand as they walked down River Street. "What was that all about?"

"My mother has suspicions about everyone," Louisa said. "She thinks Francesca is a witch."

Francesca saw James and Louisa from the fire escape. She would have said nothing if Maud hadn't nudged her.

"I see them," Francesca said, drained of blood at the sight of James with Louisa Natale.

"You've never told me they were together," Maud said.

"James never told me." Cesca pulled herself up on the railing and brushed off her skirt. The clock over the bank said 7:55. "I just knew." She realized flatly that she had known from the start.

182

Will Weaver sat in the back of Rooster's with Celia Hamilton. He was agitated. He had been all day for no reason, and now Celia, just her presence next to him, was driving him crazy. She kissed his hand or his shoulder or his cheek or his ear and he thought he was going to jump straight out of his skin. He excused himself and went to the men's room and then to the bar, returning with two beers.

"What is the matter with you?" she asked when he came back.

"Nothing. Nothing," he said. "I'm nervous. Haven't you ever been nervous?"

He had been having dreams lately about his mother. In the dream, she was dressed in a long clinging gown and sat beside his bed. She was decapitated. When he woke up from this dream, he was holding himself and the smell of her lingered sweetly in the room.

"You're always nervous," Celia said. "You make *me* nervous. I wish we could just have a relationship."

Will had only kissed her. Once he had touched her breasts and pulled away as if his hand had been injured by the feel of them. They had never been at ease together.

"We do have a relationship," Will said.

"We're business partners, that's all," she said crossly. "Business partners who sometimes kiss."

"We're more than that," Will said. He thought he loved her, but he had not been able to act on it except in the privacy of his own room or in a bathroom or in the stock closet of Leonora's, watching her in the children's section.

Sometimes he entertained an interest in men. Not that he had felt desire for a particular man, but that his problem with women had to do with a sexual aberration. The term "sexual aberration" he had read in a book. He read all the technical books on sex he could find, although unlike his brothers, he had no interest in erotic magazines.

"Did you know Billy Naylor was queer?" he asked Celia. "He's the only one I've ever known in Bethany."

"I didn't know him. I know he died in the hurricane, but I had only moved to Bethany that summer, remember?"

"Well, he was queer." He finished off his own beer and drank a swallow of Celia's.

He turned to Celia to tell her something else he remembered about Billy Naylor—something sweet—and her head was gone.

"Jesus Christ." He stood up and pushed the table away, shaking his head as if his ears were full of water. He rubbed his eyes.

"What now?" Celia said with great tiredness.

"I'm getting another beer." He didn't look at her.

"You've already had half of mine."

"Another for the concert." He wanted to be immediately drunk.

"Sit down, Will." She pulled his hand. This time when he looked at her, her head was back in place, her hair falling in a dip over her forehead as it did, her expression quizzical but not blaming.

"You're right," he said, grateful for a return to normality. "No more beers." That was it, he decided. He was drinking too much. No more beers for a while and he'd look into the problem he had with women. Perhaps his father knew of a psychiatrist in Boston who could work quickly. He didn't want bad dreams about his mother anymore.

The spotlights at Rooster's were large and bright yellow, not professionally set up. The room was black and silent when Maud took her place at the piano and Francesca came down the back stairs which her grandmother's clients had used and walked across the small stage to the microphone.

Then the lights came up and in the bright yellow glare, Francesca looked as artificial and made-up as the paper replica filling the display windows of record shops in the Northeast. Maud began with the opening bars of "Betrayal" and the crowd exploded in applause. They stood and stamped and cheered and banged their beer mugs on the polished tables. She had to stop and begin again.

Hendrik Andrews arrived late at the River entrance to the tavern and made his way through the crowd, sliding between two men who stood at the end of the bar.

Francesca didn't see him. She couldn't see anything except Maud, glittering and incomplete, in the stark circle of yellow made by the spots. The light was alarming. She sang as if blind into a small, brilliant empty space. She could hear the audience; she could almost feel them, but the sensation was strange, as if she were dead with the memory of living or had hallucinated their response. It occurred to her that she would not be able to gauge their reaction to "Billy's Love Song." They could turn on each other or come after her and she wouldn't know it.

"I can't see at all," she said to Maud during intermission.

"There's nothing to see, Ces," Maud said. "Just a crowd of people mad about us. It's plain wonderful."

"But I depend on seeing," Cesca said.

It was hot under the lights and she had on too many clothes. In the back room, she took off the high-necked cotton lace blouse of Santa Francesca's and splashed water from the sink on her perspiring breasts and under her arms and let the warm air dry her skin. "I want someone to fix the lights so I can at least see the people close to the stage."

"I'll find the technician," Maud said, surprised at Cesca's agitation.

The technician said he could turn off some of the lights but he couldn't dim them.

"You should see yourself. The light's good," he insisted. He was a small, open-faced Irishman, probably fifty but he looked like a boy. He smiled at her broadly. "You're very pretty, I think," he said. "And you sing so good it makes my heart beat fast."

"Thank you." Cesca smiled.

"I was standing out there at the bar next to a young man getting very drunk who thinks you are the cat's meow," the technician said.

Hendrik Andrews was certainly very drunk and wild in love with Francesca Woodbine—obsessed with her. He couldn't stand the sweet and foolish sentiments, but he was

185

half in love with himself at the same time.

"I've drunk too much," he said to the old man next to him named John Hammer, who had lived in Bethany seventy years, since birth, and never traveled farther than Boston. He was a serious and earnest, puritanical old man, down on himself. He had always drunk too much.

"But it's a good drunk, you see. I'm very happy." Hendrik ordered a Scotch for both of them. "Some drinking is fine and makes you very happy and some is bad and makes you miserable, you know?"

"I know about misery," John Hammer said, but he had a light in his eye and was glad for conversation.

"What do you think of that woman?" Hendrik asked.

"Francesca? The singer?" John Hammer shook his head.

"Isn't she a beauty?"

He pulled at his thick white eyebrows, narrowed his eyes at Francesca as she came back to the stage for a second set to a warm and roaring applause. He turned to Hendrik with a look of warning or confidentiality, Hendrik couldn't tell.

"She had a grandmother who was a fortune-teller and a whore," John Hammer said, not with accusation so much as a certain curiosity. "Here."

"What do you mean here?" Hendrik asked.

"Here. At Rooster's Tavern. She worked here. My father knew her."

"I see." Hendrik didn't know what else to say. "And did you know her?"

John Hammer didn't reply, but a small grin crossed his face and he lifted his empty glass in a toast to Hendrik. "I try to stick to Scotch," he said. "It's easier on the stomach."

The news about the grandmother filled Hendrik with astonishing good cheer, as if Francesca had suddenly become a mysterious character who began as a broad gesture, a woman in a novel of manners, dropping small secrets like handkerchiefs which he picked up and stuffed into his pockets until his pockets were full to bursting. She had captured his imagination. He blew her a drunken kiss.

In the second set, Francesca, accustomed to the eerie lone-liness of the bright yellow circle of light, let her voice go. It swirled, a dancer, into the crowd, permeating like weather.

Every time Francesca sang was a love affair. She could stir people to small confessions of affection, to sweet moments of passion in the midst of the long tedium of ordinary days. After a concert, she would go home triumphant, crawl into bed and fall asleep with her face buried in the soft down of the pillow, sufficient unto herself like her memory of the photograph of Santa Francesca. She wanted to sing forever.

In the second set, she sang temperate love songs, mostly ballads, some medieval, others popularized recently by folk-singers. The crowd had grown softhearted, mildly drunk like lumpish feeding pigeons who did not easily scare.

Tim Greenfield was thinking. He was a rational man who occasionally reviewed his life without self-pity for purposes of microscopic examination. Right now, he recalled the eve-ning when his cousin George had taken Francesca. He and George and Johnny Trumbull had been after her all day, but the actual idea was his. He knew very well that drunk or not, George Saunders could be persuaded, and the violation of this young woman, whom Tim had known all his life, whose grandmother had been a prostitute, pleased his fancy.

George sat forward in his seat, fixed on Francesca. He was absolutely still while the people around him moved to the rhythms of her voice.

"George?" Tim whispered. "Did you really have her after the Festival that year? Or did you lie?"

"I didn't lie," George said, provoked.

"You could have. It would have been easy."

"Well, I didn't."

"I wonder if what you did to her has had a lasting effect." Tim Greenfield was pensive.

"I don't want to talk about it," George said without taking his eyes from Francesca.

On the dance floor, Johnny Trumbull swayed back and forth, his feet planted firmly on the ground, his soft belly spilling over his belt.

"Jesus, Johnny," Tim Greenfield had said to him, "you're getting a little fat. You better take yourself in hand."

"I don't need to bother taking myself in hand any longer, thank you very much." Johnny jabbed Tim in the ribs. "I got a girlfriend don'tchaknow." They had little in common since Tim had gone off to college, except a boys' dark history of sexual games; and they always spoke together as if they were adolescent boys.

Johnny was dancing when Cesca began "Billy's Love Song."

Tim Greenfield got up and went to the bar. His hands were suddenly clammy, and the skin under his white ducks itched miserably. George followed him. Tim ordered a double vodka straight up and turned his back to Francesca.

"Big on queers in New England?" George whispered.

Tim didn't answer. He was anxious not to call attention to himself.

Johnny Trumbull had his arms around the girl from Salem's waist, and their bodies rocked back and forth. When Tim looked at Johnny for a sign of recognition of complicity, Johnny had a funny smile on his face as if the song of Little Billy Brown brought sweet memories; he nuzzled into the bird's-nest hair of the girl and closed his eyes.

"Jesus," Tim said aloud for no particular reason except he hoped to get a response or conversation from John Hammer and the young man standing next to him. But John was drunk, and the other man watched Francesca as if her gestures were sanctified.

"Nice little love song," George said to Tim. "I would like to go home. This town is beginning to make me nervous."

"We're going to leave when the concert is over, for chrissake. I was raised to be polite," Tim said.

He felt the eyes of the crowd behind him. Julian Woodbine and his family were at the table just to his left, and Dr. Weaver with a woman from Ewes, and the long table by the dance floor was filled with couples from Tim's graduating class at Bethany High.

Johnny Trumbull did not open his eyes. Maybe, Tim thought, the dumbbell didn't even know the song was about them. Maybe the dolt thought Baytown was Baytown and not Bethany. Maybe he was so stupid, he thought Cesca had made up the story.

Tim's stomach turned over with the shock of vodka, and he prayed for cardiac arrest on the spot.

Zap would go his career as a lawyer when people found out about Billy Naylor. Down the drain with his good-looking, smart wife from New Hampshire. She would take his daughter and move back to Exeter. And his poor parents, frayed from the struggle so he could have an education at Harvard, would wither away their last years. Maybe his wife would agree to stay with him if he explained he had been drunk that night and agreed to move away to Oklahoma or Wyoming.

"Shut up," he said to George, but George hadn't said a thing.

Julian Woodbine leaned towards Sophia and grabbed her hand.

"Did you know?" he whispered, distressed.

"I wrote the music, Julian."

"Did you know the story?"

Sophia looked confused. "Ces made it up," she said.

Julian shook his head. "I doubt it," he said. Francesca was a strange woman, he thought—sometimes she was his daughter only by the tawny color her skin. Her blood ran too hot to be a Woodbine's.

When the music stopped, the cavernous room of the tavern was quiet. On the planet where she stood illuminated, miles away from human touch, Francesca waited. Behind her Maud moved nervously on the piano bench. They aren't going to applaud, Cesca thought, and she was as terrified as if, for no reason, the possibility she could be murdered had occurred to her. She took the microphone. "Thank you," she said. "Thank you very much."

And a strange thing happened. People stood and clapped respectfully. There was no frenzy of musical pleasure as there had been in the first set, and no cheers.

"Have them turn down the spots," Cesca said to Maud, "and turn up the house lights."

Maud told the technician, and he turned off the spotlights, turned the house lights on. Now Francesca could see the crowd in front of her, but they could no longer see her.

"Thank you," she said again, and her voice was all that remained of her for their inspection.

Tim Greenfield made his way to the dance floor, where Johnny Trumbull stood pressed without embarrassment against the girl.

"So, Johnny," Tim said, his hand on Johnny's ample shoulder, "how'd you like the concert?"

Johnny turned his head and rolled his eyes heavy with drink.

"Good," he said.

"Good?"

"Johnny didn't like the last song much," the girl said. "He thought it was a dumb song."

"Is that so?" Tim said.

"He doesn't like queers." The girl was glad for the role of interpreter.

"You know goddamned well I didn't like that song," Johnny said. He made his way through the crowd until he was out of the tavern and in his car, where he took the girl without mercy in the back seat of his rebuilt Pontiac convertible.

"I hated that song," he said later to the girl as they drove home. "That's how much I didn't like it."

Tim Greenfield was not the kind of person to retreat from trouble. He was a strategist, too combative and curious to flee without a word to Cesca Woodbine.

"Now what?" George said. "It's after eleven."

"There'll be fireworks on the river, and people will be dancing to the jukebox here."

"I'm exhausted," George said.

"I'd like to wait until Francesca comes back and dance with her," Tim said.

"I'm not interested in dancing," George said.

After the concert Maud and Cesca changed in the room upstairs which had been Santa Francesca's bedroom and was now rented to guests during the summer months.

"I think we were terrific, don't you?" Maud asked, pulling on jeans and a T-shirt with BETHANY RESTORED, 1964 in blue letters across the back.

"Terrific," Cesca said, but her feelings were darker and more complicated than Maud's sweet elation at their triumph, which in spite of the unsettling finale the evening had been.

"Do you think any critics were there?" Maud asked.

"Maybe. Columbia said someone was bound to come to hear us the first time the album was sung live."

Cesca stood naked from the waist up in her grandmother's bloomers and looked at herself in the oak mirror over the bureau. Her breasts were smaller since the birth of Tobias, but she was otherwise fleshier than she had been as a girl. She looked at her body in appraisal, putting it forth for her own inspection, unaware exactly that what she had in mind for tonight was sex.

"Are you going out?" Maud asked, sensitive to Cesca's condition.

"I don't know," Francesca replied. "Maybe. Tobias is spending the night at my parents' house."

Maud scrubbed the bright makeup off her face and brushed her hair. Sometimes she worried about Francesca. Since they

191

had started to work together, Cesca had not been with a man.

"Do you think I've gotten fat?" Francesca said.

"I think you're beautiful," Maud said. "Now get dressed and let's go downstairs."

But Cesca wasn't ready to return to the tavern. "Maud?" She lay back and covered her eyes with the back of her arm so the overhead light didn't shine directly in them.

"Mmm?" Maud was taking mascara off her eyelashes with Vaseline.

"Have you ever fucked?"

"Cesca." Maud laughed. "You know I have."

"I don't mean made love," Francesca said. "I know enough about making love to last me forever to death."

Maud sat down on the bed and put her hand gently on Cesca's leg.

"I have only fucked. Except James. I made love to him." She hesitated. "And he dropped me."

Cesca got up and slipped on one of her grandmother's skirts. "Is it awful with the men you sleep with?"

Maud thought of the men she brought back night after night; mostly they were older than she was and gentler, with soft erections. "No," she said. "Not awful, but not splendid either."

Francesca put on a pale mauve blouse which buttoned in the back. She didn't wear a bra. Just after she turned out the light in the bedroom and followed Maud down the back stairs of Rooster's, she touched her breasts. They felt small and firm under the soft cotton blouse. Pleasing.

"The reaction to 'Billy's Love Song' was strange, didn't you think?" Maud was saying.

"I didn't understand it." Cesca said.

"I think everyone stood out of respect."

"Maybe. And worry."

"I suppose."

"You sang wonderfully," Maud said, but Cesca was preoccupied with Tim Greenfield. What she wanted to do if he was still there and without his wife was dance with him in the low lights by the music of the jukebox.

James caught Cesca at the bottom of the stairs and hugged her. He lifted her up and kissed her.

"You're a goddamned miracle, Ces," he said. "It was wonderful. Wonderful, Maud." He kissed her too.

"Really," Cesca said. She was pleased to hear it, pleased to see him and have him kiss her with such delight. But his mood was too lighthearted for James, and she was suspicious of bad news immediately.

"I've missed you," she said. "You never come home weekends any longer."

"Work, work, work," he said, winding through the crowd, who stopped Francesca with congratulations.

"I saw you come in with Louisa Natale," Cesca said when they had broken free of the crowd and walked across the dance floor to the table where the Woodbines sat with Louisa Natale. The Adlers had already left.

"I suppose you're going to marry her," Cesca said.

James looked astonished. "Who told you?" he asked. But Francesca was kissing Sophia now and Hal and Julian. Then she sat down in the seat across from Louisa. The Beatles were playing on the jukebox, the air was thick and stale with smoke and beer, people danced moving their bodies like thick rope just to the left of the Woodbines' table.

"Hello, Louisa." Cesca leaned across the table to be heard without shouting. "Congratulations."

At that very moment, Tim Greenfield tapped her on the shoulder and asked her to dance. He could not have guessed that he had joined as if in midair a significant game of catch in the Woodbine family history, but she was grateful. Over her shoulder as she danced, she watched Louisa, soft as angel hair, nestled in a chair between her mother and Prince Hal as if she were the real sister and belonged in that place. And Cesca's carefully constructed wall against bad dreams collapsed; she was flooded with memories of Colin Mallory. She wanted to do bad things. She would cut up Louisa Natale's dresses, shave off all her lush black hair, snip the long eyelashes shading her cheeks, hang up her panties on the willow branches all over Bethany with LOUISA NATALE in red lipstick on the crotch.

She wanted blood. To tear her skin off, pluck her like chicken feathers, to wring her slender neck. She wanted to bite her on the full thighs tasting of wedding champagne, to twist her limbs off and toss them into the Leonora River so only the olive-colored torso remained, her neck broken, her head a paper necklace against her chest. Call on the hawks, Francesca thought crazily. Demolish her flesh, bite by bite.

Her brain was so full of the conversation she planned to have that night with James that she didn't hear Tim Greenfield speak to her. "Ask Louisa about her swan hat," she was saying to James in the slow reel played out in her mind. "I understand she always wears it on important occasions."

"So the concert was terrific," Tim said.

They danced easily and without speaking. Perhaps, Francesca thought, he had not connected "Billy's Love Song" with Billy Naylor. The event on Marsh Road might have meant nothing to him, or he might have been drunk. He wasn't a man with a sensitive memory. She leaned back so she could see his face straight on, which she had never had the nerve to do the few times she had gone out with him in high school. He was tall, with a large but delicate face. The features were too small to suit, too finely made, better designed for a woman. Close up, Cesca decided, Tim Greenfield looked a little foolish.

Maud danced by with a man Francesca had never met.

"Are you going to the fireworks?" Maud called.

"I'm not sure," Cesca said. "Are you?" she asked Tim Greenfield.

"Perhaps. Although I'm with my cousin from Nashville."

"I saw."

"You've met him?" Tim said.

"I don't think so."

"Well, he's met you."

"He has? Well, maybe," Cesca said, put off. "But usually I remember everyone."

"He said he met you a few years back."

She could feel his erection against her pubic bone. Imperceptibly, with a slight tilt of her hips towards him, she acknowledged his desire.

"I'm leaving in a few minutes," he said. "I'll go home and pick up the car and come back here for you."

They broke apart just as James came across the dance floor. James took her in his arms and held her close.

"How did you know about Louisa?" he asked. "Nobody knew. Not even in Boston."

"Instinct," Cesca said.

When they were in high school, they used to go to dances together and play at being married or lovers or enemies or competitors or strangers on a boat or long-lost twins. They'd dance in the corner of the Bethany High gymnasium under the raised basketball net, safe for the night with each other.

"Remember how we used to be long-lost twins?" Cesca said.

"Or strangers. Or lovers. I remember," James said.

"Long-lost twins is what I had in mind," Cesca said with an edge.

"Ces"—he held her tight, but she stiffened—"I happen to have fallen in love with Louisa."

"Let's drop the subject," Cesca said.

Tim Greenfield insisted diabolically that George meet Francesca before they left for home, and George was drunk and foolish enough to agree.

"You've met," Tim said to Cesca.

"Perhaps," Cesca said. "I don't remember."

"I don't think we have," George insisted awkwardly. "I really don't think we have."

He told her that the concert was splendid, the best he'd heard in years. He had in mind to make her a household word in Nashville if she wasn't one already. It had been a pleasure to meet her for the first time. He knew, whatever Tim said, they had never met before. He always remembered a pretty face.

Francesca and James finished off the dance.

"He's a silly man, don't you think?" Cesca said.

"I wouldn't expect much more of Tim Greenfield's relatives."

"Sometimes I like Southern accents, and sometimes I don't," she said. "I'm not fond of his."

She was lost in a distraction about George Saunders. Tim could be right—they might have met before; but the memory was a hidden intimation of past life, another incarnation. She could not catch hold of the string and follow it down her mind's path home.

"She knows," George said crossly.

"I doubt it," Tim said. He put his hands in the pockets of his white pants and pulled the cloth tight and teasing over his genitals.

"I could tell by the way she looked at me, for chrissake," George said. "I'm not going to the fireworks."

"Relax." They walked down River Street. "I'm walking home with you."

"You don't need to. I can go on myself," George said.

"I want to pick up my car."

"You're going to the fireworks?"

"Yes, I think so," Tim said. But he did not have the fireworks in mind at all.

Hendrik Andrews made it to his car, which was parked at the side of Rooster's Tavern, and climbed into the back seat. He was certainly not going to make it to Boston and Emily, the skinny hen. He rolled over on his back and put his feet out the back window. *"You are very very drunky, darling Hendrik,"* he sang to himself. He had not been out of control like this since he was sixteen. And here he was thirty-one and sensible and he had fallen crazily in love for the first time ever. He deserved to be drunk. A present to himself, he thought as the car rolled over and over and the lights from inside his brain spun colors in his eyes.

196

"So goodbye Emilee/You cold-hearted chickadee/Pack up your neg-lijee/And flee from me in a hur-ree," he sang.

James and Louisa on their way back to the Woodbines' to tell James's parents passed the car with Hendrik's feet sticking out and heard him singing.

"There's a man Cesca has moved to song," James said, but he didn't bother to look into the back seat to identify the singer. So except for Mr. Hammer, who could not be counted on for accurate memories, no one in Bethany knew of Hendrik's presence at Cesca's concert except him. The next morning early, with a head the weight of a cast-iron skillet and a pain in his belly, Hendrik Andrews drove back to Boston full of dreams.

Francesca climbed into the front seat of Tim Greenfield's station wagon.

"To the fireworks?" she asked. She knew very well they weren't on their way to the fireworks. He drove down Main Street, which was full of people as if it were midafternoon. He drove slowly and looked around.

"Sight-seeing, I guess," she said.

And he laughed.

After the last streetlight on Main, past the First Congregational Church and Our Mother of Mercies R.C. Church, there was a narrow bridge over the Leonora and then a two-lane asphalt road which led to Ewes. There were no lights. On the clear summer night, the heavens were polka-dotted with stars and the half-moon made a silver path down the sky.

"To Ewes?" Francesca asked.

He reached over and took her knee.

"Not Ewes."

"Then where?"

"Guess," he said.

She knew before they got to Marsh Road exactly what Tim Greenfield had in mind.

He turned left and drove at a snail's pace along the slender dirt road between the marshes, flushing the birds and frogs

197

and snakes. Reeds and stiff marsh grasses brushed the sides of the car.

"There we are," Tim said suddenly. He dimmed his lights and turned into a curtain of cattails just wide enough for an ordinary car and pulled in far enough for the cattails to close behind them. He put the car in neutral, turned off the engine and the lights and opened the car door on his side.

"Do you know where we are?" he asked.

She opened the door on her side, pushing it against a thick army of high grasses, and stepped out. The ground was surprisingly solid beneath her feet. The marshes were phosphorescent, bathed in lavender, and noisy. The car had awakened the inhabitants, who sang or grumbled or harangued or cried against the night invasion. But Francesca was glad of company. Tim got out and lay down on the hood of his car whistling something familiar, perhaps from Gilbert and Sullivan. Cesca pulled herself up on the hood and sat beside him.

"Do you?" he asked again.

She knew where they were. She considered her options. She could pretend. "We're just off Marsh Road," she could say. "I've never actually been here before, and it's lovely at night." Which was true. Or she could make love, which was what she'd had in mind initially. Or she could ask him directly why he had brought her to the place where Billy Naylor had been humiliated.

She folded her arms across her chest and looked at Tim Greenfield in the silver light.

"Yes," she said. "I know where we are."

Separate as stars, they closed their eyes and listened to the birds argue back and forth in the low grasses.

Later that night, unable to sleep, Francesca replayed the scene with Tim, curious at the ease of their unspoken communication. They had meant to make love. Surely that was what he'd had in mind, as well as to shock her by bringing her to the place of "Billy's Love Song" just as she had shocked him with the song itself. And then they should have fallen into each other's arms, bad children capable of witchcraft, and fucked the night away. Instead, the life fell out of them and they lay stone-quiet, their eyes shut against the moonlight.

"Did the police ever find clues about Colin's death?" Tim asked finally.

"They gave up," Francesca replied. Her voice was wire-thin. She did not wish to have this conversation. She had lived months now guarding the locks on her memory of Colin, the carnivorous beast sleeping in the jungle of her mind; he was beginning to stir again.

"There are those of us who think Billy Naylor did it," Tim said. "I suppose you know that."

"But he didn't," Francesca replied.

Tim opened his eyes and looked at her.

"He didn't?"

"No."

He bent his knees so the small of his back was flat against the hood.

"You're probably right," he said, to his great surprise believing her absolutely. "It wasn't in Billy's character, even provoked."

She held herself stiff, imagining a turn of conversation, but Tim had nothing more to say on the subject. At one point, he reached up and took her hand, holding it loosely in his.

She was almost asleep when he spoke to her. He stood beside the car; she hadn't heard him get up.

"Time to go," he said. He leaned over so his face was just above her. She thought certainly he was going to kiss her, but he didn't.

"Don't tell me any more news about myself than you already have, Cesca," he said.

"I make up songs," she replied vacantly.

"Whatever." He climbed into the car. "You know what I mean."

The lights were off in the apartment when they drove down Main, which meant that Maud was either with someone or out late. Cesca decided to spend the night at her parents'.

When they stopped at the bottom of the Woodbines' driveway, she wanted to say something familiar to Tim Greenfield to honor the warm surprise of their evening together. But he was a stranger again. So she said goodbye and shook his hand.

Upstairs, she stopped at James's room to see if he was there and alone. He was, and her heart beat faster at his presence in her life again. He lay on his side curled around a pillow. A small gray cat made a fur ball at his head. Prince Hal was awake, although his eyes were closed, but she could tell by the stiffness of his body that he didn't want to be discovered thinking.

She lay in bed under the soft rose quilt and listened to the familiar night music of her childhood. Julian's breath was caught like a chicken bone in his throat; James breathed evenly, deep in a sleep where dark dreams are stored in the cellar of unconsciousness. Too many cats stirred in the corridor. Downstairs, she could hear Sophia making hot milk and honey as the prostitutes at Rooster's used to make for her when she was a child.

George Saunders couldn't sleep. He heard Tim come home and listened as he came upstairs, shut his bedroom door. He heard Mr. Greenfield in the bathroom and the dog scratching at the front door. At three o'clock by his watch, he got up, dressed in the clothes he had laid out for his return home and went downstairs. There was stationery in his aunt's rolltop oak desk, and he sat down to write Francesca Woodbine a letter. He had decided that if he did not acknowledge directly what he had done to her, he was not going to be able to sleep again. His eyes would be propped open as they had been tonight in a permanent and purgatorial consciousness. He sealed the letter and went out the back door, followed happily by the Greenfields' Labrador, glad of company.

Perhaps Francesca had slept, although when she heard steps on the wooden porch, she was already awake. She got up and went down the hall to a large cathedral window which overlooked the front yard. The outside light was on, and she could see the Greenfields' ancient Labrador peeing on the azalea bushes. Then she saw a figure—familiar to the Labrador, because the dog did not take exception—walk down the steps and turn on the brick path, and she recognized Tim Greenfield's cousin George. He walked down the driveway and up Hawthorne Street.

She went downstairs and turned on the lamp on the library table in the hall. The mail slot, a narrow slot with a brass flap on the outside of the door, was at the bottom of the front door.

There was an envelope on the grape-red Oriental rug, and she picked it up expecting the letter was for her, which it was—brief and in longhand.

"Dear Miss Woodbine," she read. *"I leave today and won't have a chance to see you in person. I doubt I will be returning to Bethany for some time. But I wanted to say that I deeply regret any harm I have caused you. Sincerely, George Saunders."*

Hal stood at the banister in pajama bottoms holding a pregnant mother cat in his arms like a baby.

"Who was that?" he asked.

"I thought you were sleeping," Cesca said.

"I hardly ever sleep," Hal said.

"Tim Greenfield's cousin," Cesca said. "He wrote me a letter."

"A love letter?"

"I don't think so," she said. "It's a letter I don't understand."

Hal followed her into the bedroom and lay down on the other twin bed with his cat. She sat against the headboard and pulled her quilt up over her knees.

Nothing this night had been as it seemed or should have been. Not the concert or her surprising tryst with Tim Greenfield. And now this letter about an injury she had never, as far as she knew, sustained.

"I used to know things about people's lives," she said to Hal. "I have known about Louisa and James for months."

"And Billy Naylor?"

Francesca thought for a moment. "Billy Naylor told me that story, but I would have known it anyway—not the facts necessarily, but the content." She turned over on her side and looked at her brother. "I've always had scenes in my mind. Now, all of a sudden, I've gone blind. I can't imagine anything about Tim Greenfield's cousin."

Cesca handed him the letter and he turned on the light beside the bed.

201

"I even know our grandfather was not a Roman count," she said.

He read the letter, folded it and put it back into the envelope.

"I didn't meet George Saunders until tonight, although he did seem familiar," Cesca said. "What do you think?"

"I don't know what to think," Hal said. "Maybe everyone's life is clear to you except your own."

He got up and left the fat cat on the pillow. "Soon enough, you'll know your own life as well. I wouldn't want to be in a hurry if I were you." He meant it as a joke, of course, but he was a serious boy.

At just about the same time Francesca was watching George Saunders leave with the Greenfields' Labrador, Father John was pacing back and forth in his apartment, too uncomfortable to sleep. The revelers on Main Street had kept him awake until midnight, and by then he was too bad-humored to sleep. He had been trying a few prayers of absolution aloud in his living room to take his mind off himself when he heard a terrible crash. His apartment was across the street and three doors down from Leonora's Books and Records. By the time he got to his window overlooking Main Street, what he saw was Will Weaver—certainly it was Will Weaver—standing on the sidewalk tossing paper in the air. It looked very much as though the front window of Leonora's had been smashed. And while he was watching, Will Weaver got into a car and drove away.

Father John called the police to say that something had happened at Leonora's. He didn't mention that he thought Will Weaver had broken into his own store. The circumstances were too disturbing, and he decided, as befitted his nature and training, to keep matters to himself.

Will Weaver received a call from the police department early on the morning of July 5 to say that sometime after midnight the bay window at Leonora's had been broken by vandals. He got dressed and went downtown.

The window had been shattered, probably with a heavy object, according to the police. There was a space large enough for a man to step through without cutting himself on the glass edges.

The albums of *Mating Calls*—perhaps fifty copies of the album had been in the window—were gone, and the cardboard Francesca had been ripped in small pieces and scattered along Main Street in front of the shops. Nothing else in Leonora's had been stolen or disturbed.

"Apparently 'Billy's Love Song' was more upsetting than I'd thought when I sang it last night," Francesca told her mother after Will had called with the news about the shop.

"Who do you think could have done it?"

"Probably kids," Francesca said.

"Do you really think so?" Prince Hal asked.

She knew what he was thinking because she had been thinking the same thing. George Saunders had done it, probably drunk, and then full of remorse, he had written her a letter of apology. But it didn't make sense.

"Nothing makes sense," Cesca said, getting Tobias his breakfast.

"The world is more fragile than we think; sometimes nothing does make sense," Sophia said.

"I hate that," Tobias said.

"Of course," Sophia agreed. "We all do."

Cesca packed Tobias' small overnight bag, made her bed and prepared to go back to the apartment. James was still sleeping, and she closed his bedroom door. On the way downstairs, she had to sit down, off balance—as if a flat world with an absolute perimeter had suddenly tilted and she was going to fall off.

2.

The Witch's Witch:
July 5, 1964

There was a legend local to coastal Massachusetts about a young girl, called Felicity, or the Witch's Witch, who lived in Salem in the seventeenth century during the time of the witch trials. At twelve years old Felicity was lovely to look at even in a drab Puritan dress, strong-minded in spite of the restrictions of her closed society, independent of spirit and curious about the women believed possessed by the Devil, unjustly tried and hanged or imprisoned. According to the story, on at least two occasions, perhaps more, Felicity attended the trials of innocent women accused of witchcraft. When the accuser entered the stand to bear witness against the woman in question—in one case, Felicity's own beloved aunt—the child screamed out from her place in the court-room, *"Devil, Devil, Devil!"* and fell over on the floor as if she had been stunned by a vision of the Devil in the heart of the accuser. So disturbing to the conduct of the trials was Felicity's behavior that the case against her aunt and perhaps other cases were put aside until her unexpected death.

She died before the end of the witch trials. Some said she had been murdered by a stranger passing through town or drowned accidentally in Salem Pond. Weeks after she was reported missing by her distraught father, her frozen body was discovered at the shallow end of Salem Pond. Her father believed and told everyone who would listen to him that she had been killed by one of the people in Salem who were convinced she had the power to see into the dark center of their secret hearts.

All over Bethany Sunday morning, the story of Francesca Woodbine was told.

Mrs. Natale, who had adjusted to the news about her daughter's marriage, got up early for Mass at Our Mother of Mercies and then went home to call her friends with the news.

"So," Edna Fergusen said. "What a good catch for Louisa."

"He's a nice boy," Mrs. Natale agreed. "And a doctor, who makes good money, you know."

"I suppose you've heard about his sister," Edna Fergusen said.

Mrs. Natale had not heard, so Edna told her about "Billy's Love Song" and how, now Francesca was on the radio regularly, all the people in America were going to know there had been a queer in Bethany, Massachusetts, and boys sinful enough to treat him terribly.

"There're queers and sinful boys all over America," Mrs. Natale said, not pleased to have her good news altered by Edna. "There's no point in thinking we're different in Bethany."

But Edna pointed out the real danger. If Francesca actually had the power to see into people's private lives, which Edna admitted she certainly doubted, then she'd sing their secrets on the radio and nobody in Bethany would be safe.

Marcia Cooper saw the situation differently. She was pleased to hear from Mrs. Natale about James and Louisa, but what she really wanted to talk about was Francesca Woodbine, who had confirmed her belief in fortune-tellers and psychics and horoscopes and the stars. "Maybe the gift is inherited from their grandmother and will pass through James to Louisa's children."

"I certainly hope not," Mrs. Natale said.

By the time Mrs. Natale called her mother, who got the town news every morning when she hung out her laundry, she had changed her opening conversation.

"I suppose you've heard about Francesca Woodbine," she

said. "Well, Louisa's going to marry her brother on the fourth of September at Our Mother of Mercies."

Mrs. Natale's mother said she'd known Francesca had sight because of her Sicilian genes from the first time she met the child. She hoped they'd change the wedding date, since her Uncle Patrick had died of liver failure on September 4, and she particularly hoped Louisa wasn't going to be one of these modern girls who use birth control.

"Tell me about the concert last night," Mrs. Natale asked when Louisa came down for breakfast at noon.

"Francesca was wonderful." Louisa checked the refrigerator.

"Everybody tells me she sang a song about Billy Naylor being queer and gave out information that was personal."

"The song was about a boy named Little Billy Brown who lives in Baytown. I don't know what you mean about personal information." She dropped two pieces of raisin bread into the toaster and sat down at the kitchen table with the first section of the Sunday *Boston Globe*.

Mrs. Natale's mother called back to say that she had kept Mrs. Natale's wedding dress for Louisa to wear and that her next-door neighbor Debbie was married to Joe Rinkle of the police force, who knew for a fact that an incident very similar to the one in Francesca's song had actually happened while he was on duty.

Mrs. Natale leaned over the kitchen sink and examined her garden out the window. "I always say the best defense is a good offense," she said. She rinsed her coffee cup and wiped the linoleum surface. She watered the African violets on the windowsill and snipped off the dead leaves and flowers from the pale pink begonias. "I think we should ask Francesca to be your maid of honor," she said.

"We?" Louisa looked up from a front-page article on Vietnam. But Mrs. Natale had gone out to the cutting garden to fill the house with dahlias in honor of Louisa's engagement to the judge of Holbrooke County's son.

Father John hadn't seen Johnny Trumbull for years—not since he was twelve or thirteen and had traded in his Sunday-morning duties as acolyte for smoking cigarettes behind Drake's Drugs with his friends in junior high. So he was very much surprised when Johnny Trumbull, in a blue polyester jacket stretched over his belly, arrived between the eight- and ten-o'clock Masses on Sunday morning to make his confession.

He opened the partition in the confession box and there was Johnny's plump face, shadowed by whiskers and stinking of yesterday's beer, a fleshy jigsaw puzzle in the small window between them.

"Bless me, Father for I have sinned," he began. "Did you know Billy Naylor, Father?"

Father John considered.

"Billy Naylor was a Protestant," he said.

"I didn't mean did you ever hear his confession. I know he didn't make confessions. Even if he'd been a Catholic, he wouldn't have dreamed of confessing to what he did."

"I remember Billy Naylor," Father John said coolly. "Why don't you begin your confession again?"

"Bless me, Father, for I have sinned," Johnny began. And he told the whole story about what he and Colin and Tim Greenfield had done to Billy Naylor and how Francesca had known it, either because Colin told her before he died or because she was a black witch, the latter most likely.

Father John listened on his side of the window, but when Johnny Trumbull had finished his confession, the priest did not offer absolution.

"I'd like to talk to you about this, Johnny," Father John said quietly, ignoring the appropriate form for confession.

"No I don't want to talk at all," Johnny said nervously. "My girlfriend's waiting in the car. I just came to make my confession. That's all."

"Why? Why didn't you come to me years ago?"

"I didn't want to then," Johnny said. "Please, Father."

So Father John gave him absolution, knowing in his heart that what Johnny Trumbull had done was not forgivable.

They said the "Our Father" together, and afterwards Johnny whispered in his deep cigarette voice, "I came because I'm afraid of Francesca Woodbine."

Father John smiled. "I can't save you from Francesca," he said.

He waited until he heard the heavy doors of the church groan shut and then he went through the side chapel door into the small cemetery and across the street to Hanrahan's. It was 9:30 on the steeple clock at the National Bank—between the Masses, and half an hour before the family service at First Congregational—but Hanrahan's was "alive and jumping," as Frank said, greeting Father John at the door. Down the street, Maud was sweeping up pieces of scattered cardboard Francesca, shattered glass sticking to the damp and mossy brick sidewalk. She wanted to have the street cleared by the time Francesca and Tobias arrived.

"Someone broke into Leonora's," Frank said to Father John. "Kids, I imagine." He handed the priest a cup of coffee. "So you must have heard about Cesca's concert last night."

"Just recently," Father John said. "Was it good?"

"Out of this world," Frank said.

There was a long pine table at the back of Hanrahan's with picnic benches and booths along the sides where the Catholics waiting for the ten-o'clock Mass had coffee and the Protestant families of Anglo-Saxon origin had doughnuts and coffee and talked—this morning about Francesca.

Maia Perrault sat at one of the round tables with her husband, Sean O'Brien, who was a shipbuilder—new to Bethany. Maia was pensive.

"So you liked the concert," she said to Sean as they waited for Mass. A sadness had developed between them lately, and for solace they had returned to the Church. Sean had given her the beginnings of three babies, only to have them slip away from her before they could survive outside her womb. He was a restless man, and Maia was afraid she would lose him unless one of the easily made little chicks took hold and grew to term. Meanwhile she kept herself pretty and tried to conceal her jealousies, which were, she very well knew, blackening a gentle and affectionate nature.

"I loved the concert," Sean said. "Francesca is a mysterious woman."

"And you want to marry her." Maia tried to be lighthearted.

Sean laughed, split a honey doughnut and put a syrupy piece of it into Maia's small French mouth.

"I'm married to you, love."

Maia was not consoled. "Cesca was going to marry a man named Colin Mallory who was murdered before you moved to Bethany."

"Of course I know that."

"Did I tell you I knew Colin very well?"

"Slept with him." He chucked her under the chin. "Yes, you did tell me that."

She finished the honey doughnut.

"He liked me."

"I'm sure he did. You're sweet with men, Maia. I've always told you that."

But she knew Francesca was sprawled across his brain and would stay there for days.

Sean stood up to get more coffee.

"I bet Billy Naylor told her that story she sang last night," she said when Sean came back.

"Who knows? It was a good song," Sean said just as Ellen Barger, who had grown up next door to Maia, stopped by the table.

"Didn't you think Francesca Woodbine was a knockout?" she said. "My mother says her grandmother was a psychic— a real one—and Francesca has inherited her brain."

"Not her brain." Maia shrugged. "Her eyes. If she comes into Hanrahan's before Mass," Maia said, unable to let go, "I'm going to ask her if Billy told her that story or she made it up."

"No, you're not, Maia," Sean said. "You're going to shut up."

Will Weaver had just finished sweeping the glass from the bay window and removing the jagged pieces from the frame when Francesca arrived with Tobias.

"Hello," she said. "It doesn't look such a mess."

"Maud helped clean up this morning," Will said. "She's in the apartment."

"You think it was drunk kids?"

"I imagine."

"The albums are all gone?"

Will nodded. "Apparently."

But he had a peculiar sense of reality, similar to that which comes with fever when internal and external events exist as part of the same strange scene. He remembered carrying a heavy stack of albums from the bay window to the basement steps. He saw himself at the top of the steps, weighted with albums, which he dropped on the dry dirt floor beneath him.

"We're going to Hanrahan's for coffee," Francesca was saying. "Do you want to come?"

"I'll be there," Will said.

There was something he wanted to do. He waited until Maud and Cesca and Tobias had gone up Main Street to the front of Hanrahan's. Then he went inside the shop. The entrance to the basement was at the back, next to The Snake Bed, and was kept locked so children would not open the door and tumble down the steep wood steps. It was locked now. He worked the combination, pulled the lock, took a flashlight from over the door and went down the steps. Halfway down, he shined the light on the basement floor. *Mating Calls* was there, all right—not in stacks but strewn all over, as if someone had dropped the albums from the top step. He closed the door, locked it, replaced the flashlight and called Celia Hamilton.

"Someone broke into the store," he said. "I'd like you to come over."

He sat down on the stool next to the telephone and stared down at the line of books, across the turquoise-patterned carpet, past the snake cages where his snakes lay coiled, comfortable and still; his eyes rested unseeing on the back garden.

After the concert, he had taken Celia home. He remembered that. She had sat curled in the front seat when they parked and talked about trouble with her father while he drifted into and out of sleep. Then he had driven by the fireworks and decided not to stop, although he did pull over by the side of the road to watch the sky explode in brilliant yellow snowflakes. His father's car had been in the driveway when he arrived, but the house was dark. He let himself in the back door, turned on the kitchen light and checked the refrigerator, which was stocked with fresh trout, so his father must have been fishing. As he started up the back stairs to his bedroom, he heard voices. He heard his father's low rolling voice and a higher birdsong whispering back. The voice of the woman from Ewes. In the dark, as if she were artificially lit, he saw his mother walk through the upstairs hall in a long robe. That's all he remembered, but sufficient for him to know that he had been in a dangerous state of mind.

He got off the stool, put the telephone back on the counter and checked the time. Then he took a hammer and broke the padlock to the basement. No one would suspect that he had been the one to break into Leonora's. When Celia arrived, he would show her where he had discovered Francesca's albums and together they would carry them back upstairs.

Hanrahan's was full of warm and curious, somewhat combative chatter about Francesca's concert as she arrived with Tobias. But when the people gathered in the sunny delicatessen saw her in the doorway, they fell suddenly silent. Cesca took Tobias by the hand, opened the screen door and went inside. A shaft of sunlight spread across her path, and for a moment before she stepped beyond the light, she was transfigured—as light will alter the fixed place and form of an object so the object suggests a mystery of form beyond itself.

At that moment, surrounded by the familiar faces of the people with whom she had lived her life, Francesca knew she had been invested with their belief in her power of sight. It didn't matter whether Billy Naylor had told her the story or she had guessed it or if the story she had sung was a made-up tale about Baytown. The moment had a quality of magic; she knew that she believed in herself.

"Look who is here this morning at last," Frank Adler said to break the silence. He went across the room to greet Francesca. "Our very own Witch's Witch."

3.

Dress Rehearsal:
September 4, 1964

The brilliant sun, a brassy general, charged through the storm clouds at noon, just as people all over Bethany began to dress for James Woodbine's wedding.

"*Sunshine!*" James shouted, making an imaginary jump shot in the middle of Francesca's old bedroom. He had persuaded her to spend the night at home so they could stay up late after his bachelor's party, but the party had not been over until three. When he arrived home, Francesca was still up, and James, combative with liquor, was interested in past grievances and Cesca's coolness to Louisa. He had fallen asleep at the foot of Tobias' bed in the middle of a long argument about morality, their grandmother's in particular. Wide awake, Cesca lay on her back examining the shapes on the ceiling until dawn.

"Time to get dressed, Ces." James did a two-step across the room, leaped sideways, kicked his bare feet together Russian style and landed half off the bed, banging his ankle on the Harvard frame. "Jesus!" he called out. "I believe I've broken my ankle."

He rolled onto his back. "I honest to God think I have." He stretched out his foot so it touched Francesca's belly. "You check it."

"You're the physician," she said, impatient with his boyishness about this wedding, his foolish confidence in bliss.

213

Prince Hal came in and leaned against the bedroom door. He was already dressed, with a cat around his neck like a fur piece, littering his black jacket with yellow hair.

"Mama says we have to leave for the church in half an hour, in case you plan to carry through with the wedding," Prince Hal said to James.

"In spite of my devoted sister's reservations about my bride," James assured him, "I plan to get married in a matter of hours." He limped out of the bedroom. "It is only a small inconvenience to have cracked my ankle in two places."

But by the time he got to his own bedroom, he was singing at the top of his lungs and walked to the bathroom without evidence of injury.

Cesca yawned. "I'm glad I've decided never to marry," she said to Hal. "I couldn't stand the state of sustained dementia."

Hal sat down on the end of Cesca's bed. "Daddy has just pointed out that you won't be marrying due to bad luck and I won't be marrying due to equipment failure. So James is his only hope."

"Some hope." Cesca opened her closet door and took down the dress she would be wearing as maid of honor.

Louisa had asked her right after the Fourth of July. She had called on the telephone and asked would Francesca be willing to serve in a voice of such formality and reserve that one would suspect the service Louisa required involved personal danger.

"What else could I do?" Francesca had said to Maud. "String her up in front of the post office? Shoot her?"

Maud was thoughtful.

"I don't particularly like Louisa, Ces," she said, "but she's too ordinary for the response you have to her."

Cesca shook her head. "She's not ordinary, Maud."

"Well, she's not evil as you seem to think."

"I don't believe in evil," Francesca said. "But if I did, Louisa would qualify."

All summer while a perennial flower garden of arrangements and celebrations bloomed around her, Francesca was distraught—caught in an old photograph of Louisa and Colin Mallory and herself. She wanted the wedding to be over. Sometimes she believed she was going mad.

"How did it feel just before you got sick?" she asked Sophia one afternoon when her mother came over for lunch to discuss the plans for James's wedding.

"You're fine, Ces," Sophia said. "You're absolutely fine."

"Of course. I know that," Cesca said bravely, although her hands and feet were always cold, her heart fluttered, as if captured like a dying bird, and all summer her brain gradually turned to stone. She sang the concerts of *Mating Calls* in Boston and New York, Chicago, Washington, D.C., and was astonished at her success in spite of the clear fact that she was exiting the world of rational men and women.

She was becoming famous. People stopped her on the street and asked if she was the gypsy fortune-teller on the radio who made up songs about her own hometown—which was the story about Francesca that Columbia Records had distributed for purposes of publicity. "I am. I am," she would say gaily, able to march through the days advancing the cardboard Francesca Woodbine so people believed they were meeting the real McCoy.

"The Queen of Hearts," one reviewer in Boston had called Francesca when *Mating Calls* was released. "The new folksinger from Bethany, Massachusetts, sees beyond our lives into the secret heart," he had written. And the name took.

"I'm afraid the mind of the Queen of Hearts is beginning to slip away, Mama," she told her mother one afternoon.

"I felt like I was slipping before I got sick," Sophia said. "Actually like slipping on ice and falling down."

"So you see," Francesca said. She agreed, as if she were coldheartedly planning her own funeral, that her mother should wear cornflower blue, since the bridesmaids were going to be in lavender, that she shouldn't cut her hair but have it done up, that the rehearsal dinner should be in the garden of the

215

Woodbine house and Cornish hen would be very good.

She began to buy *The Boston Globe* regularly, sometimes *The New York Times*, and read first the obituaries and then the entertainment page. She imagined her own obituary would be on the entertainment page; perhaps a story there with a notice in the actual obituary section. People would be moved in general to note that she was only twenty-nine when she died. In early August, she wrote a will leaving three-quarters of her estate to Tobias and one-quarter to Maud and named her parents guardians of Toby. She supposed she was contemplating suicide. Because she was of a temperament incapable of facing such an act straight on, she danced around the edges, reading the obituaries, securing Toby's future, hoping perhaps to be saved by madness.

"You are not going mad, Ces," Sophia said. "I can tell by your eyes."

She examined her eyes in the bathroom mirror.

"We don't necessarily see the same eyes," she said to her mother. "Everything is determined by the seer's state of mind."

"That may be true about eyes," Sophia said. "But I am your mother and know for a fact you are not going mad."

Will Weaver, however, was going mad. On the morning of James Woodbine's wedding, he woke up early to the sound of a woman's voice—probably his mother's, certainly hers by the softness of it—coming from the closet next to his desk. he pulled the covers up to his chest and waited for the voice to go away. Certainly he was sufficiently clearheaded to know that his mother wasn't in the closet. She was dead in Atlanta, Georgia, at the Church of the Heavenly Rest, he told himself.

But the voice persisted. He could not hear what she was saying; the sound was muffled by the clothes in the closet and the fact that the door was closed. He called his father and then remembered with fury that Sam Weaver had spent the night at the house of the woman from Ewes. So he got up. He forced himself to do chores—to brush his teeth and wash his face, to put on blue jeans and a shirt, to comb his hair, which he was wearing long, to make the bed and toss his laundry down the bathroom chute. He closed the windows against the chance of rain. He even turned on the radio, but the voice in the closet did not diminish in competition with the radio.

So he went to the closet and opened the large oak door, and no one was there but the voice, soft as silk, disengaged from human form, enunciating clearly. *"Kill her,"* the voice said, *"until her head falls off."*

He shut the door quickly, ran down the stairs, through the kitchen, out the back door to a low willow at the far end of the garden. Then he listened again. Only the sound of the birds, a woodpecker above him, the swish of wind gusts in the trees. The voice was gone.

Inside the house, he called Celia Hamilton to make arrangements to pick her up for the wedding.

"I need to talk to you first," she said.

He agreed to meet her at the shop at eleven.

Celia Hamilton took down her mother's large suitcase and packed everything in her room—her clothes; her cheerleading letter from high school; a picture of her little brother playing catcher for Little League; a picture of Will Weaver leaning against the front door of Leonora's, boyish and engaging, a sweet expression as if childhood had fixed itself permanently on his face. A snake wound comically around his waist like a belt. She packed the picture and petals of dried roses Will had given her on the first of every month. She made her bed, straightened the top of her bureau, closed the suitcase and dressed for James Woodbine's wedding in a cotton piqué pinafore reminiscent of a picture of her First Communion. When Will called, his voice remote, she asked him to pick her up early at the shop. Then she wrote her mother.

"Mama," she wrote, *"I am leaving. There is too much unhappiness in this house. When I settle, I will let you know where I am. As you certainly know, my leaving has nothing whatever to do with you, whom I love. Celia."*

She put the letter in an envelope on the kitchen cupboard, since her father by his own admission never darkened the door of the kitchen in his life except to eat.

Celia's father was a drunk. He came home more nights than not full of temper and crashed, loose-legged, around the house breaking lives like china, until he fell over the double bed he no longer shared with his wife. Sometimes he was charming. But just as Celia softened, the dark lights would ignite in his eyes and he'd lash out. In time the sweetness of her spirit spilled, and what remained was an empty container and a sense of longing, particularly for Will.

Her father had grown worse in his fifties.

"Leave him," Celia would say to her mother.

"But I love him," her mother would reply.

"How can you love him?" Celia would ask.

"I just do," Mrs. Hamilton replied, as if she too were drunk just by his presence in the house.

The night before, at an evening meal of silences, Celia had looked at her mother—at the slack skin falling from her once-pretty face, the aspect of a cadaver more evident in her eyes than life. She did not want to watch her mother's slow death, so she determined to leave.

Celia let herself into Leonora's, put her suitcase behind the counter and waited for Will.

Father John was across the street in the garden of Our Mother of Mercies, clipping the dead roses from the bushes along the fence. Celia crossed the street to see him.

"Busying myself until the wedding," he said to her. "You look very lovely. You must be coming to see James married."

"I am," Celia said. "Everybody is." It had been years since she had made a confession, but she wanted to confess. "Father?"

He put his hand on her cheek.

"I want to tell you that I'm leaving. After the wedding, Will Weaver is taking me to Boston and then I'm taking a bus to Vermont."

"I didn't know that," Father John said. "In fact, I thought you and Will Weaver had become such good friends that you might be liking Bethany better."

Celia hesitated. She had not planned to tell Father John anything at all, and now, with him, she was afraid she might tell him too much. "I like Will," she said, "but I'm not sure

218

he feels the same. He has only kissed me."

"I understand," Father John said, smiling. "Sometimes kissing is not sufficient."

"But I'm leaving because of my father. Not Will," she said. "You know my father."

"I do know your father." He wished her well, thinking sadly that weddings were never his favorite occasions—and months later, recalling his last conversation with Celia, he knew that the trouble he had sensed in the air the morning of James and Louisa's wedding was Celia Hamilton's death.

Will was not dressed for the wedding when he arrived at Leonora's to pick up Celia. He took her back with him to the house so he could change, and in the car, he listened with growing agitation about her decision to leave home.

"You can't go," he said as they pulled up in front of the house. "I need you at the store."

"You can replace me at the store," she said. She wanted him to say that he needed her for himself, but she was disturbed by his uneasiness. She did not press.

"I won't let you leave," he said.

He told her to sit in the living room while he changed. He brought her a cup of coffee and gave her an album of photographs.

"When I was little," he said, opening the leather book. "That is my mother." He pointed to a picture of a dark, willowy woman whose hair was pulled back off a face with the soft angles of Leonardo women. "You look just like her."

While Will was dressing, Celia took the picture with her to a mirror and held it up alongside her own face. There was a resemblance in the eyes, she thought, very pleased that Will had noticed.

Upstairs, Will went to his own room and in a terrible rush took his tuxedo from the closet and dressed in his father's room in case the voice started to speak again.

Louisa Natale woke up late in a black humor. Downstairs, she could hear her mother swishing through the kitchen hum-

219

ming Frank Sinatra off tune, her grandmother complaining that it was going to rain, to pour, thunder, and she'd had her shoes dyed green to match her dress.

"Think of the bride, not yourself all the time, Mama," Mrs. Natale said. "Louisa's dress will be soaked."

"I just picked the shoes up yesterday," her grandmother said. "The green will run all over the street. I object to Father John," she added without a pause in conversation.

"You're the only person in town who objects to Father John," Mrs. Natale said.

"Well, I do," her grandmother said. "He has a fancy for women. I mean I'm not expecting the worst of him, but he is a priest of God and I know for a gospel fact that he had his fortune told by Francesca Allegra when she was right in her room at Rooster's and who knows what might have happened. You know what I mean?"

"And who cares?" Mrs. Natale said, unwilling to allow her spirits to darken with the weather.

Mr. Natale was taking a long shower. Several times, his wife called upstairs to save the hot water for the bride, but Mr. Natale could not hear her.

Louisa, known for the past two months in her own household as the bride, sat up on the end of her bed. In preparation for this afternoon, she had read a book about depression in women called *Sisters in Darkness* which her cousin Maia Perrault had given her.

"I don't know what's the matter with me," she said to Maia, to whom she was as close as anyone, although only recently had they begun to confide in each other when Maia had told her about Sean's wanderings. "I go to the market," she said to Maia, "and I stand at the vegetable bin trying to remember why I've come. Once at work, I went into the ladies' and sat on the toilet for hours until one of the docents at the museum came in to find me."

"You're depressed," Maia had told her. "What you describe is a clear sign of depression," and she gave her a dog-eared copy of *Sisters in Darkness* and told her to eat nuts and vegetables—no meat.

"I don't think I want to get married," Louisa said.

"Of course you want to get married, Louisa," Maia said. "Everyone feels like you do."

"Not everyone," Louisa said.

"I promise you."

Louisa read *Sisters in Darkness* cover to cover, but there was not a single case history cited that had anything in common with her own except the state of mind as described by the women involved.

"Maybe you just have trouble with men," Maia said. "You haven't had a lot of boyfriends. You've always kept to yourself—at least since college."

"The trouble is not men," Louisa said. "It's Francesca."

One evening when Maia came over to have her bridesmaid's dress fitted by Mrs. Natale, she stayed to check through Louisa's old clothes, since she could not afford nice clothes.

"I have often wondered about Francesca and Colin Mallory," Maia said, going through a stack of sweaters. "They seemed wrong together."

"Why wrong?"

"I don't know. Just a sense I had. I knew Colin," Maia said. "I used to sit for the Mallorys. Remember?"

"I suppose I do."

"And once when I was about twenty and he was fourteen, I stayed the night with him," Maia said. "The first."

"For you?"

"Of course not. The first for him."

Louisa lay back on her bed. "Me too," she wanted to say, and then Maia would ask when and she would either lie or say that she had slept with Colin Mallory the day he died, and as she turned those thoughts around in her mind, Maia interrupted.

"Did you ever sleep with him?" she said. "I've always thought something might have happened between you the day he died."

"Well, it didn't," Louisa said quickly. "I went over to lunch. That's all. Lunch and to try out the champagne. We were friends."

"Did Francesca ever know you were there for lunch?" Maia asked.

"I never told her, but I'm sure she read the police report."

Maia checked her cousin's closet for summer skirts. From a top shelf she pulled down the broad-brimmed hat with long streamers which Louisa had worn to the Festival and put it on her head. "You were daring, Louisa. I used to think you were the most daring girl I knew. Remember how you'd wear hats all over town? Nobody wore hats then." She took down a yellow pillbox, a cloche, a rolled straw hat and the swan hat.

"Put them away, please," Louisa said. "I hate hats now."

She should have thrown the hats away that night after Maia went home. It crossed her mind, but she fell asleep, and by morning she had forgotten.

Will Weaver's oldest brother, Oliver, was coming from Providence, where he was a portrait photographer, to take pictures of the bride and her attendants before they left for the church. So Francesca arrived at the Natales' at noon for pictures. Maia was already there. Mrs. Natale's mother, dressed in a pale green silk dress, carrying her matching shoes, answered the door when Cesca rang.

"Wouldn't you know my feet would swell up like pigs this morning?" she said to Cesca without a word of greeting. She called Louisa. "The fortune-teller's here," she said. "That's what I call you to Louisa. The little fortune-teller. It's a bad day for a wedding, as you very well know." She closed the front door. "I told my daughter. Today, September fourth, is the very day my uncle dropped dead of the liver, but would she change her mind?"

Mrs. Natale came out of the bathroom in her slip as Cesca walked upstairs. "If you listen to my mother, you'll go crazy," she said. "Have the flowers come yet?"

"White roses. I saw them in the hall."

"Thank God," Mrs. Natale said. Louisa had been so difficult about this wedding that each successfully completed arrangement—the invitations, the flowers, the music, the food—seemed a small miracle to Mrs. Natale.

"It's not that I don't like the wedding you've planned,

Mother," Louisa had said. "It's that I don't know if I want to get married."

Mrs. Natale tried to ignore the news about the marriage. Louisa was going to get married and that was that. If she decided she didn't want to stay married, that was a horse of a different color, she had told Mr. Natale, who tried with some success to sleep his way through the arrangements. "Certain formalities in life have to be honored," Mrs. Natale said.

"Are you saying Louisa has to get married?" Mr. Natale asked.

"I'm saying she has to appear at her wedding," she said. "That's the end of her obligation to me."

Maia, doing her makeup in the mirror over the dresser, was immediately on edge when Cesca walked into Louisa's bedroom. She supposed it was because Sean had talked about Francesca at breakfast that morning and made her cry. He'd told her that he planned to go to Francesca and get his fortune told. What ever for? she'd asked, trying to sound undisturbed. He said he wanted to find out about the babies, if they were going to be able to have one, as well as find out about other things.

"If the babies are going to stick, they'll stick. God knows that. Not Francesca." Which was when she'd started to cry. Sean had followed her upstairs to the bedroom and kissed her neck softly, but she hadn't believed his intentions.

"It's not a fortune you want from Francesca at all," she said.

Sean shook his head. "If you were a man, Maia, you would know instinctively that Francesca Woodbine is not available."

Louisa was lying down dressed only in her wedding slip when Cesca walked in. Maia had put on her makeup: soft blush and mascara, no lipstick—a natural look, she'd said, for the virginal bride.

"What time is it?" Louisa asked. She was so absolutely tired, she wanted to die or felt as if she already had.

"Just after noon," Cesca said, and smiled at Maia. They did not know each other well, although in the first year she and Colin had been together, Colin had spoken of her often. "The baby-sitter" he had called her with some kind of implication. At the time, she thought that Colin was as inexperienced as she was. Now she imagined he had made love with Maia.

"You're getting well known, Cesca," Maia said. "I hear you a lot on the radio."

"I've been singing quite a bit this summer," Cesca said, lifting her dress so it wouldn't wrinkle when she sat down. "I hear you're working at the high school teaching French. Hal told me."

"I teach him."

"His mind isn't much on French." Cesca took off her sandals, which matched the ones Maia was wearing.

"I don't want to teach French," Maia said suddenly. "I want to have a baby. Already I've had three miscarriages." Her voice was accusatory, as if Cesca had jinxed her babies. "Sean wants you to tell his fortune," she said in spite of herself, her voice strident and unnatural.

"Once I did fortunes at the Festival," Cesca said. "But I don't tell fortunes. I don't know how."

"Then how did you know about Billy Naylor?"

There was a long silence. Louisa got up and sprayed her arms with cologne, spraying the back of her cousin's neck playfully, but Maia could not be settled.

"Well?" she asked.

"Billy Naylor told me that story before he died," Francesca said quietly.

"I thought so," Maia said triumphantly. "That's exactly what I thought."

"It's not a secret. A lot of people know. Don't you, Louisa?"

"I do know from James," Louisa said.

"And Sean thinks you're psychic. Stupid Sean," Maia said.

Just then and to Cesca's great relief, Oliver Weaver arrived to take pictures.

Oliver Weaver was a small, bright-eyed young man dressed fashionably for the occasion in a white Gandhi jacket which he wore unbuttoned halfway with a daisy in each buttonhole. He kissed Francesca. "The love of my life grown up," he said.

"Almost thirty," she said.

"Well, nearly grown up." He had been known in high school

224

as garrulous—"garrulous Ollie" he was called, but only Oliver amongst his friends knew what the word meant. "Talk talk talk talk—like having a daughter in the form of a son," Sam Weaver said of Oliver, but warmly, because Ollie Weaver was a sweet man without malevolence and Sam adored him.

Oliver told Mrs. Natale's mother that *she* looked young enough to be the mother of the bride. "Well, I'm not," she said. He rearranged the furniture in the living room for pictures and called for Louisa and Maia to hurry up or the wedding would be over.

"So, Cesca, I understand you live in an apartment above my crazy little brother. It's a good thing you're fond of snakes."

"But I'm not. I hate them. I am fond of Will."

"So is everyone, I guess. It just goes to show you what a little nuttiness can do to grab the hearts of the masses." Oliver dashed around the living room, setting a plant here, a picture there, his tripod across from the couch. He arranged Mrs. Natale's mother on a straight-backed chair and took shots of her complaining about her shoes, which sat like a child in her lap.

"My father tells me Will has a girlfriend, so he might turn out in the end to be an ordinary married man. Unlike me."

"And me." Cesca laughed.

Oliver gave a long whistle as Louisa walked into the room, a pale goddess in a white lawn dress, a circle of daisies in her black hair.

"I love brides," Oliver said. "You look beautiful, Louisa." He moved around the living room snapping pictures. "The town is beside itself about this wedding. You must have invited everyone in Bethany," Oliver said to Mrs. Natale. "When I came over, Main Street looked like a maypole dance."

"She invited everyone," Mrs. Natale's mother said. "Even the dry cleaner on Main and Tennyson. I don't believe in democratic weddings, but who asked me?"

"A very good question, Mother. Why don't you put on your shoes?"

"*You* try putting on my shoes," she said. "Maybe you are a magician at putting large items in small boxes."

"Shh," Mrs. Natale said. "Today is Louisa's wedding day."

"Is that a fact? You couldn't have given me news of a greater surprise," Mrs. Natale's mother said.

"Every time I do a wedding, there's a fight," Oliver said. "Once, last month in Providence, the father of the bride threw a Bloody Mary at his wife while I was doing the pictures before the ceremony and she refused to clean off the red splashed on her pastel dress. 'I'll just let everyone at the church know you threw your drink at me,' she said, 'and I'll say I consider myself lucky you were in a throwing and not a killing humor.' And the father replied he *was* in a killing humor but also a gentleman exercising self-control. The guests, all the same, had a wonderful time. Weddings are for guests." He took Francesca's arm. "You and Louisa sit down on the couch together, Cesca. Isn't Maia Perrault in the wedding?"

"She isn't quite dressed," Louisa said, sitting down next to Francesca.

"Okay." Oliver knelt down in front of them with his camera. "Closer together. Your heads touching. Smile smile smile." They leaned together stiffly, straight as mannikins, expressionless. "Be like the girls you used to be," Oliver said brightly. "Whisper together. Tell secrets. Surely you have secrets."

They did not look in each other's eyes.

"Relax. Deep breaths," Oliver said, kneeling at an angle. "This is not a funeral."

"Who knows?" Mrs. Natale's mother said. "A wedding is a funeral. A funeral is a wedding. Who can tell?"

"Francesca can," Maia said quietly, coming into the room.

Maia had not been dressing upstairs. After Louisa left the bedroom, she had gone into the closet and pulled down the hats from the top shelf. For a moment she stood examining them as they lay in a heap on the floor and then she picked out the swan hat, shook off the dust, tried it on her own head and went downstairs with the hat held behind her back. Until the very last moment, she didn't know what she was going to do. Later, in retrospect, when Louisa, agitated beyond sense at what Maia did do, asked her "Why?" Maia knew only that she was furious at Francesca Woodbine because of Sean's interest in her. She didn't know why the swan hat.

"I acted on instinct," she said.

"Maia Perrault—a lovely long drink of water," Oliver said as she came into the room. "I'm glad to see you. I wish you were my wife, but you refused to marry me. Remember? I asked three times on successive Thursdays."

Maia smiled, glad of Oliver Weaver's attentions, strengthened by them.

"Each time, you said, 'If I were to ask you, would you say yes?'" Maia said.

"And you said, 'Ask me.'"

"And you said, 'I'm chicken.'"

"If only you hadn't grown so tall and lovely, I would have married you twice."

Maia laughed.

"What is that you're hiding behind your back?" Oliver stood on a stool to take a picture of the Natales with Louisa. "A present for me?"

Maia's heart was beating furiously. "A surprise," she said. "Father John says it's inappropriate for young virgins to go to Mass with their heads uncovered, and so I brought Francesca a hat to wear."

With a broad sweep of her arm, she produced the swan hat, crowning Francesca before she had a chance to duck.

"There," Maia said. "You look terrific. See yourself."

The ceremony had been so swift that Cesca did not see what it was Maia had put on her head. Automatically, she went over to the long mirror, carefully placed over the piano to make the room look larger. The swan, tired and limp from its life in the closet, fell over Cesca's forehead.

"Very sexy," Oliver said.

With astonishing calm, Cesca reached up and took off the hat. "I don't look well in hats," she said. She turned away from the mirror to give the hat to Louisa, but she had left the room.

Mrs. Natale said it was nerves. Louisa never had had a good stomach. Mrs. Natale's mother tried to put her fat foot into her slender new shoe. "I think maybe the joke about the hat wasn't so good a one, Maia," she said. "But then, who cares what I think?"

There was a story Sophia had told Francesca about a time when she was five and in Miss Prickett's kindergarten. Miss Prickett was the kind of lady whom Santa Francesca would have wryly described as "a girl of high moral standing—for what that's worth" and she had been invited to tea at the Woodbine house to make amends for the terrible time she was having with Francesca.

"Miss Prickett knew who your grandmother was, darling," Sophia told Francesca, "and disapproved."

On that particular afternoon, a warm one in early fall, Miss Prickett, overdressed for tea, uncomfortable in a household of suspect genetic history, sat stiffly in a garden chair and talked to Sophia about the impossibility of Cesca's adjusting to kindergarten.

"Why don't we have Cesca out to talk with us?" Sophia had suggested. She had told Cesca to change clothes from shorts to her pale blue party dress in which she looked irresistible, an angel.

"Be sweet as you are," Sophia had implored.

Miss Prickett agreed to talk with Cesca, and Sophia called to her.

"Coming, Mama," Cesca called back. "I'll be right there."

And she came running out the French doors, flying across the garden, giddy with the pleasure of her small drama and absolutely naked.

"'H'lo, Miss Prickett,' you said, and hopped up on my lap," Sophia said. "I am sure Miss Prickett never recovered. She probably stayed awake at night and wondered why in a life of impeccable morality, she had been punished by the humiliation of that small naked child."

"Why do you think I did it?" Cesca asked.

"Because you knew she had made judgments about your grandmother and me and you," Sophia said.

"I couldn't have known that," Cesca said. "I was too young."

"We know more than we see," Sophia said. "There are small

moments in our lives in which we know everything there is to know because it's in the air around us."

"What was that all about with the hat?" Oliver asked Francesca.

"Weddings bring out the darkest side of human nature," Cesca said. "That's why you've never married, Ollie."

"Perhaps you're right," Oliver said.

September 4 was Elena Andrews' birthday, and Hendrik picked her up early at the Boston Home for Disturbed Children to drive her to their parents' house. They were going to spend the day there with presents and relatives and a picnic in the backyard. No doubt Hendrik's father would recall, as he invariably had since Elena had fallen or been pushed out the second-story window when she was two years old, the events of that afternoon. He particularly liked to stand on the exact place where Elena had fallen and in a company of relatives who seemed to enjoy the repeated account, either for the horror of it or the mystery or both, he would tell the story of Elena's fall, which had destroyed the rational mass of gray cells in the child's brain and left her a wild dance of disconnected emotions, a heart that beat double time in the brain and in the chest without the fine wire of sense running through the center. She could cry uncontrollably for hours or laugh and laugh. "Funny, funny, funny," she would say, laughing even at the sound of the word.

This morning when Hendrik picked her up—her legs were useless and so he carried her to the car, put her wheelchair in the back—she was in a good humor.

"So, you're twenty-five today, Elena. You'll get presents."

"Fun. Fun," she said, laughing merrily as they drove to North Boston. "Happy Elena." She referred always to herself in the third person—a fact that Hendrik held to occasionally with the hope that the first person lost inside her muddled brain was somehow intact. "There's sunshine in Elena's heart and dancing feet and kisses," which was the way she had

229

always talked since she learned to speak when she was seven or eight.

She was very pretty, and because the sense had been knocked out of her in the fall, her face still held the wonder of a child's. Hendrik took her hand and held it between the seats. She loved that.

"Hold Elena's hand. Hold her hand tight," she'd say.

It would be late in the afternoon when the story got told again. Elena would be in the yard playing happily with presents. She always got toys for her birthday, generally a baby doll, which would be ruined in a matter of months by either too much love or too much anger or both. Mr. Andrews would get up from a low slat garden chair, a beer in one hand, a cigarette in the other, and ceremoniously, he would move to the spot under the second-story window.

"Now, Hendrik," he would begin, "have you had any fresh thoughts about the situation during the year?" He always referred to Elena's fall as "the situation."

Once when he was fifteen or sixteen, Hendrik had lost control and shouted, *I did it. I did it. I did it on purpose*," and his mother had cried and his father had said with great calm, "I have always told you that one day, you'd remember exactly."

But Hendrik hadn't done it. Or if he had, he didn't remember exactly, so he went through the ceremony of Elena's birthday as penance because he would never know whether he had pushed her or she had fallen.

As for Mr. Andrews, Elena's affliction justified his drinking, his irresponsibility, his miserable temper, his unkindness to his wife.

Hendrik was seven years old. It was August and he was sitting on his bed with plastic soldiers which his mother had gotten him that afternoon at the five-and-ten to play war. The window over the garden was open and the bed was situated level with the window. He had been told to mind Elena while his mother put together a lasagne. Elena—and this certainly he remembered—was driving him crazy. She'd grab an important soldier just at the moment Hendrik was marching him into battle and stick the soldier in her mouth locked in her tight gums. She could be a terrible tease—even his mother agreed with that. At the time of the accident, his soldiers were battling Hitler in Germany, and he had them all standing precariously on the bed when Elena threw herself in the middle of the battle. *"No, Elena!"* he shouted, and even if he hadn't remembered shouting, his mother did, because she rushed upstairs and when she got there Elena wasn't on the bed any longer and Hendrik on his hands and knees was looking out the window.

"She fell on my soldiers," he said in horror. "I stood her up and she went over backwards." The screen had fallen easily with the weight of her small round body.

"You were angry and pushed her," his mother said, rushing downstairs and out into the garden, where Elena lay as dead underneath the window.

He hadn't pushed her. He had stood her up on his bed to get her off his soldiers. Maybe he hadn't checked to see if she was balanced properly. But he didn't think he had pushed her.

The subject of his implication did not come up again until months later when Elena was out of the hospital and the verdict was in that her brain, for all intents and purposes, was blotto; there was no hope left, only the persistent existence of a small ruined child.

"Tell the truth, Hendrik," his father had said repeatedly— an incantation. "You pushed her, didn't you?"

"You got Elena a present, Hendrik? A baby doll with fuzzy hair?" Elena asked.

"A surprise, Elena."

"Elena hopes she wets," she said, contented. "Elena loves it when they wet."

At one o'clock, Hendrik Andrews parked in front of his parents' North Boston row house.

"We're here, Elena." He kissed the tips of her fingers.

He was full of resolve. On the first of August, Emily had moved back into medical-school housing at Tufts, leaving him abruptly one afternoon with a small raccoon shut in the bath-

231

room and the cardboard replica of Francesca Woodbine in three pieces under the sheets. He deposited the raccoon at the zoo, restored Francesca to standing position and made arrangements to return to medical school in the fall. A fine and unfamiliar calm had settled on him. For the moment he was satisfied to imagine a love affair with Francesca Woodbine; soon, he would hunt her down.

Today, when his father ambled lugubriously to the spot beneath his bedroom window for the usual ceremony, Hendrik planned to stop him.

"Enough is enough, Father," he was going to say. "I didn't push Elena."

He lifted his sister out of the car into her wheelchair just as the steeple bells at Our Mother of Mercies in Bethany began to ring.

Will Weaver left the reception at four o'clock with Celia. They did not say goodbye. Celia didn't want anyone to know where she was going, and Will planned to return to the reception by evening. They stopped at Leonora's to get her suitcase.

"I brought your picture and the rose petals from the roses you have given me," she said, full of sentiment. If he had asked her to stay at that moment, she would have done so.

Will didn't reply. He noticed that his hand gripping the steering wheel was white, his head throbbed, his stomach was tender and the voice in the closet was back, faint as memory. He didn't look at Celia. He knew very well that her head was off and he was anxious not to see her that way. Even in a state of unbearable turmoil, he was clear about his intentions.

"I have two hours before my bus." Celia checked her watch. "We could stop someplace. Maybe get a sandwich."

She said goodbye to Bethany as they crossed the bridge, onto the narrow highway, which was empty—surprising for a Friday afternoon. Will drove at the speed limit. He put his hand on hers and left it there. At Marsh Road, he hesitated and then turned left, driving very slowly through the high dry grass alive with cicadas after the long summer. He turned onto a dirt road which would have been a familiar territory to Tim Greenfield and Francesca and stopped the car.

Celia believed he was going to make love to her. She leaned back against the seat and closed her eyes. He would make love to her now. After all these months when she had been willing and he had been so strange. She ought to say, "No. It's too late. I'm moving to Vermont and you had your chances."

He took her hand and covered his erection. She didn't hurry. She simply left her hand where he had placed it and knew she would do anything he asked her to do.

The voice—his mother's—was sharper now, throbbing like a persistent migraine—*Kill her until her head falls off*—chanting monotonously, maniacally, in his ears. He didn't want to kiss her, but her lips were parted and so he did. He kissed her hard. And then he took her on top of him.

In the last minutes of her life, before he put his hands on her throat, Celia knew to be afraid. He could not come, and she could feel his mounting fury. She was losing him. Then, in a move so swift she didn't have time to resist, he turned her over, face down, his knees pinning her arms against the car seat, and he strangled her. He had practiced on kittens. He knew exactly how to strangle, but it took so long for a woman to die that way. The voice in his head was as loud as percussions now: *Kill her kill her*, cheering him on until he knew for certain that Celia Hamilton was dead.

He got out of the car and fell over the hood, resting. The voice, to his great relief, was gone and he was finally at peace.

He undressed her—pulled off her panties, took off her shoes. Then he lifted her out of the front seat, walked the almost twenty yards through the dense path of cattails to the marsh and put her in the water. The marsh water was low because of the season, but she sank just below a dark and murky surface which concealed her. He got her clothes and stuffed them into a mass of cattails.

Then he went back to the car, drove out of the marshes and turned left towards Boston. At the Trailways station, he put Celia's suitcase in a locker, locked it, dropped the key in the sewer outside the bus station and drove back to Bethany, arriving easily before six o'clock for the rest of the wedding reception at Rooster's.

On the drive home, he thought about Francesca. He imagined kissing her plum lips, as he had once done while she sat on the piano bench in her apartment above Leonora's. He imagined undressing her, taking her full breast in his mouth.

Medical textbooks describing mental illness would have called Will Weaver's condition episodic pychosis—he was no doubt schizophrenic. Perhaps blood samples taken at the time of his hallucinations would have indicated a sharp chemical imbalance in a system which tested otherwise within the range of normal.

He had no recollection of feelings associated with the killing of Celia Hamilton. And no remorse. It was as if he had read about the murder in a mystery novel and recalled the details with exact precision—even the hallucinations of his mother's voice. But he had no actual connection with Celia's death.

In fact, as he walked across the patio beside the Leonora River, spotting Francesca with Tobias at a table by the tavern, he felt marvelous, as if by some miracle he had shaken the burden of terminal illness and was going to survive.

"Hello, Ces," he said, and he kissed her lips wet with the taste of champagne.

He danced with Louisa and Maia Perrault. He sat down at the table with his father and talked to the woman from Ewes. He danced with Sophia, cutting in on Prince Hal. After the reception, people in Bethany remarked that they had never seen Will Weaver so easy and relaxed since he was an adorable little boy.

Francesca put her feet up on the chair across from her, lifted her lavender skirt to the knees and pulled Tobias next to her. In the center of the patio, James danced with Louisa, lost in her, lost in the idea of her or the fact that she was his wife. She looked beyond the Japanese lanterns hanging in the willows into the darkness. Although not happy, she was pleased to be James Woodbine's wife, pleased as well to have somehow beaten Francesca in an imaginary but deeply serious competition.

Francesca saw them old. They danced at another party, also

a wedding, perhaps the marriage of their daughter. James slightly bent over, encumbered with years of disappointment; Louisa elegant and appropriate, like a purple iris spread just after full bloom. Their dance suggested choreography—an arrangement beyond these partners which left no chance for their improvisations. Seeing James in her mind's foreshadowing broke Francesca's heart.

"Wouldn't you like to dance with James? Or someone," Tobias asked, sensing his mother's sadness.

"I used to in high school. James and I went to all the dances together so we wouldn't have to dance with anyone terrible."

"Like Will Weaver," Tobias asked.

"Will isn't terrible, Toby," she said.

Tobias leaned his head against Cesca's shoulder. "You don't love him, do you?" he asked.

"I love my family and especially you." She stood up and stretched so the firelights from the Japanese lanterns danced merrily across her lavender dress, her dark face.

Book Four

Prologue

*I*n *the spring, Santa Francesca and Sophia walked along the
river paths behind Rooster's Tavern shedding the thick cocoons
of a long winter. They'd walk for hours, sometimes well beyond the
town limits of Bethany, until the sun fell and Francesca had tired
of telling stories.*

*Once in late May, the spring Sophia was eleven—she
remembered that spring in particular because during the winter she
had outdistanced her mother and on their walks together, she could
look down on Santa Francesca's soft brown hair—they took a very
long walk almost to Ewes, where the Leonora River narrowed to a
thin slow-moving stream. Francesca was telling stories about
Sicily—"Sicilian secrets" she called them. And Sophia,
sleepwalking, was lulled to safety by the sound of her mother's
voice; the world as she knew it at that moment was jewel-perfect
beyond wishing.*

*Santa Francesca saw the snake first on the rocks beside them. It
was small and elegant, beautifully coiled, its diminutive head a
brilliant orange triangle.*

"Don't move," Francesca said, quietly.

"I see it." Sophia was thrilled. "It's lovely."

Santa Francesca did not reply.

"It's much better than the brown snakes slinking around the Leonora like thieves."

"Not better," Francesca had said. "Lovelier to look at perhaps." She took her daughter's hand and turned back towards Bethany. "If snakes like that are out sunning this afternoon, we're going home," she said.

"I didn't think you were afraid of things," Sophia said.

"I have learned in America to be a sensible woman," Francesca said. "The snake is dangerous. I know because I was bitten."

She did not elaborate, and during the walk home there were no more stories.

"It's savage for God to make a poisonous snake more beautiful than ordinary ones, just daring us to touch him," Sophia said.

"That's not God's fault," her mother said. "He gave us eyes to see the troubles in our own gardens. It's our fault for being too stupid to use them properly."

"Well," Sophia said, cross at the intrusion of bad news on her lovely walk with her mother, "at least we should have better hints from Him."

The sun had fallen below the river, dusting the path with suffused light, making a world of shadows between them and Rooster's Tavern in the distance. Sophia leaned against her mother's shoulder.

"Don't be easily fooled by what you see, Sophia," Santa Francesca said. "The hints we need against trouble we must look for in our own hearts."

And they walked the rest of the way home in silence, their eyes fixed on the dark path in search of snakes.

1.

The Ballads of
An Ordinary Town

1. *"Ballad of the Undrowned Boy"*

There was a soft winter storm in Bethany the night Prince Hal left home. Dry snow from a low sky gathered on the ground, thick and airy as down. By eight o'clock, the night was quiet; yellow streetlights drew a shadow circle of dust; the pines and low bushes were weighty with a snow that would be gone by morning as if the night itself were a dream from which people would awaken altered by a memory, perhaps even a nightmare, they could not remember.

After dinner with Sophia and Julian, Hal packed. He took four cotton Indian shirts and blue jeans, one pair of shorts, a cable-knit sweater which James had given him for Christmas and he had never worn, but thought should he happen to die on this trip, he did not want James to think he had left the sweater at home. He took an envelope of cuttings from his cats, bits of hair clipped from the tails or thighs of each of them, mixed together in an envelope like ashes from the crematorium; a picture of Sophia as a girl; one of the family in the garden behind the house looking ordinary and posed; a letter from Frank Adler; a publicity picture of Francesca announcing her second album, *The Ballads of an Ordinary Town,* which would be released in the summer. He also packed his last correspondence from Amal.

He remembered Valentine's Day in particular because he was a senior and did not have a girl to take to the winter dance. At home that night, he had turned off all the lights in his room except the one bright spotlight on his desk and stripped. He examined himself without sentimentality. In the mirror on his closet door, he saw the reflection of a boy. His chest was small, concave and hairless; his nipples dimple-sweet, the nipples of a prepubescent girl; his penis plump and short, unexpansive; it looked like a lavender flower between his slender porcelain legs.

"Dear Amal," he wrote. "*I am seventeen this month and ready immediately to come to Sarasota and apprentice with you. However, I should remark that in spite of my age and, I believe, mental maturity, I am, in appearance, still a boy and may remain so for the rest of my life. Yours, Hal Woodbine.*"

He read the letter twice before he mailed it, uncertain whether Amal would intuit what he intended to say.

The letter back was prompt and simple.

"*Dear Hal,*" it began. "*If you have a man's heart and are not crippled in the legs or bald (for the impressing of people), come immediately. Yours, Amal, the Lion Tamer of Ringling Brothers and Barnum & Bailey Circus, The Greatest Show on Earth.*"

Two months went by, however, before Hal left, six weeks short of his graduation from high school. The decision to go then, late Saturday night, April 3, was not because of Julian's incessant harassment, as everybody thought, but in fact had to do with Francesca and Will Weaver.

He zipped his bag shut, turned off his bedroom light and listened. It was ten o'clock. Sophia and Julian were talking behind the bedroom door, whispering sweetly to each other; it pleased him to leave at such a moment in their lives. He didn't have to feel responsible.

He hadn't planned to leave a note. The circus was in Raleigh, North Carolina, and would be there for three days. They could find him if they wished. Certainly they'd guess

242

immediately that he had gone to join Amal. But he didn't want for them to catch up with him before he even got to Raleigh either, to drag him back to graduate.

He went quietly downstairs, opened the cupboard over the sink and took down two bags of Fritos, a box of vanilla wafers and two small boxes of raisins for the trip. On the counter was the beginning of a grocery list: KLEENEX, ASPIRIN, GROUND BEEF, FRESH TOMATOES, TOILET PAPER, CAT FOOD (LOTS), SKIM MILK. On second thought, he decided, recalling the grief Celia Hamilton's parents had suffered—he could see it in their stricken faces when they came to Hanrahan's on Sunday morning before church—he would leave a note.

"I've gone to the circus in Raleigh and will love you always, Prince Hal," he wrote under SKIM MILK. And then he left by the back door. He had in mind going to Francesca's apartment to get a ride to the bus station in Salem, which had an eleven ten to Boston and a morning bus from Boston to Raleigh, North Carolina. Or else he could call Will Weaver from the pay phone on Main Street outside the drugstore. Or get a taxi. He hoped Francesca was at home. Something had gone wrong with his friendship with Will Weaver since Celia Hamilton had disappeared.

The day after Celia Hamilton left, Will Weaver told the police his story. He had taken Celia to the bus station in Boston after James Woodbine's wedding. He knew she was running away from home, of course, because she had told him. He had tried to persuade her to stay; he was fond of her and needed her at the shop. But she was determined.

"There wasn't a love affair between us," Will Weaver said. "We were just good friends," and the police were satisfied with his explanation.

In 1964, it was not uncommon for adolescents to leave home, for people in their twenties to disappear, usually to California or Vermont or Canada. Within a month of her departure, the police had tired of the search. They had contacted Celia's friends in Montpelier, who said she had not arrived, the attendant at the bus station, who insisted he had seen at least five girls matching Celia's description and how was he to remember particulars? He did recognize Will Weaver, he said, but couldn't recall the woman with him. The police put out bulletins nationally and waited with diminishing interest for a response. They did not entertain the possibility of foul play, imagining that she was alive and well and would return home. The Hamiltons, not resourceful by nature, were quietly bereft. Occasionally Will stopped by to see them and talked for hours to Mrs. Hamilton. She was grateful for his company and the memories he had of Celia and told Father John and her friends at church what a comfort Will had been to her. No one in the town of Bethany ever thought to suspect Will Weaver. He was, after all, still the motherless child of Sam Weaver, their eccentric mascot, their darling boy.

On the night Prince Hal packed to leave home, Will Weaver sat on the top step of the ladder at Leonora's Books and Records filling the shelves under NEW FICTION with April's books. Upstairs, Francesca Woodbine was singing. She sang a new ballad he had not heard before about a man who saves a young boy from drowning and must be ever after responsible for his life.

"He'll have the young boy's life in his ancient hands/For the rest of his days," she sang the refrain.

The melody roused in him a memory of passion. Since Celia's death he had been at peace, as if the soft part of his brain had been shot through with Novocain and the demons who peopled his daily life had lost their nerve. He did not even remember Celia as a presence. Only facts about her which he told Mrs. Hamilton. Like numbers she was to him. He could call up equations between them perfectly and without emotion.

He was glad he had killed her. She had been driving him crazy.

No one in Bethany had troubled him with her absence after the general investigation was over except occasionally his father and, one afternoon in autumn at the river, Prince Hal.

It was late October and he had met Prince Hal at the usual

244

place, just below Frank Adler's old cottage. They met to hunt for snakes, but that was an excuse to be together, since Will was no longer interested in the hunt for snakes and Hal had never been. The day was cool and crisp and they sat on high rocks, just beyond the shore, took off their shoes and socks, rolled up their jeans and hung their legs in the water running winter-cold.

"Cesca's writing a song now about the night of the hurricane," Prince Hal said, standing on the slippery rocks so the river splashed his knees.

"I thought she already had, about Billy Naylor," Will said.

"This one's about us. You and Frank Adler and me," Prince Hal said. He tore a broken branch off a tree and used it as a walking stick to move from rock to rock.

"If she has to write a song about me, I'd prefer on the whole it be about lion taming than drowning," Hal said, although certainly he was pleased to be sung about all over America, as was happening with Cesca's songs.

"Pretty soon, everyone in Bethany is going to have his own Francesca Woodbine original." Will grabbed Hal's walking stick. "BETHANY, U.S.A." He held the stick aloft and waved an imaginary flag.

In the shallow part of the river, Prince Hal collected rocks— ordinary black rocks, some worn smooth and oval, some round with jagged edges, some geometric, chipped from larger rocks and without interest even for a rock collector, which Hal was not. He simply liked to collect whatever was in the vicinity. He examined the rocks, however, feigning geological interest. He washed them in the current, spread them out on the large rock where he was sitting. He was not, however, thinking about rocks. What he was thinking about was Celia Hamilton and the circumstances of her disappearance and why a sweet, sensitive boy as everyone knew Will Weaver to be seemed so little troubled by her sudden absence from his life.

"I suppose sooner or later, she'll write a song about Celia," Hal said. He rubbed a small gray rock dry with his cotton shirt and put it in a pattern with the rest.

Will Weaver crouched on a rock beside Hal, stirred the water with the walking stick he'd taken.

"She doesn't know much about Celia—not enough to write a song about her. No one did," he said.

Just beyond him, in the black water, flipping under the surface like ribbon, was a small young snake which caught Will's practiced eye. He reached out and lifted the snake with the end of his stick.

"You know Cesca sees things," Hal said, surprised at his own uncommon provocation. "That's the source of her songs."

"She doesn't see everything." Will whirled the stick with the snake around, close to the surface of the water.

He lifted the snake in the air on the end of the walking stick and flipped it like a whip in Hal's direction.

"Watch out!" he called. "Copperhead."

Hal threw his arms out in front of him and fell over, landing backwards in the cold water. The snake Will had thrown at him fell just beyond his legs. He scrambled up and looked in the water just as the snake slithered by.

"It's just an ordinary snake, isn't it, Will?" Hal asked.

"Who knows?" Will shrugged. "It looked like a copperhead to me."

By the time Hal got out of the cold water onto the bank, the snake had swum downriver to join its companions.

"You'll freeze your tail off if you don't go home and change," Will said. He picked up his tennis shoes and socks and tossed Hal's on the shore. They walked up the hill to Hawthorne silently together.

Will was on edge.

At the bottom of Hawthorne, they said goodbye.

"You really think that was a copperhead?" Hal asked.

"There may have been an orange diamond on that snake's head; I'm not sure," Will said. "Sometimes the sun plays tricks."

When he woke up Saturday morning, Prince Hal knew he was going to leave home. Tobias had come over. He lay on the wool rug in Hal's bedroom and let the cats wander without interest across his back. Occasionally, he'd grasp a tail and hold it until the trapped cat moved or turned around to bite his hand.

"Please, Toby," Hal said. "Don't tease the cats."

Toby didn't reply. He closed his eyes and grabbed another tail or leg or rolled over, trapping a small kitten beneath him.

Since Christmas he had grown leggy and awkward. The soft, fleshy baby face had given way to the sharper angles of a boy's, and his large eyes held on to trouble.

"I wish you were my father," he said to Hal.

"I'm your uncle," Hal said. "Close enough."

"I know that, dummy. I just wish you weren't."

He crawled halfway under the bed on his stomach and growled.

"What are you doing now, Toby?" Hal asked, unsettled by the changes in his nephew.

"Looking for enemies," Tobias said.

"Tobias is a monster," Hal said to Sophia at lunch.

"It's his age," Sophia said. She made tuna fish sandwiches.

"This has been going on since Christmas," Hal said. "He pulls the cats' tails. He bites and breaks things. Sometimes he acts like he ought to be institutionalized."

"He'll outgrow this stage, darling," Sophia said. "It isn't easy not to have a father."

"You think that's it?" Hal asked.

"Francesca is preoccupied."

They sat across the table from each other and listened to Tobias make wildlife sounds in Hal's bedroom—the roar of a lion, the high silly chatter of monkeys, the long screech of a coyote. Hal put his hands over his ears.

"I can't stand it," he said.

Julian burst in from the library, where he was reading.

"Sophia," he said. "It's Saturday morning. Do something."

"I'll get him." Sophia got up.

"Why is Cesca preoccupied?" Hal asked. "Her music?"

"I don't think she's preoccupied with singing," Sophia said.

"What do you think?" Hal followed his mother into his

bedroom, where Tobias stood on the top of a desk with a striped cat draped over his shoulders.

"Love perhaps," Sophia said. The idea had crossed her mind.

"Me jungle boy!" Tobias shouted, and leaped to the bed, landing to a loud screech on the cat's hind legs.

"Lunch, Toby." Sophia reached out her arms to him. He pulled away.

"Mommy kissed Will Weaver," he said combatively. "I bet you didn't know that." He picked up a golden angora kitten resting in Hal's sock drawer and kissed it firmly on the lips. "See. She kissed him like this." Smack, smack, smack, he went, and dropped the kitten back in with the socks.

Prince Hal lay on his bed. The angora, recovered sufficiently to purr in small snatches, rested on his stomach, and downstairs Hal could hear his mother easing Toby's sadness as she had done with them. The April sun slid out from between the clouds and flooded him with light; ignited, the golden kitten on his belly dazzled.

Francesca and Will Weaver. The thought made him light-headed, like the onset of a stomach virus. In the bottom drawer of his desk, he kept the circus schedule Amal had sent to him. April 3, 1965, the circus would be arriving in Raleigh, North Carolina, to play for three days. He would leave after supper.

He didn't question why Francesca and Will Weaver had settled his destiny—or even wish to know. He simply knew that the idea of Will Weaver with his beloved sister filled him with dread.

"I'm sorry to hear that Ces is interested in Will," he said to his parents at supper that evening.

"He's odd but sweet, and I like him," Sophia said. "Surely he's harmless."

"His father loved your mother for years," Julian said.

"We all know that," Hal said. And the subject of Will was dropped.

By ten thirty that evening, Hal had walked to Main Street to the taxi stand in front of Leonora's Books and Records, where the single taxi in Bethany, Massachusetts, driven either by Ace Stats or by his son, Ace Junior, was sometimes parked. Across the street, Father John walked his insomniac route from the Catholic church to Rooster's Tavern and back again, leaning heavily on a cane. He lifted his hand to Hal.

"Leaving on vacation?" he jested.

"Yes," Hal replied. "Of course."

Upstairs, over Leonora's, Hal could see the shadow of his sister against the pale walls; her hair was up, a cockeyed urn on top of her head. He could see the back of Will Weaver on the stepladder arranging books. The taxicab was there, and he climbed in. Ace Junior was driving. Ace put out one cigarette and lit another, turned on the radio to All-Music Boston.

"I'm going to the bus station in Salem," Hal said.

Ace Junior did a U-turn.

"Maybe we'll catch your sister on WQRM," Ace said. "Who knows? This could be our lucky night."

Francesca was at the window when the taxicab turned. Hal saw her there framed by the light behind her, disheveled, her hair lazily across her face, her blouse too large. Like their grandmother. There was a picture Sophia had of their grandmother on the fire escape at Rooster's Tavern. On the back, full of self-mockery, she had written "*Santa Francesca Allegra, 'Dressed for Work,' Rooster's Tavern, 1916.*"

"So," Ace Junior said, guessing exactly what was going on with Hal. "You going on a short or long trip?"

"A long one," Hal said.

"Don't stay away forever," Ace Junior said when they pulled up in front of the bus depot in Salem.

"Nothing's forever, Ace Junior," Hal replied.

In the bus station, he counted his money. One hundred fifty-six dollars. Not enough to last for long unless the circus took him on soon.

Francesca stopped in the middle of the living room and listened. Downstairs at Leonora's, she heard Will Weaver putting up books. She had expected him tonight, even though it was Saturday and late and everybody else their age and attached was dancing at Rooster's. Last night he had worked late too, and she had gone downstairs after ten to find him sitting next to the cash register doing the books.

"Hello," she'd said, suddenly shy with this man she had known since childhood. "I thought I heard you here."

"I worked late tonight so I could listen to you compose," he said. "It makes me very happy."

She sat down on a stool across from him, conscious of her body as if it were in the process of being formed by an artist in love with the pear shape of a woman's breast. She rested her chin in her hand.

"So," she said. "I'm writing about a physician who loves a woman married to someone else." She made it up. She was not writing about Sam Weaver at all. She simply wanted trouble.

"My father," Will said.

"How did you guess?" She laughed.

He reached out and touched her lips.

"I know you very well," he said. "I always have."

She smiled, flooded with sex.

He had known her forever, since childhood. Before Colin Mallory. Perhaps he even knew about Colin Mallory, or guessed at what had happened and forgave her, or loved her in spite of that dark knowledge. She knew he had watched her everywhere. And you know people you love with that kind of adoration because you memorize them. She leaned across the counter and kissed him, parted his lips with her tongue and flew inside, a small hummingbird teasing the back of his throat.

Tobias saw this. He had wandered downstairs after his mother and had stood at the door to Leonora's in darkness. He could see Will and Francesca by the desk light on the counter, but they could not see him.

When he saw his mother kiss Will Weaver, he went back upstairs, took off his T-shirt and shorts and underpants and crawled under the double bed in Cesca's room.

If she wanted him ever again, he thought, she would have to find him and pull him out and promise him over and over again "I will never kiss Will Weaver on the lips" until the words became a chant like Hail Mary, full of grace, the Lord is with thee. And he believed her.

"Tobias?" She had walked upstairs and looked in the living room for him and the bath, in the kitchen and his own room, decorated in ships. "Toby, love?" she called. She even looked in Maud's room, knocking first just in case the man with whom Maud was sleeping lately had not taken her to a hotel. She went back downstairs and looked up Main Street. There was no sign of Toby. She checked her watch. She had been with Will such a short time—less than ten minutes. She opened the door to Leonora's. "You didn't see Toby, did you?"

"No, I didn't," Will said.

She blew him a kiss.

What a funny thing, she thought. Of all of the people in the world, in Bethany at least—and "with all your opportunities" as Maud would say—to be called out of the desert by so strange and familiar a young man as Will Weaver.

She checked the closets in the apartment, even the broom closet, under the skirted table in the living room which held the picture of the Count, under the beds, and there he was, curled up next to the wall, as far away from her as he could possibly get.

She got down on her stomach and tried to reach his leg with her hand, but he pulled away wrapped his arms around his legs. "No," he said. His eyes were tight shut.

"Tobias?" she pulled the bed away from the wall, but he scrambled and kept moving to stay under it. She pushed until the bed was all the way across the room, and then she reached just in time to grab his arm and pull him, kicking, out.

He would not be touched.

"What is going on with you, darling?" she asked, sitting across from him on the floor.

His eyes flashed with anger.

"Well," she said quietly. "It's after ten and I am going to sleep."

When she came out of the bathroom in her nightgown, he had not moved from the place where he was sitting. He squeezed his eyes shut.

"I suppose I'll read *Jane Eyre* tonight," she said. "But first let's read *Charlotte's Web* together. We're on page thirty-five. Would you like some chocolate before we go to bed? I'm going to get some for myself."

She put his pajamas down beside him, but he made no effort to dress. She got into bed with *Jane Eyre* and pretended to read, but her thoughts were full of Will Weaver. She heard Toby dressing. He put on his pajama bottoms and walked over to her bed.

"I want you to promise to never kiss Will Weaver on the lips again," he said in a small, earnest voice.

She took his hand, but he pulled away and stuck his hand down his pajama bottoms.

"You followed me downstairs?" she asked.

"Promise me," Tobias said. "Please."

"I cannot promise that."

"Why not?"

Toby fell on her then and bit her shoulder hard. He pounded the bed with his fist, went to his own room, climbed under the covers and finally went to sleep.

It was Saturday, and the clock over the kitchen sink said 10:30. Downstairs Francesca could hear Will Weaver fold the stepladder. She was alone. Tobias was spending the night with Michael Sawyer, in third grade. She had expected a telephone call by now from Mrs. Sawyer to say either that Toby wanted to come home immediately or else that he'd bopped Mikey Sawyer on the head and could she come get him.

Since Christmas, Tobias had been impossible. The third-grade teacher said he needed more or less attention, she couldn't tell which—but guessed at more attention since Cesca had become well known. Sophia said not to worry, he would out-grow this stage—although today, Julian had said he could not visit unless he outgrew the stage immediately. Maud, who endured the worst of Tobias' performances, was spending her weekends in hotels with Mr. San ever since Tobias had poured cranberry juice all over Mr. San's white shirt the last time he had spent the night.

"Perhaps you should take Toby to a child psychiatrist," James had suggested. "There's a good clinic at Boston Children's. I can help you with that."

"Never," Cesca said furiously. "He's perfectly all right. It's a stage. Mama, who ought to know, after all, says he's in a stage."

She was furious at his troubles, which she believed were her own doing. After all, she asked herself, as she watched the sweet and serious boy in the terrible process of transformation, what could be expected of a child with his history— what black seed born of her own fury had multiplied in his curled body as he grew to birth?

Meanwhile, through the winter into spring, Francesca had been writing the stories of Bethany, discovering in the blighted lives of her own town, crouched just beneath the surface of pretended happiness, mysteries of the human heart.

Downstairs, Will Weaver put away the stepladder, stacked the empty boxes of books, closed the ledger and called his father to say he might be spending the night out.

"With whom?" Sam Weaver, asked, surprised. Will never spent the night out.

"I'm going out with Francesca," Will said.

When Cesca had kissed him last night, there had been no hallucinations like the ones with Celia. No demons, no messages from his mother. Perhaps, he had thought, driving home that night to his father's house, killing Celia Hamilton had cured him.

"I didn't know you were going out with Cesca." Sam was alarmed at the thought of his son with Francesca Woodbine.

"It's just beginning," Will said, full of pleasure.

"Well," Sam said. What could he say to this strange son? he thought, loading the dishwasher, scouring the one frying pan in the sink. "I'll see you in the morning."

Ever since Celia Hamilton's disappearance, Sam had feared the telephone bore bad news.

"Will is so much more normal than he's ever been," Oliver had said. "After all, he's given up snakes. He must be better."

"I suppose I preferred it when he spent the day in his room with the dreadful snakes than this worry over what is taking their place." Sam was plagued by an insistent memory of disaster which had no connection with his actual knowledge of events.

Will turned off the light, locked the door and went upstairs to Francesca's apartment. She was expecting him. She had, in fact, just checked outside to see if Will was leaving and noticed Ace Junior's taxicab make a U-turn. She didn't see Prince Hal, but Will's car was still parked at the meter on Main Street, and Will himself—she was sure that was who was knocking at the door.

"Hello." She stood aside to let him enter.

"I heard you singing," he said.

"A new song," she said. "I just finished it today."

He sat down on the edge of the couch beside the piano.

"Sing it," he said.

She was lovely, the way her hair fell just cockeyed at an angle on her head, the way her blouse billowed, the way her skirts spread soft blankets under the piano. Like his mother, he thought. And then, with great effort, he brushed that dangerous suggestion out of his mind. Not like my mother, he almost said aloud.

"I told you about it. It's called 'The Ballad of the Undrowned Boy.'"

When she had finished singing—he had not even listened to the words, so taken was he with the moment—she leaned over and kissed him. He held his hand against her breast and she fell against him, pulled him down with her on the couch.

"No one's here," she said.

He didn't know what to say.

"Maybe we should go for a drive." He got up awkwardly. "Then we can come back for something to drink. Have you ever been to the marshes?" he asked.

"I wrote a song about the marshes, remember?"

"But have you been there?"

"Once with James. That's where Louisa's car landed in the hurricane." She did not mention the time with Tim Greenfield.

"Well, it's very pretty. Full of birds."

"Then let's go," she said, and kissed the ends of his fingers, the corners of his lips, "and hurry, before Tobias bops Mikey Sawyer and has to come home."

The spring snow had stopped. The night was unusually dark, still and starless and damp enough that Cesca's hair was actually wet. Will turned the car around, passed Father John, who leaned against the black wrought-iron gate, haloed by the street light.

Father John noticed Francesca. Her head was slightly out the window, so the wind blew her hair off her face. He couldn't exactly see her face, but he could imagine that lovely face in memory. Although she didn't look like Francesca Allegra, she suggested her to him. He stood on the pavement and watched Will Weaver's car fly out of town towards Ewes. Surfacing in his mind's picture of Francesca, double-exposed, was the clear image of Will Weaver on the night before the Fourth of July ripping up the cardboard replica of Cesca Woodbine. Slowly, Father John made his way upstairs to his flat over the parish hall, struck by a cold emotion. His pulse was fast, his mouth was dry, he was light-headed, as if the moment were life-threatening.

He ought to warn Sophia, he thought. He checked the clock and it was after eleven. What would he say to her? Your daughter has gone off with Will Weaver, the beloved Will Weaver, treasure of Bethany, Massachusetts? He ought to have told someone what he had witnessed with Will at the time— Sophia perhaps, or Julian. What reservations detained him from participating in the world of human affairs? he asked himself severely.

He dressed for bed in a white dressing gown, lowered himself to his knees on the velvet cushion of the kneeling bench. But all he could think of on this prayerless night was Santa Francesca's soft sweet flesh. And how he had loved her.

Will turned left off the main road onto Marsh Road and drove past the high cattails and reeds to the narrow path that led to the deepest part of the marsh, where the white, white bones of Celia Hamilton, picked clean of flesh, lay underwater, flooded by the melting snows of New England's long, cold winter.

Prince Hal settled into the back of the bus to Boston. There were very few passengers. One tall, serene and well-dressed woman in the front seat sobbed throughout the trip. He took an interest in her tenacious weeping. She seemed too well dressed for buses, too austere for public display. He was inclined to offer his condolences.

But in Everett, she got off the bus and fell into the arms of a round bald man, smaller than she was, and Hal was glad he had not made inquiry.

What are we, after all, in one another's lives but bystanders, visitors to sadness we are pleased to have missed on this round of fortune? He thought of Francesca. What happened, he wondered, when her eyes turned inward? Were the lights out? Did they dilate in darkness so she could see trouble take form in front of her?

He could not bear witness to his family's sadness. He was glad to have left, glad especially to be on his way to a made-up life where the cats in his bedroom would be lions and he would be in charge of the magic.

Julian Woodbine was a realist. He knew his limitations; as a man who held no court with illusions, he put aside bad news. Unlike the rest of the family, with the possible exception of James, he had no romantic notions about bad news. So for years, he had not thought about the gun that had been missing after Colin Mallory's murder or the possibility of Francesca's involvement. Until lately. As Prince Hal, unbeknownst to his family, rode to Boston, Julian was thinking about Francesca. In the last few weeks something was new in his daughter's life. She was familiar to him again. He lay on his pillow in the silver moonlight, Sophia's breath soft on his neck—she was not sleeping yet—and wondered why he was suddenly reminded of Francesca as she had been when Colin Mallory was alive. He recalled her just weeks before the wedding, gently rounded with Colin's son, flushed with anticipation of a perfect life.

"Sophia"—he rolled over on his side, put his leg across her hips—"what do you think is going on with Ces lately?"

Sophia stretched. Her breast came out of the deep V of her nightgown and Julian covered it with his hand.

"Love."

"You think so?"

"She may be falling in love with Will Weaver, don't you think?"

She put her head on his shoulder.

"She reminds me of herself before Colin died."

"It's lovely, isn't it?"

"I suppose." He turned on the reading light. "But I associate that mood in her with Colin's death, not with falling in love."

"It's sex you notice." Sophia turned on her stomach.

"Danger. That's what I notice. Tornado weather."

Sophia laughed softly.

"Of course, it's always dangerous weather when you fall in love."

Outside their door, Prince Hal's cats were prowling. Julian could hear them, insomniac, stalking one another in the upstairs hall. Each time he almost fell asleep, cat sounds—a thin meow, a soft shuffle—startled him awake again.

"I'm going to put the cats back in Hal's room," he said to a sleeping Sophia, and got up.

In the hall, deaf Sebastian, Hal's all-white cat, chased a water bug across the floor. Julian picked up Sebastian, took another cat languorously clawing a cane chair under his arm and pushed open the door to Hal's bedroom with his foot. The light was on and the bed was made. Julian dropped the cats on the bed with several others already sleeping, closed the door and went downstairs. The kitchen light was on as

257

well; a small, unattractive tabby was quite happily lying in a fruit bowl, and there was a note from Hal underneath the grocery list.

"Sophia." He shook her by the shoulder. "Hal has gone."

Sophia put on her robe and went downstairs. Julian had left the note on the kitchen table. She turned it face down without reading.

"What are we going to do?" He sat across from her. "It's almost midnight."

"There's nothing to do."

"He may be at Francesca's," Julian said. "I'm going to call. I'll call the police."

No one answered at Francesca's.

"She may be out with Will Weaver. Don't call the police until morning. He says where he is in the note. Let's let him go. We can't stop him in any case."

Julian ripped the deep pink petals from the carnations on the kitchen table.

"He wouldn't grow," Julian said crossly, as if Hal had carefully chosen an affliction to diminish his father.

"He couldn't grow, Julian." Sophia slipped the note into her pocket.

Julian called James.

Hendrik Andrews answered the telephone at James's apartment. He was at James's house for Louisa's birthday. Since January, when Elena had broken her arm driving her wheelchair down the front steps of the Boston Home for Disturbed Children and ended up at Mass General, where James was Chief Resident, Hendrik and James had become friends.

James liked Hendrik enormously.

"I've never had a real friendship with a man since I was a child," he said to Louisa, "and I feel as if I could have one with Hendrik."

"He's more complicated than you think," Louisa said.

"I didn't say he was simple; I said he interests me."

"He's obsessed," said Louisa, who was herself attracted to Hendrik Andrews and pleased to have his company.

"I don't know what he's obsessed with. Maybe his sister. Not the toy store."

"He just strikes me as a man obsessed," Louisa said. "That's why I find him interesting." She would have been disturbed to know that the obsession she observed in Hendrik had to do with Francesca Woodbine.

"You've gone cockeyed," his mother said to Hendrik. "I wish you'd sell the toy store, go back to medical school and get married."

"It's enough to have one demented child, not to mention a perfectly normal son in love with the voice of a rock star," his father said.

"Folksinger," Hendrik had replied.

"Big difference," his father said.

Shortly after she departed without her raccoon, Emily had told his parents about Francesca. She thought of herself as family, she said, and expressed a serious concern about Hendrik's mental state. She described the scene of his dancing with a cardboard replica of Francesca Woodbine and suggested the family seek professional advice.

"Of course she thinks I'm mentally incompetent," Hendrik said. "I wasn't in love with her."

"Maybe you should find a nice girl from your own class," his mother said.

"The nice girls of my class are fat and have been married for years, as you very well know."

"Yes," Mrs. Andrews said sadly. "They are quickly fat. It's tragic." She tried another tactic. "So if you like this girl who sings dirty songs about queers on the radio, why don't you ask her out, like any other normal boy would do?"

"I'll give that some thought, Mother. I'm a methodical man and it will take time," he said. But the fact was he had made plans to lie in wait. Instinct told him that Francesca was not ready.

During the gray days of winter when business was slow at

Uncle Ben's, he played *Mating Calls* until Francesca's deep, resonant voice was a part of him. He imagined her everywhere—in the kitchen, familiar as the smell of coffee; her long gown brushed his bare knees. In the living room, framed by the morning sun, she stood in a long skirt, her breasts uncovered. She brushed her hair, knelt where he was sitting and spread her hair softly over his legs. Sometimes he thought, with impressive objectivity, that he had fallen off the edge of sanity and would never be a normal man again. If anyone could examine the scenes on the inside of his brain, he would be institutionalized. Perhaps he was ill. Nevertheless, the illness gave him such pleasure, he hoped it would last forever.

Francesca lay on the hood of Will Weaver's car and looked at the sky. The air was dusty with wet snow, not cold, and her face was pleasantly damp. Will had left the headlights on. Otherwise it was too dark to see. And quiet. No bird racket in the gentle storm to disturb the silence.

"It's better in summer," Will said, lying on the hood of the car beside her. "The sounds are spectacular."

Cesca took his hand and held it against her lips.

"I like it with the snow." She put his wet fingers in her mouth.

He lay with his eyes closed and concentrated. He was afraid he was going to say something about Celia which would suggest her presence close at hand. Or else, he was afraid she could materialize in this white air, brushing their bodies with her breath.

"Will." Francesca turned towards him.

He didn't open his eyes.

"Do you ever miss Celia?" she asked.

"Yes, of course," he said quickly. "I miss her." And he kissed Cesca hard on the lips.

In the car, Francesca turned on the radio very low.

"You never mention her at all." She pulled her knees up under her skirt and rested against him.

"I suppose I think she's dead." Will backed the car slowly along Marsh Road.

"Dead?" It had occurred to Francesca that Celia was dead. She was fascinated by the thought of her death or the manner of it. On several occasions she had started to write a song called variously "Cora," "Mary," "Sasha," about a girl who leaves home and disappears. The girl in her songs was on a search. In "Cora," she went from bus station to bus station; in "Sasha—gone, forever gone for now," Cesca wrote from the point of view of the lover left behind—Will's point of view—and in "Mary," she wrote about a gentle girl who runs away to join a group of political revolutionaries and is burned up when the house in which she is living explodes from bombs kept in the cellar. But none of the songs seemed true to the actual character of Celia as Cesca had known her. Celia was simply not the kind of woman to disappear. She was solid and simple; she would not leave without a forwarding address.

Ever since Will Weaver had blossomed spring peonies in her mind, Francesca's imagination was full of Celia Hamilton: what had gone on between them; had he loved her? had she loved him? why had she left when their lives seemed inextricable?

Recently, driven to write about Celia, perhaps even jealous of this absent woman who might return in a swan hat and steal Will Weaver away from her, Francesca had started a new song called "The Girl with Ribbons in Her Hair." The girl, dizzily in love, allows herself to be seduced into the woods by a young man who in the act of seduction is transformed into a monster and strangles her with the ribbons in her hair.

"That one is simply too disturbing to record," Maud said to her.

"I know," Cesca said. "But I can't get it out of my mind." So she tore it up—lyrics and music both, because the composition simply called forth the same story every time she tried to put new words to it.

"She could have been hit by a car," Will said, turning onto the main road. "Or died of pneumonia in San Francisco. Ter-

261

rible things happen to these young runaways. She could have been murdered, I suppose."

"Otherwise she would have written," Cesca said. "She wasn't the kind of girl to lose contact."

Will put his hand on Cesca's and kissed her lightly on the neck.

"I suppose you could die without any identification and the police would give up trying to find relatives. But I don't think she was murdered," Cesca said.

"Why?" Suddenly Will wanted Cesca to know, pleased with himself to have managed to kill Celia, to have been yards away from her bones just now and Cesca, with all her powers of sight, had not suspected.

"It's statistically unlikely. I don't believe there could have been two murders in Bethany in so short a time. The town is too small."

"Colin was murdered for reasons. Billy Naylor did it—you know that. And Celia Hamilton wasn't from Bethany." Will was determined.

Cesca kissed his hand.

"I don't want to talk about Celia," she said. "Why don't you come upstairs? Maud's out all night."

Upstairs in Francesca's bedroom, they would make love, he thought. She would take off her full blouse and her breasts would fall, peach flesh, into his mouth. He took her hand.

The lights were out in her bedroom, and he stood in the doorway while she walked across the room to turn on a small lamp on a round table beside her bed.

There, seated in a flowered chair next to the lamp, was his mother. She had taken the straps of a long white gown off her shoulders so her breasts fell free, and her hands were folded in her lap. She wore a heavy diamond pendant around her neck; and her head was gone. "Turn off the light," he said.

"Can you see without it?" Cesca asked.

"I can see fine."

She came across the room to him, lifted her arms, opened his lips with her finger and kissed him.

"Come." She took his hand.

"Keep the lights off, please," he said.

There was, she remembered much later, a feeling of desperation about his person, but at the time she believed he was full of desire.

He had imagined this moment long ago when he was a boy. She sat on the high four-poster bed and he unbuttoned her blouse. It was soft cotton, silky after many washings, and he pulled it off her arms, dropped it on the floor and gently brushed his hands across her breasts.

At that moment, Mrs. Sawyer called. She had been calling since ten thirty, she said. Tobias had hit Mikey Sawyer with a baseball bat intentionally, and they'd already been to the emergency room. Could Francesca come immediately and pick Tobias up. "I have been trying to get you for two hours," Mrs. Sawyer said. "I called several times from the pay phone at the hospital."

Francesca fell across the bed.

"I have to go," she said. "Tobias has made trouble."

Will was grateful for the interruption. "Don't worry," he said. He did not want anything to happen to Francesca. A part of his rational mind wanted desperately to protect her from himself. "I'll take you to pick him up and then go home."

Later, Francesca put Tobias to bed. She kissed him good night and said they'd talk about the incident in the morning.

"I want to move to Salem," Tobias said.

"Why Salem, darling?"

"I want to live with my other grandparents," he said combatively. "Or else New York City and live in an apartment with an elevator.

The telephone was ringing.

"That's probably the police," Tobias said. "They're calling to arrest me."

The call was James in Boston.

"Where were you?" he asked. "I've been calling for hours."

"Out with Will Weaver and then picking Toby up at a former friend's house."

"Will Weaver?" James asked. "Are you seeing Will Weaver?"

"I'm in love with Will," Cesca said. "Why?"

"I am just surprised. That's all."

He had called about Hal.

"He should have finished high school," James said crossly.

"He couldn't finish," Cesca said. "He simply couldn't."

"Of course he could," James said. "He wouldn't."

She did not go to bed. She lay down on the living-room couch, still partly dressed, with the lights off, and looked out the front window into the black night.

On rare occasions, songs arrived complete. They flew into her mind like butterflies, and paused long enough for her to see their design. That night "The Ballad of the Snake Boy" came to her just before she fell asleep.

She turned on the living-room light, sat down at the piano and worked.

Across the street, Father John, unable to fold his old body into bed, was at the bay window overlooking Main Street. He saw the light go on in Francesca's apartment and could see her at the piano. For a while he stood and watched her. Tomorrow, he decided firmly, he would tell her what Will Weaver had done the night before the Fourth of July. She should be warned.

At the bus station in Boston, Prince Hal bought a postcard and sat on one of the wooden benches to wait the night out for the morning bus to Raleigh.

"Dear, dear Cesca," he began. *"I'm off to the circus, as you've guessed. I'll call as soon as I get safely to Raleigh. Please be careful. Love, Hal."* He bought a stamp and mailed the card immediately. Then he curled up on the wooden bench and fell asleep.

It was four o'clock when Cesca finished "The Ballad of the Snake Boy." She lay down on the couch, pulled an afghan up to her shoulders and fell into a deep, innocent sleep dreaming of Will Weaver.

2. Queen of Hearts

At dawn on Sunday morning, Francesca awoke suddenly and in a cold terror. Something had happened. Somewhere in Massachusetts or Bethany or in her own house, there was a disturbance to the order of the day. She knew it.

She slid quickly out of bed and ran to Tobias' room, where she found him as usual splayed across the bed on his stomach, quite alive in the pale light of early morning. She called her parents, and Julian answered in a clear voice, unfazed by sleep, as if he had passed from one level of consciousness to the next without sacrificing absolute control.

"Is everything all right?" Cesca asked.

Everything was fine, he said, except Prince Hal, which she already knew and was to be expected, after all. He seemed relieved by Hal's departure, as if his worst fears had been realized and were mercifully not unbearable.

"I'm sorry to call so early," she said. "I woke up with premonitions."

She put on coffee and took a shower, but the fear had grown as distinct as another body in the shower with her.

In the kitchen, she turned on the radio to her own voice singing "Betrayal" again. She changed the station. She took a peach out of the refrigerator, poured Grape-Nuts and sat down to listen to the 7 A.M. news.

The news from Boston was local: A one-year-old boy from Watertown had been run over by a train. There'd been a four-car collision on Route 9 in which two people had been killed, one an infant girl sitting on her mother's lap. A fire in Dedham had destroyed an apartment building, but no one had been injured. A young man in Boston had been arrested on suspicion of killing his wife, a former twirler at East Wing High School, by beating her with her own baton. The local news

265

was all bad. Cesca's mind wandered to the possibility of killing a grown woman with a baton. She got coffee and went into the living room to wait for morning to arrive in full force, for the street to fill with people going to church or Hanrahan's, for Tobias to wake up. They'd go on a trip today, she thought; maybe to Boston to see James. She wanted Maud to come home so she could sing "The Ballad of the Snake Boy" to her.

By the time Tobias did wake up and wandered sleepily into the living room, Francesca was locked in her seat overlooking Main Street, paralyzed by familiar dread.

At eight thirty, Will Weaver called to inquire about Tobias.

"That's sweet of you," Cesca said. "I haven't found out what happened last night yet. He just woke up."

He asked if she'd like to go for a long walk in the marsh. There is a path at the marsh, he said, which goes completely around the lake. The day was beautiful, the snow had gone and birds should be in abundance.

"Bring Toby," he said.

"I'll call you back," she replied. "I feel strange today."

"Are you ill?"

"Not exactly." But it was like an illness which she had had before.

After Colin died, she had felt ill for weeks, certain that everyone in Bethany, Massachusetts, knew. So why now? she asked herself. Was it Tobias' recent alteration—as if the seeds of her destruction had been planted deep as blue eyes in his genes?

"So, darling," she said, touching his hand lightly, hoping that her voice betrayed nothing but maternal confidence, "what happened last night?"

"Not much," Toby said. "I don't like Mikey or his mother." He sat down across from her with his cereal. "He teased me. He always teases me. He says you write dirty songs and everyone in Bethany is afraid you'll write songs about them. He said his parents talked about you at the dinner table. So I hit him."

"You should not pay any attention to him," Cesca said.

"I said you were at home writing a dirty song about him. Which I hope you were."

"You won't be invited for sleep-overs if you fight," Cesca said.

"I don't want to be invited for sleep-overs," Tobias said. "I want to move to someplace like Kansas with you. I don't like Bethany any longer. It's full of retarded people."

Maud called to say she would not be coming home until that night and Sophia called to ask if Cesca had heard from Hal, and James to invite Francesca to dinner with Hendrik Andrews, which she refused, and Will Weaver to ask again about a walk in the marsh.

"Not today," Francesca said. "I think I'll spend the day with Tobias." She went into the kitchen after she had hung up with Will.

"Would you like to go for a long walk in the bird preserve?" she asked.

"Not with Will Weaver," Tobias said.

"With me."

"What's there?"

"Birds. Turtles, I suppose. And snakes."

"Is that all?" Tobias asked.

"Maybe we'll find something exciting," Cesca said, and she went into her room to change her clothes.

Father John, standing at his window, saw Francesca get up. He would telephone her immediately. Already this morning he had heard four confessions—a long one from Mrs. Hill, who came every week—and much as he wished she would do something sinful enough to keep him awake, the most Delia Hill could manage was a thimbleful of hatred for her mother and occasional lust for Mr. Hill's twin brother. Maia Perrault had come and listed a series of ordinary sins mostly having to do with avarice, but he knew she had something more to tell him. He didn't press for information. He was no longer interested in personal lives. More and more lately, his affections floated inwards, traveling the back paths of memory. He liked the daily and impersonal habits of living—the order of his apartment; the time it took to make toast and spread it with marmalade, to sit at his breakfast table with a mug of coffee and vase of sunny daffodils overlooking the order of the day as it started on Main Street. He liked the business of survival—his teeth, his cassock musty with his own odor, the making of his bed with the sky blue coverlet smooth as paper. He never changed the sheets. He was not an unclean man; he peed in the bowl and even with age didn't drip, like the old men smelling of urine who shuffled into the confession box with nothing to confess—not even fantasies flooded their lives any longer. He liked to read, although his eyes were not very good; he'd read a paragraph of Saint Augustine or Thomas Aquinas and test himself. Could he think about the paragraph in philosophical terms? Could he hold a concept in mind for long enough to give consideration? Could he recall details? On the whole, he was very pleased after these exercises. His mind was good—perhaps even excellent for a man his age.

He had not lost sympathy for humankind, but his sympathy was general. "Lambs of God" was how he thought of his parishioners: a little stupid, perhaps, and ordinary; nevertheless he had compassion and counted himself amongst them.

But he missed the bright meteor of feeling he remembered like the taste of chocolate from his youth. If he had a wish for his age, it was not, as the old men in Bethany often said to him, to die a peaceful death, but on the contrary, to shoot out of the world unanesthetized—to know once more in the marrow of his bones how it felt to be alive.

After four-o'clock Mass every afternoon when the business of the day was done, he played Mozart. Always the radio was turned to the classical-music station; in the late afternoon, he sat down in the low leather chair with a sherry, sometimes two, closed his eyes, put his feet on the coffee table and listened to Mozart concertos. In this ritual hour between day and night, Santa Francesca came home to him.

Tobias answered his call.

"She's dressing," Toby said, but he decided he ought to get her if a priest was calling.

"I saw you in your window this morning while I was having my breakfast," Father John said, his heart beating foolishly, "and I was reminded there's a matter I want to speak to you about."

He paused. He had not really considered this conversation—whether he would tell her about Will Weaver on the telephone or ask her to come over now before the ten-o'clock Mass. The matter seemed suddenly pressing; or was he, he asked himself, just an old man anticipating death so all matters seemed either insignificant or pressing?

"In the afternoon, I have sherry and listen to Mozart," he said. "Perhaps you could come today."

"I'd like to very much," Francesca said.

"About five," he said. He hung up the telephone, his face flushed—with pleasure, perhaps, or excitement; he didn't know exactly, but the day suddenly took on meaning that had not accumulated on the calendar for years.

The morning was bright and wet from the soft snow of the previous night, and the marshes were like an oil painting in their brilliance. Cesca parked her car just off the path and walked with Tobias through the high reeds and cattails to the slender path that circled the marsh. The water was high and muddy. Beige stalks danced on the surface in a light wind which blew that morning across the coastline. The air was rich with vegetation, ringing with the songs of birds.

Francesca and Toby walked single file, Toby first. He carried a long stick with which he brushed the tops of the cattails. Occasionally he left the path, slogged through the low marsh water up to the top of his Bean boots and stirred the water with his stick: "Looking for surprises," he told Francesca. "Maybe dangerous ones," he said happily. He held her hand.

"I don't know why you like Will Weaver," Tobias said, picking up another stick the same size and using them both as crutches, hopping along the path.

"I can't understand why you *don't* like him, darling," Cesca said. "Everyone in Bethany does."

"I'm different," Toby said matter-of-factly. "I'm just different because my father was murdered. I don't know anybody in the world whose father was murdered. Or at least, not in Bethany."

A small brown snake wriggled across their path unafraid,

269

and Tobias picked it up, let it weave its long slender torso back and forth across his hands and then put it down again. "I ought to move to Salem and live with my grandparents," he said again solemnly. He knew how upset that made his mother.

"Don't you think it would be a good idea for me to move in with them for a few years so I can learn about my father? You don't tell me anything about him."

Cesca hesitated.

"I am my father's son," he said, checking her face for a response. Sometimes she could be sloppy, and he liked that. She could say, "I've wanted to be the best mother in the world to you to make up for the fact that you don't have a father" and he would shrug and retreat happily into victory.

"I knew your father," Francesca said. "You are not entirely your father's son."

"Then whose son am I?" Toby asked.

"Also mine, of course."

Toby left the path again, swinging on the two sticks towards the water. He crouched down at the edge and plunged his sticks into the mud, playing an imaginary game. Cesca leaned against a slender tree and watched him stir the mud off the bottom of the lake so a chocolate brown ribbon wound across the surface. She was daydreaming, off in another world, when Tobias discovered the bones.

"Mama." His stick had touched something hard. He pushed it underneath and lifted.

"Look."

Cesca looked. She took his other stick and lifted so the skeleton rose from the water, bent at the waist—"bowing," as Toby said. There was a flurry of bird wings at the disturbance, and the bones actually rattled and separated. They laid the skeleton on the wet shore in the shadow of marsh reeds.

"I think we ought to go home now," Cesca said. "We should tell the police what you have found."

She backed the car quickly out of the marshes, onto the main highway, and drove into Bethany sightless—or so it seemed, for she had no memory of the road, of the yellow lines or the bridge over the Leonora or the stop sign at Main or the traffic light before the churches. She parked, got out, took Tobias' hand still carrying the sticks that had touched the skeleton, went upstairs and called Bill Becker, who was Chief of Police and had been when Colin Mallory died.

"Who do you think it is?" Tobias asked, hushed with the excitement of the moment. He sat down next to her on the couch. "Someone we know?"

Francesca shook her head. "I hope not."

She felt peculiar, separated from the ordinary world, floating just above her own life; the terror which had overcome her like sickness that morning was no longer mysterious.

Tobias lay down and put his head on his mother's lap.

"That was very creepy, wasn't it?" he said quietly.

"It was."

He looked up at her. "Did you know there was a skeleton in the marshes like you sometimes guess at things?"

"No, darling. Of course not," Cesca said. "*You* found the skeleton by accident."

But in fact the discovery had not seemed an accident at all—rather inevitable, like a perfect tale whose conclusion is anticipated from the start.

All afternoon while she and Tobias played war and Scrabble and listened to *Peter and the Wolf* on the record player, still-life photographs of Colin Mallory dead surfaced in the dreamy darkroom of her mind.

The casket had been gunmetal gray, expensive—"the best," according to Colin's sister Miranda. And he lay in a plush bed of maroon velvet, his eyes closed, his hands folded at his stomach. No one had told her and she had been unable to go to the viewing, but that was how she had imagined him and how she saw him now.

Had the flesh gone after these years? Were the bones like any other bones, filling the inner earth with the residue of human life? His splendid Irish face faded pale blue in death, the energetic hands laced like slender toothpicks across what had been his midriff. Long, foolish bones lost in the wide wool trousers Mrs. Mallory had insisted he wear for eternity. "Wool," Miranda had told her after the funeral, because of the damp, cold winters in coastal Massachusetts, even though he had died in summer. His sex would be gone. Only the high, narrow pelvis of a man.

She could see him now, handsome, full of life at thirty— thirty-one the second of January. His hair thinned slightly at the temples, lines around his eyes and mouth which softened the striking appearance of his youth. She had not ever thought of him specifically since he died. Now she saw him naked in her bedroom on Main Street, a wonderful-looking man. Had he survived her passion, they could have lived out a life and forgiven transgressions.

She was too preoccupied for games with Tobias. She went to the kitchen to make cookies, chocolate-chips. On the floor Tobias zoomed his cars around the legs of the kitchen chairs, forcing accidents at high speed, cars flipping, crashing into the table legs. He looked like Colin—more Irish than Italian, with high color in his cheeks and broad-set eyes, porcelain blue. He could have had a father sufficient to the terrible boys in grammar school like Mikey Sawyer and Tommy Boom Boom. She saw Colin Mallory on the steps of Bethany High School, his hair blown, his shirt open, his eyes blazing with the old promise of conquest. For the first time, the bottom fell out of her, as if the vital organs had actually dropped, afterbirth exposed to the open air. And she knew in the center of her being the consequence of his death.

Father John changed his mind about telling Francesca.

She looked so small to him in the high-backed velvet chair in his study—although she was larger than he was and surely than her grandmother. But she looked like a child, and he didn't want to worry her with dark news.

She drank the sherry he gave her too quickly.

"It should be drunk slowly," he said, but he gave her a second glass nevertheless. "It can go to your head."

"I'm thirty," Cesca said. "Not a girl."

"You look like a girl," he said.

272

He had decided instead to tell her another story and hope she could make the connection.

"I'll tell you a story about snakes, and your grandmother, who was my very good friend," he said.

Cesca was pleased.

This afternoon with Father John had seemed like the beginning of a love affair. She dressed carefully for the occasion—even lilac perfume, the deep scent of late May, which Sophia had told her was her grandmother's favorite. She imagined as a woman does at the beginning of a love affair that her dress should be beautiful as it comes off, the underclothes soft and delicate. She smiled at the thought of this fine old priest with only the memory of desire for a woman undressing her. But that was happening, wasn't it?

"I just wrote a song about snakes," Francesca said. "I'll sing it to you after you tell me your story."

"About Will Weaver?" Father John asked.

"In part," she said.

"Your grandmother was not familiar with snakes when she came to this country," Father John began. "In the small village in Sicily where she grew up, there were no dangers. Stray cats, I think she told me, and a kind of biting spider—but the only real dangers were familial. People with long histories, like Sicilians who live in villages without great possibilities, live safer lives than we do in America. So she came to Bethany innocent of snakes."

According to the story which Father John told, Santa Francesca took a room at Rooster's when she arrived and planned to make an occupation as a shopkeeper. But pregnant women did not work in shops or let themselves be seen on the streets. So all that winter before Sophia was born, Santa Francesca would walk along the paths of the Leonora River—blazing the paths, in fact; no one in those days walked along the river because of snakes. She saw brown snakes on her walks and paid them no attention, knowing they were harmless. But once in late spring, she came upon a very beautiful snake—small and slender, with a finely woven pattern on its skin, and its tiny head a bright orange triangle. She crouched down to inspect the snake more carefully, reached out her hand to touch its head and in a flash, before she even knew to pull back, its tongue flew out, its head whipped towards her and it bit her on the wrist. Four tiny viperous marks broke the skin.

"She was quite sick, although the proprietress at Rooster's knew exactly what to do, and she recovered," Father John said. "But after that encounter she understood things are not always what they seem to be. That which is beautiful can be dangerous," Father John said, pleased with himself, glad to have remembered a story of warning without telling Francesca exactly about Will Weaver.

The story was true. Santa Francesca had told him on one of those long afternoons they spent together between Masses when Sophia was at school and after Francesca had come to him for confession.

"I've never seen a copperhead in Bethany, but my mother says she did when she was a little girl."

Francesca stood, arranged her skirt, folded her hands at her waist. "I'll sing my new song for you if you'd like. There happens to be a poisonous snake in it."

"I'd very much like to hear you sing for me."

And he closed his eyes to listen. But he didn't actually hear any of the words, his mind transported to another time by the smell of lilacs.

The first time Father John met Santa Francesca—although he'd certainly heard when she arrived in town pregnant by a count she'd left behind—she came to him for confession. He was very young, just out of seminary, with the kind of humorless, earnest manner employed by the young in dealing with a world they believe would be in good order if only they were in charge of things. He was disapproving of Santa Francesca.

She had come to tell him the truth about herself. That the baby was not a count's baby; it was the child of a violation which had taken place on a visit with her cousins in Rome. All she knew of the man who had raped her was that he was an American.

She refused absolution.

"This is not a confession," she said. "I don't need forgiveness."

"What did you come to me for?"

"To tell you."

"And what am I to do with this information, if you are not confessing sins?"

"Listen," she said fiercely.

She lifted the shawl from around her shoulders over her head. He could see her from the tiny square that separated them in the confession box framed in her lavender hood. She leaned into the box so close that Father John could feel her breath.

"You are too arrogant for friendship, Father," Santa Francesca said, "but friendship is what I am after in this isolated country of buried dreams."

He fell in love with her then. He watched her walk saucily out of the church, in a regal gesture swing the shawl across her chest. She looked back once as if she knew he watched her, and left.

That afternoon at the pub where the Presbyterian church now stood, a group of men, his own Irish parishioners, were drinking and talking before going home to their chiding wives; the subject was the Sicilian whore.

"So Father, what do you think about the new Italian girl? We are taking bets on who the father is and whether he would ever marry her."

Father John poured himself a lager and drank it in a single gulp. "The father is a count who could not leave Rome for reasons of business," he said. "And they are married." He spoke with the accumulated authority of a priest; in his presence the subject of Santa Francesca did not come up again.

"You weren't listening, were you?" Cesca said.

Father John opened his eyes. "I was reminded of your grandmother with you in my study," he said. "I don't stay put so well in time as I did when I was younger."

"What can you tell me?" Francesca said.

275

He shook his head. "Someday perhaps I'll remember a story to tell you if you promise not to sing it on the radio."

He pulled himself out of the chair. "What can *you* tell *me*?" he asked.

"About my grandmother? Almost nothing," Cesca said. "But I can tell you one story. Today while Toby and I were taking a walk in the marsh, we found a skeleton." The sherry had rushed to her head and she wanted to tell Father John everything—how she had awakened that morning with a sense of dread which she recognized as familiar. She wanted to ask him did he as a priest believe in signs—did he acknowledge symbols? Because the bones she had discovered in the marsh seemed personal.

The apartment was very warm, the sherry burned her stomach and stories stuffed in the back cells of her brain dashed forward to the front line unselectively. She realized she was capable of confessions. She was going to confess Colin's murder. She could actually feel the words forming. But instead, she said, "At the Festival of Fortunes when I was fourteen, out of nowhere, a man or a boy, I don't know which, raped me in the woods behind the high school."

Father John turned the Mozart concerto down and poured himself a second glass of golden sherry. He rearranged a candlestick and pillbox on the pine table beside his chair and turned the lampshade to the side, away from him. Santa Francesca used to say she could see his mind.

"Everything, my treasure," she'd say.

"Not everything," he had said to her. "Desire, but that's no trick."

"Everything touched by the stars," she'd said in her simple, confident way.

"How is it you tell me about yourself this afternoon?" he asked Francesca. Although as a priest he thought that nothing in life surprised him any longer, he had been astonished to hear that Francesca had been raped, as he always was to learn behind the confessional curtain about repeated lives.

"With all of this sherry, I was feeling confidential," she said. "Actually, I thought I was going to tell you something else and the rape came out of the blue as if rape had been the conversation we'd been having."

She was ready to leave. The study was hot and oppressive, and she didn't wish to surprise herself with more confessions.

"Do you want to tell me anything else?" Father John asked.

Cesca laughed. "I didn't come for absolution, Father."

"Just friendship." He recalled her grandmother.

"No." She leaned over and brushed his cheek with her own, touched his face lightly with her fingers. "Just sherry," she said.

When Francesca arrived home from Father John's, flushed and light-headed, Hendrik Andrews sat in the rocking chair beside the grand piano talking to Toby.

"Why, hello," Cesca said.

She had drunk altogether too much. The carefully constructed walls of her mind had fallen. Nothing was in place. Was there such a thing as forgiveness? Had she told Father John everything right there in the parlor of his apartment without the protective curtain of the confession box, would he have forgiven her? And what if he had, or allowed her penance—would the walls have flown up again, the rooms intact?

She smiled a cockeyed girlish smile at Hendrik Andrews.

"Do you remember me?" Hendrik asked.

"Of course." She fell onto the couch. "You're the doctor from the hurricane. I remember."

"What a perceptive child you are."

She could hardly hold her head up. "I'm not perceptive," she said. "I have X-ray vision because I was born with a membrane over my eyes." She rested her chin in her hands.

"You were just walking down Main Street looking for victims of the hurricane who might still be lost in the shuffle and *kazam*, here you are *chez moi*." She threw her legs over the arm of the couch. "Did Toby tell you that victims of the hurricane are popping up like mushrooms? We found one our very own selves this morning."

Toby examined his mother with displeasure.

"I told him, Mother," he said earnestly.

"Boy or girl? Which do you think, Toby? I think a girl."

He had not seen his mother behave like this before.

"I think I'm calling Grandmama," Toby said.

"To tattle." She looked at Hendrik devilishly. "So I'm very glad to see you. I was expecting you, of course. I woke up this morning and saw you, in my overpopulated brain, leap out of bed, dress in the very jeans and shirt you are wearing now, jump in your car and drive straight to my house as if by accident."

Toby sat down in the corner of the couch.

"You probably don't know this," he said to Hendrik: "there are people in Bethany who think my mother sees things like a magician. But they're wrong. She's perfectly normal," he said, full of hope. "I know because she's my mother."

"But in this case, she's absolutely right," Hendrik Andrews said. "Except I didn't leap out of bed this morning. I was up all night."

Hendrik had in fact been up since 2 A.M., when the telephone in his apartment rang and it was a physician at Mass General calling to say that Elena had fallen from a window and was in a coma in intensive care.

According to the nurse at the Home for Disturbed Children, Elena must have thrown herself out the window in the nurses' quarters sometime after midnight. No one knew exactly how she could have gotten there. She had been put to bed at ten and was sleeping, or seemed to be sleeping, when the nurses did rounds at eleven. Her wheelchair was beside her bed as usual. Just after midnight, the head nurse returned to her own bedroom to discover Elena's wheelchair pushed up to the open window—and Elena unconscious on the ground below.

At seven, Hendrik drove to South Boston to pick up his parents, who rode silently to the hospital in the back seat of his small car. Once in the waiting-room corridor outside intensive care, however, his father could not stop talking.

"She wasn't trying to commit suicide," he said to a young father whose child had fallen off a horse. "She had an accident when she was young and was simply trying to re-create the

278

accident. Her brother"—he indicated Hendrik—"pushed her out the window accidentally," he added.

The doctors, when he repeated the story for them, showed no interest in past details.

"I suppose it would be just as well," Mr. Andrews said. "She's been half a person for years."

"Hush." Mrs. Andrews put her hand on his arm. "Please hush."

"We don't know about this kind of head injury except to say it's very serious," the doctor in charge said. "It is difficult to determine the degree of hemorrhaging."

"I can imagine what went on," Mr. Andrews said to the man whose daughter had fallen off a horse. "She was thinking, Why should I live like this? You know, she was an absolutely beautiful child before her face went blank after the accident."

At noon, James Woodbine came on duty as Chief Resident and spoke with the other doctors about Elena.

"You may be here for a long time," James said to Hendrik. "You may be here for days. Weeks. There's a good chance she will never wake up."

"I know that," Hendrik said. "I ought to take my parents home for lunch and to rest. My father is driving everyone crazy."

"And *you* go do something for a few hours," James said. "In fact, you can do me a favor."

Hendrik followed him to his office. "I have a picture for my sister's birthday weeks ago—a sort of a joke. You can drive to Bethany, which is a nice drive, and take it to her. Maybe you'll have a chance to see Maud, the girl I want you to meet."

Hendrik smiled. "Maybe so," he said.

James walked out to the parking lot with Hendrik and his parents.

"She was the first woman I loved."

"Francesca?" Hendrik asked.

"No, Maud." James shrugged. "I suppose you're right. Francesca really was."

Hendrik pulled the framed poster from behind the chair where he sat. "I have actually come on a mission. From your brother."

"For our birthday," she said. "He always forgets to give me a present on time."

The picture was a poster-size playing card of the Queen of Hearts.

Cesca laughed. She read the card aloud: "To the Queen of Hearts from the King of Hearts."

"He said you'd understand."

"So thank you," she said, and kissed Hendrik's hand. "Would you like some wine? I think I have some wine—don't we, Toby?"

"No," Toby said, not willing for his mother to have more to drink. "We have milk and orange juice, and also I broke the last wineglass."

"We'll have red wine in paper cups. I know we have some."

"I shouldn't," Hendrik said. "I have to be back in Boston right away."

"I shouldn't either. You're quite right."

"Because you are already drunk, I think," Tobias said.

"Just a little, my sweet, and so we will have just a little wine."

Which she poured into paper cups with HEY DIDDLE DID-DLE THE CAT AND THE FIDDLE printed in blue and yellow on the side, and toasted Hendrik.

"To us and Toby."

"Not to me," Toby said. "I am going to Grandmama's. Don't you even remember that Uncle Hal ran away to the circus last night?"

"Oh, Toby." Cesca ruffled his hair. "It's not so awful. Hal wanted to be a lion tamer more than anything, and now he will be one. And I have drunk sherry with Father John, which is not the worst thing either."

"I'm going to call Grandma anyway and then get ice cream," Toby said. "She wanted to be an opera singer—she told me—and she didn't run away from home," he said crossly.

"Maybe she should have," Cesca said. "So to us." She toasted Hendrik again. She slid into a chair and closed her eyes. "I have been married to a lot of people," she said coquettishly, "but never a doctor. Why don't you marry me?"

"I'm already married to a cardboard singer," he said. "One singer is enough."

"Cardboard?" She was very sleepy, she thought. Perhaps she should get up. Perhaps she was very drunk. "Would you like me to sing you a new song I just wrote last night? If I can remember."

She sat at the piano.

"It's about a boy who loves snakes and collects and trains them like my brother Hal did with cats in preparation for lions, if you get what I mean." She played the melody first without singing. "But there isn't any preparation for lions, of course. So one day, the boy's pet snake turns on him and bites him fatally. Although I can't decide whether the bite should be fatal or not. What do you think? Do you prefer fatal or nonfatal bites?"

And she sang, forgetting some of the words as she went along, too light-headed to see the score on the piano in front of her.

"I hate that song." Tobias flopped face down on the couch. "I hate Will Weaver too."

"The song isn't about Will, Toby."

"Who else is it about, then? He's the only person we know with snakes." He rolled off the couch to a sitting position. "I'm going to Hanrahan's to get ice cream. So I'll see you later," he said to Hendrik.

Francesca wandered to the sofa and sat down, spinning.

"I think the bite should be fatal," Hendrik said.

"Me too," Cesca agreed happily.

"And now I have to go back to Boston," Hendrik said.

"Thank James when you see him," Cesca said. "And thank you."

"Are you okay for me to leave?" He put his hand on her forehead.

"Just fine. I'm whirling into a rainbow. At least, I think it's a rainbow. I've never done this before. Goodbye. I don't remember your name."

"Hendrik Andrews," he said.

"Dr. Andrews. I wish you could make my head settle down." She turned on her side. "And if you could do that right now this minute, I'd love you instead of the snake tamer."

"If I were really a doctor, I could do anything, of course," Hendrik said, and kissed her lips. "Goodbye."

Elena died that night. Hendrik was with her when the coma deepened. He had taken his parents home after supper. Once, either waking or sleeping, he thought he heard her say—or else he dreamed it—"Elena jumped."

"She couldn't have talked, could she?" he asked James, who was on night duty.

"No, she couldn't," James said.

So he had dreamed it.

When she stopped breathing, he kissed her hand, called the nurse and waited in the hospital dispensary until dawn to drive to his parents' house to tell them Elena was dead.

The Chief of Police called Francèsca the following morning to tell her he was going to check the dentists in Bethany and around Holbrooke County to see if the skeleton could be identified by the teeth. She hung up the telephone. Any news, even that the bones belonged to a stranger, was going to be bad.

3. Tornado Weather

The teeth were Celia Hamilton's.

On Monday, after Francesca had spoken with him, Bill Becker contacted all the dentists in Holbrooke County. Only Dr. Wade, a small weasel of a man with a gift for detail, as suited his profession, practiced in Bethany. The other dentists were in Salem and Ewes and Haymarket and Sealsville. They all agreed to check their records for patients unaccounted for. Also, by Tuesday, the Chief of Police had a list of five people from Holbrooke County alone who had simply disappeared. Fallen off the globe without a trace. A Mr. Ian Hughes of Ewes had not been seen for months— a fact that had gone unreported by his neighbors. When the Chief of Police checked his house, Mr. Hughes, who had been dead for several months, was seated at the breakfast table in an advanced stage of decay with a newspaper spread out over a bowel of Rice Krispies.

There was a piece in *The Boston Globe*, page 4 of the Metro section, with a picture of the bones on the marsh bank and a paragraph explaining that the police department planned to conduct an investigation through dental records to determine the identity.

Mrs. Hamilton saw the piece. Since Celia's disappearance, she had lost interest in living. Until the article in the *Globe*, nothing had caught her attention. Mr. Hamilton blew into and out of the house, wind puffs of his former self, in various stages of inebriation. Philip was consumed by sports and spent what time he was at home at the dining-room table keeping statistics of whatever sport was presently in season. And Mrs. Hamilton lived a daily life of isolated grief.

When she saw the article in the paper, however, she was revitalized. If only she knew where Celia was, she could recover. Even if her daughter were dead. She called Dr. Wade, who checked his records. Yes, he said, he had seen Celia twice to clean her teeth, but he had no record of X-rays. She should call Celia's childhood dentist in Norton. Which Mrs. Hamilton did.

On Thursday, the dentist in Norton determined that indeed the teeth were those of Celia Hamilton.

Francesca found out at noon. She had made herb bread and minestrone Thursday morning and invited Will Weaver for lunch. It was the first time they had seen each other since the weekend, and she noticed that Will was preoccupied and melancholy as he used to be when he was young.

"I read in the paper about you," he said, sitting down at the kitchen table. He had picked up the paper on Tuesday morning, glanced quickly through the first-page national news, turned to the city section for more personal stories and was turning to the obituaries, which he always read with care, when his eye caught the headline BETHANY SKELETON DIS-COVERED. He scanned the story quickly and then with an enormous weariness sat down in the living room and read the column word for word.

On Wednesday, he stayed at home with a migraine headache. He could go away, he decided. He could join Hal with the circus or simply vanish. Go to Mexico or South America. He would lie about Celia if they discovered the identity of the skeleton. When Francesca called to find out if he was ill, he said he was quite ill and could not see her.

That afternoon, he had recovered enough to go to Leonora's and order the summer books. He called Hal in Raleigh, North Carolina. The woman who answered the Ringling Brothers number said the circus was headed north and he could catch up with it in Richmond, unless it was an emergency, in which case she would notify the police.

"I don't need you to notify the police," Will said.

On Thursday, he was better. Rational, he thought. He had slept well Wednesday night; his appetite was good. At dinner, his conversation with his father had been unexceptional.

Thursday morning in the shop he had a momentary sensation of hallucinating, but in fact nothing from his own brain displaced the objective world of the bookshop. The brightly colored stacks of books; Sarah Pillsbury, who had replaced Celia as his assistant, in her maroon tunic in The Snake Bed; customers in and out, in and out. He was pleased. Perhaps he could get by the investigation of Celia's death without serious event. When Francesca called to ask him up for lunch, he agreed to go.

"Remember Celia Hamilton?" the Chief of Police asked Cesca when he called.

"Of course," she said.

"Well, that's who you found in the marsh," he said. "Bones because the birds, hawks mainly, had eaten her flesh." He promised to be in touch.

Will was expectant. "So who was that?" he asked.

She did not want to be the one to tell him.

"Do you want wine?" she asked, stalling for time. "I have wine, although I drank too much the other night and I don't want anything but tea for a while."

"No wine." Will shook his head. "Tell me who called. It was about the skeleton, I bet."

"Bill Becker," she said. "He's an odd man, but he was often very kind after Colin died."

"Whose bones were they?" Will asked. "Someone we know."

Cesca nodded.

"Celia's," he said. "*Celia Hamilton's*. That's right, isn't it?" He looked at her insanely. "*You found Celia in the marshes, for chrissake.*" He walked drunkenly across the room and down the stairs. She heard the front door slam and his car start up.

"Will was devastated," Francesca told Maud when she came back from her doctor's appointment with the news that she was pregnant. "I ought to do something for him. But I don't know what to do."

"He looked crazy when he found out," she told Sophia. "Perhaps you ought to call Sam at the hospital and tell him."

Sam knew already. The sergeant was in Emergency with a boy from Bethany Grammar who had broken his leg, and he told Sam Weaver it was Celia's bones that had been discovered.

"Murdered or drowned," the sergeant said, not displeased to have a little excitement in Bethany. "Up for grabs which one."

Sam set the boy's leg and went home. The Chief of Police was parked in front of the house when he arrived.

"You know what's going on?" Bill Becker asked.

Sam nodded.

"We have to check everything, of course," the Chief said. "We have on record that Will took Celia Hamilton to Boston to catch a Trailways bus to Montpelier. That's confirmed. There was a witness to that. But we have to investigate again because it's unusual, as you'll certainly agree, for Celia to surface in our own marshes, miles from Boston. You understand, don't you?"

"Of course I understand," Sam said.

"He's brokenhearted," the Chief said. "I'm sorry this has happened."

Francesca called in the evening.

"I'll do anything you'd like," she said to Will. "I feel terrible for you."

The whole town of Bethany felt terrible as well.

"Poor Will Weaver," people said to one another at Hanrahan's and in the supermarket, at church on Sunday, at Sunny's Ice Cream Parlor. "Such bad luck for a boy who lost his mother."

Will retreated to his room and read scientific books. He reread the books he had about reptiles. He read zoological studies from his father's library, a scholarly book about reptiles and evolution. He discovered one of his father's college texts from a sophomore course in entomology and was fascinated to read about rare insects in South America and Africa. He was particularly intrigued by the *Enola varelii*, a winged South African insect with two long antennae, a body protected by thick black fuzz, lavender pattern on the wings and a stinger located in the tail which killed both the enemy and the insect when used. There was a beautiful full-page glossy of the *Enola varelii*, exact and delicate as a Japanese watercolor. Will looked at it for hours. In self-defense against what he was certain would be a recurrence of hallucinations, he lost himself in zoological texts.

He left the house only once in a week, to go with his father to a Mass for Celia. The rest of the time he remained secluded in his room.

Elena Andrews was buried the same day Mass was said for Celia Hamilton in Bethany. The service for Elena was at home in the small, shabby living room of the Andrews row house, with a few friends in attendance. No one came from the Home for Disturbed Children.

"I shouldn't have had her there," Mrs. Andrews said. "If that's all it matters to them to have a child die, I should have had her here in her own house."

"She wasn't a child," Mr. Andrews said. "She was twenty-five. She could have been married if things had been different."

There were casseroles in Corningware spread out on the plastic lace in the dining room for a lunch after the service. And flowers—a large arrangement of white roses on the coffee table from James and Louisa Woodbine, several pots of gladiolus.

"Of course, I'm sad it's over," Mrs. Andrews said to Hendrik as she walked him to his car that afternoon. "It has been so long and difficult. She would not have gotten better."

Hendrik kissed his mother and got into the car elated about his departure, which seemed somehow permanent. As he turned off Euclid Street, his eyes in the rearview mirror caught the row house where he had grown up, undistinguished except for a large pot of white chrysanthemums on the front porch to honor Elena.

He had one more responsibility.

At the Boston Home for Disturbed Children, Elena's room was locked in anticipation of his arrival. A supervisor opened it for him, provided him with a stack of empty boxes and stood at the door while he packed up. She was a supervisor he had not met—sullen, but pretty in a youthful way and interested in him.

"I understand she'd been here forever," the supervisor said. "I only came in February."

"Twenty-three years," he said.

"She was going to have to move anyway," the woman said stupidly. "The oldest one we have now besides Elena is nineteen."

Her clothes in her dresser smelled old and of mildew. He packed them quickly.

"Do you have any place like the Salvation Army where these might go?"

287

"Value Village. They come by once a month."

Down the corridor, there was a long screech and Hendrik started. The supervisor shrugged.

"Marianna. She's practicing dying. She practices dying every day."

In the top drawer Elena had kept mementos—plastic flowers in plastic bags tied with ribbon.

"She loved flowers," the supervisor said. "'Elena loves flowers,' she'd say to me. And so we'd give her plastic ones from arrangements."

There were birthday presents—sweaters, perfume, nightgowns, art books, still in their wrappings with the notes attached. There were letters and cards, sweet-smelling sachets, an announcement of the opening of Uncle Ben's and a picture of Hendrik when he was thirteen years old, a first-year student at Boys' Latin. On the back, written in her child's scrawl, was *My dear brother.* He put the picture in his pocket, packed the coverlet and sheets, took down the reproduction of Gainsborough's *Blue Boy* and stacked the boxes on the bed.

"Finished," he said. "Should I call Value Village?"

"I'll call," the supervisor said. "You carry the boxes down to the basement."

He picked up the boxes and followed her to the basement room where extra beds and dressers were stored.

"Aren't you going to take anything of hers?" the supervisor asked, shaking hands with him.

"I took something," Hendrik said. "A picture of myself."

"Conceited, aren't you," the woman said brassily.

"You should have come to her funeral or sent flowers."

He turned and went quickly down the long cement steps, got into his car and drove home.

He was not unhappy about Elena, although he would certainly miss her. Perhaps he had been responsible. Perhaps not. He would never know, and what a waste of life it would be fettered to an inexplicable past. He had done his best. He was, after all, her "dear brother."

The town of Bethany's reaction to the death of Celia Hamilton was extreme. The subject of Colin Mallory came up again. The town was suddenly a dangerous place to make a life. There was no question of accidental drowning. How, people asked themselves, can a grown woman drown in a shallow marsh by accident? Someone either drowned her in the marsh or killed her elsewhere and brought her there or killed her there. In any case, she had certainly been murdered. That conclusion was sufficient to set the citizens of Bethany on edge.

The Chief of Police called in detectives from out of town and doubled his efforts at investigation. He could not afford to keep his job with the town's distrust. There were no clues.

Will returned to work several days after the funeral. He was subdued and people left him alone. He would have nothing to do in a personal way with Francesca Woodbine.

"You'll have to understand, Ces. Celia's death has been an awful shock."

"Of course I understand," Francesca said. But she did not approve. His withdrawal possessed her.

She thought of him all the time. Nothing else filled her mind. Not her work on the new album nor trouble with Tobias, who was required by the principal of Bethany West to see a psychologist because he'd become, as she put it, "unnaturally violent." Nor Maud's pregnancy, nor calls from Hendrik Andrews inviting her out. Nor even the visions of Colin Mallory dead which had unsettled her life since Celia had been discovered. Will Weaver was stuck in her mind, lodged like an oversize piece of furniture between the portals of her brain.

"I simply don't understand you," Maud said on the train to New York in early May to cut the single of "The Ballad of the Snake Boy." "You are a sensible woman."

"I can't help it," Francesca said.

"You act as if you don't have a choice."

"I don't," Francesca said, and she was serious. "It's like gravity."

She was magnetized, drawn to him as if her natural immune system had broken down and Will Weaver invaded her cells.

"You're being awful with Tobias," Maud said. "He may be asked to leave school."

"Then he'll stay home with us," Francesca said. "Learn to play the bass."

She was distressed about Tobias, but in a distant way.

"My heart isn't with him as it was," she told her mother.

Sophia was not concerned.

"That's natural from time to time," she said. "I remember watching you and James one afternoon when I had my illness—so lovely together, but you were as strangers to me. I felt nothing but a passing visual interest at the sight of you."

"I'm not having a breakdown, if that is what you mean."

"Not precisely," Sophia said.

"Maybe we should go on the road," Maud said. "This summer, with the new album."

"I don't want to do concerts," Cesca said. "We made a decision to stay in Bethany."

"That was for *Mating Calls*," Maud said. "I think we should reconsider. Now we have a reputation."

"Our reputation is based on staying at home," Cesca said.

And they were silent the rest of the way to New York.

The front page of the Bethany newspaper included a daily report of the investigation of Celia Hamilton's murder. All over town, people read about the murder first before national news on the front page. Before sports. Then they discussed the latest information. If Will Weaver had let her off in Boston, which was what he said—and everyone believed him except Tobias, who said out loud in Miss Fulcher's third-grade reading class that probably Will Weaver was lying, which caused such an uproar that Francesca was called to the principal's office again—but if Will Weaver had let Celia off in Boston, how did she happen to get back to the marshes three miles away from Bethany? Had she met someone in Boston, or hitchhiked home, and been killed in the marshes? This theory was popular amongst the citizens. It wasn't possible to determine when she had died, but people were inclined to believe that she had changed her mind about running away shortly after Will Weaver left her at the bus depot. That she'd met a man there who offered to drive her back to Bethany and that he had killed her between Boston and the marshes and dumped her in the lake.

Then Tim Greenfield, home one weekend to visit his mother, suffering from cancer, told Frank Adler, who told the Chief of Police, that no one unfamiliar with the marshes could know that particular section of water.

"It's where we all went as kids for sex and trouble," Tim said.

The report in the *Bethany News* on Monday, May 17, referred to Tim Greenfield's observation. The citizens who had grown up in Bethany agreed. No doubt, they decided, the murderer was a man, perhaps on drugs, and Celia Hamilton had taken him to the marsh. They were on their way back to Bethany to meet Celia's family and had stopped off there, knowing that at Celia's family's house their time together would be restricted.

The former Mayor of Bethany, Colin Mallory's father, read the *Bethany News* on May 17. His wife was dead. His children were grown and had children of their own, with whom he was in regular contact except for Colin's son Tobias. He practiced law, feigning interest in the daily tedium of domestic and tax law, and he drank too much. He had always drunk too much, but particularly since Colin's death had forced him to leave Bethany. Drinking made him bad-tempered. Even at sixty, he was always on edge, ready to fight.

He was ready to fight when he read about Celia Hamilton's murder and the conjecture that she had been murdered by someone from out of town.

"Horseshit," he said to the Chief of Police, whom he called early that morning. "Colin and Celia were murdered by someone in Bethany."

He wrote a passionate letter to the editor of the *Bethany News* in which he said the evidence pointed to someone from

291

Bethany who knew the habits and hidden territories of the town like the Mallorys' cottage by the river and the small lake where Celia's bones had been discovered. "Why don't you look in your own backyards?" he wrote. "Perhaps the same person killed both Colin and Celia. Or perhaps you're a town sufficiently violent to nurture two killers."

There was a wind change after the ex-Mayor's letter. The possibility of an insider had been rationalized after Tim Greenfield first suggested it. A connection between Colin Mallory and Celia had now been discussed. People took up arms and locked into battle positions. No one could be trusted any longer. Underneath the general spirit of conviviality and petty curiosities and affections which had flourished since the hurricane, dark suspicions scattered, invisible as ragweed.

On Friday morning after the ex-Mayor's letter, Frank Adler suggested that Francesca be brought in to help the police. He mentioned it to Bill Becker, who had stopped by for coffee just after the nine-o'clock shift went on duty.

"I'm thinking of going door to door with a lie-detector test," Bill said to Frank.

"No clues?"

"How can you have a clue with only bones? And now Colin Mallory's risen from the dead again."

"Why don't you ask Francesca Woodbine to help you out?" Frank said.

"Francesca?"

"People in this town actually believe she has access to secrets," Frank said.

"So I'd use her as a psychic detective," the Chief of Police said. "I don't know about that."

"Why not?" Frank asked. "What's to lose?"

"You really believe she has powers of that kind?" he asked.

"I don't believe anyone actually has psychic powers," Frank said. "But Francesca has an understanding of people's lives which certainly isn't ordinary."

The Chief of Police finished his coffee and ate a doughnut.

"Anything's worth a try, I suppose," he said.

Will Weaver woke up to the sweet smell of perfume in the air. He got out of bed and knew uneasily that the hallucinations were coming back. He dressed for work pleased that at least his mother had not materialized in his room while he had been sleeping. She was, however, at breakfast in the chair beside him. He poured cereal and sliced bananas. It felt as if she were breathing on his face. He did not turn around to check.

"I wish they wouldn't investigate Celia's death," Will said to his father. "What can they find?"

"Perhaps they'll actually find out who killed her," Sam said.

"How?" Will was distraught. "How in Christ's name can they find out anything from bones?"

Later Sam recalled that his son's eyes were distended that morning like the eyes of a patient in the advanced stages of thyroid disease. And his body moved in the slow staccato of metal joints.

Will drove to work. The scent of his mother was light in the air, mixed with the stale smell of the cigarettes he smoked one after another.

When he arrived, Celia was in the shop crouched in The Snake Bed arranging books on the bottom shelves. He had almost expected her to materialize that morning. Later he had called Sarah by Celia's name and seen Celia's sweet, open face imposed on the slender, sallow one of Sarah Pillsbury. His brain hammered against the skull; he knew that he was going mad again.

He saw Francesca, dressed as he had seen her once at the Festival, in a full beige blouse and cranberry skirt, walk with Tobias to school. She was innocent, he thought, like his mother. He couldn't bear her sweetness. She was his mother exactly, and Tobias, walking with her, hand in hand, was himself.

According to the book he had read on insects, the *Enola varelii* chooses the end of its life. Unless trapped, it will live out an ordinary life and at the appropriate moment, just short of natural death, will choose a victim—rarely a human being, usually a small animal. It will sting the victim, and within a minute both will convulse and die.

If the hallucinations pursued him as they had before Celia's death, Will knew he would kill Francesca Woodbine. And then he would kill himself. Somehow it pleased him completely to think of Tobias left alone as he had been.

Francesca was lying face down and at an angle across her bed when Will came into the apartment without knocking and saw her. At first he thought that she was dead because she was so still. That his powers of wishing were such as to cause her death.

"Cesca?"

She was hiding from the light of day writing lyrics for a new composition. She had written the melody first without the help of Sophia and without an idea for the lyrics. The tune was somber and quiet, like her mood lately, and did not call to mind a story. Perhaps it should be about Father John, she thought, although he was not essentially a somber man. She wondered if he had had love affairs—or one great love which temporarily filled his life with light. She thought of Maud Hanrahan, who had gone to Boston for an abortion.

"Have the baby," Francesca had said. "You would be a lovely mother."

Maud wanted a baby. She wanted a baby to dress in soft kimonos and tuck into bed with her, lost in her arms. She could imagine no greater happiness or safety. She had no pleasure in men except the tiny pinprick of satisfactory sex, fleeting as days. She did not like the fleshy-bellied man with toothpick legs, too short for his torso, who had fathered this baby. And he certainly wasn't interested in a baby. He had five children at home and did not want trouble. He agreed to pay for the abortion "and then some," he said. If she had an abortion, she would pay for it herself, she said.

For weeks, almost too many weeks to be safely aborted,

Maud fretted over whether to keep the baby or not. She changed her mind several times a day.

"You'd better hurry," Cesca said.

"I can't make up my mind," Maud said.

Finally Tobias made the decision for her one morning at breakfast while Cesca was reading the latest report on the murder of Celia Hamilton.

"Do you remember Tommy Tyler?" he asked his mother, spooning extra sugar on his Cheerios.

Francesca nodded.

"I think I hate him completely," Toby said.

"We don't hate, darling," Cesca said absently.

"I do. I hate Tommy Tyler," Toby said. "Sometimes a lot. Yesterday at recess he teased me about not having a father, and as usual everybody copied him."

"That's because something has happened in your life which frightens them. So they tease you in self-defense. Pay no attention and they'll stop."

"It's too hard to be a boy without a father," Toby said earnestly. "Sometimes I wish I had never been born."

Maud made her decision for an abortion then.

"I don't want to raise a child alone," Maud said to Cesca later. "If you can't do it, then no one can."

"Francesca?" Will walked to the bed and put his hand on her arm.

She turned over, flushed with the warmth of the wool blanket against her face."

"Hello. I didn't hear you."

"Hello." He sat down beside her.

"What time is it? I've been working and have lost all track of time."

"Ten," he said. "I just opened the store and came up to apologize to you for being remote since Celia was discovered."

"Of course." She sat up and crossed her legs. "I certainly understand."

He gently brushed her hair off her face.

"You're very beautiful," he said. "You remind me of my mother."

"I do?" Cesca was pleased.

"She was also beautiful." He kissed her lips softly.

"Will you be here alone all day?"

"Until Toby gets home from school," she said. "Maud's in Boston."

"I'll be back later, then," he said. "Maybe at lunch."

All morning in high spirits, Francesca sang old sentimental songs. She danced through the apartment in long scarves, passing by the mirrors on her dresser, over the buffet in the living room, on her door, pleased to see her own reflection. She kissed her own lips lightly in the mirror.

At noon, Maud called from Boston to say she did not feel well enough to come home and planned to spend the night with James and Louisa. Hal called from Columbus, Ohio, to say that he was getting his first chance to help Amal in the ring with the big cats, as he called them. And then, just as she was expecting Will Weaver, the doorbell rang and the Chief of Police with a detective from Salem she had never met arrived to ask for Cesca's help.

They told her about a psychic who was brought in to help the police solve a series of murders in Mendocino, California.

Francesca was not enthusiastic.

"I'm not psychic," Cesca said. "I'm a looker."

"This psychic didn't solve the murders because she had special powers," the Chief of Police said.

"Deductive reasoning," the detective said.

"I have a curiosity about people and an eye for the patterns in their lives. I make things up and sometimes they turn out to be true. Sometimes not. That's not deductive reasoning."

The Chief of Police insisted. "You may not think you have powers, but other people in this town do," he said.

Francesca was thoughtful.

"If I were to actually use deductive reasoning, the only person in Bethany who could have been there to kill Celia is

Will Weaver. And that's not possible. We all know that."

"Improbable," the Chief of Police agreed.

"So what good can I be to you?"

But she was finally persuaded.

"Nothing will come of this," she said as the Chief of Police and the detective were leaving.

"Something will, I am sure," the Chief of Police said.

When they left, she bolted the apartment door, trapped as she had imagined she would feel if she had been caught for Colin Mallory's death. In a way, she decided later, she had been.

She slipped into her nightgown and got back into bed to work on lyrics, but she couldn't think. She turned her radio to Boston's all-music station. Occasionally she slept, comforted from time to time by the sound of her own voice.

When Will banged on her door in the early afternoon, she was just waking up.

"Coming," she called, but drugged, she got out of bed slowly, pulled to consciousness from a bad dream.

"Coming," she said to Will, zipping up her skirt, brushing her hair, which had tangled in her sleep.

"It's just Will," he called from the door.

She didn't tell him immediately that she had agreed to help the police department with its investigation of Celia's death. When he asked her why the Chief of Police had come that morning, she said it was to talk about the ex-Mayor's letter to the editor in the morning paper—to ask her whether she thought there was any connection between the deaths of Colin and Celia Hamilton.

"Do you?" Will asked.

"Of course not," she said.

"Do you think the person who killed Celia is from Beth-' any?" Will asked. "There seems to be some feeling that he is."

"Who's to say she didn't kill herself?" Cesca said.

"So you believe it could have been suicide?"

"I believe nothing," Cesca said. "What I'd really like to do is join the circus with Hal and leave Bethany for a year."

"As a lion tamer?"

Cesca laughed. "I'd be better on the high wires balancing without a net."

Julian read the morning paper, folded it into a small square and propped it up against the vase of daffodils on the kitchen table.

I would like to go on a trip," he said to Sophia.

"A trip?" Sophia leaned against him. "I don't believe we have been on a trip since the children."

"Well, I'd like to go on one now."

She sat down in the chair next to him, brushed his hand lightly with her arm.

"For several weeks. Out of the country. Perhaps to Italy."

"Italy?"

"You haven't even been there. You must have a score of relatives in Sicily."

"The Count, of course, in Rome," Sophia said.

"Of course."

"We had a card this morning from Hal," she said. "Perhaps instead we could go see the circus."

"We'll see the circus when it comes to Boston," Julian said. "In the meantime, I'd like to give away the cats forever and leave the country as soon as we can get passports."

Sophia cooked eggs lightly over, poured orange juice, unfolded the paper and read first the news of the investigation and then the editorial page with former Mayor Mallory's letter.

"Poor Thomas Mallory," she said, folding the paper beside her plate. "He simply can't get on with his life since Colin died."

"He's a drunk," Julian said. "He's a furious drunk."

She cleared the table, clipped the dead daffodils, fed the cats, who slunk around the kitchen complaining, opened the window over the sink just barely for fresh air.

"You hated that letter, didn't you?" she said to Julian, who was gathering his papers for the day, taking out an umbrella.

"I objected," Julian said. "I don't want to stir up our lives again with Colin's murder. It's sufficient bad fortune for this aging lawyer to accommodate a son who is a lion tamer."

Sophia laughed and kissed him softly on the lips.

"And so we'll go to Italy," she said.

"As soon as possible."

"It's no country for lawyers," she said.

"They'll have to adjust."

In the car, he rolled down all the windows and drove to work the back way through Marsh Road. Certainly, he thought, driving through a low gray mist, damp on his face, the person who killed Celia Hamilton was not the same one who had killed Colin. For a long time, he used to think about the revolver missing from his desk drawer. But Cesca had never mentioned it, as certainly she would have, at least to Sophia. Now the former Mayor had brought up Colin's death again, and the doubts lingering just under the surface of his consciousness were back. His mind filled with dark thoughts of Mayor Mallory's death. Perhaps his liver would give. Or his heart.

They could move to Italy for a year or two. He had plenty of money and could retire. He'd take Francesca and Tobias. She could learn to sing in Italian. Perhaps there were circuses in Sicily with slim-lined lions, deceptively fierce, pussycats at heart, as suited the Italians.

He was glad to finally get to work and lose himself in the myriad of petty details with which he protected himself from the business of living.

May was wet on the coast. It was always gray and rained steadily, so the days turned into night without a perceptible change in the amount of light. The Festival was postponed to late June because the ground was soft enough to sink to China, as Frank Adler said. There was a general sleepiness, and for the moment people lost interest in the murder of Celia Hamilton. Except Francesca.

She had made discoveries. She had talked to the dentist in

299

Norton, Massachusetts, and a boy in Taunton called Slim Steve who said he was the first one to kiss her, in seventh grade, and she was the sweetest girl he'd ever known before or since. One afternoon she went to Celia Hamilton's house to talk to her mother.

"You should see her things," Mrs. Hamilton said. "Maybe you can find something." Her things were in a large box the size of a steamer trunk marked CELIA'S with tiny yellow tulips Mrs. Hamilton had painted all over the top "so people will know when I'm dead she was a happy child," Mrs. Hamilton said.

The box was full of Celia's favorite clothes from child-hood—a sailor dress, a white pinafore stained with chocolate, a pale blue formal with puffy sleeves and a crinoline skirt. Scrapbooks, carefully kept, with a medieval sense of order, arranged in chapters of Firsts: "First Prom," "First Kiss," "First Football Game," "First Folk Concert," "First Year in High School," "First Sorrow"—and the sorrow described at length was the move to Bethany.

There was a five-year diary completely filled in, each day of which began: *"Boys, boys, boys, boys, boys, boys, boys."* Nothing in the diary, however, indicated that boys were more than a hope present in her world. Her life, boxed and tied in ribbons, was undistinguished, interchangeable—except for the care she had taken to preserve her own history—with the life of any teenage girl in the late fifties.

"She was not a girl to go on drugs," Mrs. Hamilton said, sitting on the pink fluff comforter on Celia's single bed. "There was mention of drugs in the paper. I tried not to read those articles that kept coming out after we knew it was her who died."

"The mention of drugs in the paper was speculative," Cesca said. "The article suggested she might have met a boyfriend and he could have been on drugs."

"I don't know why people want to make up what might have happened to her. What use is that?"

"No use really," Cesca agreed.

"But you don't see anything in the box about drugs?" Mrs. Hamilton asked. "I got a cleaning lady to pack the boxes. It was the first time I've ever had a cleaning lady, but she was worth it. I couldn't have done it myself."

"There's nothing in the box about drugs." There was an orderly innocence about Celia's things, no suggestion of danger, of longings unfulfilled.

"Maybe she could have been attracted to a boy on drugs, although I doubt it. Will Weaver was more her type, and he was such a good boy and kind to her," Mrs. Hamilton said. "He didn't even try anything, you know." She gave an odd laugh, brassy, like a snort. "'I just wish he would,' she said to me—and we didn't have that kind of relationship, with confessions, like some girls have with their mothers."

In the afternoons, if Maud was out, Will and Francesca had lunch and lay together on the high four-poster bed. The afternoon following Cesca's visit to the Hamiltons', Will was in her kitchen when she came back. He stood at the window overlooking the backyard.

"Maud let me in," he said. "She's at the market and then she's going to Salem to get a new dress. She told me you might begin to do public performances when this new album is released."

"I don't think so." Cesca took an apple from the bowl on the kitchen table and offered one to Will.

"What were you doing at the Hamiltons'? Maud told me you were there. I didn't know you even knew them."

"Just talking to her mother about her."

"What did you discover?" Will asked, nervous but self-contained.

"The life of a saint." Cesca pulled Will towards her. "You didn't kiss her enough. That's what Mrs. Hamilton said."

Will straightened.

"I'm teasing you, Will."

"I didn't want to kiss her," he said.

Cesca stood on tiptoe and laid her cheek next to his.

"You take everything seriously, don't you?" She put her hand gently on the back of his neck. "Come," she whispered.

She pulled back the comforter and took him down with her on the bed.

He closed his eyes, pleased with the smell of clean sheets and the absence of perfume. What he liked about Francesca was maternal. He liked the way she took him by the hand or touched his face or put her cheek against his chest or her hand on his breastbone—softly, softly. They had not made love. There was no sense of urgency; she had not insisted, as Celia had.

Francesca had waited. He would undress her to the waist. He liked to lie with his legs tangled in her skirts, with his face against her breasts. She wanted to make love always, but was afraid to press him.

This afternoon, however, in the shadow of Celia Hamilton's ordered life, and some knowledge of destiny or simple curiosity about Will's secret life, she was impatient. When she felt the beginning of his desire, she led him inside, and for a small moment he filled her.

She leaned against the headboard of her bed and he lay face down on her lap, buried in her musty-smelling skirt. "Never mind," she said, running her fingers through his hair. "Don't worry."

At the bottom of a long and narrow well, lit from behind as if the sun had fallen to the center of the earth providing light from the inside out, he saw his mother.

That night, agitated by longings, Francesca could not sleep at all.

When she was a child, she and James had read a series called "The Book House" with romantic full-page glossy pictures and unexceptional stories. She recalled one of the pictures titled "Girl with Her Skirt Caught in a Freight Train." She didn't remember the story at all, but the picture showed a girl whose long blue-gray skirt was caught in the door of a moving freight train and the girl sailed behind the train, exhilarated and doomed.

The picture had fascinated Cesca. She loved the girl's long

hair, the perfect pleasure she seemed, by her red-lipped smile, to take in her predicament.

"How do you think she got stuck like that?" Cesca had asked James, who did not like the stories in "The Book House," but he particularly didn't like the romantic pictures.

"She probably put her skirt in the door herself," James had said. "Stupid girl."

"She's going to be killed," Cesca said, thrilled with the thought of the girl's death. "In the next picture, she's going to be killed."

"It'll serve her right," James said. "And besides, you know very well there is no next picture."

Lying in bed, tossing back and forth, Cesca could not get the picture of the girl out of her mind.

Hendrik Andrews had met Maud Hanrahan that evening at James and Louisa's apartment. James was always introducing him to unexceptional women, and this one, whom he actually liked, reminded him somehow of his mother. She was a woman of real sweetness who expected nothing of relationships and was rewarded in kind. But he was interested to hear her talk about Francesca.

"I suppose you've heard about Will Weaver," she said to James.

"Even Cesca has told me about him," James said.

"The trouble is not Will Weaver. He's very sweet," Maud said. "It's Francesca. She's obsessed with him."

"I'm not surprised," James said. "It's been such a long time since Colin died, and no one in between. But she hasn't the temperament to be obsessed."

"That's exactly the temperament she does have," Louisa said. "Sometimes I am astonished at how little you know her."

"Cesca is a source of disagreement in our house," James said to Hendrik.

"She is *the* source of disagreement," Louisa said crossly.

"Whatever her temperament, Will Weaver has overtaken her life," Maud said, "and I hate it." She turned to Hendrik

Andrews. "Why don't you sweep her off her feet?" she said. "Someone has to."

In the morning, as Toby was leaving for school, Hendrik called to invite her to bring him to Uncle Ben's.

She hesitated.

"I am involved with someone," she said. "Perhaps you know about that from James."

"I do," he said. "I'm not asking you to marry me."

She laughed and said after the new album was finished she would like to come. To call her again.

Will Weaver woke up early the next morning, got dressed, called Sarah Pillsbury to open the store for him and drove to the marshes. He had not been back to the marsh since Celia was discovered.

There was a thick mist dividing the horizon. He had to drive slowly on the highway, close to the right side of the road. Headlights from the oncoming cars were barely visible; the yellow line was gone. At Marsh Road, he drove from memory to the place where a path hidden by cattails, obscured by the early-morning fog, led to the lake where Celia Hamilton had been.

He sat in the car with the engine running, the heat on, the defroster, the radio turned to Boston's all-music station and watched the fog lift, rising like a gray velvet stage curtain to reveal a scene of precision and perfect stillness. High bronze reeds and marsh wheat stood military guard. The lake was black and tranquil. His mind was sharper and more settled than it had been for weeks. Cold-blooded. His brain felt re-frigerated.

He got out of the car and walked through the dense path to the edge of the deep water where he had left her. The fog had lifted as high as his shoulders when he stood, but he had to duck in order to see. The early-morning sun burned through the mist, dusting the vegetation with light, dancing across the surface of the water, illuminating the white bones which lay on the shore.

He had not expected anything out of the ordinary at the marshes, but he was not surprised. Nothing surprised him. He knelt down and touched the folded right leg. The skeleton was taller than Celia had been, supernaturally white. He turned her over on her back so that she lay flat. The skull was nowhere in sight.

He opened the trunk of the car, moved the snow chains, the summer fold-up chairs, his brother's camping tent, a six-pack of warm Budweiser, a suitcase full of snake skins which his father had packed and put in the trunk because, he said, they smelled up the house, although as far as Will could tell there was no odor whatsoever from the dried skins. He would have to destroy the evidence.

The skeleton was intact except for the missing skull. He lifted it and laid it gently in the trunk. Then he drove out of the marshes and turned left towards Boston. At Danvers, he stopped by Dunkin Donuts, got two chocolate doughnuts and a cup of coffee and called Bill Becker, the Chief of Police. He told him that he'd been to the marsh that day just to see where Celia had been discovered, which was the reason for the tracks on the lake path, in case the investigative detective became suspicious. He was still concerned with survival.

He would leave the skeleton in Danvers. No one would make a connection. Danvers was a dark, dreary mill town, bleak even in sunlight, with a small commercial district and a park called Simon's Memorial to the south. He drove to the park, which was empty. There were tennis courts, a playground, picnic tables in a grove of trees and several large trash cans lined with plastic around the edges of the parking lot. He backed up to one of them and opened the trunk.

Everything was there—the snow chains, the folding chairs, the jack, the suitcase full of snake skins. He took everything out and put it on the ground until the trunk was absolutely empty. The bones had simply vanished.

He had felt them in his arms. They had actual weight. Even if his eyes had deceived him, he could not have imagined weight. He closed the trunk, got back into the car, started the engine and checked his face in the rear-vision mirror for familiarity—chilled by the extraordinary power of what must have been a hallucination. The fog had lifted completely to a perfect day, and he drove too fast back to Bethany.

Everybody in Francesca's immediate life arrived at once. She had a call from Toby's school to say that he had stomach flu and could she pick him up.

"I'm quitting school," he said on the way home. "It makes me sick."

"You *are* sick, darling," Francesca said. "You have a perfectly normal sickness. A virus."

"I'm sick every day because of Will Weaver."

She put Toby into bed, covered him with a quilt and was just making hot tea when Maud, milk-pale, walked in from Boston and slid into a chair in the living room.

"You look beat," Cesca said.

"That baby took my life," Maud said. "I'm the kind of woman who wears thin like old cotton."

"You'll recover."

"Not soon," Maud said.

Cesca was just taking the tea into Toby's room when Will Weaver bounded up the steps and knocked on the front door. He was flushed with excitement. He grabbed Cesca by the shoulders. "I was at the marsh this morning on a walk tracing the path you took with Toby and I found Celia's clothes," he said. Just as he ran upstairs to Cesca's apartment, the lie had come to him complete. "I saw them on the other side of the lake." He had arrived in Bethany from his abortive trip to Danvers without a plan. He knew he was driven to see Francesca, to take her with him. He wanted to drive his car with her in it, beside him, as fast as the wind. He wanted to die with her. The thought was exhilarating.

"We'd better call the police," Cesca said.

"Come with me first and then we'll call the police. You're

the psychic, aren't you? You have to see for yourself." He went into the kitchen to get coffee.

"You're sure the clothes were hers."

"Positive."

"Toby's home sick."

"We'll be gone less than an hour."

"You're sure."

"I have to be back in the store," he said.

Toby had a tantrum.

He was going to throw up, he said. He was going to throw up without stopping the whole time she was gone if she left him. He would probably choke to death. He stood up to go to the bathroom and pitched straight forward on his face.

Cesca knelt down and took him on her lap.

"See," he said triumphant. "I fainted."

"I'll stay with him, of course," Maud said. "You didn't actually faint, Toby."

"I did so," Toby said. "Dead away. Just for a second."

She lifted him into bed.

"Will Weaver makes me sick, I think," he said, leaning against Maud's full breast. She pressed his head against her, comforted this morning after the taking of her baby to have him there, finally sleeping beside her.

"I wanted to go to the marsh and see what it was like beside the lake where you found Celia. I'd never been there by daylight," Will said. "I was walking around the edge on that muddy path and ahead of me I saw some color under the ferns. I went over to the low bushes and there were her clothes. It's amazing no one has seen them there before. The same ones she wore to James's wedding."

"The same ones?" Ces asked.

"Exactly," he said.

"That's very strange."

"You are beautiful, Ces. I used to watch you when I was young. Did you know that?" He did a U-turn on Main Street and drove across the bridge over the Leonora River.

"Snake River," he said. "I wonder who named that river for a girl."

"Why do you think she was wearing the same clothes she wore to James's wedding?" Cesca asked. "They weren't clothes to travel in."

"She wore them to Boston. She didn't change while I was with her," Will said.

"Maybe she died that night," Cesca said.

The light on the far side of the bridge was red. He could feel his mind slipping away, separating. He wanted to tell her everything.

"She died that night," he said.

After the light, the car picked up speed.

"Do you know about hallucinations?" he asked. "Natural ones, without drugs?"

"About them, yes," Cesca said.

"I have them."

The speedometer was at 65 on a narrow road with a solid yellow line. Cesca put her hand gently on his arm.

"I hallucinate my mother without her head."

"You're going seventy," Cesca said. "Slow down."

"I have to drive fast." He pushed the car to 75. "I'm pressed."

They were going to have an accident, Cesca thought. He had it in mind to crash, she could tell.

His voice, however, was even and controlled.

"She is sitting in a peach gown," he said. "I can even smell her."

"Please, Will."

"She told me to kill Celia Hamilton."

Francesca was not astonished.

"I know," she wanted to say. "I know exactly."

They passed the town limits of Bethany. Seven miles to the marshes—five minutes at 70 miles per hour if what he had in mind was killing her there where Celia had died. Five minutes to the end of her life. Or perhaps no time at all.

"I killed Colin Mallory," she said. Had she said that aloud? Could she hear her own voice in the soft air cocoon of Will Weaver's car? "I shot him with my father's gun." Her heart was beating in her mouth and she could not breathe. *"I killed him! I killed him!*" she shouted over the roar of the engine, and she was convulsed as if the words had ballooned, exploded in her brain, shot out like ammunition—a self-inflicted mortal wound. On her knees, she grabbed Will's arm and shook him. *"Did you hear me? I am the one who killed Colin Mallory. Me. Francesca Woodbine. Can't you hear what I'm saying?"*

But Will seemed not to have heard her. His eyes were fixed on the road, which was empty and flat, a straightaway without curves to the marshes. The speedometer wavered at 75. Perhaps he would turn the wheel to the right and they'd fly out of control, over the embankment, into the dense woods. Certainly they'd die.

At a distance, she saw them—charmed children of Bethany, Massachusetts, locked together in a private desperation.

"I killed Colin Mallory." She threw herself against him. "Not Billy Naylor at all. I did it, with my father's gun. Please, Will." Her voice was paper-thin now. "Listen to me."

But Will simply smiled strangely as if the face of a circus clown had been painted on his own.

She fell exhausted against the front door of the car. She was going to die, and she should. She did not deserve a life, had not earned one; had not—for that matter, *could* not suffer sufficiently to atone for the life she had taken.

Although they had been raised Catholic by Sophia, she did not believe in God. But she did believe in certain inevitabilities, causal relationships at work in the physical universe, seeds planted deep in the black earth which grow towards the light around roots and rocks and other impediments aboveground and bear fruit.

She believed in fortune. There was no real surprise that she should be locked in a death dance with Will Weaver. Doomed to this moment when she had killed Colin Mallory. An act of passion woven in the life of Santa Francesca, passed down in some strange collective memory to Cesca, already vulnerable after the violation on the high school grounds at the Festival in 1949.

The car shimmied back and forth. Francesca was shaking; she held her jaw with both hands so she wouldn't scream. She could not catch her breath.

"I love you!" Will called out in a high singsong voice. "I love you with all of my heart." And then it was as if his voice had fallen in his throat and stuck there on a single note, a low, tormented wail.

"Will!" Cesca shouted, terrified more by the sound of him than by the speed of the car.

The car was barely under control. It wavered across the yellow line, shook like a body convulsed. Will hunched over the steering wheel, his face almost against the windshield, half-standing, pressed the accelerator to the floor.

She had lost her sense of place. The landscape whipped by so quickly it was as if she were exiting the world conscious of the passage through of the speed of days, hardly a breath in time. The car was moving up to 80 miles an hour. The marshes surfaced above the windshield, and suddenly an instinct for survival overtook her and she wanted to live.

She reached over and touched Will's hand—terrified, but the gesture was instinctive and correct.

"I don't want to die," she said.

He looked at the steering wheel. His mother's hand—a thin white hand with lavender veins—was on his brown one. Without turning to look, he saw her in Cesca's face and soft hair. He could smell her sweetness. He put his foot on the brake. Slowing the car—to 60, to 55, to 50 to 45 to 40 to 35.

"I can't stop entirely," he said. "I'm in too much of a hurry. *Jump*."

Francesca pressed the door handle, pushed against the door held by the wind's velocity and tumbled free of the asphalt down a small embankment.

She rolled. The ground was soft, with low brush; a small hill dipped into a gully. She rolled on her side, her knees up, and landed against a large tree, unharmed. She got up, checked herself for damage and climbed the small incline to the road just before Will Weaver's car went over a hill and disappeared. He was going to crash. She knew that.

"I don't want to die," she had said, calmly, calmly. And he had attended.

In the rear-vision mirror, Will Weaver saw Francesca stand

up. But it wasn't Francesca he was seeing in the softly blurred figure of a woman.

He pushed the accelerator to the floor. *He had saved her*, he thought, jubilant. *He had saved her at last.*

2.

"The Ballad of the Snake Boy"

In the days that followed Will Weaver's death, the town of Bethany had fallen silent. Shops were closed without question—no one was in a shopping mood—except Hanrahan's, the supermarket, the drugstore and service stations. Even some offices shut down until his funeral. People gathered quietly at Hanrahan's or Rooster's Tavern at night; on the street corners, leaning against parked cars; on the front porches of the bungalows; by the river; on the benches in the churchyards of First Congregational and Our Mother of Mercies, R.C.

Slowly the news of Celia Hamilton's murder slipped into the town's consciousness. People were stunned. They talked about Will's death as if it were significant beyond Will Weaver and marked the death of treasured innocence for the town itself. They had misunderstood him completely, invested him with their own vulnerable dreams.

No one spoke of the murder of Celia Hamilton. Their recognition of the truth was too great to bear. They did not blame Will. He was beyond blame. Rather, they held themselves responsible for failing to see the irreparable tear in Will Weaver's heart.

Francesca stayed at home in her nightgown as though she were ill. She kept Tobias out of school and made a bed for him to sleep in next to her own. They stayed close, almost tripping over each other, as if the apartment were too crowded to accommodate them. Even the air outside carried dust and silica dangerous to breathe. They made cookies and ginger-bread cakes and caramel flan for which they had no appetite. They read books, and Cesca taught Tobias to play the piano—which he had no interest in learning, but he liked to sit against his mother with the long line of her warm body beside his own.

"Do I have to go back to school?" he asked Francesca.

"After the funeral," she said.

After the funeral, she would get dressed and work again.

Maud was an angel floating silently through the house—there in her room or in the kitchen baking, on the couch in the living room with a book. She was as Sophia had been when Colin Mallory died. She did not ask any questions.

"Don't leave," Francesca said to Maud. "Not until after the funeral."

"He might have killed me. He was going to," Francesca told her mother the day of the accident.

On Tuesday morning, in the left-hand column on the front page of the *Bethany News* which had been saved in the past weeks for information regarding the murder of Celia Hamilton, there was the story of Will's death. BELOVED TOWN MASCOT KILLED WHEN CAR HE IS DRIVING SWERVES OUT OF CONTROL.

"The story is written as if he had no choice," Francesca said to Maud, putting the newspaper down on the kitchen table.

There was no mention in the newspaper of suicide and only a small note on the bottom of the obituary page on Friday, the morning of Will's funeral, which said that the investigation of the death of Celia Hamilton of 12 Waterway, Bethany, Massachusetts, had been closed.

313

Amongst the papers and books in the kitchen where Grace's cookbooks were kept, Sam Weaver found the recipe for chocolate cream pie which had been her favorite when they were young.

The pies had been Sophia's idea. She had come over after the news of Will's death and stayed with him until his sons arrived. The house was full of people that afternoon—a constant stream of people, and too much food. Late in the evening, Sam took Sophia onto the sun porch.

"You know about Celia," he said.

Sophia knew, the way news slips in unspoken.

"I have to do something for the Hamiltons."

She suggested the pies. "Make something of Grace's, something personal."

"That's nothing," Sam said.

"Anything is too little," she said.

So Sam made pies while his sons watched, bemused. He took them over to the Hamiltons' the day after Will died, and the four of them—Philip Hamilton was at home—sat at the Formica kitchen table under a fluorescent light and ate the whole two pies while they talked uneasily in monochrome voices about the loss of children.

On the morning of Will Weaver's funeral, Francesca got up early and dressed with intent. She had not slept at all since Will died, her brain muddled with daytime nightmares. But this morning, she was clearheaded and certain that what she must do was tell the truth about Colin Mallory's death. Tell everyone was what she had in mind—one person after another, until the story, the words recounting and recounting the actual event, lost its terrible power and she could sleep.

First, she thought, she would go to Bill Becker, and after the Chief of Police explained her rights to her, she would tell him. Then she would tell Father John. He would tell her in return exactly what rituals she must perform to be forgiven. She imagined leaving the confession box light on her feet.

She went down the front steps to the back of Leonora's and

got into her car rehearsing her conversation with Bill Becker. She would tell the story in sequence and not mention Louisa. It was not until she was driving on Main Street and had passed the police station that she knew exactly what she was going to do.

The Holbrooke County Courthouse was located in Ewes, the county seat, on the main street, Route 127, set back from the road. Although Julian Woodbine had been the judge of Holbrooke County when she was born, Francesca had been to her father's office at the courthouse only twice.

Once when she and James were in high school and Sophia was ill, he had invited them to a trial for armed robbery at which he was presiding. They went once for the final day.

The bank in Ewes had been robbed by a young and frightened man and his girlfriend, who had hanged herself the day they were arrested, so the man was on trial alone. Francesca could not take her eyes off him. She was fascinated by his plight, by the look of terror in his eyes, around his lips. He did not look like a man who could shoot a woman in the back, but according to the reports he had. The clerk was there, a young, quite pretty woman who did not show evidence of violence. But when she took the witness stand, she cried and wound her handkerchief in her hand and said the young man, shaking in his seat, had ruined her reproductive life. The prosecution presented a physician's testimony to that effect, and the young man shook his head back and forth saying audibly, "I'm sorry, I'm so sorry."

Julian, angular and remote in his black robe, was appropriate for a judge. Francesca had felt unrelated to him—closer, in fact, to the frightened gunman, who was given thirty years that afternoon.

As children, she and James used to pretend or believe— she was never sure which—that they had been adopted by Julian. Sophia's illegitimate twins, they'd pretend, fathered by Dr. Weaver perhaps, or the football coach at Bethany High, which pleased James, or their Uncle William Woodbine, a failed actor, who used to entertain them with wonderful stories of an invented career on holidays. Once Sophia overheard their conversations and was surprisingly cross.

"Of course you are your father's children," she had said. "Look at you!"—as if the evidence were clear in their faces.

But the fact was that until they grew older they often didn't feel like Julian's children, and so the imaginings continued.

Francesca parked the car beside her father's, walked around the courthouse to the front of the building and went into the long, sterile hall hung with the dark oil paintings of former judges of Holbrooke County. A middle-aged secretary with gray corkscrew curls led her to her father's office.

"Miss Woodbine," she announced as if it were an initial introduction and the secretary knew the business at hand was serious, demanding ceremony.

Julian, in a gray business suit with wide lapels and a striped tie, was on the telephone, which he hung up without formalities.

"I'll get back," he said.

In the rest room, he washed his face with cold water and stood to look at himself, aged beyond retirement, in the yellow light.

He knew, inexactly, why Francesca had come this morning and did not wish to hear her news.

When his father died, a pale telephone pole of a man, rigid for days under the white sheets, he had been out of the room.

"Wait," his mother had said, grabbing his wrist.

He had been waiting for days.

"I have to buy cigarettes," he said, and left.

"You missed the passing," his mother said on the automobile trip home. "You could have waited for cigarettes."

"I did not want to know what it was like," he said.

"Like nothing," she replied.

"That makes no difference," he said. "I didn't want to know that either."

316

Neither did he wish to witness Francesca's confession which he knew with a terrible certainty she had come to give.

He sat down behind his desk and loosened his tie, choked by a tightness in his throat.

"People are beginning to talk about the possibility that Will Weaver killed Colin Mallory," she said. "Maud told me. She's been at Hanrahan's."

Julian nodded. He had heard.

"And he didn't," she said. "I know that."

The muscles around Julian Woodbine's heart constricted. There were shooting pains in his arms; his breath came staccato—not enough oxygen to keep a man alive for this event, he thought. He got up and opened the window behind him.

"On the afternoon that Colin died, he was with another woman."

Her father lifted the telephone.

"Please, Daddy." She meant to stop him.

"I need to call your mother," he said, desperate to interrupt this moment. "It will just take a minute." But he laid the telephone receiver on his desk, his hand tight on the cradle to silence the operator's chattering signal.

"I suppose I lost my mind when I saw them," she said.

He looked at her without sight, his eyes fixed as if he had suffered a cerebral accident.

"Are you listening?" she asked.

He did not reply.

"Do you remember the loaded gun kept in the side drawer of your desk?" she asked.

He had seen it on Tuesday. After learning of Will Weaver's death, he had gone into his study at dusk, turned on the desk light and opened the left-hand drawer where the .22 revolver lay on top of a yellow legal pad, where he had placed it himself years before, the day Chief Becker came to talk to Francesca about Colin's death.

He replaced the telephone on the hook.

"I buried the gun near the fishpond," Francesca said evenly.

Julian Woodbine laced his fingers together and rested his

chin on his hands, looking just beyond Francesca at the door to his office. He remembered that afternoon after he discovered that the revolver he kept for protection was missing. He had examined his gun collection. There were seventeen guns on the wall above the highboy—he had counted that day; he had never counted before—some from the Civil War, one from World War I which his brother had given him, a few from World War II and three revolvers similar to the one he had kept in the drawer for protection. He had taken a revolver off the wall, loaded it with ammunition he kept in the highboy and put it in the top left-hand drawer. Then he had looked at the collection again.

If the Chief of Police were to return with further evidence and ask to see the gun collection, he would notice that the shape of a revolver remained on the wall as the paint around it had darkened with age. In the basement there were other guns from his brother's house when he died. Julian had gone to the basement, searched through a cardboard canned-goods box and come up with a Luger which he placed on the nail where the revolver had been. Only a small rectangle of light paint remained under the handgrip of the Luger. Relieved, he had drunk a Scotch from the bottle in the highboy, gathered his papers and left for the office. He had in mind to call Anthony to check if he had borrowed the gun for shooting beaver, but he never did, guessing the answer that Anthony would give him.

"The gun is still in the drawer where I put it years ago," Julian said in a last effort to allow his daughter to maintain the illusion of innocence, this time for his sake and not her own.

"That's not possible," Francesca said.

"I saw it three days ago."

And suddenly she understood what he had said.

"You replaced it." She was stunned by the recognition of his act.

He looked like a cadaver—ashen, ancient as civilization, blue with grief. The stark horror on his face was beyond

Francesca's assimilation, beyond any possible forgiveness, beyond forgetting.

"Are you all right?" she asked. "Are you going to be all right?"

She stood up.

"Do you want me to tell you everything?" she asked.

"No." He opened the drawer of his desk. "I don't want you to tell me any more."

In the car, she turned on the engine but she could not drive. She could not even put the gear into reverse, but sat there on a misty morning of creeping sun with the engine going and waited.

She did not know how long she waited, her head on the steering wheel, empty of thought, but there came a point when she knew she would not be able to drive the car back to Bethany. She turned off the engine and got out.

The sun burned through the mist; the air was syrup-sweet; the landscape took on an eerie, supernatural unfamiliarity. For a while she leaned over the hood of the car, too exhausted to go back into the courthouse. Anyone who saw her there would have thought she was either ill or crazy; but no one did. And she was neither ill nor crazy—perhaps for the first time since Colin's death.

She had at last acknowledged his murder. What she knew of this moment and the rest of her life was the fact that her responsibility would remain as an aberration of the heart, a permanent malformation which must be attended with vigilance. There was no forgiveness. That was plain in the horror on her father's face.

She opened the door to Julian's office without knocking, and he stood in his robes at the window, looking out on a long field of wildflowers and high grass. Like an old man wise with the salted hopes of years and history, he clasped his hands behind his back. Seeing him there, she was full of love for this reserved and rational man for whom honor counted above all passion and who in spite of that had known his daughter's secret and protected her.

"I cannot drive the car," she said.

He turned.

"I thought perhaps someone could drive me home. Your secretary, or the janitor."

He gathered a stack of books from his desk.

"No," he said. "You will have to drive yourself home," he said, and he crossed the room, leaving by a side door which led directly into the courtroom.

She did drive. Her knees shook, her hands perspired on the wheel and her mouth was steel-wool dry. She had to pull over once just to breathe.

But she made it to Bethany, and as she drove down Main Street, past Rooster's Tavern and the stucco houses into the quaint refurbished commercial district, full of people, friends, about their daily lives, she knew she would not tell the citizens of her town, not the police nor anyone, even Father John, however much the telling would unburden her. They did not want bad news. And if she chose to live out her years amongst them, she owed them the illusion of her imagined life.

Everyone in Bethany was at First Congregational on Friday morning. There wasn't room to sit. Those who came later milled around the churchyard, on Main Street, in a light drizzle and waited for Dr. Weaver to arrive with his sons. His sons, however, came first and alone. Walking down Main Street with Styrofoam cups from Hanrahan's, they entered the side door to wait in the sanctuary for their father.

Just before eleven, the familiar green Oldsmobile drove down the street and pulled into the parking lot opposite Our Mother of Mercies, and Sam Weaver and Mrs. Hamilton got out.

The night before, quite late, Mrs. Hamilton had called Sam; he had gone to bed, although he was certainly not sleeping.

"I'll come with you tomorrow," she said. "You pick me up."

He thought she might have been drinking because her words

were thick. But he decided later, the thickness was from weeping.

"I didn't think you would come tomorrow," Sam had said.

"Of course I'll come," she said simply. "What else?"

Sam put up his large black umbrella and walked across the street with Mrs. Hamilton through a hushed crowd who parted to make a path for them into the church.

In Hanrahan's, George Saunders waited for his cousin. After the last summer he had not planned to come back to Bethany for years, but his aunt, Tim's mother, was ill with cancer and would not, according to the doctors, live until summer. So there was no choice. Maia Perrault, pregnant and too nauseated to go into the church, sat on the stool next to him. They were the only customers; everyone else had gone to the funeral.

"That's Cesca Woodbine singing," she said to George. "Do you hear?"

Faintly he could hear Francesca's voice.

"She's singing about Will Weaver. Creepy. The song is just out on Columbia Records and now he dies."

"Tim told me she's half-psychic."

"She makes up songs about people in Bethany," Maia said. "If you're not careful, she'll make up one about you."

"No, thanks," George said. "I don't plan to remain in Bethany for long enough to be the subject of songs." He took a honey doughnut from the cake tray and poured himself a cup of coffee.

Francesca was the first to leave the church right after the service. She was light-headed, as if she were drunk—perhaps from singing, she thought, or nerves. Her feet did not even seem to touch the pavement. She walked up the street to Hanrahan's, where people would be coming after the service, and pushed open the screen door, and sitting at the counter were Tim Greenfield's peculiar cousin from Nashville and Maia Perrault, just leaving for the ladies' room.

321

"Hello," she said to George Saunders. "Remember me?"

"I remember."

She poured coffee and took a doughnut. "Tim must have told you about Will Weaver."

"He did," George said. "He told me you were in the car with Will when he died."

"Not when he died," Cesca said. "He stopped the car and let me out."

"You're lucky," he said.

"I don't so much believe in luck," she said.

The crowd poured out onto the sidewalk, down Main Street, towards Hanrahan's. Frank and Dottie rushed in the side door to make preparations for lunch.

"I've been hearing you in Nashville all winter," George Saunders said. She hadn't realized how slow and Southern his voice was, and familiar—not just the Southernism of it, either, she thought.

"Everyone asks do I know you," he said, "and I'm always glad to say that I do. They always ask why a woman from a Puritan town like Bethany, Massachusetts, wears gypsy clothes."

"They're my grandmother's," Cesca said. "I have her name."

"I remember Tim or Colin Mallory told me about your grandmother."

"She was a fortune-teller," Cesca said. "Everyone came to her for fortunes."

In the fluorescent light, George Saunders was florid, with pouches of fat around his chin and cheeks, small green eyes too close together, a birthmark across his temple in the shape of a salamander which she had not noticed before.

"How did you know Colin Mallory?" she asked.

"I used to visit my aunt and uncle every spring when I was a teenager. Mostly at Festival time."

"How come I never met you?" Cesca asked.

"You did," he said; he was confused. "You knew about me."

She was walking through the woods behind the high school at dusk, only it was darker in the long shadow of the trees, and the ground beneath her was uneven with exposed roots. She had to walk carefully and was full of the preoccupations of young adolescents, unaware of someone behind her until he was right there—his arm across her face, blinding her, tying her hands, stuffing a cloth into her mouth. His body was heavy as he pushed her down to the ground on her back. She could not even scramble or turn, as he hammered on top of her. There might have been another one, her hands and eyes had been so quickly tied—but only one lifted her dress, pulled down her panties and took her. She felt the wet leaves against her hair, the dank smell of new vegetation on the ground, the heat of his breath on the side of her face as he pounded her into the earth.

Hanrahan's was filling now. She heard Tim Greenfield's voice calling "George." She heard her father and Oliver Weaver.

"Do you remember what you said to me?" she asked George Saunders.

He shook his head. "When? I don't remember anything."

"You said my grandmother was a whore."

He got down off the stool, but she had hold of his wrist; her nails were ripping the skin.

"And you were misinformed. She was a fortune-teller. That's why I wear her clothes."

George Saunders wrenched his hand free.

"I wrote you. Don't you remember? I apologized."

He made his way through the crowd to the front door, through the door and up Main Street to Hawthorne, where he turned right and ran like an old bulldog to the Greenfields' house.

Everyone wanted to touch Francesca. People touched her arm or her face or her hair. They embraced her, held her hand, her fingers, kissed her cheeks. Even people she didn't know.

Outside, Tobias leaned against a streetlight. She made her

way through the crowded room warm with the hands of friends and strangers to be with him.

"You sang the song too high," Tobias said contentiously.

"I sang it just right," Cesca said. "Do you want to come in for chocolate and a doughnut?"

"Not now."

She followed him to the large store window. He cupped his hands around his eyes to lock out the sun and peered inside.

Inside was like the end of a war fought in the trenches. Neither side has won or surrendered; the losses have been too great, sufficient for peace.

People held on to one another, unguarded in their sudden emotions; they wept without regard for privacy and laughed easily. No one went home until evening; no one wanted to be alone.

That night, after dinner with James and her parents and a call from Prince Hal playing in Indianapolis and a long, long hour with Sam Weaver and Oliver without mention of Will's name—"Sometime later when the air clears," Sam said, but they both knew that night the air was as clear as it would ever get—after the lights were out all over Bethany, Francesca lay across Tobias' bed and waited for sleep to flood her weary bones.

The room was dark. Maud sat in the rocking chair in her flannel gown, her feet on the bed.

"My room's too empty," she had said. "We should all sleep here."

"I'm not sleeping tonight," Tobias replied.

For a long time they were silent, waiting for a change like miners trapped in a mine shaft who see the light of day, who know they will with any luck be rescued but must wait for the shaft to be opened wide enough to allow a man passage.

"I didn't understand today," Tobias said at last.

"What did you expect?" Cesca asked.

"That people would cry and then go home and hate Will Weaver forever," Tobias said, "and instead it was like a party at Hanrahan's all day long."

Francesca sat up against the wall.

324

"You could tell me a story," Tobias said, "as long as you don't sing it."

"I suppose I could." She took Tobias' head in her lap.

"I hope it's a mystery."

"If it's any good, it will be," Cesca said. She put a pillow behind her back.

Once upon a time, years ago in an ordinary town, there lived an ordinary blind girl with brown curly hair and wide hips and a large heart easily broken. She lived in a cottage on the bank of a river with a monster, and the monster helped her to cook and clean, bring in wood and water.

She had not always been blind, but as I have mentioned she had the great misfortune of human girls to be born with a heart easily broken. When she was first sent into the world full of innocence and wonder and faith to find a husband, the splendid husband that she found without even having to leave the ordinary town broke her heart.

And so she cut off his head. The man, still full of energy in spite of the loss of his fine blond head, raced after her and blinded her with his long fingers and then fell over dead.

When she returned sadly to the cottage where she lived alone, the monster had appeared, but she didn't know he was a monster, of course, being recently blind. He sat at her kitchen table with a bowl of applesauce and a glass of cranberry juice, quite at home.

"Hello," he said to her. "I am a darling boy and have come to take care of you since you are no longer able to see. I will take care of you for the rest of your life but in exchange you must promise me one thing. You will never go out into the world of men."

The ordinary blind girl was pleased to make that promise, since she no longer had an interest in the world of men on account of her recent tragedy. So for years, they lived quite happily in the cottage by the river. In time, she even confessed, as heavy-hearted girls will do, the reason for her blindness and he said not to worry; he knew already. He had always known, of course.

One day, however, late in the year near Christmas, after the monster and the blind girl had been together for seven years, there was a knock

325

and she opened the door without even thinking of her promise to the darling boy.

"I am lost in these woods," a wonderful voice said to her. "I need your help."

The voice was warm and deep and comfortable. She opened the door wide and invited the man to come inside her cottage just as the darling boy was coming in the back door with two pails of water for her morning bath.

"My God in heaven!" the warm, deep voice said. "A monster just walked in the back door of your cottage."

"A monster?" the blind girl said. "I'm sure you're incorrect." She heard the water pails rattle and knew her darling boy had just arrived. "That's not a monster at all," she said. "That's my darling boy."

"He doesn't look like a darling boy to me," the warm voice said. "He looks exactly like a monster."

"You have broken your promise!" *the monster shouted.* "You have broken your promise after seven years and now I will have to kill you."

And he leaped on her back, put his hands around her throat.

"And so she killed him," Tobias said. "Right?"

"No," Francesca said. "He died on the spot of natural causes and a broken promise."

"And then she could see again and married the man with the wonderful voice and they lived happily ever after."

"Not necessarily. But she could see again. And when her eyes were opened, she saw that the darling boy had indeed been a monster."

"And then what?"

"And then she went out into the world and could see every-thing there was to see."

"And married the man."

"Maybe."

Tobias turned over. "That wasn't a mystery," he said. "I wanted a real mystery."

"That was a real mystery. You don't even know who the monster was or how he got there."

"I don't care. I liked him because he had the saddest life," Tobias said.

"Yes, he did," Francesca said. "Now go to sleep."

"Good night, Mama. Good night, Maud."

"Good night, Tobias."

"Good night, my sweet."

"Good night."

"Good night." And their words were whispered into the darkness like a warm circle of breath on a cold, cold day.

Prologue

I *n the Sicilian village where Santa Francesca Allegra grew up,*
the only holiday to rival Easter was the feast day in late
September honoring Saint Theresa. Saint Theresa had been a
Carmelite nun in France who dealt in ordinary miracles amongst
people who lived quiet desperate lives and very often died young.
Each year, she was celebrated in small French and Italian villages
with a festival of roses to recall the legend accorded her in which
she had promised these simple people that at her death the sky would
shower them with roses.

Once, when Francesca Woodbine was quite small, she had come
upon a wooden box full of dried rose petals Sophia kept in her top
bureau drawer under her slips; she opened it and spilled the petals
on her lap. The roses were soft dried and had not lost their scent.

"They were my mother's, gathered when she was a girl in Sicily
and when she died." Sophia sat down on the bed with Cesca.

According to Sophia, the Festival of Roses in Santa Francesca's
village promised romance, not sacrifice, and had little to do with
the saintliness of Theresa. At an appointed hour on the day in
September, young men of the village rushed to the tops of the clay-
and-stucco buildings around the square with armloads of roses,
which they tossed to the girls and women and children milling on
the cobblestones at the festival below. The Festival of Roses was
Santa Francesca's most treasured day—and Theresa, misunderstood

by Francesca as a figure of romantic love, was the origin of the name—Santa—which she carried with her to America.

Like all the young girls, Santa Francesca collected the rose petals, and when she left for America, amongst her few possessions was the box of petals she had saved.

When Santa Francesca died in her sleep on September 29, 1933, Sophia found her just before daylight in her room at Rooster's where, years after her working life was over, she had been allowed to remain. Sophia and the other prostitutes at Rooster's Tavern planned her funeral, a simple, economical service, with Father John saying Mass and burial in the small churchyard beside Our Mother of Mercies R.C. Sophia had assumed that only the women at Rooster's would attend, the proprietor, a few shopgirls her mother had come to know through the years, perhaps some of the church's parishioners.

Instead, to Sophia's astonishment, the church was full. People she had never known and others whose association with her mother had seemed incidental. Two hundred people at least filled the tiny churchyard on a lovely warm September morning.

At the end of the Mass, just as Father John splashed holy water on the oak casket, the roar of a propeller plane overhead drowned out his voice and the sky was suddenly full of roses—peach and plum and magenta, rose, yellow, white and orange, pale pink, multicolored petals. Cascades of perfect roses in tight bud fell on the gathered crowd.

"Who might have sent them?" Francesca asked.

According to Sophia, Father John didn't know.

"Someone who adored her," he said as he and Sophia wandered through the churchyard, gathering rose petals to fill the box from Sicily once again.

1.

The Last Epistle:
August 28, 1965

Father John woke up early to a smoky gray morning with the taste of death in his mouth.

He heard confessions as usual. Maia Perrault was there, full of child, to tell him carnal secrets; but he was not interested in Maia or Mrs. Hill or James Mahoney, wishing to quit a world he had already quit years before. After the ten-o'clock service, Father John knew without sorrow he would not say another Mass. He was moved only by the sound of his own voice in his ears; the words of the Mass, intaglio on his brain, had held nothing for him as long as he could remember.

The chapel was cold—cold around his shoulders, creeping up his body—his blood cooling in anticipation of final rounds. He did not wish to be detained after Mass and left by the side door, up the back steps, breathless at the top. He had to sit down. He must have slept sitting in the high-backed chair in the hall, because the day had altered when he was conscious again. Sunbeams spilled through his apartment.

He had not known until this moment of brightness how shabby the objects of his daily life had become. They would have to be thrown out, no use to anyone except on welfare. The material was worn down to the stuffing; everything in the parlor was the brown of tobacco-stained fingers, the brown of the earth in the winter north of Boston.

Out the window, Francesca Woodbine caught his attention for a moment. She got into her father's car with Tobias. Then Maud climbed into the front seat next to Sophia. The Adlers' blue station wagon pulled up behind Julian's car. They were on their way to Boston to see the two-o'clock matinee performance of the circus.

Weeks ago Francesca had asked him to go with them, but he knew he was too old for the circus—the long trip to Boston and the steps and the crowd.

"Tell Hal I am restored by his young life," he had said.

"I will tell him," Francesca replied.

"And give yourself my love."

Her laugh was girlish and had pleased him.

He stood in the middle of his living room, not wishing to sit down again. Rest, even a plan for a brief rest, could be permanent. His apartment looked like the quarters of an old man who had acquired what was necessary for existence early in the century. There were shelves and shelves of books, all of which he had read, some several times; what else was there for a priest, not predisposed to prayer, to do with his nights? And silver, quite a lot of that, kept polished by Maria, Anna Wheeler's cleaning woman and friend—she had confessed to him the nature of their friendship years before and he had been pleased to know they had a life together. She seemed more deserving, if such a thing as deserving could be taken into consideration, than most people he had known. The silver would be sold at auction; the profits would go to the Church. There was nothing else of value.

Pictures, hundreds of them through the years, of his family in Ireland, trips he had made to Paris and London, Grenoble for a year, Jerusalem, Italy for several months. He had many pictures of parishioners, inscribed to Father John from the O'Malleys or the Fergusens or the Connellys or the Graingers—photographs of the family lined up on the settee on the front porch or beside the mantel with Father John amongst them. Many letters, mostly letters from parishioners, impersonal in nature in keeping with the relationship between a priest and his people. He had no letters from Santa Francesca, but he did have one picture taken when she was in her thirties on the fire escape at Rooster's Tavern. He kept it in a silver frame by his bed, along with his missal; the picture of his sister Rosemary, who had died of tuberculosis the month he left Dublin for America; and a small cobalt blue vase from Santa Francesca which Maria kept filled year round with flowers. He liked that. His mother, even when darkness overtook her life completely, months before her own death, had taken the trouble to have fresh flowers.

He had no legacy. His family had been dead for many years. No one would have an interest in the pictures or the letters. People might want the books but not for personal reasons, and the furniture could be re-covered by young married couples short of money. The apartment would be cleaned out immediately; the walls painted, the floors refinished. Father Seymour of Salem, who would no doubt take over his pulpit, was a fastidious man and would not consider living with the lingering smell of death. Unlike Father John, he was a priest who believed in eternal life and ghosts.

The only interest Father John had ever had in immortality was under the dark brown earth of the churchyard of Our Mother of Mercies with the bones of Santa Francesca Allegra, with whom he had spent those moments sweet beyond wishing which transcended his daily life.

And suddenly, he knew there was something to leave. An actual will. A bequest. He was struck that he had not thought of it before.

He went into his bedroom and took the picture of Santa Francesca, with the idea of putting it in the pocket of his cassock so he would be found with her. Then he sat down at his desk and wrote on a church envelope: *"For Francesca Woodbine: An Epistle.*

"My Dear Francesca," he wrote. *"You have often asked me to tell you what I remember about Santa Francesca Allegra, and so in parting, I leave you the gift of one small story.*

"There was a count—not the father of your mother, but a count

335

nevertheless—who went by another name and who adored her beyond his own life.

"I have no other will except this news for you.

"Yours, Father John"

2.

"The Greatest
Show on Earth"

The Ringling Brothers Circus was in Boston for three days. All over Bethany on the morning of the twenty-eighth of August people were getting dressed to go.

The Festival of Fortunes had been called off for the first time since 1913. May was too wet, and then Will Weaver's death altered the spirits of people in Bethany. A certain joy had gone. An arrogance and promise captured in the brief life of Colin Mallory. There was no faith in an imagined future. And in the place of the old dangerous innocence, a new spirit of calm and humor which comes of knowing the dark side of the soul and surviving with a capacity for hope had settled in the New England town.

"It's not the year for a Festival," Frank Adler wrote in the *Bethany News.* "Instead, we should all go to Boston in late August and watch Prince Hal Woodbine charm the big cats at The Greatest Show on Earth."

"How do they know the circus is the greatest show on earth?" Tobias asked his mother. "Who says?" He had been dressed for the circus since seven in new jeans and a T-shirt Hal had sent—twice his size, with a yellow lion on the front and "THE GREATEST SHOW ON EARTH" on the back.

"The people who make the circus say so," Francesca said.

"How can they know?" Tobias asked. "Have they been all over the world to see?"

"They believe it," Francesca said. "So we believe it too. We have been promised."

"They could be wrong," Tobias said darkly.

"They could be, of course. But when we are at the circus, it doesn't make any difference," Francesca had said.

She stood in front of the long mirror on her closet door. Her hair was wet and she couldn't decide whether or not to cut it. Someplace in the back of her mind, she had a memory of Hendrik Andrews at the emergency room during the hurricane when she had felt the first stirring of an attraction. The memory had to do with the length of her hair. Had he said she should cut it? Or leave it long?

"Should I cut my hair?" she asked Tobias.

"If you cut it, I'll move to Kansas," he said.

"Again?"

"I haven't been to Kansas yet," he said.

In the kitchen, Maud listened to WQRM Boston. The station was playing "The Ballad of the Snake Boy." Some papers in America had already carried the story of Will Weaver, although Francesca had refused to talk about the relationship between his life and her song. The record had been released late. In August, she and Francesca had recorded *The Ballads of an Ordinary Town* to be released in September.

They were going on the road. Six months all over America in coffeehouses and small concert halls. If everything went well, which was to say if the album flew as Columbia expected it would, they'd go to Europe in March.

"Paris," Maud had said. "Perhaps we can visit the South of France while we are there."

Francesca was recalcitrant. "I don't want to leave Tobias," she said.

"We'll take him," Maud said. "Do you remember when you gave me France as a fortune at the Festival?"

"As a choice," Francesca said. "And I made no mention of taking me with you."

But in fact, Francesca was beginning to have daydreams of performances. In her favorite one, which she regularly replayed, they were in Chicago. She was singing the last of *The Ballads of an Ordinary Town* to a wonderful applause. Full of affection, the crowd began to advance on her, to raise her up on their shoulders, to carry her victorious through the concert hall. As they approached, she rose of her own accord, sailing above them, just out of reach beneath the crystal chandeliers which sparkled across her cranberry skirt, her grandmother's black cape, her long black hair.

"Should I cut my hair?" Cesca had come into the kitchen with her hair folded in order to determine how it would look short.

"Shhh," Maud said. "Listen." They had not heard "The Ballad of the Snake Boy" on the air before.

"Well?" she asked when it was over.

"We sound full-grown," Cesca said.

"But that song is creepy," Tobias said. "I think it's the worst song you've done."

In the weeks after Will Weaver's funeral, there were stories. Someone remembered the Festival when Francesca was a fortune-teller—perhaps Johnny Trumbull, who had been outside the fortune-teller's booth at the time. Frank Adler overheard Johnny tell Tim Greenfield about the brown snake that had crawled up Francesca's leg while she was telling Colin Mallory's fortune.

"I bet Will Weaver put that snake under the booth with Cesca," Johnny Trumbull said. "I thought so at the time, but Cesca made such a fuss of protecting him."

"Why would he do such a thing?" Tim Greenfield had asked. "Since I can remember, he was in love with her."

"Jealousy," Johnny Trumbull said. "He was jealous of Colin. And crazy."

"He was certainly crazy," Tim agreed. "You might be right.

I never really thought Billy Naylor had the temperament for killing. And clearly, Will did."

Gradually through June and July, the people of Bethany accepted that Will Weaver, driven by a kind of madness—no one tried to understand the nature of it—had killed Colin Mallory.

"You've heard?" Sam Weaver asked Francesca on one of her frequent visits to his house after Will's death.

"I don't believe he killed Colin," Francesca said.

"It doesn't matter anyway whether he did or someone else," Sam said. "For the peace of this town, it's just as well to believe the case is closed."

One night in late July, Francesca woke with a start from a nightmare she could not remember. She got out of bed and sat on the small upholstered chair next to the window overlooking the back garden, wrapped in a blanket because it was chilly. She was afraid to sleep again. When she drifted and her head fell forward on her chest, she saw Will Weaver lying across the hood of his car just after the accident as he had been found by Anna Wheeler on her way home from Salem.

"I killed Will Weaver," Francesca said to Anna Wheeler, relieved to tell someone. "You can tell the people in Bethany that I did it."

She had gone to the kitchen to make chocolate, stood by the window in the living room overlooking Main Street, which was dark—even Father John's apartment was unlit—a song coming to mind about a love affair between a mad boy and a young girl full of remorse; too late, as language always comes too late. The song simply rushed through her mind as she stood there as if the lovers themselves had fled across a path, disappeared deep into a woods.

At the end of the Woodbine garden, she remembered, where she and James had read about the white man's rape of the Indian women, where she had buried her father's

340

gun, there was an old rope swing frayed from years of use and weather.

When Prince Hal was small, she had sat him on the swing between her legs, told him to hold on tight and she would pump the swing until it flew to the top of the trees. Just short of the top of the trees, the rope went slack and shook the wooden seat turning it perpendicular to the ground. Hal clutched the rope of the swing and shouted happily, *"Jump!"*

"Hold on tight," Cesca said.

"Jump, Ces, and you'll fly!" he called.

And she did jump. Just as the swing was descending, she let go of the rope and flew into space.

Hal stopped the swing with his feet and ran over to her where she had fallen.

"Why did you do that?" he asked. "We were too high to jump. I was pretending."

"I just did," she said crossly, rubbing her twisted ankle.

"You forgot gravity," Hal said, walking back to the house with her.

"I didn't forget," Francesca said. "Sometimes you do something out of your heart instead of your brain."

"Not with gravity," Hal said earnestly.

"Well, I do, even with gravity," Francesca replied.

On and off that night, she slept in the living-room chair; she did not go back to bed.

Gradually, dawn filled the dark morning with a quiet light, just enough to outline the shape of things. It was the time of day she loved for its imprecision and ambiguous promise. Perhaps it would rain. Perhaps the day would be splendid. But whatever the weather, the world outside her window rose to define itself once again.

Maud followed her into the bedroom.

"Hendrik Andrews is meeting us at the circus?" she asked.

"He is," Francesca said. "He called last night."

341

"He's called plenty of times before and you never wanted to see him."

"This is the first time he has called since Will Weaver died," Francesca said simply, as if the explanation were clear.

Hendrik Andrews opened the front door to Uncle Ben's early on Saturday morning and carried a bag of groceries upstairs. After Elena died, he had made a small apartment at the top of the shop and lived there. He did not mean always to live there, since what he intended to do was spend his life with Francesca Woodbine. But for the moment, it was an inexpensive way to live for a man returning to medical school. He planned to keep the toy store and had found a manager to run the shop beginning in September. He put away the groceries for dinner, set a table for two on the loft overlooking the main floor and then dressed. Just before he was ready to leave for the circus, he sat down at the table and imagined Francesca there as she would be tonight.

Sophia played Francesca's new album during breakfast.

"I simply love it," she said to Julian. "Don't you?"

"Some of the songs," Julian replied.

"Most of these she wrote herself, without me." She poured coffee and sat down next to him.

"Are you ever envious of her music, Sophia?" he asked.

"Never. I think never," Sophia said. "The life I wished for came to be in her. And that, to my surprise, is enough."

Sophia told the truth. She had ever understood her own life only through her children. That her daughter had realized the gene of her promise was sufficient. The demons had fled her mind; their absence was enough for happiness.

She and Julian had gone to Italy in June—gone to Sicily and met Santa Francesca's relatives; to Rome and Florence and Umbria, where she had cousins. The trip was "perfect," Sophia had said on the plane home.

"We'll do it next year again. We'll do it every year." Julian was pleased to have finally made her happy.

342

"Never again," Sophia said. "If a moment comes perfect, you should let it go."

"We ought at least to find the Count," Julian said.

"I found him," Sophia replied, and although Julian did not understand exactly, he knew he was meant to and didn't pursue the conversation.

At breakfast, Julian was full of nerves. He drank too much coffee.

"Tell me, darling, how does a man whose son is the assistant lion tamer behave at the circus?"

"Like yourself," Sophia said.

"Myself wouldn't be at the circus, of course," Julian said.

Prince Hal's last letter was propped against the empty vase on the kitchen table with pictures of the lions in color—Samantha, Andrea, Leonidas, Bartholomew and Jack. There was a picture of Hal from the back and taken at a distance. He was wearing a cape.

"I don't like to see a man in a cape," Julian had said.

"He has to wear a cape, darling," Sophia said. "It's part of his costume."

"Do you think he'll ever outgrow this stage?"

"I don't think it's a stage," Sophia said.

"Dear Mother and Daddy," the letter began. *"I have wonderful news. Amal is allowing me one show in Boston, the matinee on August 28, just so all of you can come. I'll be solo for the first time.*

"Life here is more than I could have wished for. I have become close friends with Teensy, who does the poodle act. I often have dinner with her, although her trailer smells awful because she lives with the poodles and sprays the place with cheap cologne to boot. I also like the Flying Wallendas—Carlotta, who is hot-blooded and stubborn, reminds me of Cesca sometimes. I have become particularly friendly with D.O.A. (Dead on Arrival), the laconic and depressed clown who is also the treasurer of the circus.

"Amal and I get on very well, although he's bad-tempered with the lions, probably because of his heart. The lions are fine, particularly Bartholomew, who licks my bare feet and eats out of my hand. I am teaching him a special trick for the time you come to the circus, one never done, as far as I know, by lions. Only cats. The lions are more nervous than they should be because of Amal's temper. He's become

343

impatient with age. The other day Jack objected to the hoop and gave Amal a scratch on the back, right through his shirt. And in Detroit Samantha left the ring. I got her back with Gravy Train, which Teensy, who is the act after ours, uses for her poodles.

"Last night we had a talk about my taking over, perhaps in two years. He admitted he has been losing his touch, but as he says, what's out there in the world for an old lion tamer except grandchildren, and he hasn't got any of those? So by the time I'm nineteen, I could be running things here.

"I've moved to a trailer with the Yugoslav cyclists, who never speak English, although they are perfectly able to, but we go to bed so late or else are packing up at night to go on the road that speaking English hardly matters as long as they're polite.

"Francesca wrote to me about what has gone on in Bethany since Will died. She didn't mention Colin, but James wrote to say that people have accepted Will's responsibility for Colin's death. All of this seems too unreal, miles away from home, living the kind of life I do now. But I do remember one incident with Will which I never mentioned to anyone because I was small at the time and what happened scared me. I was probably about six and Will was fifteen and we were playing bear hunt in the garden as we often did in those days. We used to get on the rope swing and hunt down bears for our squaws and children. At one point, Will plunged towards the rope swing as if to grab someone who was sitting there. Then he rolled over and over, down the small incline shouting, 'I've caught you. I've caught you at last.' I asked him what he had caught, thinking it was a hawk, since we were often pretending to catch hawks, and without a moment's hesitation, he said, 'My mother.' He was a very strange man, and I worried a lot in the months that Francesca was gone on him.

"Don't be concerned about me when you come to the circus. I will be having the time of my life.

"Mr. Malone, who runs the show, gave a speech the other night, as he does from time to time just before we played in Cleveland. 'We have one job on earth,' he said. 'To entertain. For two hours a night, it is our great privilege to send the sorrows of the world downstream.'

"I can't wait to see you. Love forever, P. Hal"

Julian glanced over the letter again.

"I'll be glad when this day is over," he said.

"Pretend," Sophia said. "You can certainly pretend to have a lovely time and tell Hal what pleasure he has given you."

"I have never been much good at pretending, as you know," Julian said.

"You can learn." She took Hal's letter and the pictures and put them in her purse.

"Time to leave," she said. "The Adlers are following us to Boston."

"Who's coming from Bethany? Do you know?"

"A lot of people. The high school is sending all its buses. Sam's taking Anna Wheeler and Maria. Mr. Mallory is coming. Even Bill Becker."

Julian took an umbrella and his briefcase just in case he could not bear to look.

"How dangerous do you think lion taming actually is? Has Hal ever said?" Julian asked.

"I have never wanted to know," Sophia said.

At noon, or minutes after—depending on whether the clock at the bank, which said 12 exactly, or the clock on First Congregational, which said 12:04, was correct—Father John slipped out of the world.

He was asleep, too old to resist dying. He lay in full sunlight on the couch in the living room, where he would be discovered that afternoon at sunset by Maia Perrault, who had come to see him for personal reasons. She would be able to announce to his parishioners and friends that he had died in his cassock, a few wispy strands of white hair across his forehead—his eyes closed, his face at peace. "Absolute peace" was how she described him; but the peace she witnessed was an absence in the brain and not a coming to terms. No man who had held on to the private hearts of generations in a small town could be at absolute peace until those secrets had ceased fluttering in his brain.

The lions were not impressive. They were Amal's lions, each one of them, except Bartholomew, old when the circus bought them, bored with their routines, unhappy in captivity. Amal got on with them well enough; they suited his bleak assessment of the world, his occasional rage. But Prince Hal, whose intuitive sense for animals was out of the ordinary, believed these lions, like old men, were sullen and stubborn and would not learn new tricks or disturb the peace.

Francesca had written Hal to ask about the circus. Was he really in danger? Were the lions unpredictable? Could they escape? And he wrote back with Amal's answer to the illusion of the circus. "There are two things to remember," Amal had said to him on the first day in North Carolina. "One is that the crowd, deceived by the bright lights, thinks you are at great risk. The other is that you think you are safe."

In the months that he had been with Ringling Brothers, he had taught one lion, Bartholomew, a new trick, in which he left the center ring with the lion and taught him to sit down on his haunches, face to face with Hal, and lift his paws benevolently, or so it would appear from the audience, to Hal's shoulders.

"Too risky," Amal had said. He didn't like the fact that Hal left the other lions in the ring on their stools, from which they could easily escape. He didn't like the chance Hal was taking with Bartholomew, who might decide to eat before he did his trick. In fact, Amal didn't like Bartholomew. Always if there was trouble at a performance, Bartholomew was the one to cause it.

"Do your trick when your family comes if you insist," Amal said gloomily. "But don't come whining to me if Barto decides to eat you."

Prince Hal left the trailer, where the Yugoslav cyclists were having an argument in their own language which resulted in one cyclist's throwing his bowl of soup at another who was already in costume for the performance. Hal had put in a request for a change of trailer, although the only one with any room at all was Teensy's, and he didn't particularly want to live with the poodles either.

He was dressed in yellow tights, blue satin shorts and sleeveless yellow shirt. His cape was long and black and extensively eaten by moths. He wore makeup—Pan-Cake and rouge, mascara and lipstick, which he planned to remove before he saw his father. He passed the rest of the trailers to the large cages where the lions were kept. Amal was already dressed, sitting on a stool outside the cages eating a pastrami sandwich.

"So," he said. "I almost had a heart attack this morning." Frequently, Amal had a near miss with a heart attack. "I won't be long. That much I know."

He was forty-eight, with a good body—at a distance he looked like a man in his twenties—but up close without makeup, he was an old man with a bad heart.

"Barto's in a stinking mood," Amal said. "He shouldn't even go on today. He might eat a child. Right, Barto? You have no discrimination, stupid lion."

"He'll be fine," Hal said.

"You've known Barto two months," Amal said. "I've known him twelve years. He should have been put down in '62 when he did this to my face." He turned his head so Hal could see his face, but no mark was apparent. "Do what you will. It's your funeral. But don't, for chrissake, take a risk with the crowd."

"I would never do that," Hal said. "So hello, Bartholomew, my one true love," he said. "It's our big day."

The dark yellow lion was uncommunicative. He raced up and down his cage, rubbed his matted fur against the thick wire, roared low in his throat to no one in particular. Intentionally he ran into Samantha, who lay in the cage nursing an injured paw.

The Woodbine family arrived early and sat in front at the center ring just as the concession stands were beginning to open.

"Too close," Julian said crossly.

"We'll be able to see if there are tricks," Tobias said.

"Tricks?" Sophia asked.

"Make-believe lions," Tobias replied.

"The lions are real," Sophia said. "That much is certain."

Maud sat at the end of the row; then Julian, Sophia and Tobias and Francesca and Hendrik Andrews, who had arrived with James, Louisa and the Natales, who had come in spite of Mrs. Natale's arthritis, and Frank Adler with Miranda, his miracle daughter, and Dottie. Next to Dottie were Sam Weaver, aged by circumstance, and Oliver, his son. Scattered through the rows at the center ring were others from Bethany—Maia Perrault and Sean; Tim Greenfield and his wife carrying twins, holding their daughter on her lap; Anna Wheeler and Maria; Mrs. O'Malley, who came to the circus every year without fail; Johnny Trumbull in his police uniform, although he was off duty; a lot of the students from Hal's class at Bethany High, who had graduated in June.

Julian had changed since Francesca's attempted confession. He was an old man. Occasionally when he was unaware, she looked at him stricken by the alteration in his eyes. She had forced on him the announcement of his death. They were polite to each other, but he could not meet her look directly and he could not touch her.

Some days she wanted to call him: "Will you forgive me? Will you ever forgive me?"—but it was not a matter of forgiveness. What had been done was absolute, and she would live out her life with that knowledge.

Now Sophia leaned towards him, put her hand on his cheek; her lips brushed the side of his face, and Cesca was glad to know she had not cost her father everything, that at least he could close her out and live on accessible to her mother.

The summer of 1965 had been hot and dry. The circus rings were dusty; a thin film rose from the ground. In the center ring, a red-haired clown with a belly the size of a beach ball and long shoes that swept upwards towards his knees watered down the ring.

The front row at the center ring was unnaturally quiet.

At one point, when the tin-band circus music began to play, the performers lined up to march in their colorful procession around the enormous tent, James leaned across Hendrik and touched Francesca's hand.

"Love you," he said to Francesca, as if he were anticipating disaster and wanted to settle the score in advance.

He dreaded this performance, she knew—imagining catastrophe, Prince Hal maimed beyond recognition by the lions, humiliated in front of a crowd of strangers.

Lately James seemed to her like a young man too soon complete. He had surrendered his childhood dreams as spoils in a war that had not been fought. Somehow Louisa had robbed him. At thirty, he was a finished character without future possibility, and it was strange to be his twin.

Louisa, thick with child—a pregnancy that wrapped around her like an inner tube—sat between her mother, who chattered away about motherhood, a book she had committed to memory, and James. She looked aged.

Francesca had a sack doll when she was very young—called Sack Doll because her body was a muslin flour sack stuffed with unbleached cotton. She had no arms or legs. For reasons which seemed at the time entirely plausible, Francesca did not like Sack Doll. So one afternoon, she had taken her mother's makeup and aged the cherubic plastic face with wrinkles and downward-turning lips and brown spots on the cheek.

When Francesca looked at Louisa Natale this afternoon, she did not feel the familiar quickening. No swan hat arched provocatively on Louisa's pretty head. What Francesca saw was Sack Doll, aged by makeup, discarded as her own doll had been, at the back of her closet. She could not call up those old feelings, only the memory of betrayal as fact. But the passion she had so long felt was stilled as death.

Francesca leaned against Hendrik Andrews with intention. Their legs touched, their arms pressed bone to bone.

Free as air, she felt. Shimmering with life—as if Pandora's box had not held the dark secrets born with her, realized in a terrible moment of distorted love, but to her astonishment, the box when finally unlocked, bloomed a flower open-petaled to the light of day.

The circus had begun. "Welcome, everyone, children all, to The Greatest Show on Earth."

And the rings filled with poodles and unicyclists, clowns spilling one after another out of a tiny car, jugglers and acrobats, ladies in short pink dresses balanced barefoot on the haunches of galloping horses. Elephants labored to dance.

Prince Hal was the fourth act in the center ring, after the cyclists, before the Flying Wallendas.

"And now," the ringmaster announced, "in the center ring—introducing, for the first time under the big top, Prince Hal, with the lions."

Hal, larger than life under the lights, marched out, his cape flying. He snapped his whip as one by one the old lions meandered out of the cages, growled low in their throats, rolled their enormous heads and got up on stools.

Once Hendrik put his large hand over Francesca's. She was pleased to see the size of it—square and brown, with broad fingers, the hand of a carpenter. It covered her own entirely.

The lions bowed and roared, walked mouth to tail around the ring, jumped through low hoops and back to their stools obediently. Only once did Samantha lift her injured paw and bat at Hal. There was no other complication.

"And now, for the first time—in the center ring, Bartholomew, most ferocious of Amal's beasts, will perform a new and dangerous trick taught to him by Prince Hal," the ringmaster said. "Sit very still. Don't even whisper. Hold your breath."

"Just wait," Amal said to Teensy, who stood with her poodle backstage. "There's going to be trouble."

Prince Hal put down his whip, took up a small stick the size of a twig and tapped Bartholomew on the shoulder. Bad-tempered Barto left the stool with easy grace, cocked his large head and followed Prince Hal languidly out of the ring. Behind him, the other lions, impatient for the show to be over, impatient for dinner, sat on their stools and did not move.

Outside the ring, directly in front of the center aisle, Prince Hal dropped his stick, put his hands on his hips, spread his legs enough for balance in case Barto decided to give him a paw across the shoulder and waited for the lion to amble over, as he had been trained to do day after day after day for the months since Hal had arrived. In Hal's pocket, as Barto very well knew, was a beef-flavored dog biscuit. Sometimes Barto waited for the biscuit after the trick and sometimes he went after it and didn't bother with the trick.

"Don't count your chickens," Amal had said.

"Down, Barto," Prince Hal said. "Sit down."

Bartholomew sat.

Across the space of seats the Woodbine family locked hearts.

Prince Hal stepped towards Bartholomew, close enough to dance.

"Up," he said in a strong voice. "Up, boy. Give me a hug."

Bartholomew rolled his head. He lifted a paw and batted at Prince Hal.

"Up, now," Prince Hal said.

Barto checked Hal's pocket with his nose, but not obtrusively.

"Now," Hal said.

The old lion rested on his haunches, lifted his two front paws onto Hal's shoulders and roared—his wide mouth open to the dark cave of his throat.

From the grandstand, it looked as if Bartholomew could swallow Hal in a single gulp.

Quickly Hal embraced the lion, who was not fond of demonstrations of affection. And then Hal jumped away, gave a quick bow, tossed the lion the biscuit and pranced back into the ring

The crowd cheered. The lights went out. The ringmaster in a far corner announced Teensy and the poodles, and the lion act was over.

"It's done," Julian said to Sophia, still half-hidden behind her hands.

One by one the lions returned to their cages until only Hal was left in the light circle, bowing and bowing.

"So," Amal said as Hal walked behind the tent.

"So it worked," Hal said. "And it's a very good trick."

"But it's a trick, and you were lucky," Amal said.

The circus went on and on that afternoon; but in her mind Francesca had left after the lions. She was in a large room

351

with toys and a table with candles—a small table. She was seated in a child-size chair across from Hendrik Andrews, and all around them music was playing.

He leaned over, lifted her hand from the table and asked her to dance.

"Here in this toy shop?" she asked.

He was tall and straight and formal.

"Of course," he said.

And she stood, put her hand in his hand, her arm across his shoulder. Their bodies were almost touching. She imagined her electric hair brushed his lips.

"I have danced with you before," he said.

"I don't remember," she said.

"I've held you in my arms like this—lifted you just off the floor so your feet didn't touch. You don't remember?"

She laughed into his warm cheek.

"I remember," she said. "I remember everything."

The room was dusky with candlelight, and he swung her around the table, in between the rocking horses and bright red fire engines, spinning through the dollhouse and the puppets and the dolls, across the open floor under a circus tent in which circus music was playing until, done with dancing, they fell together into a soft corner of the room.

The circus was over while Cesca was dreaming. The horses and elephants and poodles and puffy-dressed ladies and clowns, Prince Hal and Teensy and Amal and the Flying Wallendas and the ringmaster and the cyclists walked triumphantly around the large ring, waving and waving.

Tobias sat down on the seat next to her, full of pleasure and excitement.

"They were right," he said. "It is the greatest show on earth."

Later, in the parking lot, the Woodbines waited for Prince Hal to arrive in street clothes, scrubbed clean of makeup.

"He looks regular," Tobias said. "Like himself."

"He is," Francesca replied.

"But he wasn't when he tamed the lions," Tobias said matter-of-factly.

At dawn, the beginning of a painted morning, blue-gray and wet with the smell of autumn in the air, Hendrik Andrews drove Francesca to Bethany, over the Leonora, through the blinking red lights, past her apartment, past the pastel stucco houses to the end of Main Street which was Rooster's Tavern. He stopped his car in the empty parking lot.

"I was here once before, on the Fourth of July," he said.

"You heard me sing?" she asked. "Nobody told me you were here."

"Nobody knew." He got out of the car and stretched.

She stood next to him.

"My mother grew up at Rooster's," Francesca said. "There." She pointed to a room. "My grandmother worked here."

"Someone told me that."

"James?"

"No. A man at Rooster's when I came to hear you sing."

"Did he tell you she was a prostitute?"

"No, he told me she was a fortune-teller."

He reached out, turned her towards him, took her hand in his. "I wanted to dance with you on the Fourth of July, but you were too busy."

She put her hand on his shoulder, her cheek against his cheek.

"There isn't any music," she said.

"You can easily make the music," he said.

All over Bethany, along the coast of Massachusetts, in Boston, people were beginning to rise. Sophia stretched, leaned against Julian and kissed his bare shoulder.

"I'm certainly glad that ordeal is over," Julian said.

"It wasn't so bad," Sophia said.

"Now that it's done," Julian replied.

Tobias climbed out of bed, went down the corridor and into his mother's room. Her bed was empty.

"Maud!" he called.

She answered in a sleepy voice.

"Where's Mama?" He went into her room.

"Out to dinner with the toy-shop man," Maud said.

"But it's morning," Tobias said.

"She'll be home soon. Right after breakfast, she told me."
He poured Grape-Nuts and sat down at the breakfast table.

"He invited me to the toy store next week," he told Maud
when she came in to make coffee. "He said I could spend the
night if I wanted."

In Boston, Louisa lay on her back with her hands on her belly
and felt the baby kick. He ran his foot or hand across the surface
of her stomach. James had gone to the hospital at dawn. She
picked up the telephone to call him. "Come back," she wanted
to say. "Come back because I hate to be alone." But he was in
Emergency and couldn't be interrupted, according to the nurse
who answered the telephone. He would call back later.

Prince Hal got up in the dark to feed the lions. Amal was
already at the cages, watering down the floors.

"I thought you were going to sleep all day," Amal said
crossly.

"I changed my mind," Hal said. "So, Barto." He put down
a tray of food for the lion. "We were wonderful yesterday,
you and me."

"Wonderful?" Amal shook his head. "Some kind of wonderful. So now your parents think you're a real, honest-to-
God lion tamer, right?"

"Right," Hal said. "And I am."

"Over my dead body," Amal said.

Prince Hal nudged him gently in the ribs.

"Be careful of your heart," he said.

And in the parking lot of Rooster's Tavern, the sun, stretched
over the horizon, shimmered on Francesca, dancing barefoot,
her hair flying. For a single moment, in advance of day, the
summer sky was ablaze with roses.